Spec

SINCERELY, YOUR INCONVENIENT WIFE

JULIA WOLF

Copyright © Sincerely, Your Inconvenient Wife by Julia Wolf

Special Edition

All rights reserved.

No portion of this book may be reproduced in any form without written permission from the publisher or author, except as permitted by U.S. copyright law.

Edited by: Monica Black, Word Nerd Publishing

Proofreading by: My Brother's Editor

Cover Design: Y'All That Graphic.

To getting up after you're knocked down and making your own kind of beautiful.

CHAPTER ONE

Saoirse

THE THING ABOUT ALWAYS saying yes was sometimes I wound up regretting how indiscriminate I was.

Those regrets usually didn't last, though. I almost always found a bright side, even in the most boring, tedious, and uncomfortable situations.

I didn't regret tonight's "yes" yet, and I doubted I would. Spending my evening in a penthouse unlike any I'd ever seen was worth it for the experience alone.

Kara pressed into my side as we made our first round through the spacious living room, with its twenty-foot ceilings and unobstructed views from every angle. Even the curved staircase leading to the second floor had Lucite rails to not block the light streaming in from the double-decker windows.

I made a mental note to venture onto the balcony later once Kara found the man who'd invited her here tonight.

This wasn't his home, but according to Kara, he'd been given permission by the owner—his cousin twice removed or something like that—to hold a party here.

I hoped that was true. And if it wasn't, I hoped I had enough time to explore before we were all kicked out or arrested for trespassing.

"Where is he?" Nudging Kara with my elbow, I took stock of the fairly plentiful crowd. Everyone was beautiful, fitting in well with the magnificent space. Women dripping in jewels and designer dresses amid couches shaped for style rather than comfort. Men in bespoke suits, power emanating from their stances, standing around sculptures made of marble and steel, probably worth millions.

Kara, who was more of an acquaintance than a close friend, was shaking. Since we weren't close, it was hard to tell if it was from excitement or nerves. Although why she would be nervous, I didn't know. With her hourglass frame, soft ebony waves, and cherry-red dress that molded to her every curve, she fit in with this crowd to a *T*.

"I don't see him." She hooked her arm with mine. "Don't leave me. I'll die before I walk around this party alone."

"I have no plans of leaving you until you find your Vincent."

"But you can't leave even when I find him. If you do, he'll know I only came for him."

I tugged her to a mirrored bar set against one of the few walls in the wide-open space. There, I poured us both a generous glass of Pinot Gris and handed her one. She took a long pull, swallowing almost half the wine in the glass.

"How many rooms do you think are in this place?" I asked under my breath.

"Five bedrooms, six baths, eight-thousand square feet," she answered far too quickly and with entirely too much precision.

"Have you been here before?"

"No." Her shoulder lifted. "I looked it up online when Vincent gave me the address."

"Whose place is it again?"

She shrugged again. "He just said a relative he's staying with while he's in the US."

It was beginning to look more and more like this evening would conclude with me dashing for the exits to avoid another trespassing arrest.

Just when I'd resigned myself to the fact that Vincent either wasn't real or he wasn't here at all, a grinning man with a boisterous Italian accent in a suit that fit his body like a second skin strode toward us, his arms outstretched.

"Kara, you have come. I was getting worried, *bella*." He clasped her shoulders and leaned in, kissing both her cheeks.

Her arm unhooked from mine the moment she'd spotted him. She went a step further to distance herself from me now that her dream guy had arrived by moving in front of me. At that point, I was shocked I hadn't received a shove to top it all off.

Too bad Kara was a smidge over five feet tall and I was a hairsbreadth under six. Blocking me from view was impossible. But her message had been received loud and clear. I turned toward the bar again, refilling my mostly full glass.

"And who is this you brought with you?"

My shoulders stiffened at the rowdy voice drawing near. I was here for the vibes, not to poach Kara's man. But I couldn't exactly stare at the wall all evening.

I slowly turned around, making eye contact with Kara first. Hers flared, and her head tipped subtly to the side. I nodded once in understanding.

"Hello. It's nice to meet you." I started to hold out my hand, then accidentally on purpose jerked my other hand, sloshing wine onto the bodice of my dress. Luckily, it was black and the wine was white.

My sacrifice wouldn't do long-lasting damage. "Oh no. I made a mess of myself."

Vincent pulled a silky handkerchief from his pocket. "A dreadful shame, *bella*. To ruin such a lovely dress." He came close, his intent to blot the wet spots on my chest and stomach clear. Kara latched on to his elbow.

"I think Saoirse should take care of that herself, Vinny. Is there a restroom nearby?" she cooed.

His lids lowered, and some of the puff in his chest deflated. I supposed he'd been looking forward to patting me down. He would have been severely disappointed since my tits were primarily made of a really good push-up bra and hopes and dreams.

I scrambled in the direction Vincent pointed, not escaping soon enough, judging by the pointed glare Kara shot me. I remembered then why we weren't close. I considered myself to be a girl's girl, while Kara was more *every man for himself*. One on one, she could be fun, but toss a guy into the mix, even one I wasn't the slightest bit interested in, and the claws came out.

Throwing wine on myself had been half an excuse to leave. The other half had been self-preservation.

Unfortunately for me and my sodden dress, the bathroom off the living room had a line of people waiting to use it. The woman at the front rolled her eyes when I peered at the closed door.

"Someone's fucking in there," she deadpanned.

A laugh burst out of me. When she didn't laugh with me, I realized she wasn't joking. Then I heard the moans and skin slapping and continued on my merry way, following the hallway deeper into the condo. Surely, with six bathrooms, there wouldn't be a line at all of them. The wet spots on my dress were getting cold, and my skin was starting to feel sticky.

The first room I came upon seemed to be a den. The couches actually looked cozy and plush. My attention caught on a throw blanket hanging over one of the windows. Someone had haphazardly tacked it up there. Compared to what I'd seen of the rest of the condo, this touch stuck out like a sore thumb, which intrigued me about its owner.

Before I could check out the rest of the room, I had to dry myself off a little. I locked myself in the attached bathroom and found a towel I used to soak up as much wine as I could.

Once that problem was mostly solved, I looked around the spacious bathroom. I'd been inside many nice homes in my life. My best friend and roommate, Elise's boyfriend, Weston, lived in the penthouse of our building. This kind of place wasn't brand new to me, but there was something about it that was a notch above everything else I had ever seen. The art, the modernity, the nod to luxury in the more public spaces and comfort in the private spaces like the den. I *really* longed to explore the rest of the place.

The bathtub was freestanding in front of a wall of windows. For a moment, I imagined myself having a bubble bath and watching the sunset.

Then I moved on.

The party seemed to have filled in more. I wove through the mingling crowd, wondering if the fucking couple had vacated the bathroom yet. Kara and Vincent were in a small group near the windows. She'd tucked herself to his side, but when her eyes flickered to me, she tried to merge herself with his ribs.

Unoffended, I gave her a smile and strode directly to the bar to fill my wineglass. Then I found some cheese and crackers, which I folded inside a paper napkin, and carried my loot back to the cozy den.

As much as I would have liked to nose about this glorious condo, I had manners, so I would refrain. Though some might say eating crackers on a stranger's couch in a room I hadn't been invited into was rude in and of itself, and I wouldn't argue that point.

But no one was around to tell me I wasn't allowed in here, so I kicked off my heels, sank down on the cushions, and relaxed.

CHAPTER TWO

Luca

MY HEAD THROBBED. WITH each beat of my heart, it expanded and contracted, skull, gray matter, the whole package.

It had been a long day. A long two weeks, if I was counting. And there was no end in sight. I'd accepted that, but today's series of meetings had been the cause of the spike in my skull.

If my head had been pounding less, I wouldn't have bothered getting on the elevator to my condo. Riding my bike in this condition wasn't smart, though. That wasn't to say there wasn't a time in the recent past I would have thrown caution to the wind and gone for a ride anyway.

As the consultants had drilled into me today, my age of recklessness had ended.

I stepped off the elevator and opened the door leading to my entryway, where I was greeted by lights, music, people. Somewhere in the recesses of my tired mind, I remembered my cousin, Vin, who was here from Italy for an undisclosed period of time, had asked if he could have a *few people over*.

This was more than a few people. At least fifty strangers were milling around my living room.

I shouldn't have been surprised. It was typical Vin. He had friends, acquaintances, and business partners on every corner of the globe. The last time he'd visited Denver and stayed with me, he'd had a party twice this size.

He probably considered this showing restraint.

If my brain didn't feel like it was being liquefied, I would have poured myself a drink and joined in. As it was, I had no inclination to make small talk. I was all talked out.

As I stood there, surveying my home, Vincent moved through the crowd, coming my way. A petite brunette who had attached herself to him came with him.

"Luc, you're here," Vin boomed. He leaned forward, cupping my face and air-kissing both my cheeks. "Come in, get something to drink. There's food in the kitchen."

I pulled back from him, frowning. "You realize this is my place, right?"

He laughed, throwing his head back. "Of course, of course. Have you met Kara?" He pushed the small woman toward me. "Kara, this is my cousin, Luc."

His woman's cheeks flushed as she raked her big brown eyes over me. There was interest in her gaze, which immediately turned me off, even though she was attractive. Disloyal women were one of my biggest turnoffs, and considering she was here with Vin, she shouldn't have been looking at me like I was an option for her.

I kept the introductions short and broke away from the two of them. Hunger gnawed at my stomach, so I used that as an excuse to duck into my kitchen. Obviously catered food lined the counters. Every surface was covered with some type of dish.

"Jesus, Vin," I muttered as I grabbed two bottles of beer from my fridge and the box of prosciutto pizza from the counter.

I took my food and drinks to the part of my condo where I spent most of my time. Even more than my bedroom lately, though that hadn't been entirely by design. Suddenly working twelve-hour days had taken more out of me than I'd expected. I often found myself startling awake in the morning on my couch in the den, having passed out cold the night before.

Striding by the strangers standing in my halls, I shut myself in the den, locking the door behind me. There was a light on in the bathroom. I didn't remember leaving it on, but I wouldn't have put it past myself.

Not bothering to turn on any other lights, I put my beers and pizza on the tray atop the ottoman in front of the sectional, kicked off my shoes, and yanked the tie off my neck. Once that was tossed aside, I unbuttoned my shirt partway and rolled up the cuffs.

Only then did I sit down and release a long exhale.

A glint of light coming through the center window brought me out of my moment of respite. That window was the bane of my fucking existence, with its forever-breaking automatic blinds and direct line of sight to a glaring spotlight on top of a high-rise tower.

Two nights ago, I'd solved the problem by nailing a throw to the window frame since I didn't have time or the will to call a repair person. Why wasn't it working now?

I started to get up to see if it had fallen down when I noticed the lump on the other end of the couch. A lump covered with my fucking throw blanket.

"Who are you?" I barked.

The lump stirred, and a soft sound, something like a moan, came from them. The person beneath the blanket straightened, and the light spilling from the bathroom illuminated them.

Her.

She found me in the dark and jumped slightly. "Oh, hi. I think I fell asleep." Then she pointed to the corner I'd started to settle in before spotting her. "Fair warning, this couch eats your energy like a snack. I wasn't even tired when I sat down, then boom, I was out like a light."

I knew that, of course, since the couch belonged to me. But I found myself staring at this woman, trying to understand her presence in my home. In my personal space.

"What's your name?"

She'd just lifted her wineglass to her lips and answered me around it. "Sasha." She took a long sip then raised a brow at me. "What's yours?"

Interesting. She didn't know who I was. Either that, or she was playing coy. Generally, women in my social circles in Denver recognized me, if not by my face, then by my name. To be completely honest, my name was recognizable far outside of this city too.

"Luc," I answered, which wasn't a lie, but it wasn't the complete truth either. If she truly wasn't aware of who I was, I wanted to keep it that way. It was easier for me.

She nodded toward the pizza box. "I stole some crackers, but I'm impressed with your plunder. Is that a whole pizza?"

"It is."

"Well"—she scooted forward, her eyes darting from me to the box—"are you going to share? Some of us are starving."

"I was planning on eating it all myself."

She shifted closer to me and the pizza. "That isn't nice, Luc. If I'm going to share my hiding spot with you, it's only fair you share your food. I promise to only eat two or three slices."

Reaching an arm out, I snapped on the table lamp beside me, then turned back to my intruder. In full light, she was even more gorgeous than I'd suspected. And I'd suspected she'd be beautiful. A woman didn't have the type of easy confidence she did if she wasn't used to moving through the world on a path made by all the lesser beings who willingly stepped aside for her.

"Fine. Two pieces are your limit."

Her full, pink lips spread into a wide smile, revealing a row of straight pearly-white teeth that were almost too big for her face but suited her impeccably. She leaned forward to flip open the box, and my gaze drifted to the subtle swell of cleavage peeking from the top of her corseted, black dress.

She straightened back up, holding a slice victoriously. "It's cold, my favorite."

"Really?" I lifted a brow while snagging a piece of my own.

"Yes. I can eat it faster this way." She crammed a large bite into her mouth to demonstrate. It wasn't a sexy move, but it did something to my cock anyway.

But this was what I meant. A woman who looked like her could get away with *anything*, and idiots like me would think it was adorable or quirky. Look at me, sharing my pizza and my haven for no other reason than Sasha intrigued me. And she intrigued me because she might have been one of the most beautiful women I'd ever laid eyes on.

We ate in silence for a few minutes. I didn't protest when she went for piece number two and three. I would have eaten the entire pie, but sharing wasn't a hardship when it meant I got to listen to her breathy little moans as she bit into another slice and she crossed and uncrossed her mile-long legs as if the flavor was so incredible she couldn't sit still.

"You never said why you're hiding in here when there's a party going on out there."

She wiped her mouth with a crumpled paper napkin and patted her flat stomach. "I only came because my friend asked me to."

"Do you do anything friends ask you to?"

"I have this thing—" Her mouth twisted, and she didn't elaborate.

"Thing? Explain."

"I say yes when I'm asked to do things if I think there's even the smallest chance I'll get something out of it."

She only became more and more intriguing as time went on. "Your friend asked you to come to a party with her, and you said yes because you thought you'd get something out of it?"

She nodded.

"What do you think you'll get out of being here tonight?"

"That's yet to be determined." She uncrossed and crossed her legs again. "Friend isn't really the right word for Kara anyway. We temped together last year, and we still hang out every once in a while."

"Kara? Small, red dress?"

"Mmhmm. Do you know her?"

"No."

"Oh." She huffed lightly. "Well—"

"That's what you do? You're a temp?"

By the nature of their job, I never had a chance to get to know my temporary employees, though I was certain we employed them from time to time. I was also certain they did not look anything like Sasha.

She waved her hand around. "I'm not ready to settle into a career, much to my mother's displeasure. I've tried it, and it didn't suit. I get bored easily."

I related to that on a visceral level. "It sounds like you haven't found the right career."

Her full mouth tipped into a tepid little smile. "I like things temporary. It makes life more exciting. What about you, though?"

"What about me?"

She gestured to me then my boots piled on the floor. "By the looks of you—the Rolex on your wrist and Tom Ford boots you kicked off—you have money and a good deal of it. My guesses are a trust fund baby, a foreign prince, some bigshot CEO, or a Mafia don."

I lifted an eyebrow, amused by her guesses, especially with how close she was to her target. "Which one do you want me to be?"

She hummed and tapped her cheek with her forefinger. "CEOs and trust fund babies are a dime a dozen. You don't have the right accent to be a foreign prince." Her eyes flicked over me. "The all-black clothing gives you a sort of villainous edge, so I'll go with Mafia don. Am I right?"

Leaning forward, my elbows on my knees, I leveled her with a hard, unflinching stare. "If I told you...well, you know the rest."

"Yeah, yeah. Death, destruction, that kind of thing." Her lips curved into a sexy, amused grin. "Can we circle back to Kara? You don't know her?"

"I don't. I had the pleasure of being eye-fucked by her before I retreated in here."

Laughter floated like bubbles on a clear, blue sky. "That sounds like her, although she came for this other guy, so I'm surprised she was hitting on you since she seemed so into him."

"Vin?"

"Yes, that's his name. Vincent. I spilled wine on my dress to give them alone time while I cleaned up. I'm hiding in here now because when I came out of the bathroom, Kara looked like she was going to murder me."

I scrubbed at the scruff on my jaw. "You...purposely spilled wine on yourself for the sake of someone who's not even a good friend?"

She lifted an elegant shoulder. I wanted to press my mouth there to see how smooth her fine skin was. "It isn't a huge deal to me. The dress is dry-cleanable."

"Why not leave instead?"

"I promised I'd stay."

"That simple?"

"Well, that and I fell asleep in here. If you know the owner, don't tell him." She picked up the blanket and waved it around. "I kind of pulled this down from the window. I think the blinds are broken, so I feel bad, but also, he should invest in more blankets. Who only has one throw blanket? Then again, maybe he spent his fortune on art and concrete slabs and this one puny blanket is all he can afford. In which case, I feel doubly guilty since I ripped the corner a little."

I had to laugh, and that was when I noticed the ache in my head had all but vanished. I could have given credit to the beer and pizza, but I seriously wondered if some of it had to do with this pretty blonde who continued to surprise me each time she opened her mouth.

"I'll make a note of it," I quipped.

She froze as she tucked her long hair behind one ear and her soft-brown eyes rounded. "Oh shit. Is this your place? Have you been humoring me to keep me here until the cops show up to arrest me?"

"Why would you think that?"

Her hand fell to her lap, where she twisted her fingers into knots. "Which part? That you're the owner or that you called the cops?"

"Either. Both. You sound experienced with having the police called on you. Should I worry I'm alone with a criminal?"

"I've only been arrested once, and the charges were dropped. It was a nonviolent crime, so you're safe." Her eyes narrowed, and she actually did seem worried. "You never did answer my questions."

I snagged the blanket from her lap, examining the corner, which was in tatters. Then I put her out of her misery. "Yes, this is my place, and no, I didn't call the cops. As long as you don't steal anything besides my pizza and some crackers, I doubt I will."

She licked her lips then rubbed them together. My cock noticed all of it, even though I was pretty certain she wasn't flirting. "But you're not making any promises?"

I raked my gaze over her, letting the voices in the back of my head, telling me I had to clean up my act, dim.

"When it comes to trouble, I make no promises."

Chapter Three

Saoirse

Luke was flirting with me, and I was absolutely receptive to it.

Who wouldn't have been?

He was fricking gorgeous.

Even sitting down, I could tell he was tall, most likely taller than me. His limbs were long and lean, and the skin peeking out from his partially unbuttoned shirt was golden, with just a hint of black hair in the center of his chest.

His dark eyes were heavy-lidded and gave off a sensual glint. My grandmother once mentioned her favorite actor had *bedroom eyes*, and this was the first time I really understood that term.

Those eyes, compounded with his sharp, square jaw lined with dark scruff and his thick black hair, which seemed to have a mind of its own, continually flopping across his forehead after he scraped it back, made Luke *devastating*.

Internally, I was panting like a little puppy.

I really hoped I was playing it cool on the outside.

"Since I'm already in trouble, can I push my luck and ask for a tour? I've never been in a home quite like this."

He stared at me for so long I was preparing myself to be rejected. Just when I was about to take back my request, Luke unfolded himself from the couch and rose to his feet. Then he offered me his hand. I slipped my hand in his, allowing him to pull me upright.

He tugged just a little too hard, and I ended up flush against him. "Well, hello." My hands went to his chest, and his landed on my hips.

I had to look up at him. Not far, maybe two or three inches, but I appreciated that he was taller than me.

"I'm not used to a woman being at my eye level," he uttered lowly, his gaze sliding across my face.

Neither of us seemed to be in a hurry to pull back.

"What do you think about it?"

He smelled good. Like spice and fresh air. I had to stop myself from shoving my nose in his throat to see if his scent was more concentrated there, right over his thrumming pulse. I bet it was.

"I have a lot of questions I didn't have before."

My tongue darted out to wet my upper lip. "Ask them."

One of his hands dragged from my hips, along my ribs, trailing over my arm and shoulder to the side of my neck. He watched me as he moved higher up my body as if waiting for an objection, but I found nothing objectionable about being in this man's arms.

His thumb stroked the underside of my jaw, gently tipping my head back.

"Some things can only be answered through experiencing them." His eyes never left mine as he closed in on me at an achingly slow pace.

Impatience spurred me to rise ever so slightly on my bare toes and press my mouth to Luke's. He grunted, deep and rumbly, then tugged me deeper into his body, his fingers tangling in the back of my hair and clasping my hip even more firmly.

Despite the almost rough way he held me, his lips were soft and searching. I'd shared drunken kisses with strangers in bars before, but this was nothing like that. Not at all. He was slow and thorough, tasting every inch of my lips before coaxing them to part and sliding his tongue against mine.

My toes curled into the plush rug beneath me, and my entire body melted into Luke's. His hold on my hip loosened, and he slid his palm to my lower back, teasing the top of my ass. My fingers slipped into the back of his hair, drawing his face nearer to mine.

He tasted delicious, like beer, mint, and something decidedly exclusive to him. I lapped at his tongue and the back of his teeth, and a moan slipped out of me without my permission.

He smiled against my lips, easing back to pepper them with light kisses before pulling away entirely.

"Come on, pretty girl. I'll show you around."

<hr />

Luke led me from room to room, but I barely noticed the contents of any of them. His thumb rubbing the back of my hip had a direct line to my clit, and by the time we were climbing the spiral staircase to his bedroom, I decided I wanted this man and didn't want to wait to have him.

He pushed open the door to his bedroom and allowed me to enter ahead of him, but he never let go of me. His hand seemed to be permanently molded to my hip, and I had no problem with that. I liked it there.

He stood behind me while I tried to take in his room. A bed, tables, art, lights—that was all that registered. Most of my focus had been stolen by the man pressing his thick erection against my ass as he dragged his lips along my bare shoulders.

"There's something to be said for a woman almost as tall as me," he murmured against my skin.

I arched my spine and hooked my hand on his nape. "It's really convenient when things align."

"Hmmm." He sucked on the place between my shoulder and neck. "I'm all about convenience."

I spun to face him, draping my arms over his shoulders. His fingers dove into my hair, angling my head the way he wanted, then his mouth was on mine. God, did this man know how to kiss. He went in lightly at first, taking almost gentle sips from my lips. It was maddening but, at the same time, addictive.

"You're good at that," I told him.

"Your lips taste like fucking sugar." He pulled away just enough to look at them. The heat swelling behind his gaze was so massive it almost knocked me backward.

I knew he meant it—and not just from his expression. In the next moment, he was sucking and nipping them, trying to steal the flavor off my lips. And I wondered if it was possible to come from kissing. I had to press my thighs together to help with the ache Luke had caused, but it didn't do much good.

While he was devouring my mouth, his fingers toyed with the straps of my dress, slipping them down my shoulders. His fingers trailed over my collarbone and the slight swell of my cleavage before venturing around me, where I knew he'd find the zipper.

He didn't ask. One moment, I was secure in my dress, and the next, it was open and sliding down my body. Luke allowed enough room between us for it to fall all the way to the floor.

Breaking away from my mouth, he hooked his fingers in my panties and pulled me toward the bed. He sat down, bringing me to a stop between his spread legs. Lips parted, he took a long, thorough once-over of my body in lacy black panties, a black push-up bra, and absolutely nothing else.

"*Fuck*. The things I want to do to this body." His open mouth landed on my belly button, leaving a trail of wet kisses along my abdomen while he cupped between my legs. "I need to eat your pussy."

I nodded, willing to do almost anything to keep his mouth on me. "Take off your shirt first. Let me see you too."

He let go of me, leaning back on his hands on the bed. "You do it."

His low command hit me in the belly, and I dropped to my knees, sliding my fingertips down his exposed chest to the top button. He had already done half the job, so it took no time to unbutton them all and push his shirt open.

My mouth watered at his tautly muscled torso. I was tempted to use my tongue to follow the line of black hair dividing his abdomen and leading into his trousers. But Luke had other ideas.

He grabbed me and tossed me on the bed. Standing over me to shrug his shirt the rest of the way off, he swept his hungry eyes along my exposed flesh.

"Bra off. Get that fucking bra off now, pretty girl."

My spine bowed at his command. I reached beneath me to unclasp my bra and toss it to the side. Once my breasts were exposed, I had a moment of apprehension. My little tits were my biggest insecurity. But Luke's gaze became darker, going from hungry to starving. Heat scorched my skin as he drank in my body.

He fell over me, his lips closing around one of my nipples, sucking hard enough for me to arch into his mouth and moan. My fingers tangled into the sides of his hair, and my legs pressed and squirmed.

This wasn't me. Kissing strangers in college was as daring as I'd been with men I didn't know. But there was something about this man that had set me alight from minute one. I knew if I said no to this particular experience, I'd regret it forever.

"Luke...oh please." What I was asking for, I wasn't sure. Just *more*. All the promises he'd made while ravishing my mouth.

He lifted his head from my breasts, cupping one of them in his wide palm. "These need more attention. Your nipples are as sweet as your lips." He gazed down my belly. "I bet you're even sweeter between your legs, aren't you?"

"I don't know. You'll have to tell me."

One hard kiss to my smile and he was moving down my torso, licking my nipples and then sucking the skin below my belly button. My panties were removed like the lash of a whip, fast and smooth. Luke wasted no time in spreading me wide and taking his fill of the sight of me.

"*Jesus. Fuck.* Even your cunt is pretty."

Palms spread on the backs of my thighs, he pushed my knees to my chest and dropped down to devour me.

And that was what he did.

There was no teasing. He took one long swipe of me, from end to end, groaning when my flavor hit his tongue, then he speared me with two thick fingers and latched on to my clit.

My neck arched, eyes opening wide to the ceiling. This part rarely worked for me, and if it did, it took a long, long time. But Luke had started the blaze before he even touched me. When his fingers curled inside me, finding a spot I heretofore believed to be a myth, and he sucked my clit between his talented lips, I became a shaking, moaning, wanton little addict.

He'd hooked me in under a minute.

His gratified grunting as he licked and pleasured me only pushed me closer and closer. Because he was getting off on this. He wasn't just doing it for me. This man clearly enjoyed the work he was doing.

I never wanted him to stop.

But I didn't even try to hold myself back. My climax barreled into me with unimaginable force, knocking me for a dizzying loop. A knot deep, deep within me sprung free, and rivers of heat gushed through me. And out of me.

My grip on his hair was solid as I rucked against his waiting lips and tongue, calling his name at a volume that must have reverberated off the walls. My ears were ringing, and I'd lost control of what was leaving my mouth. If everyone at the party downstairs heard me, then I hoped they were happy for me because I'd just had the best orgasm of my life.

My eyelids fell closed as I panted and quivered from aftershocks. Luke let my legs fall to the side as he stroked my inner thighs and the curve of my waist.

"Look at me, pretty girl."

Soft, but it was an order which my eyelids obeyed. Luke was kneeling between my thighs, his pants open, the tip of his cock bulging over the waistband of his black underwear.

I licked my lips.

He chuckled. "Eyes up here."

Our gazes met. If possible, there was even more heat behind his now.

"Did I make a mess of your sheets?" I asked.

His head cocked, and he swiped his index finger along his mouth and chin, then slipped it into his mouth and sucked. The rumbling groan that came from him had my hips rising off the mattress.

He laid his palm on my belly and pressed me down flat. "You improved my sheets. They were missing a pool of hot fucking candy made from your cunt."

"I've never done that before," I admitted.

"It won't be the last time." He pushed a finger into me and twisted. "I'm going to fuck you now, gorgeous."

I nodded. "Please."

He had to climb off the bed to grab a condom from his nightstand. Watching the sensuous way his limbs moved, the rippling of his abdomen, and that dripping purple head practically ripping out of his underwear, I had never wanted anyone more.

This was crazy. Not me. I never lost it over men.

But Luke was in a league of his own.

Just as he tossed the condom on the sheet beside me, someone banged on his bedroom door.

"Luke! Is the tall blonde in there with you?" The thick Italian accent made Vincent easy to identify.

"Fuck off," Luke shouted, his fingers clenching at his sides.

Then Vincent yelled something in Italian. Luke responded in equally rapid Italian, his throat and face reddening.

I scooted upright, suddenly feeling exposed and strange, even though Vincent couldn't see me through the locked door.

Luke turned around to look at me, his hands on his hips. "Don't move. I'm getting rid of him." Then he went back to yelling in Italian.

Normally, this man speaking Italian would have done it for me, but there was nothing normal about this situation.

Embarrassment was sinking in. We should have at least exchanged last names, and I definitely should have inquired about his sexual health.

Kara's voice coming from right outside the door was the nail in the coffin of this evening.

"Sersh, can we go? I'm ready and don't feel safe catching an Uber on my own," she whined.

I already had my dress halfway on when Luke swiveled back around to face me.

"Yes, give me a minute," I called. "I'll meet you downstairs."

He stared at me as I darted around his room, grabbing my panties and bra.

"We weren't finished," he grumbled.

I stopped in my tracks, clutching my underwear to my stomach. "I know, and I'm really sorry to leave you in this state...but it's probably for the best. We don't even know each other."

He huffed. "That was the best part." His gaze lingered on me, and I tried not to react to his hurtful admission. I couldn't even pinpoint why it hurt, but it did.

I covered it up with a coquettish shrug and a little grin. "At least one of us experienced the *best part*."

He strode up to me with a dark expression, and my heart leapt into my throat when he spun me toward the door.

His warm breath touched my ear before his gravelly words did. "I'll bill you for the sheets." Then he gently tugged my zipper up and smoothed my dress along my sides. "I've never tasted sweeter than you, pretty girl."

Then he opened his bedroom door and sent me on my merry way.

CHAPTER FOUR

Luca

FOR ONCE, I ARRIVED at the gym on time.

Only a half hour after Elliot and Weston, which was on time for me. With my late nights, mornings were a struggle. But last night, once I'd cleared Vincent's guests from my apartment and taken care of the raging erection left by the leggy, quirky blonde who'd utterly destroyed my sheets in the best way, I'd slept like a fucking baby.

Only to wake up early this morning rock hard, the memory of her taste still sweet on my lips.

Elliot Levy, my friend since our Stanford days, lifted an unimpressed brow through his reflection in the mirror as he did bicep curls. My definition of early differed from Elliot's by a mile. He had never once arrived anywhere more than a millisecond past the appointed time.

I climbed on the open treadmill beside Weston, the third member of our trio. He'd have said I was the third member since he and Elliot had been friends since childhood, but I had shoved myself snug in the middle of the two of them, so there was no way I was number three.

Weston glanced at me while he kept up his fast clip. "You look rested for once."

"I am. I was asleep by eleven."

"In your own bed?"

"Yes." I punched some buttons on the control panel, and the treadmill got started. "All alone too."

On fresh sheets, which I didn't mention. Though a sick, filthy part of me had been tempted to lie in that pretty girl's mess. If I had, there wouldn't have been any sleep for me, and my dick would have ended up chafed from a night of stroking it.

He tapped a button, slowing his pace to match mine.

"You went to bed alone?"

"You sound like you don't believe me, West."

"It's not that." He swiped his sweaty forehead with the collar of his shirt. "You're not one to brag about sleeping alone. That leads me to believe there's more to this story."

He had me. I needed to talk about what had gone down with Sasha last night, but for the first time, possibly ever, I really didn't want to share any of the finer details. Weston would be grateful for that. He always humored me, but he wasn't on tenterhooks to hear about my hookup's tit size or the joys of bedding a former gymnast. West was quiet about it, but he'd had his fair share of women over the years. No doubt anything I had to say was old news.

Now that he was with Elise, who happened to be Elliot's younger sister, those days were history for him. The fucker was the happiest I'd ever seen him too.

"There was a last hurrah," I told him.

Elliot strolled over, wiping his face with a small towel. "Why last?" He sat down on the circuit machine in front of the treadmills.

"I met with the consultants the board hired yesterday."

Elliot's chin lowered. "And? What did they have to say?"

"I have a bad reputation."

Weston barked a dry laugh. "That's an understatement. Were consultants necessary to tell you that?"

"Like I said, the board brought them in. They did a top-to-bottom evaluation of my image."

Elliot paused his leg press. "And what did they conclude?"

I shook my head and let out a humorless laugh. "That it's a bad look for the new CEO of Rossi Motors to be dubbed 'The Playboy CEO' by CNBC."

Weston chuffed. "Let me guess, they conducted a focus group and wrote a ten-page report to deliver this information to you."

"Wrong." I flashed him a grin I didn't quite feel. Having my life taken over wasn't exactly conducive to good humor. "Fifteen."

"And how did they advise you to change your image?" Elliot asked.

With a groan, I shoved my fingers through my hair. "I'm to stop going to events and clubs with women I'm not in a relationship with."

"Which means you'll be going alone," Weston supplied.

"Right," I agreed.

Since unexpectedly taking over my father's position as CEO of our family's company, Rossi Motors, everything he'd done now fell on me. That meant the dinners, conferences, charity fundraisers—each drier and more boring than the next—would be my responsibility. I'd done some of that in my role as VP, and the only thing that made them slightly tolerable was the open bars and surety I'd be sinking my cock into whichever beautiful woman I brought with me as my date.

Elliot stopped again. "They told you you're not allowed to date?"

"Not in the way I currently *date*. In fact, I was told CEOs who are married inspire seventy-five percent more confidence in shareholders."

Weston slowed down a little more. "So now you have to get married?"

Elliot made a strangled, choking sound. "How does one get married without first dating?"

"I don't know. It's all bullshit, and everyone knows that. I don't leave the office until eight at night on a good day. Since stepping into this position, my entire lifestyle has changed. I haven't even had time to get laid, and I see no end in sight. I've changed without trying."

And it pissed me off to no end. These days, I was either tired or angry, and the throbbing headache that had taken up semipermanent residence behind my right eye didn't help anything.

"If you have no time, what was this 'last hurrah' you mentioned?" Weston asked.

"It was more of an almost hurrah," I admitted. "Vin threw a party at my place last night."

Elliot winced. "I don't know why you allow him to stay with you for weeks on end. He's worse than a frat boy."

"It's funny because I seem to recall you labeling me a debauched frat boy more than once," I volleyed back, even though he had a fair point about both me and Vin.

Elliot was unbothered. "If the shoe fits." He got up from the machine, stretching his arms over his head.

Weston cleared his throat. "I think Elliot's trying to say that while you both party, Vin doesn't respect your home. Didn't he break one of your sculptures the last time he visited?"

I flinched at the memory. "Almost. He tipped it, but I caught it before it could fall."

And I tore him a new asshole, but he'd been chagrined all on his own.

"Aren't we getting off track?" Elliot asked.

"Yes. We were going to hear about the almost hurrah," Weston said.

"She was in my den." I almost allowed my eyes to close so I could bring back the image of her curled up on my couch. But the last thing I needed was to get hard in front of my best friends at the gym. "Long, long legs, silky blonde hair, and a sassy as hell mouth. We talked, clicked, I gave her a tour, she gave me a tour of *her*."

Elliot rolled his eyes, but he didn't walk away to his next machine. As dismissive as he was, he was interested, so I went on.

"Sweetest thing I've had in my bed in a long time. The chemistry was shockingly strong." I shook my head in mourning. "We got interrupted before I got off. The friend she came with wanted to go, so she went."

Weston's brow pinched. "And that's it?"

I lifted a shoulder. "It is what it is. If the circumstances were different, I would hunt her down to finish what we started, but as it stands, I shouldn't have gone there last night."

Elliot nodded. "You have to guard the brand, Luc. Bringing random women into your bed isn't wise. She could have been planted there to extract blackmail material. Think of what you'd have to pay not to have a sex tape leak."

"I don't think she—"

Elliot leveled me with a *come the fuck on* stare. "Do you know anything about this woman?"

She was sexy, funny, liked pizza, trying new things, and her taste was forever ingrained in my memories.

I conceded his point. "Not enough to trust who she presented herself to be at face value."

"It's a big change for you," Weston added. "You weren't ready for it."

"He'd known it was coming," Elliot argued.

The pulse behind my eye was beginning to throb. "Eventually, not *now*, and sure as hell not as suddenly as it did."

Weston gave my shoulder a pat. "How's Vic?"

"Snarly."

My father, Victorio Rossi, who, up until a couple weeks ago, had been the CEO of Rossi Motors. He'd been doing the job more than twenty years, since his father had stepped down. He'd have held on to the title for another twenty.

I wouldn't have had a problem with that.

His heart had other plans.

Elliot's normally impassive expression grew sympathetic. "It can't be easy to go from ruling a Fortune 500 company to being told what to do, down to what he can eat. I don't think any of us would handle that well."

"Hell no," I agreed. "I just wish he wouldn't take his anger out on my mother. She's waiting on him hand and foot, like always, and he's being a dick to her."

One sunny morning, my father had a heart attack in the middle of a board meeting. Our family gathered at the hospital, waiting hours to see if he'd make it out of surgery alive. The first thing he wanted to do when he woke up was check his emails.

My mother's sobs had flipped his switch, though.

He'd retired almost immediately, much to everyone's shock and his doctor's delight. That meant I went from vice president—which had been a cushy title allowing me all the freedom I desired to pursue my passions and, as Elliot had put it, debauched lifestyle—to running my family's company.

And we weren't some mom-and-pop small business. Rossi Motors was the largest producer of motorcycles in America.

"I'm surprised Vic is capable of being a dick to Angelina," Weston said.

"Me too." I shoved my fingers through my hair. I'd been so busy talking I hadn't even broken a sweat yet. "He'll regret it when he comes out of this fog."

My parents were disgusting. They were always kissing and laughing together. He pinched my mother's butt whenever she bent down, and she sent him off every morning by straightening his tie and whispering secrets in his ear.

My sister and I used to gag at their public displays of affection, but as our friends' parents got divorced, or worse, stayed in toxic marriages, we saw how lucky we were.

Which made my father's treatment of my mother even harder to bear. She was his treasure, but he was acting like she was his jailer.

The pulse slammed behind my eye, and I was done. Done working out, done thinking about this, done talking. Circumstances were what they were. Fighting against them wouldn't make anything easier.

I accepted who I was. Luca Rossi, CEO of Rossi Motors, soon to be the owner of the loneliest dick in Denver.

CHAPTER FIVE

Saoirse

TODAY WAS THE FIRST day in a long line of first days. I never tired of the anticipation of walking into a new office where anything could happen.

I flattened the *V* neckline of my cream silk blouse and smoothed down my leather pencil skirt, turning to the side to examine my reflection. Elise pushed into my room while I was in the middle of considering my outfit.

"Is leather office appropriate?" I asked her.

She stood behind me in one of her cute tops with a bow tied at the throat and a pair of smart trousers. I almost burst out laughing at how different our workwear was. Elise had honed her style years ago, and she rocked her librarian chic look. It helped that she was all curves and made pretty much anything look hot.

She tapped her chin, taking my question seriously. "What kind of company is this job at again?"

I turned to face her, my dearest best friend since we were randomly assigned as roommates our freshman year at CU Boulder. She'd moved back to Denver from Chicago a few months ago, and we'd joined forces once again, sharing an apartment like old times.

Except her boyfriend, Weston, occupied the penthouse, and she spent a considerable amount of time up there. But Elise was Elise, and she made sure we shared at least one meal a day together so I wouldn't feel abandoned, which I never did.

I was a West-and-Elise fangirl. I didn't begrudge even a minute they spent together. It didn't hurt that when he sent Elise flowers, he also sent a small bouquet for me because Elise had once told him how much I liked them.

"Didn't I tell you?" I shoved an earring through my lobe. "I'm in the marketing department of Rossi Motors. Maybe I'll finally get to meet the elusive Luca."

Her hands shot to her hips. "Um, no. I think I'd remember if you told me you were going to be working at Rossi."

I shoved the second earring through my other lobe, wincing at how painful it was. *Note to self: wear earrings more often so I don't have to draw blood to get them in.*

"I only got the call last week, and I was finishing up my last job. One of their marketing assistants had her baby early, so they needed me to start right away." I twisted back to my reflection. "You never told me if leather is okay. I thought yes since they make motorcycles, but now I'm worried this is a little too on the nose."

She stood next to me, eyeing the mirror. "You look hot, yet professional. I'm a big fan of the skirt. You know how I feel about your legs."

I grinned. "The same way I feel about your tits. Too bad we can't donate a couple inches to each other."

We'd had this conversation many, *many* times, and I loved that about us. My life was a constant whirlwind of changes, but my friendship with Elise had remained constant for nearly a decade.

"I'll have to text Luca to look out for you." Her mouth twisted. "You probably won't see him, though. He's pretty much buried with taking over his new position."

"I didn't figure I'd be chilling with the CEO, but maybe I'll spot him exiting his limo."

Elise laughed. "Luca doesn't ride in a limo." Then she grabbed her phone. "I'll text him anyway, just to let him know you'll be in the building. If he has time, maybe he'll introduce himself so you both can finally put a face to the name."

Luca Rossi was good friends with Weston and Elliot, Elise's older brother. Stars had never aligned for us, and our paths had yet to cross. Mostly, I was curious about the third member of the "Hot Boss Musketeers." I'd heard Luca's name in passing for several years, and I'd always wondered if he lived up to his charm-the-pants-off-anyone reputation.

"Sure. If it happens, it happens. I'll be there at least a month." I smoothed my skirt again and nodded, decision made. "This will do."

———— ◆ ————

My first week at Rossi was everything I wanted in a temp job. Loads of interesting work, good snacks in the break room, friendly coworkers. Since my positions were always temporary, sometimes I found no one could be bothered to get to know me, but that wasn't the case at this job.

I'd even been invited out for happy hour on Friday.

There were ten of us crammed around a small table on the patio of a bar near the office, seven women, three guys. Someone had shoved me toward Charlie, the single guy of the group.

Not very subtle.

Charlie leaned closer to me, his beer resting on his knee. "Where did you work before this?"

Charlie smelled good, even after a long day. He had a full head of thick, floppy hair and tattooed forearms I imagined stretched into full sleeves beneath his clothes. Thin and rangy, he was perhaps an inch or two shorter than me, which wasn't a deal breaker in terms of attraction. Charlie was good-looking, for sure, but I didn't feel any kind of spark of interest. These days, I listened to my initial gut feeling. Charlie was a coworker and a potential friend, but no more.

"A marketing firm, actually." I sipped my cocktail. "That's what I went to college for."

"And you haven't been able to find a permanent job?"

"No, I have. I've found I'm more of a temporary girl."

He raised a brow. "In all things?"

"So far."

"Are you looking for something?"

"That's a good question, Charlie. I don't really know, but moving on almost always feels right. For instance, I enjoyed my last job, but I like this one more. If I'd settled there, I wouldn't have gotten to work at Rossi."

"So, you're a rolling stone?"

I winked at him, feeling loose from half a drink and a long, happy week. "I gather no moss."

From my other side, Amelia, one of the leads of the department, asked, "Is that the same with boyfriends? Never settling?"

I turned to her. "Well, I hope when I find the right guy, it won't feel like settling."

Not that I had much hope for that, nor was I actively looking for anything.

The woman on her other side, Niddhi, guffawed. "Good luck with that. It's all rainbows and moonbeams in the beginning—and then you realize those rainbows were an illusion and the moonbeams were actually the phone he was using while you were sleeping to sext girls on Only Fans..."

Amelia patted her knee and steered the conversation in another direction. I turned to Charlie, a little slack-jawed.

"What was that?" I whispered.

"She's going through a bad breakup."

I nodded. "Uh, yeah. I gathered that. Wowza, poor thing."

"Her ex spent twenty grand on cam girls before she caught him."

I slapped my forehead. "What an idiot. Why do men throw away real relationships for a minute or two of gratification? I'll never understand it."

"Not every guy is deceitful." The eye contact he kept with me was steeped in meaning, and I got the drift. Charlie *wasn't like other men*. But in my experience, if a man had to say that, he probably was *just* like other men.

I placed my empty glass on the tiny table and hopped up. "I'm going to the restroom. Be back."

"I'll save your seat," Charlie called to my retreating back.

There were perks to being tall, one being catching bartenders' attention easily. I waved my hand at the pretty woman behind the bar. She started toward me, her steps stuttering as a long arm reached out in front of me to flag her down. When she regained her composure, she walked right past me to wait on the person who'd squeezed in behind me.

She propped her elbows on the bar and leaned forward, putting her tits on display. "Hello, handsome."

"Good evening, *bella*. It seems our waiter has gone missing. Is that something you can rectify?"

I recognized that smooth, silky timbre. The slight edge of impatience had been absent last weekend, but there was no mistaking who'd stolen my bartender.

She ran her finger along the line of her cleavage. "I think I can take care of you, handsome. Give it to me."

"I'd be more than happy to give it to you."

Oh, wow. This guy was a smooth-as-shit flirt, wasn't he? No wonder he'd gotten me into bed with barely any effort.

Luke recited his order, and the bartender jumped into action. I swiveled around to express my displeasure.

"I know we discussed your rudeness when you wouldn't share your pizza, but I thought we'd conquered that bad habit."

A flash of recognition lightened Luke's dark eyes. Momentary disbelief gave way to a sexy smirk. "Are you still talking about that?"

"I would have let it go if you hadn't cut in front of me. That bartender was mine."

He cocked his head. "If she was yours, why did she serve me first?"

I gestured to his face then the rest of him. "You're hot."

"And?"

"Hotness tends to strike some people stupid."

"Not you though?"

I tucked my hair behind my ear, playing coy, but, man, I actually felt somewhat bashful in front of him. He was more attractive than I even remembered, which seemed impossible since I remembered him being devastating to look at.

"I'm not so shallow." I tugged on his tie, which was snug at the collar, despite being in a bar during after-work hours. "You look serious."

His gaze drifted over me, and I'd never been more grateful for my small collection of leather. My leather shift dress did wonders for my figure, giving me the illusion of being far curvier than I was.

"You look gorgeous." He gave me those bedroom eyes and bit down on his bottom lip.

Belying his words and the heat behind his gaze, he kept a respectful distance between us.

"Thank you. You do too. Serious, but still gorgeous."

His slow, easy grin made my stomach flip and drop. I had to stop myself from reaching for the bar for support.

"What are you doing here?" he asked.

"Having a drink with some of my coworkers."

He glanced around. "Where are they?"

"Outside on the patio."

His eyes narrowed. "Likely story. Are you sure you aren't stalking me?"

I let out a surprised laugh. "If I was, I would never admit it. You're probably wearing a wire. Anyway, you weren't *that* good—not enough to go psycho-stalker over at least."

He gave me that grin again and ran his hand down the front of his shirt. "That isn't true, and I have the sheets to prove it."

Heat shot to my cheeks and throat. "Did you really have to bring that up?"

"I can't believe you're actually embarrassed over that, pretty girl. You don't strike me as someone who gets embarrassed easily."

"I'm not." I pressed a hand to my flushed cheek. "I wasn't prepared for you to talk about the sheets, which I really hope you've washed."

He cocked his head. "They're safely tucked away in an evidence bag."

My nose wrinkled. "Gross."

"Excuse me." We both turned to find the bartender propping her boobs up again. "Your order is being taken to your table, handsome. Is there any other way I can help you?"

Luke ran his hand through the side of his hair, mussing it up deliciously. "What do you want to drink?"

I tried to meet the bartender's eyes, but she was stuck on Luke. "I'll have a margarita on the rocks, please." I flicked my attention back to Luke as she started on my drink. "Are you here with friends?"

He shook his head. "No. Business associates. Work isn't over for me, unfortunately. I should get back to them."

"Right. Well, it was good seeing you. Maybe we'll run into each other again."

"If you *are* stalking me, I'd work on your subterfuge. Hanging out in the bar closest to my office is less than subtle."

I rolled my eyes. "I got what I wanted from you. Why would I need to stalk you?"

He dipped closer to me, bringing his mouth near my ear. "Because you recognized there was so much more you missed out on." His cheek brushed mine, then he pulled away, taking a step back. "Until next time, pretty girl."

He tucked his hands in his pockets and strolled away.

I really doubted there would be a next time, but it had been fun while it lasted.

CHAPTER SIX

Saoirse

I'D BEEN PLAYING THE long game with the honey guy at the farmers' market. Every week, I flirted a little more, slowly luring him to my hook. Not that I'd know what to do with him once I caught him, but the game was fun.

Today, I'd come away with a free pack of honey sticks, one of my favorite snacks. I supposed they weren't exactly free since I'd jumped in to help Mick while he was in the weeds with a long line of customers. I wasn't an expert like he was since he was the beekeeper, but after a summer of stopping by his booth and sampling all his goods, I could answer questions and bag up purchases.

Of course, my impromptu job meant I was running late for brunch with Elise, Weston, Elliot, and Luca.

I was finally going to meet him, and I was just a little bit giddy about it. Technically, he was my boss, but I was trying not to think about that. Having brunch with my boss was somewhat intimidating.

I made it to the brunch spot with a minute to spare, so I ducked into the restroom to wash my hands and make sure my hair didn't look too crazy from my morning outdoors.

Pleasantly surprised to find my hair cooperating, draping over my shoulders in soft waves and my cheeks slightly pink from the sun, I passed inspection. I smoothed out my red-polka-dot wrap skirt and tugged down my cropped white T-shirt then pushed open the door, intent on finding my friends.

But I ran straight into a man. He caught me by the arms so I wouldn't fall backward after bouncing off his solid chest.

"Excuse me, *bella*."

My eyes jerked up, but not far, finding Luke was the delicious-smelling obstacle.

"What—?" So shocked to see him for the second time in less than twenty-four hours I couldn't get my mouth or brain to function.

Luke had no such problems. He dropped my arms like he'd been scalded and practically leapt away from me.

"What the fuck is this?" he hissed. "I was joking about you stalking me, but Christ—"

"Wait a second. You think I'm *stalking* you?"

His heavy, dark brow furrowed into a furious line. "This isn't a coincidence. It's impossible. And since I'm sure as hell not stalking *you*, it's pretty clear what's going on here."

Incensed at his ridiculous accusation, I folded my arms over my chest. "You're nuts, aren't you? How do I know you aren't following me? That's much more likely. Or...I don't know. We both ended up at a popular brunch spot on a day when half of Denver goes out to brunch. Did that occur to you?"

"No." He folded his arms over his chest. "You aren't the first girl to chase me like this, but it ends now. If I see you again, I'll be forced to take action."

"Go for it, buddy. And see how stupid you feel when you're proven pathologically paranoid."

I stormed by him, making sure not to touch even a thread of his stupidly fitted T-shirt. What an egotistical bastard. The idea that I'd ever stalk a man. Pfft. It was outrageous.

When I found my friends, I yanked out my seat and flopped into it. Their conversation came to a standstill, all eyes on me.

"Bad day at the farmers' market?" Elliot deadpanned.

Mentally, I was flipping him off, but I refrained since there were children present around us. The stink-eye I gave him conveyed my displeasure at his condescending question just fine.

"I just ran into the biggest a-hole in Denver, that's all."

Elise had been thoughtful enough to order me a mimosa, which I slammed back. Of course, champagne and orange juice weren't meant to be chugged, so I choked on my own fucking drink. Weston patted me on the back, and Elise took the glass from me, placing it gently on the table.

When I stopped coughing, I wiped my mouth on my napkin and waved them off. "I'm fine. Sorry to make such a dramatic entrance." I glanced around the table. "Where's Luca? Is he not coming?"

"He's making a call." Elise glanced over her shoulder. "Oh, there he is now."

Time stood still when I spotted the man in question. Tall and lean, wearing a fitted black T-shirt and dark-gray pants, Luca Rossi strode to our table. But Luca wasn't Luca. He was Luke.

Or...Luke *was* Luca?

Oh shit.

He spotted me at the same time, and his expression was thunderous. Did he think I'd stalked him all the way to this table? Was he not putting the pieces together like I had?

Dummy.

Elise hopped out of her seat and grabbed Luca's arm, steering him directly in front of me. I slowly rose, leveling him with a gaze filled with more confidence than I felt.

"Luca, I'd like to finally introduce you to my best girl, Saoirse Kelly. Sersh, meet Luca."

I held out my hand. "Hi, Luca. It's nice to meet you after all this time."

After a beat of hesitation, his hand enclosed mine, and he squeezed slightly too hard. "Saoirse. Do people often mispronounce your name and call you Sasha?"

"All the time." I blinked at him. "Do you ever go by Luke?"

"Sometimes."

I tried to pull away, but he held on, searching for something in my gaze...or my expression. With a huff that sounded like frustration, he dropped his hold and turned away from me, placing a swift kiss on Elise's cheek, then took the empty chair across the table from me.

Once we were all seated and had ordered, conversation picked up between the five of us. While I was still trying to wrap my head around the fact that I'd hooked up with Luca Rossi, my technical boss and Elise's friend, I attempted to play it cool.

"By the way, I have a present for everyone." I picked up my canvas bag from where I'd stashed it beneath my chair and reached in, grabbing the first item. "These are for West."

I handed him the six-pack of hand-embroidered cloth napkins. His brow crinkled as he studied them, and I laughed at his befuddled expression.

"They're cloth napkins. I know how important the environment is, so I thought you might like these instead of using paper. I bought some for Elise and myself too."

"Thank you." Weston smiled gently at me. "That was really thoughtful."

"Changing the world one napkin at a time," Elliot intoned.

"That's right." I was used to him, so I never let his teasing get to me. And that's what I'd decided it was. Despite how closed off and uptight he was, he wouldn't be mean to me simply because I was Elise's friend. "Don't worry, I got something for you too."

I handed him the beet I'd chosen just for him. He immediately dropped it on the table to stare at it. "What is this?"

"A heart-shaped beet, Elliot. I saw it, and it reminded me of you."

Luca's low snicker drew my eyes to him. I grinned at him, and his humor fell away. He straightened in his seat, composing himself.

"Oooh, El, I'll send you a recipe for beet salad." Elise scrolled through her phone. "I haven't made it myself since...you know, cooking and I don't mix, but you're much better in the kitchen than I am. You can handle it."

"Thank you, El. I can't wait," he remarked with the enthusiasm of a corpse.

I sputtered a laugh. Elliot Levy was the best.

"Don't tell me you left Luca out," Weston prodded. "He's looking rather sad over there."

Luca held up his hands. "I'm just fine."

"What kind of person would I be if I didn't bring Luca a gift?" I reached in my bag and withdrew the grand prize, handing it to Elise. "Pass this to Luca for me."

He took the cutting board from Elise, staring at it in the same befuddled manner Elliot had with his beet. I'd been excited to give this to him before we'd met, but now I was a mess of trepidation.

My love language was gifting, and though Luca and I hadn't met—or so I thought when choosing his present—I'd wanted to give him something that showed him how excited I was to get to know him.

Now it just seemed over the top, especially after our bitter exchange outside the bathroom.

"It's a play on words," I explained. "It's a cheese board with a crown on it because you're now king of the boardroom."

On top of the cheese board, I'd given him honey, jam, and a few different cheeses I'd selected just for him.

"Oh my god, that's so cute," Elise cooed.

"Very thoughtful," Weston added.

Even Elliot had something kind to say. "Good going, Kelly."

"Thanks, Levy," I croaked before taking a long sip of my water.

All of us waited for Luca's reaction. Before he could say a single word, a horde of waiters brought our food, and Luca set the board down on the ground.

On. The. Ground.

He tossed a perfunctory "thank you" my way, then dug into his omelet like a starving man. Fortunately, Elise steered the conversation away from his nonreaction to a safer topic: Mick, the honey guy.

"He's the reason I was a little late. I helped him run his stand."

Elliot frowned. "You just…jumped behind the counter?"

"I asked before I did so, but essentially, yes."

He shook his head, and I grinned.

"Did he pay you?" Weston asked.

"In honey sticks."

"I can't believe you." Elise shook her head much the same way her brother had. "Poor Mick is probably planning how he's going to propose."

"Why poor Mick? He's playing the same game I am. We're having fun, babe. It doesn't have to mean anything."

"What does that mean?" Luca barked. "What game?"

"They have been flirting and bantering all summer," Elise supplied. "Saoirse's been slowly reeling him in."

A deep crevice formed between Luca's eyes. "What happens once you reel men in?"

I lifted a shoulder. "It depends on the man."

"Cut them loose?" he pressed.

"Again, depends on the man." I tried to keep my answers light, but Luca wasn't even attempting to disguise his disdain.

Elise shoved Luca's arm. "Relax. Mick is a grown man, and he's been flirting right back. Plus, he got free labor today. As far as I'm concerned, he's a few points ahead in this little game of theirs."

After a tense beat, Luca blew out a heavy breath. "I'm sorry. I haven't gotten enough sleep this week and my head hurts. I'm being an asshole."

Now that I was really looking at him, compared to the man I'd met last week, he seemed beaten down. He was impeccably dressed and groomed, but his shoulders were slightly slumped, and there were purple smudges beneath his heavy-lidded eyes.

"That's okay." I tossed him a saucy smirk. "I know I probably give off the impression of being a femme fatale, but I assure you, it's an illusion. I have never once broken a man's heart, nor do I want to."

"Can you say the same, Luca?" Elise asked.

He gave her a slow, crooked smile. "I've never broken a man's heart, *bella*. I can promise you that."

She snorted a laugh. "Shut up and eat your food. You're ridiculous."

Brunch went on with slightly less animosity after that. Elliot told us about the property his development company was considering investing in, and the guys debated the economics of it. Though I listened, I didn't have a lot to add. It wasn't that I didn't have a mind for business, but I was more of an idea person. Numbers were like Sanskrit to me.

Elise leaned closer to me, zoning out of their conversation. "What are you doing tomorrow?"

"I have coffee scheduled with Maritza, but I'm free after that. It'll be a laundry and veg day."

"Who is Maritza again?"

"I met her at a hostel in Croatia, remember? She's from Berlin, but she's moving to Boulder and starting a boutique gardening business, which is why we're having coffee."

"You're helping her with her plans?"

I nodded. "She wants me to look over what she has."

Elise's mouth flattened. "And knowing you, you'll probably end up spending hours and hours reworking everything."

"That's an exaggeration, but yes, I have a tendency to get carried away with ideas."

"You shouldn't be giving your time and effort away for free. I don't know why I have to keep telling you that."

"It's just fun for me."

I had a propensity for picking up friends and acquaintances wherever I went. Elise called me the Pied Piper of needy people, which was an overstatement of facts, to be sure. Besides, I enjoyed helping people out. Lately, my friends and acquaintances had been coming to me to go over their business plans, and I'd been helping them refine them.

Like I'd said, it was fun. A brain exercise for me.

But in the back of my mind, I'd been toying with the idea of turning this into a true business. It was only the beginning of a daydream, though. I wasn't even sure I had it in me to run my own business. If it came to fruition, it would be way down the line.

"If you say so." Elise sighed. "I just don't like you being taken advantage of."

"I'll stick with temping for now."

"Speaking of..." Elise tapped Luca's forearm. "Were you aware Saoirse is Rossi Motor's latest employee?"

He went still, his gaze flicking to mine. "I wasn't aware of that. When did you start?"

"I've been at Rossi for a week. It's only temporary," I explained.

"In which department?"

"Marketing."

He regarded me carefully. "Are you enjoying working for my company?"

"I like my coworkers, and the job is interesting. Plus, there're biscotti in the break room, which ups the cool factor tremendously. Oh, and Gina brings in donuts and éclairs every Friday."

His brow winged. "Gina?"

"Mmhmm. Gina's the department manager, and she has the hookup. Her uncle runs a bakery."

"So, what you're saying is, you enjoy working for me based solely on the snacks?" The corners of his mouth tipped slightly in amusement.

"I did mention the work was interesting, but it could be dull as toast and I'd still look forward to coming in every day simply for the biscotti. No doubt I'll gain ten pounds before I leave Rossi, but it'll be worth it."

Luca's gaze slid to Elliot's. "Is she for real?"

Elliot folded his hands on the table and inclined his chin. "Welcome to the wild and wonderful world of Saoirse Kelly."

I gasped. "You think I'm wonderful, Levy? I'm so flattered."

Elliot made a grunting sound and returned his attention to his mostly empty plate.

"Don't tease my brother," Elise admonished. "He doesn't know how to handle it. He might implode."

"But it's so fun," I whispered. "And yes, Luca, I'm real. Snacks are important in a workplace. I read over your employee surveys. I bet you the marketing department is the most satisfied, and it's all due to Gina and her magical baked goods."

"I'll be sure to look into that," he replied without a hint of sincerity.

"You honestly should. Employee satisfaction is vital to any business."

His nostrils flared. "I wasn't aware you've run a company."

I refused to be spoken down to. "If you think someone has to run a company to have common sense, you're more out of touch than I realized."

He straightened, leaning forward. "I'm not out of touch."

I shrugged. "Okay. If you say so."

Our friends carried on around us while Luca continued giving me a dark stare. As soon as the bill was paid, he shot out of his chair, mumbling excuses and saying goodbye to everyone but me. In the flurry of his sudden departure, no one else seemed to notice the slight, but I had.

And I hated how much it stung.

CHAPTER SEVEN

Luca

FOR THE FIRST TIME in weeks, I was alone in my home. Vincent had flown back to Italy, taking all his chaos with him.

I'd spent my evening in the blessed quiet, eating a meal I'd cooked without anyone talking over my shoulder and drinking the scotch I'd hidden from him so he didn't pour it over one of the women he'd paraded through here.

That wasn't paranoia either. A year ago, he'd cracked open the bottle of Macallan I'd been saving for a special occasion and drank it off the body of a woman he'd met that evening. Most of it had ended up soaking into my guest bedroom mattress, and I'd nearly wept at the waste.

I also hadn't allowed him back into my condo for a year. The only reason I had this time was because of my father's heart attack. Vin had provided a much-needed distraction from the worry.

Now I was settled in my den, a heavy pour of Macallan in my glass, my laptop on my lap, devouring the employment file of one Ms. Saoirse Kelly.

She had letters of recommendation from her past ten employers, and they were all glowing. I'd come to the reluctant conclusion none of what she'd told me the night she was here had been a lie. My fucking ears had just heard her name wrong. If I'd heard Saoirse, I would have asked questions because there weren't that many six-foot-tall blondes named Saoirse walking around Denver, and I'd been well aware of Elise's best friend since I'd been hearing about her for years.

But how had she not known who I was?

My need for answers beat out my common sense. I logged into my company email to fire off a message to her.

To: saoirsekelly@rossimotors.com

From: lucarossi@rossimotors.com

Saoirse,

Did you know who I was?

-Luca

It took less than fifteen minutes for her to reply.

To: lucarossi@rossimotors.com

From: saoirsekelly@rossimotors.com

Luca,

Well, hello to you, sir.

No, I didn't know who you were. You told me your name was Luke (which I now realize you meant Luc, but I didn't know at the time), and I had no reason to suspect you were anyone I should have known.

If we can put our first meeting behind us, that would be great. We share the same friends, and I'm working for your company for at least the next month, so it would be easier to act like it didn't happen, don't you agree?

Sincerely,

Your Inconvenient Hookup, Saoirse-not-Sasha

Falling back against the cushions, I read and reread her response. She was just as sassy through emails as she was in person.

And she was right. Hooking up again was out of the question. Not just because we were both deeply enmeshed in the same circle of friends, but because I wasn't fucking allowed to *hook up* anymore.

I was playing the straight and narrow now.

Yet, despite all those reasons, I found myself emailing her back.

To: saoirsekelly@rossimotors.com

From: lucarossi@rossimotors.com

Saoirse,

I apologize for getting your name wrong. If you'll remember, you were taking a sip of wine when you told it to me. Also, it's not a name I hear often or ever, so forgive my mistake. It won't happen again.

I agree, we should put it behind us, but I won't be able to forget it. When I move my lips the right way, I still have some sugar on my tongue. Then there's the evidence bag...

Here's wishing you another pleasant week working at Rossi Motors.

-Luca, your boss

⸻ ◦○◦ ⸻

Monday morning, I strode across the lobby of Rossi, nodding to the guards at the security desk. I was late due to an early morning video conference I'd taken from my home office, so the elevator bank was deserted except for one lone woman.

Of course.

Saoirse Kelly was juggling two trays of coffee and a large paper bag as she looked up at the illuminated numbers above the elevators. Her long legs—made longer by her high heels—were crossed at the ankle, propping her delicate hip to the side. Her hair spilled down her back in soft waves. Standing still, she gave off the impression of a fifties movie star. She had a Grace Kelly way about her.

Until she opened her mouth.

"Do you need help with those?"

She swiveled around, her rosy lips popping open when her eyes landed on me. Her surprise didn't last long, though.

"Thank you, I really do." She held out one of the trays.

Raising a brow, I took it from her. "They have you fetching coffee?"

"The machine broke. Add on that it's a Monday and half the team is on a tight deadline, and it's an actual disaster. I volunteered just to get away from the uncaffeinated grumpiness."

The elevator doors slid open, and I stepped in behind her. She hit the button to her floor and her hand hovered over the panel.

"There's no button for the executive floor."

"No." I pointed to the sensor above the numbers. "I have to swipe my card, but I usually just take the executive elevator."

Her eyebrows shot up. "Wow. Sounds cushy. You don't have to ride with the plebes."

"There are some perks to the job."

She sucked in a deep breath. "Thanks for emailing me, by the way."

"I noticed you didn't reply to the last one."

Her nose scrunched. "Well, it was kind of inappropriate, coming from my boss."

For the first time today, I chuckled. "The whole boss thing is still settling in. I'll work on it."

"I still can't believe you're *Luca,* Luca."

"I'm finding it hard to believe you're not Sasha."

The doors slid open on her floor. I hesitated to follow her out, and she twisted around, her head canted.

"Aren't you coming, or are you stealing my coffee?"

"I'm coming." I stepped out, the door closing behind me. "I haven't been on this floor...I don't know. Maybe ever."

"Really? Haven't you worked here a long time?"

"Since I graduated college. I stay up top."

"Weston regularly visits every level of his building, according to Elise."

"I'm not Weston." And I didn't like being compared to him by Saoirse.

"No, you're not. From what I've heard and experienced once, you're ten times less grumpy than him. Though you're not exactly proving that right now."

Impatient for this conversation to be over, I jerked my chin. "Fine. Lead the way."

The smile she rewarded me with was wide and gleaming, lighting her up to the tips of her toes. "All right, boss. Let's go."

My sister was waiting in my office when I arrived, working on her laptop at my desk.

"Get out." I said this with no heat or energy.

Clara looked up from her computer for a flicker, then her eyes returned to her monitor. "You're incredibly late, Luca. You told me you were leaving home ninety minutes ago."

"I did. I've spent the last hour in marketing."

Her attention shot to me again. "What? Why?"

I smoothed my hand over my tie and plopped down in the leather and chrome chairs in front of my desk. "I'm taking a page out of Weston's book."

"Weston Aldrich runs a very different company than we do." She rubbed her lips together, her eyes narrowed. "Still, it can't hurt to give our employees face time, especially since you've been an absent executive all these years."

"I thought so too."

I propped my ankle on my knee and regarded my sister. At thirty-four, Clara was three years older than me and all business. She was the golden child of the family, serious and committed to Rossi Motors basically since birth.

She looked good behind the CEO's desk. A natural. But the mantle hadn't fallen to her. Clara was Rossi's COO and a damn fine one.

If she'd been eyeing the job I now had, she'd never said. It was always understood it would go to me when the time came, but I didn't think any of us predicted the time would come so soon.

"What are you doing in my office?" I asked.

"Waiting for you, obviously." She clicked her laptop shut and circled the desk. It still unsettled me to see her protruding belly. Four and a half months along with my future niece, Clara acted like nothing had changed, except her normally efficient, waifish figure now had an ever-growing bump in the front. "I read over the consultants' report."

"So, you wasted your time reading bullshit?"

"They have a point, Luca. There's no denying married CEOs are seen as more trustworthy than single ones."

"Again, it's utter bullshit." My fingers sliced through the side of my hair, giving it a hard tug. "How many of Mom and Dad's friends regularly cheat on their wives? I would say most if not all."

"Be that as it may, it's about perception." She pushed her dark-rimmed glasses on top of her head, leveling me with her version of sympathy. "I'm going to send you a list of acceptable women you should get to know. This doesn't have to be painful."

"Says the woman who chose her own husband."

Miller Fairfield was a good-on-paper husband, which meant my parents wholeheartedly approved of him. So much, he'd recently been promoted to Rossi's CFO. Personally, I thought he had the personality of paper, and I'd never once seen him look at Clara the way our father looked at our mother: like she was a treasure, and he knew it. But he'd been around for a decade now, so I'd accepted he was a permanent fixture in the family. Fortunately for me, he was easy to disregard when I didn't have to deal with him directly.

Lately, though, he'd taken to giving me daily updates on a mom-and-pop business blog that, according to Miller, had a hard-on for reporting Rossi's missteps. The new habit was fucking annoying, but as long as I nodded and grunted when he did, he left me alone once he was done ranting.

I imagined Clara never heard the end of it. Then again, she could handle herself and her business, so maybe she shut him down easier than I did.

"I chose a husband who would benefit this family and our company, Luca. I didn't go out cavorting, getting my picture taken snorting cocaine off random whores' breasts in nightclubs."

I held my hands up. "That has never happened. Is that what you imagine I do?"

She groaned under her breath. "Whether you've done it or not, it's perception. You often *do* get photographed stumbling out of nightclubs with different women on your arm. The public—*our shareholders*—fill in the blanks on what you're doing inside those clubs."

Before I could launch my rebuttal, Clara yelped, her hands flying to her belly. I scooted to the edge of my chair in alarm.

"Are you okay?"

She nodded, her mouth tight. "The baby's swimming. She must like your voice."

In an instant, I was on my knees in front of her. She took my hand, guiding it to the side of her belly. My niece instantly let her presence be known, fluttering against my palm with all her might.

"That's crazy," I uttered.

"I know," she whispered. "Sometimes she gets hiccups, and it blows my mind to think there's a tiny person inside me hiccuping."

I met my sister's soft gaze. "You really think she likes my voice?"

"She might. She got lively while we were talking."

Leaning closer, I had a chat with my niece. "Hi, *bella*. It's Uncle Luca. I'm fucking dying to meet you."

Clara kicked me in the knee. "Don't curse at the baby."

"Shit." I winced when she kicked me again. "Sorry, *bambina*. Uncle Luca's going to work on that before you're born. We're going to have so much fun. Your mom and dad are nice, and they're going to love you like mad, but I'll be the one to teach you all the wild things they won't let you do. It'll be our little secret. You and me, kid."

Clara shoved my forehead, knocking me back on my knees. "You will not corrupt my daughter."

I held up my thumb and forefinger an inch apart. "Just a little?"

She bit down on her bottom lip to hold back her grin. "No, Luca. By the time she's here, you'll be reformed anyway."

"I agree to clean up my image, but you'll never force me to be Miller."

She rolled her eyes. "No one wants you to be Miller. Be yourself, just...a quieter version with a beautiful, respectable wife on your arm. Is that so awful?"

"It wouldn't be if it were my decision."

She patted my shoulder. "I get it, but we all have to make sacrifices. Besides, this could be the best thing that ever happened to you."

When she finally left, with a reminder to look over the list of *acceptable women* she was going to send me, I sank down in my chair and rubbed my right eyebrow.

This was part of my job, and the pressure was on me to excel at it. Not just from board members and shareholders but from the greater Rossi family, most of whom made their living from the company.

There was nothing like knowing almost my entire extended family's wealth depended on the job I did in a position I did not want.

Want it or not, it was mine.

An email came in from Clara. Her *list*. The idea of shopping for a wife in this manner turned my stomach. My sister was one of my closest friends, but we were vastly different people. There was absolutely no way any of the women she deemed acceptable would interest me.

I opened her email anyway.

Sometimes sacrifices had to be made.

CHAPTER EIGHT

Saoirse

ALTHOUGH I'D RECENTLY TURNED twenty-seven and had been living on my own since I'd left for college, my mother treated me like an incapable child. It was only bearable because she was states away and too busy to pry into my life on a daily basis.

But when she found the opportunity, whew, did she dig in.

She'd booked a phone call with me during my lunch hour. Being written into my mother's calendar wasn't unusual and had stopped bothering me a decade ago.

She was who she was, and I strove to be the polar opposite—which was why I was sitting on the patio of a café, picking at my sandwich, responding to her questions in the manner I knew would satisfy her. That was the easiest way to handle my mother.

"How is Elise?" she asked.

"Really great. She loves her job at Andes, and of course, I don't know how I survived without her in Denver all these years."

My mother huffed. I could practically hear her indignation through the phone. "It isn't as if you've been in Denver all this time. You were traveling more than you were home."

"You know me. If I'm in one place too long, I get antsy."

"All fine and good, Saoirse, but you're getting too old to play the part of a hostel-staying, broke backpacker. It isn't cute anymore."

I rolled my eyes. My mother had no idea where I stayed when I traveled or what I did. She had an image in her mind, and she couldn't let go of it.

"I don't have any travel plans right now," I told her, which was strictly true. But I wasn't much of a planner, so that didn't mean I wouldn't be traveling in the near future.

"Good. Then you should be looking for a permanent position. With your experience, there isn't a reason to continue temping. It's beneath you, but aside from that, you're taking positions from people who truly need them. I know that isn't something you would willingly do."

Oof. That one actually got me good. I was overqualified for most of the positions I took, that was true, but my work history wasn't exactly glowing to potential long-term employers. The longest I'd stuck to a job was six months, and I'd been crawling out of my skin by the end.

"I'm looking, Mom. But I won't settle. Besides, I'm enjoying working at Rossi, and my contract has been extended another month."

I wasn't looking for another job, but as long as I told her I was, she normally laid off until the next phone call. And it wasn't that she was stupid and actually believed me, but my promises assuaged her "mom worries" enough to drop the subject and not think about it until we spoke again.

"A motorcycle company, Saoirse? I don't see you staying there long term. What about the marketing firm Peter told you about?"

"I'll look into it."

I wouldn't, and we both knew it. We were dancing the dance we always did.

She sighed her tired, put-upon sigh I knew all too well. My poor mother had been blessed with two children who were nothing like her, and it would forever rankle her. Fortunately, she had Peter, her right-hand man and protégé, who allowed her to shape him like he was a lump of clay.

"Let's talk about brighter subjects. Tell me what you've been up to in your downtime."

This was code for, *Who are you dating?* I wasn't really in the mood to disappoint her yet again.

"I've been helping a friend with her new business in Boulder. It's consuming a lot of my time right now. Other than that, you know me, I'm a sun junkie. I'm outside whenever I'm not in the office. The farmers' market—"

"And are you spending time outside with anyone special? If you're not, Peter has a college friend who recently moved to Denver. He went to Yale, skis like you do...I know you'd get along, and he could use a tour guide for all the hidden local spots."

I closed my eyes, cringing hard. I'd let her set me up on dates before and smiled my way through them to make her happy, but Peter was such a tool. Anyone he was friends with had to be equally awful.

"I'm seeing someone," I blurted out.

"Oh." She went so quiet I could hear a pin drop. "Is this new?"

"It's—we've been friends for a while, but now, it's more, and it's serious." Why were these words coming out of my mouth? What was I even saying? She was going to have questions, and I had no answers. I was the worst liar who'd ever lived.

"Is it...not Elliot Levy?"

"No, why would you think that?" I almost gagged at the idea. Elliot was sexless to me. He might as well have been a Ken doll. Sure, he was hot in his own buttoned-up way, but in my eyes, he had no dick.

"You mentioned you were friends, and I'm not really aware of you having other male friends. Unless—"

"No, I'm not a lesbian."

"It would be fine if you were, Saoirse."

"I know, but I'm not. The person I'm seeing is very much a guy."

"Won't you tell me who he is?"

I scrambled for an acceptable answer. If I made someone up out of thin air, she'd know because she'd sic Peter on the name the second we hung up. Probably before, if she could swing it.

Puffing up my cheeks, I slowly exhaled. "Luca. I'm seeing Elliot and Weston's friend, Luca."

She paused. "Rossi?"

"Yes," I pushed out, hating myself for lying to my own mother.

"And it's serious?"

"We're committed. He's my boyfriend."

"Is *he* committed?"

"Yes, Mom. I wouldn't be with him if he wasn't."

"Of course you wouldn't. You're smarter than that."

Was I? I was feeling pretty freaking stupid right now.

She peppered me with a few more questions that I shut down as well as I could, then, at exactly twelve thirty, she let me go. It must've been time for her next appointment.

With a groan, I let my head drop into my hands. I'd have to make up some spectacular breakup story before our next scheduled call. At least I could tell her I was too heartbroken to date and buy myself some leeway.

The chair across from me scraped on the stone patio. I looked up, shocked to find Luca Rossi settling across from me, a devious smirk playing on his lush lips.

"Hello, Saoirse." My name slipped from his tongue like rich, smooth cream.

"Hi, Luca."

He leaned back in his chair, draping his long arm across the back of the one beside it.

"We're dating, are we?"

My nose crinkled. "Did you really have to hear that?"

He chuckled, low and silky. "I don't know if I had to, but I did."

"I'm not crazy," I told him.

"I find sane people don't have to tell others they're not crazy."

"Well, maybe I am crazy, but I'm not delusional. I know we're not dating. I was speaking to my mother, and she was threatening to set me up on yet another date, so I told her I had a boyfriend, and your name was the first that popped into my head."

His brow winged. "Why is that? Have you been thinking about me?"

"It's hard not to when your last name is all over the building I've been going to the last three weeks."

He hummed, his eyes raking over me. "Why does your mother want you to date so badly you feel the need to lie to her?"

I lifted a shoulder, not wanting to reveal the inner workings of the Kelly family, but since I'd dragged him into it, I guessed I owed Luca.

"If you can imagine someone who is the polar opposite of me, that's my mom. She's known what she was going to do and who she was going to be her entire life."

"And what's that?"

"She's a California state senator. Her father held the position before her, his father before him."

He dropped his arm onto the table and leaned forward. "Interesting. You're clearly not on that path."

"No." I snorted a laugh. "No one would elect me to make political decisions. I'm not that person, which my mother recognized long ago, to her great disappointment."

His brows dropped heavily over his narrowed eyes. He seemed like he was going to say something but shook his head and pressed his mouth into a flat line.

I flicked my hand, aiming for airy, but I had a feeling I came off as manic. "Sometimes it's tiring to constantly disappoint her, and that phone call was dripping with it. So, I lied when she asked about who I was seeing, and for once, she didn't end the call telling me how worried she was about me. I'll have to set her straight when we speak again, but it'll be a few weeks. I am sorry I dragged you into it, though."

He rapped on the table with his knuckles. "Apology accepted. I hope our breakup isn't too painful."

I grinned. "It'll be your fault. You're going to break my heart."

That earned me lowered lids and a soft curve of his mouth. "I would *never, bella*."

I tipped my head to the side. "*Bella*, huh? No more 'pretty girl?' I get lumped in with all the others?"

He chuckled, and some of his wayward hair flopped onto his forehead, giving him a roguish quality that suited him immensely.

"Is this the beginning of the end of our fake relationship?" he quipped, ignoring my question. Which was fine. I didn't really want to know why I'd been downgraded to *bella*.

"We were doomed from the start."

He turned his head, still smiling slightly. "I have to get back."

"Me too."

He rose to his feet, and that was when I noticed he had a cup of coffee. It surprised me that he'd been out fetching his own, but maybe he'd needed a break from the office too.

I gathered my things, and we strolled back to the Rossi building together. As we approached the entrance, two men with professional cameras came out of nowhere and started snapping pictures.

Luca immediately tensed. His arm banded around my shoulders, pulling me so tight into his side I was almost behind him.

"Who's that, Mr. Rossi? Are you on a date?"

"Is this your girlfriend, Luca? What's her name?"

"Is she a model? Does she know about your reputation?"

"How do you feel about the low stock prices?"

"Are you going to be replaced as CEO?"

"Is your father dying?"

That last question thrown at us by the two men caused Luca to stop walking. His hand tightened on my shoulder, and every muscle in his body went rigid.

I circled my arm behind him, rubbing the center of his back. "Come on, Luca. Let's go inside," I murmured. "We need to get in the building."

When I pressed on his back, he finally began walking again, steering me into the lobby, away from the intrusive shouts of the photographers.

"Wow, that was intense and really invasive."

Luca's sharp jaw ticced. "Just another day."

Without another word, Luca walked away from me into his executive elevator, where I couldn't follow even if I wanted to.

An email appeared in my inbox at the end of the workday. Since it was from my boss, I decided not to ignore it.

To: saoirsekelly@rossimotors.com

From: lucarossi@rossimotors.com

Saoirse,

Please come to my office first thing in the morning. Security will have an elevator card for you.

Yours,

Luca

What the hell could this be about? I couldn't even begin to fathom why he'd need to summon me to his office so formally. It was annoying he was making me wait until tomorrow to find out.

To: lucarossi@rossimotors.com

From: saoirsekelly@rossimotors.com

Luca,

I'd call you the king of edging, but that wouldn't be accurate since I know you're into immediate gratification.

I'll be there in the morning, sir. Bells will cost you extra.

Sincerely,

Your Inconvenient Hookup, Saoirse

A minute later, another email popped into my inbox.

To: saoirsekelly@rossimotors.com

From: lucarossi@rossimotors.com

Saoirse,

It would be most appreciated if you stopped referring to yourself that way, especially through company email.

To your first point, I'm a man who is flexible in the way I get things done. Sometimes, it's slow and deliberate. Other times, it's fast and repeated.

We can discuss all this in the morning.

Yours,

Luca

CHAPTER NINE

Saoirse

THE EXECUTIVE FLOOR OF Rossi was intimidating the moment I stepped out of the elevator. A beautiful chrome-and-leather motorcycle was mounted to the burnt-red wall beneath Rossi's insignia. To its left was a glass-and-chrome reception desk, which was empty. That made sense, though. Most employees didn't start arriving for another hour.

I strode past the empty desk, swiveling my head left and right. The offices up here were all glass, so it was easy to see most were still unoccupied. The glowing light coming from the corner acted as a beacon. I didn't know for a fact it was Luca's office, but I could take a wild guess.

As I drew closer, I spotted Luca behind his desk, typing away at his computer. The top button of his shirt was undone, and his tie was loose around his neck. He looked more himself than when he was perfectly tidy and coiffed. The stiff, starched version didn't suit the man I'd met a handful of times.

I knocked on his open door. "Good morning."

His head jerked up, startled. "Hey. Shit. Time escaped me. Come in, and please close the door behind you."

It seemed silly to close the door when the office was made of pure glass and no one was around to hear us, but then Luca picked up a remote, and the glass became opaque.

"Wow." I spun around to check out the unexpected turn of events. "That's pretty badass."

He chuckled, but it sounded strained. "Another perk of the job."

I faced him and, without invitation, sat down in one of the chairs in front of his desk. "Private elevators and remote-controlled windows. What will you tell me next? You have access to the water cooler?"

This time, his laugh came out a little more freely. "I can drink all the water I want. It's the only reason I haven't quit."

I grinned at him. "That would do it for me. Though, if this is how early you normally show up to work, it might not be worth it."

"Not a morning person, Saoirse?"

How did this man make me go from lighthearted to drenched panties from the simple act of saying my name? My thighs pressed together of their own volition, and I shifted in my chair in an attempt to cover up the move.

"No, Luca. I'm definitely a night owl."

He leaned forward on his forearms, clasping his hands together on his desk. "As am I. My lifestyle has done a one-eighty since I took this position. I've already hit the gym with Elliot and Weston."

"I won't pretend I've done anything other than drag myself out of bed and get dressed. Are you going to explain why I had to show up so early?"

"I have something I want to discuss with you. A business proposition outside the scope of your job at Rossi."

"Okay. You have me intrigued. Shoot."

He turned his head to read something off his computer screen. "Your mother is Senator Lily Smythe-Kelly, correct?"

My stomach instantly dropped, but my disappointment in Luca didn't pin me to my chair. I was up in a flash, indignation spurring me on.

"I won't discuss my mother with you. If Rossi wants to open a plant or store or whatever in her district, you'll have to go through the normal channels like everyone else. I have no power over my mother's decisions and—"

"Saoirse, you misunderstand me." Luca rounded his desk, taking my elbows in his hands to keep me in place. "I'm interested in what it was like growing up in that world. I don't want or need anything from your mother. Your father either, though I wouldn't mind visiting his ranch when I'm not buried under responsibilities."

My face burned while my mind whirled with confusion. What the hell was going on here?

"You researched my family?" I spit out. "Why would you do that?"

"If you'll sit down, I'll explain in a moment." He released one of my elbows to gesture toward the chair I'd just launched myself out of. "Please."

It wasn't as if I was going to storm out of this office without answers, and Luca had to know that. Still, I stared at him, giving him major eye daggers so he knew how displeased I was.

"Fine. But if you cross the line, I'm out of here, *and* I'll be telling Elise everything that happened."

His flinch was slight but perceptible. I appreciated that he didn't want to disappoint my best friend. That was something I'd have to remember.

This time when I sat down, Luca took the chair beside mine and wasted no time explaining himself.

"The reason I brought up your mother is, I assume, growing up in a political family, you have an understanding of the importance of image."

I nodded slowly. "I do, which is why I don't live near my mother in California. I'm not a show horse for her to trot out in front of her donors and constituents."

His mouth flattened, and he inhaled deeply through his nose. "I get that more than you know. When I took over as CEO, a consulting company was hired to analyze my image and presented me with a fifteen-page report telling me all the things I had to change about myself."

I groaned. "Ugh, I am familiar. I went through that in high school when my mother was considering a run for governor. Try being a seventeen-year-old girl reading one of those reports."

His hands balled into fists as I spoke. "That's utter bullshit." Then he shoved his fingers into his hair. "That's the last time I complain about my situation."

"They can both be bad, Luca. It's never fun to have strangers pry into your private life."

"Right." He nodded hard, then smoothed out his ruffled hair. "I'm going to level with you on why I asked you here. I've been told being married will make me something like seventy-five percent more trustworthy. My sister, Clara, has given me a list of acceptable women to date with the intention of marrying. I tried to pick one or two out that sounded interesting, but they were all basically clones of Clara, and I couldn't bring myself to do it."

I stayed silent, waiting on tenterhooks for the other shoe to drop.

"We were photographed together yesterday, and the pictures were published this morning with conjectures you and I are dating. That, along with the story you told your mother, led me to the best possible solution for both of us. Marry me."

A loud laugh popped out of me. "I know you're joking, but you really had me in the first half."

He shook his head. "I'm not joking, Saoirse. I'd like us to enter into a temporary marriage contract. It will take the pressure off us both."

"Stop it, Luca." I swatted his knee. "I'm not falling for this."

He nodded toward my purse. "Check your email. You should have a preliminary contract from my lawyers you'll want your own counsel to review."

Just so this stupid ruse would end, I took out my phone. When I saw the very official-looking email from a well-known law firm sitting at the top of my inbox, I nearly tossed the thing across the room.

"You're serious."

Luca's gaze never left mine. "Completely. We can discuss the terms and details as much as you'd like to be comfortable, but I've thought it through, and I see this as mutually beneficial. You won't have to lie to your mother again, and I'll be able to focus on my job rather than my personal life."

"You said temporary. How long would we be married?"

I couldn't believe I was even entertaining this idea, but now that it had sunk in that Luca was serious, my curiosity had been sparked.

"At least a year, but more likely two. It can't be shorter than that, or it will make me look unstable, which is the opposite of what I'm going for."

"Two years is a long time. What if you meet the woman of your dreams in that time?"

He huffed. "I'm not worried about that."

I wondered if he'd thought of anything other than the bare facts. My mind went to the logistics of being married for two years to a man who was little more than a stranger.

"What do you see our marriage entailing, Luca?"

"We would be seen together at events. You would accompany me to business dinners and conferences. We would obviously live together too."

"And what about our family and friends? Would they be in on it?"

"No. To everyone but us, it would be a real marriage."

I crinkled my nose. "I'm a terrible liar."

"You won't have to lie. We will be legally married."

"You're speaking like it's a foregone conclusion I'll say yes."

He raised a brow. "Weren't you the one who told me you say yes when there's the smallest chance you'll get something out of it? I'm surprised by your hesitation."

I had to laugh at that. "You're asking me to marry you, Luca. I may be spontaneous, but even I need to think this one through from all angles. Besides, what would I be getting out of this marriage?"

His lids lowered, and he slanted his body toward mine. "Me, as a husband."

Oh, he was turning on the charm. He must've really wanted this.

"Is that supposed to be an incentive?"

"I do have a really nice condo."

"You do, although I love living with Elise."

"She'll be moving in with Weston before you know it."

A thousand questions battled for first place in my mind. The most inappropriate one claimed victory. "What about sex?"

"I like it."

"Shut up, Luca." I couldn't stop myself from grinning. "I mean, are you going two years without getting laid? Or will you be bringing home random women?"

"Are you taking yourself off the menu?"

"This is your idea. Surely you've thought about this."

"What about you, Saoirse? Can you go two years without getting laid?

"Sure. I've done it before."

He winced. "Why?"

"Despite what you may think based on our first meeting, I don't like casual hookups. That's one thing I rarely say yes to."

"Won't you get anything out of it?"

I chuffed. "Not often."

"Then why did you say yes to me?"

I pulled my bottom lip between my teeth. "Because I was pretty certain I *would* get something out of being with you."

He blinked slowly. "And you were right."

We exchanged a long look, but I didn't have to say anything. We'd both been there. He knew exactly what I'd gotten out of being with him.

He propped his ankle on his knees and rubbed his chin. "To answer your question, no, I won't be bringing random women home. That's not a good look for a married man, and I can guarantee it would get out. As for us, if we fuck, it'll be outside the confines of our agreement."

"What does that mean?"

He dropped his hand, his fingers curling around the arm of his chair. "Eventually, I would like to have a real marriage, much like my parents'. Marriage means something to me. That isn't what this is. I'm marrying you because it's convenient for both of us, mutually beneficial, and I have a feeling you're not looking for a husband, or you would have found one."

"I'm definitely not. I never want to get married."

He considered me, raking his dark eyes over my face. "Never? No dreams of a big, white wedding?"

"No. Never." I twisted my lips. "I like dresses, but I'm not a traditional kind of girl."

"Good, then you won't be disappointed that we'll be eloping in a private ceremony."

I snorted. "You've really planned this out, haven't you? I suppose I won't be getting a honeymoon then."

"I can't exactly take a vacation right now." His jaw flexed as he stared at me intently. "I would like to save all those traditions for my future wife. I won't say no to a wedding night, though."

"You'll ditch all the traditions except the one involving sex. That makes sense."

"We're coming at this from opposite directions, but we're meeting at the same point. This is a business transaction. Sex isn't business, so when it happens, it won't have anything to do with our marriage."

I rolled my eyes. "Again with the foregone conclusions."

"I don't waste time pretending, Saoirse."

He had me there. If it weren't for us having this outrageous conversation, I might've liked to climb into his lap and pick up where we'd stopped.

"I'll have to think about this."

Something in him deflated. "I thought you said yes to experiences."

"I did, but you're asking me to do something I don't believe in."

"All the more reason to do it. If you don't believe in marriage, what's the harm in entering a fake one with me?"

I folded my arms over my chest, refusing to be convinced by this very convincing man. "We'll have to lie to our friends and family. That's the harm."

"That's the downside, I agree. But when we divorce, it'll be amicable. We won't force anyone to choose sides since there won't be a rift."

He was so calm and slick with his answers I wanted to shout and ruffle him up a little. This man was asking for a lot while behaving like it was nothing.

"I can't say yes right now. I'm sorry if that's disappointing, but I need to really consider this."

There was a tense moment where it seemed he was poised to argue with me but then released a long exhale.

"Of course you can have time. Send the contract to your lawyer—"

"I don't have a lawyer, Luca."

"Right." He slid his phone from his pocket, tapping something on the screen. "I'm sending you the name of another firm I trust. I'll let them know to expect a call from you. Obviously, I'll be paying all legal fees."

"Obviously."

Luca walked me to the door. Before he opened it, I spun around to face him.

"You realize this is nuts, right?"

He paused, staring at his hand on the knob, then lifted his gaze to mine. "I do, which should tell you how fucking desperate I am to be out from under some of the weight pressing down on me."

It only lasted a few seconds, but in that time, Luca's charm fell away, letting me see his fatigue and turmoil. It was almost enough for me to agree right then and there, but I was smarter than that.

Saving Luca couldn't be the only reason I said yes.

<hr />

Charlie was hanging around my cubicle when I hustled into the office. Though I'd shown up to Rossi at the ass crack of dawn, somehow I was running late.

Well, not somehow. I knew how. After Luca's sneak attack of insanity, I'd gone to my favorite nearby coffee shop. Over a latte and croissant, I'd gotten lost in my thoughts and time had slipped away from me.

"Hey," I chirped. "Good morning."

Since I'd started at Rossi three weeks ago, Charlie had been nothing but friendly. There was an underlying interest there, but he hadn't acted on it or made me feel uncomfortable. Even at the weekly office happy hours. He made it a point to sit beside me, and maybe after a drink or two, he got a little flirtier, but not so much I had to turn him down.

That was a relief since I'd be working here for at least another month. The last thing I wanted was an awkward workplace situation.

"Good morning." He grinned, sweeping me with his gaze. "Running late?"

I smoothed a hand over my hair and smiled back. "Wild morning. I hope it's not a sign of what's to come for the rest of the day."

He tucked his hands in his trouser pockets and rocked back on his heels. "It seems like maybe you had a wild day yesterday too."

I paused with my hand on the back of my chair. "Really? What do you mean?"

"You, with Luca Rossi. Amelia and Niddhi were talking about pictures of the two of you. Did the paparazzi really chase you?"

I rolled my eyes to deflect his interest. "That was nothing. We just happened to arrive at the same time. I feel sorry for actual celebrities. The press will twist the smallest thing to make it seem much bigger."

Charlie eyed me with something a little less than belief. "I assumed it was something like that. There's no way someone like you would actually be with someone like him."

My spine stiffened. "What does that mean?" My question came out slightly sharper than intended, but I didn't like the undertone of his question.

"No shade on you," he amended, "but everyone knows what Luca Rossi gets up to."

"How do you know?"

He jerked slightly at my whiplash question. "Well, I've seen the pictures, read the articles—"

"The pictures? We just finished talking about how the press makes things up. Maybe judge him by the content of his character, the type of boss he is, how he runs Rossi—not fictitious stories published for sensationalism."

I tugged my chair out from under my desk. "I'm sorry, but I have a lot to do today. We can chat later."

"Oh." Charlie ran his fingers through his hair. "All right. I'm sorry if I offended you—"

I held my hand up. "No, it's fine. I've had a weird morning. Sorry I snapped."

He shot me a smile. "No worries, Saorise. Have a good day."

I collapsed at my desk and groaned. I had a feeling this wasn't the last I'd be hearing about those pictures.

<hr />

I didn't have to wait long. At the start of my lunch hour, Peter, the douchelord himself, texted me.

Peter: *Ms. Smythe-Kelly has seen the pictures of you with Mr. Luca Rossi. She would like to add a meeting with you to her calendar within the week. We'll need to allot an hour. Please let me know your schedule at your earliest convenience. Ms. Smythe-Kelly is waiting.*

Peter was a thirty-five-year-old man who made a living kissing my mom's ass. He also referred to my own mother as Ms. Smythe-Kelly when texting me, which was beyond strange. But that was him.

I did not want to talk to my mother for an hour about the pictures of Luca and me. I'd rather be shot from a cannon into a moat full of hungry sharks during my period than have that conversation.

If Luca and I were married, I could rope him into speaking to my mother. That would have to be a stipulation of our marriage contract. There was no way I would be springing the news on her by myself.

I emailed him my thoughts.

———◦———

To: lucarossi@rossimotors.com

From: saoirsekelly@rossimotors.com

Luca,

I have a condition: you will be there when I tell my mom we're married. Actually, now that I think about it, you'll have to come to Wyoming with me when I drop the news to my dad and brother. They're very big, and they won't be pleased.

Are you rescinding your proposal?

Sincerely,

Your Inconvenient Maybe-Fiancée, Saoirse

———◦———

When I got back from lunch, there was an email from Luca waiting for me.

To: saoirsekelly@rossimotors.com

From: lucarossi@rossimotors.com

Saoirse,

First condition agreed to. Mothers find me charming.

As for Wyoming, I look forward to it. We'll take my bike.

Anything else I can do to make it easier to say yes?

Yours,

Luca

———◦———

I already knew I was going to say yes.

It was crazy, but now that I'd had a few hours to process everything, Luca's proposal wasn't so outlandish.

A year or two wasn't a long time in the grand scheme of things, and living in Luca's penthouse wouldn't exactly be painful.

Getting married had been off my radar for a long time, but now I'd get to have that experience under my belt without all the ties that came with it.

Above all that, when I searched my heart, I came back to Luca's fatigued expression and his raw admission at buckling under the pressure of his new life. If I could ease some of it and some of my own pressure, it would be selfish not to.

But I had one more condition.

To: lucarossi@rossimotors.com

From: saoirsekelly@rossimotors.com

Luca,

There's something else that's more of a request than a demand.

I want a cat.

Are you opposed?

Sincerely,

Your Inconvenient Almost-Fiancée, Saoirse

His response came swiftly.

To: saoirsekelly@rossimotors.com

From: lucarossi@rossimotors.com

Saoirse,

I'm not opposed.

You can have a cat as long as it doesn't shit on any of my furniture or destroy my belongings.

Yours,

Luca

My heart lodged in my throat. I'd wanted a cat since I was a child, but my mother had never wanted one, and when I'd later moved out on my own, I'd traveled too often to really consider adopting one. But I'd be settled here in Denver for a while.

I could have a cat. No, I was *getting* my cat.

I was smiling.

Luca and I were getting married.

CHAPTER TEN

Luca

IT WAS MY WEDDING day.

Strange to even think those words in my head.

In a few hours, I would have a wife. I'd be a husband. Fake or not, those would be our titles for the foreseeable future.

Though I didn't dread entering into this agreement with Saoirse, I couldn't say I'd been looking forward to this day. There was something so inherently wrong with having to do this. But I felt like I'd been left with no choice.

The women Clara had sent me had been so out of line with the type I would be interested in it hadn't been funny. Just reading their profiles had been unbearable. A lifetime with any of them would have been torture.

And I did view marriage as a lifetime contract, which was why I'd never pursued it. I had never felt ready for that step. The attraction of no commitments and living for moments of passion and excitement was still far too strong to give it up.

Until I'd been forced to.

Saoirse arrived at my condo an hour before our private ceremony was to begin. She stepped out of the elevator, her hand over her eyes.

"If you're there, don't look at me, Luca."

I stared at her. "What are you doing?"

"You're looking at me, aren't you?"

"Of course I am. Why wouldn't I be?"

She stomped her foot, and I took note of her flip-flops. "It's bad luck, obviously."

"If this were real, I would agree, but we both know it's not." I eyed her feet again. Her toenails were painted like ballet slippers. "Are you wearing flip-flops for the ceremony?"

She held up her arm, which was draped with a garment bag. "I'm not. But if I were, I would expect you to bite your tongue like a good husband."

I closed the distance between us, slipping the garment bag from her arm. "That's the last time I mention anything you're wearing. Are you going to open your eyes, or do I have to lead you to your bedroom?"

"I've been in your place once. Even if my eyes were open, you'd have to lead me."

I stared at her for a moment, but the hand over her face wasn't budging. "Are you always this superstitious and stubborn?"

"Won't it be exciting for you to find out when I'm Mrs. Luca Rossi?"

My breath caught. My stomach clenched with discomfort. *Mrs. Luca Rossi.* What the fuck was I doing?

Saoirse clutched my arm until we reached the guest bedroom where she'd be getting dressed. Tomorrow, all her things would be moved into the bedroom beside mine upstairs and this illusion would really begin. For today, she was still a guest.

I laid her garment bag on the bed before facing her and grasping both of her elbows.

"You can back out of this. This is your opportunity to tell me to go to hell."

Instead of instantly agreeing, a smile spread across her delicate, lovely face. "Why would I do that? I've already signed a thousand contracts. I also gave you my word, which means something to me. Plus, I'm getting a cat out of this."

"You could get your own cat, you know."

Her brows rose above her hand, and I wished like hell she'd just look at me. "Do you want to back out, Luca?"

"We have to do this."

"We really don't have to. I'm all in, but I completely understand if you've changed your mind. Just say the word and—"

"No. We're doing this." I let go of her arm, backing toward the door. "I'll leave you to get ready. The officiant will be here in an hour."

She chewed on her bottom lip. "If you're sure."

"I'm sure. See you soon."

I closed the door, leaving her alone, and walked upstairs to get dressed for my wedding.

CHAPTER ELEVEN

Saoirse

LUCA WAS PACING THE living room, a beer bottle dangling between his fingers. Every once in a while, he stopped to take a sip, then started pacing again.

He hadn't noticed me standing there, so I took a moment to look at him. My almost husband.

He'd changed from jeans and a T-shirt into a suit. Not the kind he wore to the office either. In a deep-burgundy three-piece with a black shirt and tie, he looked like he'd stepped off a runway. The jacket was fitted to his broad shoulders and tapered waist to within an inch of its life, and I had a feeling if I lifted the back, his trousers would mold lovingly to his ass.

"What are you wearing?"

Luca's loud, abrupt bark made me jump. My tongue was stuck to the roof of my dry mouth. My heart was fluttering wildly in my chest. I pressed my hand over it as if that would do anything to calm it.

Luca dropped his beer on his glass coffee table and strode toward me, his brow heavy and low. "I asked what you're wearing, Saoirse."

I looked down at my dress to ensure I hadn't unknowingly spilled anything on it. I'd been careful, but things happened. Not this time, though. The pink slip dress fell, sleek and silky, over my body, nearly reaching the ground.

"It's a dress, Luca."

He stopped two feet from me, raking his gaze over me. "I didn't expect you to wear a gown."

"Are you mad?"

His jaw worked from side to side for several beats before he shook his head. "You caught me off guard, that's all."

"Well..." I swiveled from side to side so the fabric swished around my legs, "I thought, since this will be my only wedding, why not do it up? There are only so many chances a girl has to wear a silky pink dress."

"There's a flower in your hair," he blurted.

I touched the silk orchid tucked over one ear with my fingertips. "I know. Isn't it pretty?"

His eyes narrowed into slits. "You're taking this a lot more seriously than I assumed you would."

"I know. You thought I'd wear flip-flops. But, like I said, this is my one and only wedding, so I went a little over the top. Besides, look at you in your suit. I bet your tailor worked overtime to make you look like that."

"Like what?" He tugged on the knot of his tie, still eyeing me like I was the enemy.

"Handsome, Luca. You look incredible, and you make that suit look good."

He turned his head, staring out the wall of windows. "Thank you."

"And?"

His attention slowly returned to me. "And...what?"

I did a smooth pirouette, allowing him to see the draping that exposed my back to the base of my spine.

I blinked at him over my shoulder, pleased to find he was rapt by the sight of me. "Do I look nice, Luca?"

There was a long pause, followed by a chuff. "I suspect you know exactly how you look."

Before I could ask him to expand on that—and possibly fish for a compliment I'd been hoping he would have given freely—there was a knock on the front door. Luca tore out of the living room without another word, leaving me disappointed and confused.

But I supposed he'd set the precedent for what our marriage would be like. I wouldn't go to him for assurance or even a simple compliment. We were business partners who might fuck if the mood struck, but that was it.

It would serve me well to remember that.

Luca escorted a man in a suit, who introduced himself to me as Judge Hernandez. *He* told me I looked nice. When I glanced at Luca, he averted his gaze back to the windows.

"I thought we'd do this on the balcony," Luca said.

"Yes," I agreed. "I love it out there."

I'd never been, of course, but Judge Hernandez didn't need to know that.

Luca straightened his tie again. "I'll meet you out there." Then he swiveled around and disappeared into the kitchen.

I smiled at the judge. His kind, almost sympathetic smile in return struck me in the gut. One look at us, and he obviously suspected this wasn't a love match.

Or maybe I was reading too much into his expression.

We went to the balcony door, but since I had never actually unlocked it, I didn't know how.

"I'm sorry. Luca always opens the door for me," I explained like a brainless, kept woman.

"It's all right, Ms. Kelly. Would you allow me?" More sympathy from Judge Hernandez. He got the door open in one move and allowed me to go outside first.

Luca appeared seconds later, carrying a compact bouquet of red roses he shoved toward me.

"Your flowers, *bella*."

"Oh. How silly of me to forget when they're so beautiful." I took them from him, bringing them to my nose to smell them. "I love roses."

The corners of his mouth twitched. "I know."

"Do you?"

His head cocked slightly while I smelled the flowers again. I mouthed, "Thank you," and he nodded, facing the judge.

"We're ready to begin."

The ceremony was short and to the point. We both said, "I do," and when it came time to exchange rings, Luca produced a simple platinum band that fit my finger perfectly. Then it was my turn. I slipped off the loose silver ring I'd kept on my thumb, and his brows shot up.

I smiled at him. "Did you really think I'd forget to get you a ring?"

"You didn't have to," he uttered.

"Well, I wanted to." I took his left hand in mine and slid the hammered white gold snugly onto his finger. It was rugged yet understated. Not plain. A plain band wouldn't do for Luca. It had taken me a while to choose it, and I was pleased with what I'd found.

His fingers curled into his palm. He didn't even look at his ring. My stomach plummeted with disappointment. I'd really wanted him to like it.

"You are now man and wife." Judge Hernandez probably had a great smile. I could picture him hanging out with his family, his eyes crinkling when his kids did something funny, looking at his wife dancing in the kitchen as she cooked. But I could only imagine it because it wasn't on display for Luca and me.

"You can kiss," he added quickly.

I stepped closer to Luca, and in my heels, I didn't even have to raise my chin to bring us to the same level. His gaze was locked on my face, sweeping from my eyes to my mouth. I took another step, flattening my palm to his chest. His finger came up to my chin, drawing me in with barely a touch.

His warm breath brushed my lips only a moment before his mouth did. For a few thunderous beats of my heart, we were sealed together, then his lips parted, taking our union slightly deeper.

My fingers curled around his lapel, and Luca dragged his lips from mine, straightening to his full height. It took me longer to snap out of the heat of his kiss. When I did, I smiled at Luca.

"We're married."

He nodded once. "We have to sign the papers."

"Oh, right. Of course."

The judge cleared his throat. "Would you like me to take pictures of you two?"

Luca said no at the same time I said yes.

I pressed against his chest. "We should. Our parents will probably want to see us all dressed up when we tell them we got married, don't you think?"

His nostrils flared as he inhaled deeply. "You're probably right." He turned to the judge. "Thank you. We'd like a few pictures."

With the sunset off to the side and views of mountains in the distance, the backdrop couldn't have been more beautiful. Luca pulled me into his side, cupping my hip in his palm. The judge used Luca's phone to snap us in several poses, and I could tell this wasn't his first time taking pictures of newlyweds. It would have been cute and fun if Luca hadn't been so fricking stiff the whole time.

I patted his middle and tipped my lips to his ear. "Relax, Luca. I'm not going to bite you, and these are my one and only wedding pictures. Try to look like you're happy to be here."

He turned, bringing his face a whisper from mine. "Thank you for being here, Saoirse."

"Of course. You're my husband."

His next breath was harsh, and his hold on me went tight. "You'd do anything for your husband?"

"I won't hide the body, but try me, Luca. I said yes to this. I'll probably say yes to most things."

His mouth curved into a near smile.

"Okay, I took about a hundred pictures. We should be good to go," Judge Hernandez announced. Luca dropped his hold, stepping apart from me. "Let's make it official."

We went inside to sign the license, which took barely a minute, then the judge departed without any fanfare. He probably couldn't wait to get out of this loveless affair.

Or maybe he was just hungry. Judge Hernandez would forever remain a mystery to me.

Luca swiveled around when the door closed, rubbing a spot near his brow with his right hand, his left still curling into a fist. I was pretty sure he hadn't looked at his ring even once.

"I'm going to get changed," he announced, barely looking at me. "You should too."

He swept upstairs without another word.

We'd been married fifteen minutes and I was already wondering if I'd made a huge mistake.

CHAPTER TWELVE

Luca

I FOUND SAOIRSE IN the den an hour later. Curled up on the couch, her legs tucked under her, she seemed vulnerable. Smaller. Out of place. A small wave of guilt hit me at leaving her to fend for herself, but I'd needed that time to get my head on straight again. Otherwise, I might have been a bigger asshole than I already had been.

"We're heading out at seven."

She turned away from the TV to raise her eyebrows at me. "Seven?"

"We're meeting everyone for drinks tonight. Elise and West had something come up and can't do brunch tomorrow." I sat down near her, raking my fingers through the side of my hair. "It's better this way. We'll get it over with sooner."

Tonight would begin our announcement tour. We'd planned to drop the news to our friends over brunch tomorrow, giving us time for reality to settle in, but plans had changed.

Saoirse swallowed, her hand flying to her hair then her T-shirt. "I don't think I'm ready."

"You are. It'll be fine."

"They're going to have questions, Luca. We haven't even talked about what we're going to say."

"Let's talk about it now. We have time."

She squeezed her eyes closed. "I don't think you understand just how bad I am at lying. It's going to be a shit show."

Seeing her freak out soothed me. At least I wasn't the only one unsettled by what we'd done today, although Saoirse didn't seem to mind being married. Her sticking point was having to tell other people about it.

Then again, marriage meant nothing to her.

"Did you open the ottoman?" I asked.

Her eyes flew open. "What—? What are you talking about?"

I nodded toward the ottoman in front of the couch. "Open it and I'll explain."

She unfolded her long legs and stretched out her arm, opening the hinged top. Her mouth popped open when she peeked inside.

"Blankets!" She pulled one out and clutched it to her chest. "Were these always here and I missed them?"

I shook my head. "Nope. Someone told me I needed to buy some, so I did."

Her brow dropped. "But what does this have to do with our story?"

"Everything. We're going to tell the truth."

———◇———

Our friends beat us to the restaurant, which was my fault. Saoirse had been waiting for me by the door by the time I finally got my shit together. In cuffed shorts and a loose T-shirt, she looked drastically different than she had a few hours before, but she'd kept the orchid tucked behind her ear.

It was a constant fucking reminder of what we'd done. Not that I needed it. The metal band around my ring finger and the invisible one around my chest were enough for me to never forget.

The rooftop casual lounge was buzzing but not too crowded. We easily found Elise, Elliot, Weston, and his younger brother, Miles. They'd claimed a corner with padded wicker seats and vintage-style lawn chairs atop Astroturf. The place was designed to look like someone's backyard. Not my style, but I hadn't picked it, and Saoirse seemed perfectly pleased with the choice.

None of our friends blinked at Saoirse and me arriving together. In fact, Elise and Miles were in the middle of a game of cornhole, so we barely got more than a wave from them.

Elliot stood with his beer in one hand and shook mine with the other. "You're almost not late," he greeted.

"I'm turning over a new leaf. I told you that."

Weston chuckled as he leaned in to brush Saoirse's cheek with a kiss. "Did you two find each other on the way up?"

Her eyes slid to mine then back to Weston. "No, actually. We came together."

His brow winged. "Did you?"

"So that's why you're on time." Elliot brought his beer to his lips. "Good job, Kelly."

She huffed. "Thanks so much, Levy. You know I live and die for your approval."

Weston was still eyeing her. "Why did you come together?"

"Why not?" Saoirse shrugged and walked over to an empty chair, swiping the menu left there. "Oh, yum. Are we ordering food? I missed dinner, and I'm starving. There's no way I can drink unless I eat something. Where's the waitress?"

Her manic display caught both Weston's and Elliot's attention. Weston stared at her with a crinkled forehead. Elliot's expression was less discernible, but he was studying her just as intently. Maybe because her hands were fluttering and she was reciting her favorite things from the menu—which seemed to be all of it.

She hadn't exaggerated. Subterfuge and Saoirse didn't gel.

Elise threw her arms up. "Yes! I told you I was good at this."

Miles kicked a beanbag. "Why do you have to be good at everything, Lisie?"

"I'm terrible at convincing you to stop calling me Lisie."

They joined our group, Elise tucking into Weston's side, Miles shaking my hand then pecking Saoirse's cheek.

"What's happening over here?" Miles asked, peering at the menu in Saoirse's hands.

"I'm trying to decide what to order." She studied the menu like it held deep, meaningful secrets.

"Saoirse and Luca came together," Weston informed his girl and brother.

"You did?" Elise stole the menu from her friend. "You and Luca drove together?"

Saoirse nodded. "We did."

Elliot tipped his beer at her. "Care to elaborate?"

I'd noticed at brunch the two of them had this *thing*, which was continuing tonight. He acted like he didn't like her, and she baited him to drive him nuts, then they called each other by their last names. Cute to some, but I wasn't much of a fan.

I curled my arm around Saoirse's shoulders. "It's Rossi, actually."

Elliot's brow furrowed. "What does that mean?"

"Exactly what I said. She's not a Kelly anymore. She's a Rossi."

Saoirse crossed one leg over the other and wiggled her fingers in front of her. "Surprise."

Our friends glanced at each other, then all eyes were on us. Miles took charge.

"Either you adopted Sersh, or you got married. Since marriage would be crazy, I'll be the first to say congrats on your new hot blonde daughter." Miles winked at me and patted his pockets. "Sorry, I'm fresh out of cigars, otherwise I'd offer you one."

Saoirse let out a wobbly laugh. "Can we sit down? I would love to sit down."

"Sure. In a minute." Elise tugged away from Weston to round on Saoirse. "What's going on with you and Luca? And why are you being so manic?"

"Well..." she curled her arm around my back, gripping my shirt, "it's been kind of a crazy day. The past few weeks have been, really."

I had to put all of us out of our misery, especially Saoirse. Her nails were seconds away from shredding my shirt from how hard she was digging into me.

"We're married."

Elise's hand flew to her mouth. Miles chuckled. Weston and Elliot stared at the two of us. Like they were waiting for me to drop the punch line.

Elise was the first to act, picking up Saoirse's left hand and rubbing her thumb over her ring. "You don't believe in marriage."

"I didn't. Until Luca," Saoirse whispered.

"But—you didn't even tell me you were together." Elise rolled her lips inward. "Why didn't you tell me?"

"I'm sorry. I didn't mean to hide it from you. Like I said, it's been a whirlwind. But you guys are the first to know. We haven't even told our parents yet."

"But *married*?" Elise was stuck on that. I guessed Saorise had been truthful when she'd told me she didn't believe in marriage.

"Married," I confirmed. "We kept things quiet in case it didn't work out between us."

Saoirse nodded. "We didn't want any awkwardness in the group."

Just as Elise seemed to accept that answer, Elliot interjected. "Is this because of the consultants?"

"What consultants? What are you talking about?" Elise demanded of her brother.

He raised his chin toward me. "Rossi's board hired consultants to go over Luca's image. They wanted him to get married. And lo and behold, he's suddenly married to Kelly, who's adamantly against the institution but also has a dire habit of saying yes to shit she shouldn't."

Everyone went quiet, even the background noise. I glared at Elliot, annoyed at him for challenging me. If I'd expected him to flinch, I would have been disappointed. Luckily, I knew better than to expect Elliot Levy to back down.

Fucking Elliot and his logical, suspicious mind. I should have known he'd question us down to the bone. That was him. He'd had to grow up fast with only himself to rely on. He never took situations at face value.

Still, it pissed me off he was questioning *me* after all the years he'd known me.

But hell, maybe that was exactly why he was questioning me. He knew me too well.

Saoirse laughed the motherfucker right off without a beat of hesitation. "Did you really think I would buy a stranger a cheese board? That's such a 'couple' gift. I'm surprised you didn't guess right then and there. Luca and I were already together the last time we saw you." She snuggled into me and laid her hand on my chest. "We met at a party and haven't spent any time apart since. I apologize again for keeping it a secret, but we are married, and we hope you'll support us. It would mean a lot if you did."

She slid her hand up my neck to my jaw, turning me to face her, and pressed her lips to mine. The connection was soft and almost chaste, but she lingered so long I pulled her against me and wrapped her in my arms.

Her eyes fluttered open, locking on mine. We were too close for me to see her lips curve into a smile, but the glint in her eyes gave her away.

A loud clap interrupted the moment. "I'm convinced." Miles rushed over and hugged us both at the same time. "Congrats. I wish you nothing but the best."

Saoirse broke away from me to hug Miles fully, and I had to stop myself from yanking her back. Elise did the job for me, stealing her friend from Miles to embrace her. They whispered to each other, rocking back and forth. I left them to it, moving closer to West and Elliot.

"Prick move," I gritted out.

Elliot blinked. "You have to agree the timing is suspect."

Weston patted Elliot's arm with the back of his hand. "Couldn't it be the timing is a happy coincidence?" Then he narrowed his eyes on me. "So Saoirse is the blonde you told us about weeks ago? The last hurrah?"

I lowered my chin. "I said those things before I knew she'd be my wife, but yes. That was her. We've pretty much been together since then."

"The consultants will be thrilled," Elliot intoned.

I folded my arms over my chest. "I won't ask *you* to be thrilled. I know that's outside your wheelhouse. But how about keeping the smart-ass quips to yourself like a real friend? Can you do me that favor?"

He sighed and shoved his free hand into his pocket. "I don't like being taken for a ride, Luca. If you're on the level, I will wish you the best. But if this is all some elaborate cover and you're standing there lying to my face, I won't react well."

Two years. I'd have to look my best friend in the face and lie to him for two years while hoping like hell he never found out the truth.

"I'll accept your apology when you're proven wrong."

God, I am such an asshole. So far, nothing about being married had provided any relief. If anything, it had added another layer of problems to my already laden shoulders.

"It looks way too serious over here." Saoirse came up beside me, circling her arms around my middle. "Are you going to feed me before I wither away, husband?"

Giving Elliot one final glare, I looked at Saoirse, who was currently the only reason anyone might believe our story. For the terrible liar she was, she was playing the role well.

"Of course I'm going to. I just found you. I can't lose you now."

Grinning, she pecked the hinge of my jaw. "Sweet husband."

"Hearing you say that is going to take some getting used to," Weston said.

"I'm practicing saying it myself," Saoirse admitted.

Elliot continued being a suspicious asshole. "That's what happens when you marry a stranger."

Saoirse's happy bounce deflated. "You know what might be nice? Some support. Luca and I didn't come here today to ask you what you think of us together. We're telling you it's a done deal. You don't understand it, and that's fine. I guess, as a friend, it would be nice if you'd reserve your judgment."

Elliot canted his head. "That's fair."

Her eyes rolled. "Glad you think so." She kissed my cheek before breaking away from me again to join Elise and Miles, who were in the midst of giving their order to a waitress.

Weston offered me a measured grin. "I'm beginning to see it. I'll echo Miles and wish you the best."

Elliot brought his beer to his mouth. "Good luck."

I pointed at Weston. "Thank you for being a good friend." Then I jabbed my finger at Elliot. "Thanks for consistently being a dick."

"I do my best," Elliot answered.

Weston reached out to squeeze my shoulder. "It's a shock for all of us. Guarantee he'll be less of an asshole next time."

I eyed Elliot, who was smirking and telegraphing his thoughts loud and clear. He was saying, "*I wouldn't bet on it.*"

———◦○◦———

The drive back to my place was subdued. The night had taken a smoother turn once the shock of our announcement had somewhat worn off, but the underlying tension had never really left.

"That didn't feel good, did it?" Saoirse asked.

"No. Not so much. You sold it well, though."

"Yeah," she sighed. "I hardly wanted them to find out we were deceiving them."

"Grace under pressure," I murmured.

"That feels like a compliment."

"It was. If not for you, no one would have believed we were married for real reasons."

"They were real reasons, Luca. Just not the reasons other people get married."

In my peripheral, I saw her spinning her ring around her finger. "We'll get you an engagement ring tomorrow."

"Oh. No, that's not necessary."

"It really is. My wife wouldn't be walking around without a diamond on her finger."

"I don't like diamonds."

My hands tightened on the steering wheel. "Fine. You'll choose a ring you like."

"Do you like yours?"

"My ring?"

"Yes. Do you like your ring?"

My eyes flicked from the road to the metal wrapping around my fourth finger. "It fits well, but it'll take some getting used to."

"I—" She shook her head, whatever she'd been about to say lost. "Okay."

Saoirse spent the rest of the ride looking out her window while I tried to figure out why I couldn't let myself tell her I'd been surprised she'd gone out of her way to buy me a ring and if I'd had to pick one for myself, it would have probably looked a lot like this.

CHAPTER THIRTEEN

Saoirse

I HADN'T GROWN UP poor by any means. We'd been more than comfortable, and I'd never wanted for anything tangible. But Luca's wealth was in another stratosphere. I wasn't sure I even understood how deep the Rossi family coffers were.

Today, I learned they were shut-down-an-entire-jewelry-store rich.

As soon as we stepped into the store, glasses of champagne entered our hands, and we were waited on by soft-spoken, unobtrusive staff. They had to have been briefed because none of the rings they showed me had a diamond center stone.

And each one was larger than the next.

Luca sat beside me on a sleek little padded bench, using his phone while I tried on ring after ring. I stopped showing them to him after the fourth or fifth one he'd barely looked at.

I supposed he wasn't playing the role of doting husband today. It was strange, but as soon as we entered into this arrangement, he'd become entirely different than who I'd first thought him to be. The charm, flirtation, and ease had disappeared. He was stiff and distant, really only interacting with me when he had to.

It had only been a day, though. I might have been overanalyzing him.

After the fiftieth ring, I sighed, and Luca looked up. "Did you choose one?"

"No, I haven't." The saleswoman's flattened mouth was subtle, but a sure tell she was getting just as tired of this process as I was.

He scanned the rings displayed on black velvet. "There isn't anything you like?"

"They're all beautiful but—" I was being silly. Luca didn't need to be involved with choosing my ring since none of this was real. The ring was nothing but a piece of jewelry.

He set his phone face down on the glass counter and turned to me. "What are your favorite pieces you own now? We can have something custom-made in that style."

"I think you're going to be very disappointed to hear I don't own any fine jewelry. My most precious pieces are things I've bought during my travels." I held up a finger. "Before you start thinking I'm some Mary Sue who thinks she couldn't possibly deserve anything fancy, that's not what I'm saying. It's just... I've never wanted to invest in that kind of thing."

The saleswoman covered her mouth as if she was aghast to find I wasn't swimming in jewels. Luca didn't seem any less disapproving.

"We'll have to remedy that, Saoirse. You're a Rossi now." He picked up a ring with a large, emerald-cut aquamarine on a platinum band. "This one. Give me your hand."

He took my hand without waiting and slipped the ring over my wedding band. It was the simplest of the bunch, even though the stone was enormous. Since I'd refused diamonds, I had a feeling Luca wasn't going to let me get anything smaller.

He ran his thumb from the ring to the tip of my finger and back down again. "Looks good on you," he gruffed. "What do you think?"

I stared at my hand in his. Being tall, I had long fingers, and it took a lot for my hands to feel dainty, but they did in comparison to Luca's broad palm and thick, blunt-tipped fingers.

"It's pretty."

The saleswoman cleared her throat. "That is five-carats and natural AAAA quality. You couldn't have chosen better."

Luca nodded decisively. "We'll take it. Now we want to see necklaces and earrings. No diamonds."

"Luca—"

He squeezed my knee. "Humor me. Let me buy you a few pieces, so I know you'll have something to wear when I need you to come places with me."

"I have to look like a Rossi."

He chuckled. "You should see my mother's jewelry collection. She could fill this store and still have some left."

"All gifts from your father?"

"Mmhmm. He celebrates every holiday by buying her jewels. He'll make something up if he finds a piece he thinks she needs. One Flag Day, he gifted her a ruby cocktail ring."

That made me laugh for the first time today. "Flag Day?"

"Gotta celebrate the flags, Saoirse."

"I've been remiss by not celebrating them all this time. This year will be different."

He leaned in closer, speaking conspiratorially. With his hand still on my thigh, he had my full attention, even as the salespeople buzzed around, selecting more jewels for me to look at.

"If you're good, you might end up with your own ruby cocktail ring."

I gave my head a little shake. "I don't even know what that is."

His brow arched. "Being good?"

My laugh was huffy. "Yes. That's exactly what I meant."

Moments later, an army of salespeople presented us with millions of dollars' worth of jewels. I allowed Luca to take the lead since this was a lot more his thing than mine. Not that I didn't appreciate it. My heart was beating a mile a minute just looking at all the beauty. My mind just hadn't connected the shiny jewelry to me yet.

Luca had no such qualms. He plucked up a platinum lariat with a round ruby dangling from the end and draped it around my neck. The ruby dipped between my breasts. Luca fixed that by sliding his finger from my throat down my chest, venturing past the V-neck of my shirt. He hooked his finger around the gem, pulling it out to lay over top of my shirt.

"You're getting this one." Swiveling away from me, he pointed to several more pieces. So many my throat went dry. The lariat was the only thing he had me try on. The rest, he chose quickly and with confidence.

He tilted his face toward me again. "Do you see anything else you would like?"

In a daze, I shook my head. How had I gone from a simple, single life to married to a billionaire who seemed to have every intention of showering me with jewels?

It seemed like a very strange, unbelievable dream.

Luca took charge, picking out several necklaces, bracelets, and earrings. He draped each of them on me, studying the way they looked on my chest or around my wrist.

"Blue suits you." He grazed my lobe with his fingertip. "Do you like earrings that dangle?"

"Sometimes, but I think you've picked out enough. I'm covered for at least several occasions."

He dropped his hand to his lap. "Most women would kill to have a shopping spree here."

"Don't make me say I'm not like other girls, or I'll never forgive you."

That earned me a soft chuckle. "All right. I don't want that. We should probably leave while you're still speaking to me."

"I think you're right. It's a razor's edge right now."

Like a perfect gentleman, Luca stood and helped me up, rubbing his thumb over my knuckles.

"It's time to go anyway." Luca checked the time on his phone. "The movers will be at your place in an hour."

"Oh, right. That's happening."

The corner of his mouth hitched. "Can't sell a marriage if we're living apart."

"Let me be bummed, Luca. It's a big change. I'm going from living with my best friend to living with a boy."

That earned me a legitimate laugh. "I'm hardly a boy, Saoirse." He pressed a hand to the small of my back. "Once we get all the hard parts over with, we can get back to some semblance of normalcy."

"Normalcy dripping in jewels."

He leaned in, his mouth brushing my hair. "You say that like it's a bad thing."

"It's a thing."

He chuckled again. "Let's go, wife."

When it was all said and done, I couldn't bring myself to completely move out of my apartment. I left some clothes, bedding, and toiletries so I'd have a place to retreat to if I needed to be alone or a crash pad in case this all blew up in my face.

Besides, we had another six months on our lease. There was no rush to remove every trace of myself from my old life.

Luca wandered into my new bedroom, which was beside his. My things were scattered everywhere as I attempted to reorganize my new life.

"Do you need any help?"

I blew hair out of my face and glanced around. I'd taken things out of boxes, and now it was just a matter of finding where to put them.

"I think I have to do it myself, or I won't know where anything is. You could recycle the boxes for me if you're in the mood to be helpful."

"Sure. I'm going out for a while. I'll take them on my way." He moved deeper into my room, where I'd piled the broken-down boxes beside my bed. With his hands on his hips, he studied my possessions spread across the king-size mattress.

I turned to hang dresses in my walk-in closet. "I'll never be able to fill this closet. Who needs a closet this size?"

"I do. Mine is the same size and it's full."

I came out and flicked my eyes over him. Even casually dressed, he was stylish. "You're much more fashionable than I am."

"We'll have to remedy that. I'll take you shopping."

"You took me shopping this morning."

"For clothes. You have to have clothing that matches your jewelry."

I scooped up another stack of my subpar clothing to hang up. "Fine. I wouldn't want to make you look bad when I'm by your side."

This time when I came back out of the closet, Luca was holding my vibrator. "You have quite a collection." He nodded toward my pile of toys.

I shrugged, refusing to be embarrassed. "I like to come."

His nostrils flared, and he made a low, guttural grunt. Some of his stiffness from this morning returned. Not the reaction I would have expected from a man holding *my* vibrator.

"Nothing beats the real thing," he replied.

"Oh, I don't know. There's something to be said for getting off then rolling over and going right to sleep."

He dropped the toy on my bed and bent to pick up the stack of boxes. "I'll leave you to your solo fun. I might be out late, but text me if you need anything."

He left without an explanation. No word on where he was going or what he'd be doing. It left me with a sour taste in my mouth. It was my first night officially living here, and I was already on my own. If this was what it was going to be like being married to Luca, I supposed it was a good idea to know early on.

Once I was unpacked, I wandered downstairs into the kitchen. I hadn't explored here last night or this morning, so I planned on poking around the sleek, white space before I found something to eat. There wasn't much to see, though.

The counters were bare except for one lone piece of wood. My heart stopped when I realized what it was.

The cutting board Luca had barely acknowledged.

It was sitting on the counter next to the sink, a place he would see whenever he used the kitchen. I wondered if it had been here since I gave it to him or if he'd just put it on display for my sake.

Probably the latter, but my heart fluttered when I further investigated by peeking in the refrigerator. It was well stocked with fruits, veggies, yogurts, and other sundries, which surprised me. I held my breath as I pulled open the cheese drawer.

The cheeses I'd given him had been sampled, one much more than the other two. I was a gift giver to my bones, and my toes curled with pleasure, knowing he'd enjoyed what I'd given him, even if he hadn't expressed it.

It made the sting of being alone in this huge, empty penthouse slightly less sharp.

I gathered some snacks and a drink then headed into the den, the one room I truly felt comfortable in here so far. With one of the throws Luca had bought spread across my lap, I settled myself on his soft couch. The glint of my oversize engagement ring caught my eye. No one could relax with ten pounds of aquamarine on their finger.

Slipping it off, my wedding band too, I placed them on the ottoman. I'd put them back on later, but for now, I sighed with relief.

Chapter Fourteen

Luca

I HAD NOTHING LEFT in me when I arrived home.

Usually, I welcomed the quiet, but I was taken aback to hear nothing when I walked in. It was only eleven, still early for me. Then again, Saoirse's definition of being a night owl might have been different from mine.

I knew almost nothing about my wife.

Her room was still as I stood in the doorway. Not even the slight sound of breathing. I turned on the light, finding an empty bed. The chaos from this afternoon had been tamed, her belongings put away. It was almost like she'd always been here.

I walked into the room and cracked open the drawer of her bedside table, smirking at the contents. Saoirse was an undercover dirty girl. She didn't own just one vibrator. She had a variety.

Pulling the drawer open fully, I paused on the contents near the back. Two bottles of lube and an opened box of condoms.

An open fucking box.

Without giving my compulsion to act a second thought, I picked up the box and crumbled it in my fist. She could keep her toys, but she wasn't bringing something she'd used with another man into my house.

I charged down the stairs and out of my apartment to the trash chute, tossing the box and its contents inside to be incinerated. Because fuck that.

Not in my house.

Storming back in, I went in search of my wife. We obviously needed to have a conversation.

Clarity struck through my thundercloud of displeasure when I noticed the pool of light in the hallway coming from the den.

Of course she was in the den.

And sure enough, I found her curled up under one of the throws I'd bought with her in mind.

I took in the scene.

An empty bottle of water on its side on the ottoman with a crumb-covered plate next to it. Saoirse was in the corner of the sectional, her head against a cushion. The TV was off, the remote resting on the palm of her slack hand.

Sound asleep.

She was so still I would have suspected she was dead if not for the gentle rise and fall of her chest.

I crouched down in front of her, pushing her hair back from her face. "Saoirse. Time to go to bed."

Her eyes fluttered but remained closed. "I'm sleepy."

"I know, pretty girl. But you'll have a better night's sleep in your own bed." Removing the remote, I took her hand in mine, stroking my thumb over her fingers.

"Not my bed," she mumbled.

"It's your bed now." My thumb landed on her ring finger, and the absence of her rings brought me to a standstill. "You took your rings off?"

Her fingers flexed. "That was a long time ago."

"How long?"

Her mouth curved. "Years."

"And where did you put them years ago?"

Her hand flopped in the direction of the ottoman. I turned back, immediately spotting them near her plate. How I'd overlooked them, I had no idea, but I picked them up and easily slid them back on her.

"That's better," I murmured.

Her fingers flexed again. "It's so weird."

"They look good on you, though."

She peeked at me through a slit in one eye. "Shhh." Then she tapped my lips with her fingertip. "No more talking. I'm sleeping here."

I peeled back the blanket, and she responded by curling into an even tighter ball. "Wake up for me."

"Mmm...no. Not right now. Try back later."

She was cute, but I was too tired to battle her.

"Come on." In one fell swoop, I had her up and in my arms. "Let's go."

Startling, her arms looped around my neck. "Luca! What are you doing?"

"Taking you to bed."

"I'm not helpless, you know." Her head fell against my chest. She inhaled deeply. "You smell good."

"That's what showering will do."

Her eyes finally opened. They raked over me, a line forming between her brows. "I can walk." She kicked her feet. "Put me down."

"Stop moving, or we're both going down." I strode up the stairs and down the hall to her bedroom. At the threshold, I relented to her repeated requests, setting her on her feet. She stumbled a little but caught herself on the frame.

"I think the last two days are catching up to me." She yawned to punctuate her statement.

"Me too." I swiped my hand over the top of my head. "I'll see you in the morning."

She caught my sleeve as I turned away. "Are we driving to work together?"

"It's better we're not seen together again until we tell our families."

She nodded. "Sure. That makes sense. Good night, Luca."

"Good night, Saoirse."

Stripped out of my clothes, I lay in bed, wide awake, despite being dead on my feet. I'd hoped working myself to the point of exhaustion would have dulled my thoughts enough for me to ignore them, but no dice.

I was facing another week in a job I had heavy doubts I was capable of.

Keeping a motorcycle company afloat and profitable in an electric age and downward economic trends.

My entire extended family counting on those profits for their livelihood.

The reality that my father wasn't the invincible force of nature I'd always viewed him as.

My mother worrying herself into knots over the heart of the man she'd taken care of her entire adult life.

The wife sleeping in the room beside mine.

My fucking dick swelling in my pants at the very thought of her. My desires couldn't even give me a break. Not even my constant stream of worries would cut off my forceful attraction to Saoirse.

I accepted sleep wouldn't be coming until I did. With a frustrated groan, I yanked back the covers and took my cock in my palm. And like I'd done dozens of times since the night we met, I closed my eyes and pictured Saoirse writhing on my sheets, the memory of her taste on my tongue.

When I was finished and sated, undeserved resentment toward her rose in the place of desire. But at least I was finally able to shut everything else off and fall asleep.

My next week was so tightly packed I barely had room to think, which I now viewed as a good thing. It was only when I got home, the quiet presence of Saoirse in my den, the place that had been my retreat, everything flooded back.

She was as unobtrusive as possible. She hadn't asked anything of me since moving in. No chirped greetings in the morning or demands I have dinner with her in the evening. We were barely roommates, and we'd yet to discuss how it would go when we went public with our marriage. We hadn't talked about much of anything.

That would have to change. In order to be a believable couple, we had to know each other. Beyond the background check I'd had done on her, I only knew vague stories I'd heard about her over the years.

With that in mind, I emailed her Tuesday morning from my desk.

———◦◦◦———

To: saoirsekelly@rossimotors.com

   From: lucarossi@rossimotors.com

Saoirse,

If you have time today, join me for lunch.

Yours,

Luca

———◆———

Her reply was immediate and to the point.

   To: lucarossi@rossimotors.com

   From: saoirsekelly@rossimotors.com

Luca,

Hey, thanks for the invite. I actually have plans for lunch today.

What about tomorrow?

xoxo,

Saoirse

———◆———

I stopped myself from demanding to know what plans she had. It wasn't my concern. Saoirse could have lunch with the president if she liked, as long as she understood, in public, she was my wife.

———◆———

To: saoirsekelly@rossimotors.com

   From: lucarossi@rossimotors.com

Saoirse,

Then I will see you tonight for dinner. We should talk about how we're going to handle telling our parents, which is something that needs to happen soon.

Yours,

Luca

Prompt as ever, she replied in minutes.

To: lucarossi@rossimotors.com

From: saoirsekelly@rossimotors.com

Luca,

You're actually going to be home tonight? I wasn't sure if you even lived there anymore. I'll have to cancel the rager I had planned.

I'm up for dinner and talking. I would like that very much. We can also discuss the cat you promised me.

xoxo,

Saoirse

I pressed the heel of my hand into my eye. This woman. I'd forgotten about my promise to let her have a cat. Clearly, she hadn't.

Clara popped her head into my office. "The baby is in the mood for Thai. Take me to lunch?"

I dropped my hand, narrowing my eyes at her. "Don't you have a husband for that?"

"Miller doesn't like Thai food and you know I hate eating on my own. *Please*, Luca? We can talk about the new list of women I sent you."

"Is that supposed to be an enticement?"

She rubbed her protruding belly. "Your niece is craving chicken satay. Would you really deprive her of that?"

I shook my head. "At some point, you won't be able to hold her over my head to get your way."

She wagged her finger at me. "Fortunately for me, that day is not today. See you at noon."

Chapter Fifteen

Saoirse

Niddhi, Amelia, Charlie, and I were out to lunch at Niddhi's favorite Thai place. She was still in a downward spiral over her ex, who now had a serious girlfriend and was blasting their relationship all over social media.

This was a cheer-up lunch, and I was more than pleased to have been invited into this tight little group.

Plus, the pad thai and gaeng daeng were off-the-charts delicious. Better than I had when I'd visited Thailand.

I felt a little bad for being in such a good mood when Amelia had just swooped a tearful Niddhi to the bathroom to help her clean up her makeup, but I was. Luca and I were finally going to talk tonight, and maybe I'd get my cat soon.

Charlie reached across and swiped a piece of fried basil from my plate. "How is this so good?"

I swatted his arm. "Watch it. I take my food seriously. The next time you steal from me, I can't promise I won't stab you with my fork."

He gave me a playful shove back. "Sharing is caring, Saorise." His playful expression suddenly dropped. "Oh shit. Why is the CEO looking at us like that?"

Turning my head, I followed his line of sight, landing on Luca. He was on the other side of the restaurant, his thunderous glare aimed directly at the two of us. I gave him a small smile, which seemed to cause his frown to deepen. I didn't know what else to do since we were still under wraps. It wasn't like a temporary employee could waltz over to the CEO for a chat.

"He's not going to last, you know."

I whipped around to face Charlie. "What do you mean?"

"Have you heard anything about Luca Rossi?"

I shook my head. "Not really."

He leaned in, speaking low, even though there was no chance Luca would be able to hear him from the other side of the restaurant. "He's at clubs every weekend, always getting his pictures taken. I've heard rumors he's had multiple DUIs, which have been dismissed from bribes. They also say his sister is the one who really runs the company. He's just the face of it...for now."

"That sounds like a lot of rumors based on nothing but gossip." I had to fight the snarl that wanted to come out and play. I barely knew Luca, but by the nature of our relationship, he had my loyalty, and I didn't love the way Charlie was speaking about him. "Besides, I don't think it's a great idea to root against the CEO of the company you work for."

He shrugged. "I was a big fan of his father. I'm reserving my judgment for the son."

A laugh burst out of me. "This is you reserving your judgment?"

He snickered. "I guess not. But you're right. I should give him a chance." He peered in Luca's direction. "Looks like he's gone now. We can relax again."

Niddhi and Amelia chose that moment to bustle back to the table, Niddhi's streaks of mascara all cleaned up. She dove straight for the plate of spring rolls in the middle of the table.

"What did we miss?" Amelia asked as she shook out her napkin.

I waved my chopsticks at Charlie. "Just a little bashing of the CEO, that's all."

She rolled her eyes. "Charlie only dislikes Luca Rossi because he's hotter than him."

Charlie made a strangled sound. "That's—"

She pinned him with a hard stare. "It's true and you know it. But Luca Rossi is hotter than ninety-eight percent of the male population, so don't get too disheartened."

When we arrived back at the office, I noticed a few people looking at me as I walked by them on my way to my desk. I wondered why I was suddenly so interesting. I checked the compact mirror I kept in my desk drawer. There wasn't food on my face or blouse, so I shrugged it off. I had a full inbox of emails to answer and tasks to complete before the end of the day.

The subject of the company-wide email from Luca Rossi, CEO of Rossi Motors, stopped me in my tracks.

Personal Announcement

Holy shit. He couldn't have.

I clicked it, the blood draining from my face when it opened. At the very top of the email was a picture Judge Hernandez had taken of us on our wedding day.

He'd done it.

He'd really done it.

Without any discussion, Luca had announced our marriage to the entire company.

Dear Rossi employees,

It is my intention as your CEO to be honest and open with you. Sometimes that will mean sharing bad news and personal failures, but other times, like now, I'll share my triumphs.

It's with great happiness I announce my marriage to my new bride, Saoirse Kelly-Rossi. We were married in a private ceremony at our home, and we're looking forward to what the future has in store for us.

Thank you for your continued support of Rossi Motors, the Rossi family, and of me.

Yours,

Luca Rossi

As soon as I finished reading, Charlie walked into my cubicle, waving his phone around.

"Is this you? Is he talking about you?"

Swallowing, I nodded slowly and forced out a grin. "Surprise!"

The furrow in his brow belied his carefully measured words. "Congratulations are in order then."

"Thank you, Charlie."

Silence stretched between us as he stared at my computer monitor. I realized belatedly my wedding picture was filling the screen.

I was all out of grace and subtilty when I minimized it, but it snapped Charlie's attention back to me.

"You could have told me at lunch instead of letting me spout off. I feel like an idiot."

"No, don't." I was going to kill Luca for putting me in this position. "You didn't do anything wrong. And don't worry about what you said. I won't repeat it."

His shoulders slumped forward. "Thanks for that."

I fielded several more visits before Amelia sent out a department-wide email reminding everyone it was still a workday and to keep private matters outside of the office. The visits petered out after that, but I had no doubt I was the subject of many interoffice private messages.

And yet, I hadn't heard a single thing from Luca.

Foregoing an email, I texted him.

Me: *Send me the code for the elevator. We need to talk.*

Luca: *I'm busy now, Saoirse. We'll talk tonight as planned.*

Me: *A little late for that, isn't it? While you're locked in your executive tower, I'm with the rest of your employees. Send the code, or I'll "reply all" to your email and tell everyone about your fetish.*

Luca: *What fetish do I have?*

Me: *Don't be coy. I know all about your collection of toenails.*

Luca: *Jesus. Why did I think you'd make my life easier? Check your badge. You'll find you now have clearance to the executive floor. Perks of being my wife.*

Me: *I'm on my way. Prepare to meet your maker, Rossi.*

Luca was sitting calmly behind his desk when I arrived.

"Are you kidding me?" I seethed, charging toward his desk. I braced my hands on it, leaning down so we were face to face. "This isn't what we planned."

He lifted a shoulder. "Plans change. We would have discussed it over lunch, but you were busy."

My eyes flared. "I know you saw me with my coworkers. I saw you too."

"Coworkers? I only saw one, and the two of you looked really familiar with each other."

"You only saw one because two of them were in the bathroom." Straightening, I slapped my forehead. "Is that why you did this? You sent a company-wide email because you were jealous?"

"Jealous? No." He pushed back from his desk, stood, and rounded to my side. I turned to face him head-on. His eyes were nearly black as they flitted back and forth between mine. "If I'm going to be inconvenienced by having a wife, I expect her not to date other men during our marriage. That's not asking for too much, is it?"

My breath caught at his harsh manner. "Inconvenienced?"

He picked up my left hand. "Is it too much to ask for you to wear your rings?"

"Are you wearing yours?"

His jaw tightened, and he leaned in so our foreheads were almost touching. The heated way he looked at me made me unsure whether he was going to throttle me or kiss me. I was millimeters from taking the decision from him when his office door flung open.

"Married?"

We jumped apart at the indignant screech. A smartly dressed pregnant woman with tidy hair and Luca's eyes stood in the doorway, her head swiveling back and forth between us.

Luca's arms crossed over his chest. "Knock next time, Clara."

She cupped her round belly. "You're married, Luca? Are you kidding me? We just had lunch and you didn't say a single word."

A man hovered behind her. He was what my sister-in-law, Elena, dubbed "Medium." Everything about him was in the middle. Height, coloring, looks. For Clara's sake—since I recognized him as her husband, Miller Fairfield—I hoped he had the personality to make up for his lack of everything else.

Clara strode right to me, holding out her hand. I took a step to meet her, sliding my hand into hers to shake. Then I used my best training from my life as a politician's daughter.

"Hi, I'm Saoirse. It's really nice to meet you, even under surprising circumstances."

That wasn't a lie. I wanted to meet all of Luca's family, but Clara had intrigued me the most since she was his big sister, and from all accounts, they were fairly close. Also, I'd always had an interest in high-powered women. And Clara Rossi-Fairfield exuded power, even flustered and red-faced.

Miller followed his wife, shaking my hand after her. "Miller Fairfield. Rossi's CFO and Clara's husband."

"It's nice to meet you too."

My nose twitched since this was less than the truth. I knew nothing about Miller, but his immediate vibes were so blah, they were off-putting.

The corners of Clara's eyes pinched. "I wish this wasn't the first time I'm hearing of you, Saoirse. If I'd known my brother already had a wife, I wouldn't have spent so much time trying to fix him up with a suitable woman."

I let out a soft, breathy laugh. "It would be great if you didn't push my husband to date any longer."

Luca's presence hit me a beat before he wrapped his arm around my back, settling his palm over my hip. "Clara, Miller, this is my wife, Saoirse. We were going to tell the family together, but I was hit with a sudden surge of possessiveness this afternoon and couldn't stop myself from informing everyone this beautiful woman is mine."

She gave him a very sarcastic thumbs-up. "Cool. Next time, get her name tattooed on your bicep. We don't send emails to the entire company on a whim, Luca. I think you know the minimum you should have done was run it by me, but really, legal should have been pulled in as well."

His fingers curled into my hip. "In the future, I'll do that. But what's done is done. I can't exactly unspill this news."

I slid my hand over his, weaving our fingers together. "I would have stopped him if I'd known he was going to do it. But we both know when Luca has an idea—"

"There's no stopping him," Clara finished. "Yes. Thirty-one years of Luca Rossi has taught me that."

Luca cleared his throat. "Well, you've met. Now you can go, and we can all get back to work."

She scoffed. "Do you actually believe that's the end of it? I have questions, Luca, and you *will* answer them." Then she smiled at me, and there was a heavy dose of kindness behind it. "You're beautiful and elegant and seem to like my brother for some reason. I'll get your number from Luca—"

He chuffed. "I don't want the two of you meeting without me."

"Bypass Luca and email me. It's my first and last name at Rossi Motors."

Her brows rose. "You're a Rossi employee?"

"Only a temp."

Luca cleared his throat again. "Actually, as of five minutes ago, your new email is Saoirse Rossi at Rossi Motors dot com."

I bit down on my tongue. Hard. Luca was obviously used to making unilateral decisions, but that wasn't going to fly. Still, I knew enough to discuss this in private.

Clara pressed her hands together. "You'll have an email from me with all my contact information very soon." She jabbed a finger at her brother. "We'll talk later."

"Uh, Luca." Miller held up a finger. "We need to set aside some time to discuss the Grave Business Report. They published an article—"

"*Miller.*" Clara's sharp tone and clenched jaw drew everyone's eyes to her and stopped her husband in his tracks.

What the hell is that about?

Luca filled the thick silence. "Send me the link and your thoughts, please. I'll get back to you as soon as I have the chance."

Mollified, Miller nodded and let his wife lead the way out of the office, his hand on the small of her back. As soon as they crossed the threshold, they went their separate ways without a word to each other.

Luca circled his desk, taking his seat behind it. I stood there with my hands on my hips.

He raised his eyes to me. "I can't do this right now."

"Are you going to actually come home tonight?"

"I come home every night."

"Pfft. After I'm asleep, and you leave before I come downstairs. Can you try to be home earlier so we can make a plan?"

He folded his hands on a tidy stack of papers. "I'll be home by seven. We can have dinner together and talk." Then he waved me off. "Order takeout. I'm good with whatever you like."

I blinked at him, not feeling like much of a fan of CEO Luca. "Am I being dismissed?"

"You can stand there for as long as you want to, but I have a lot I need to get through in order to leave the office before your eight o'clock bedtime."

"I don't go to bed at eight." It was more like ten, but still. Couldn't a girl like her sleep without being judged?

"Close enough. I'll see you tonight, Saoirse."

Spinning on my toes, I headed for the door. With my hand on the knob, I looked over my shoulder. Luca's eyes were on me.

"Your sister seems pretty amazing."

He lowered his chin, his mouth curving slightly. "Yeah, she is."

"Your brother-in-law, though..." I rolled my lips over my teeth, and Luca's shoulders vibrated with silent laughter.

"Yeah, he is."

<hr />

I was sifting through Luca's pile of take-out menus he kept in one of his kitchen drawers. It seemed, like me, he was a fan of holding a menu in his hands rather than scrolling through them on his phone.

I was thinking we'd have burgers for dinner. I had no idea if Luca even liked hamburgers, but he'd left me in charge, so he'd have to live with whatever I decided.

A knock on the front door interrupted my rumination. Before I could even hop up to answer it, I heard the sound of the dead bolt clicking, followed by two voices.

"Luca?" A woman.

"He's not home yet. I told you that." A man.

Oh shit. What was I supposed to do? I was in the kitchen, so I had my choice of weapons, but maybe hiding was the best plan. Thieves didn't typically steal from pantries, did they?

My feet were still glued to the floor in panic when the intruders rounded the corner into the kitchen. The three of us stared at each other for a long, tension-filled moment.

As I took them in, it became crystal clear they weren't thieves. The woman looked to be a well-kept sixty, with a thick, creamy blonde bob and elegant understated makeup. There was nothing understated about the rock on her finger or the gleam of rubies in her ears.

The man was of a similar age. Dressed in tailored trousers and a starched button-down, he towered over the petite women by his side. His salt-and-pepper hair and the subtle wrinkles on his angular face did nothing to take away from the stark resemblance to his son.

There was no question these were Luca's parents.

I raised my trembling hand. "Hi. I'm Saoirse. You must be Mr. and Mrs. Rossi."

His mother covered her mouth with one hand and clutched her husband's arm with the other. Mr. Rossi's reaction was more subtle, rocking back on his heels as he took me in.

"We thought Luca was playing a prank on us." He cleared his throat. "It appears his news is legitimate. You're married to my son."

I nodded once. "I am. And believe me when I say I wish you hadn't found out this way."

Mrs. Rossi sucked in a breath, and I braced myself.

It was a good thing I did because the next thing she did was rush at me.

CHAPTER SIXTEEN

Luca

I MADE IT HOME by seven thirty. Later than planned, but Saoirse would still be awake, and we could get this hashed out.

The scene I walked in on was not the one I expected.

The first sign something was off was the laughter coming from the kitchen. Then there were the scents of cooking and the pop of oil in a pan.

Kicking off my shoes and dropping my bag, I rounded the corner to be greeted by the sight of my mother and Saoirse standing side by side at the stove while my father leaned against the counter, watching over them.

He was the first to see me. Instead of the frown of admonishment I'd expected, he grinned at me.

It was a punch to the gut. His smiles had been few and far between since his heart attack. He wasn't adjusting well to all the changes in his life. Yet here he was, standing in my kitchen, looking as happy as I'd seen him in ages.

"Luca's home," he announced.

My mother and Saoirse whirled around at the same time. I walked over, pecking my mother's cheek before moving on to my wife.

"You're late," she teased. "But it's a good thing you're here now since dinner's almost ready."

I took her chin between my fingers, studying her expression for stress or anger, but I couldn't find it. She leaned in, offering me her lips. I took them, pressing a lingering kiss to her mouth.

"This is a surprise," I murmured.

Her mouth stretched wide into a smile. "A good one, I hope. Ang, Vic, and I have gotten all the preliminaries out of the way. They know all about how we met and our balcony wedding. Now we can just relax."

I felt my mother's eyes on us, so I turned to her. "Is that true? Can I relax?"

She reached out and swatted my arm. "No, you can't. You kept this wonderful news from us for some reason, so you'll have to pay. Go set the table with your father."

I planted a kiss on the top of her head. "Aye, aye, captain."

My father's regard was a lot heavier than my mother's had been while the two of us set the table as instructed. I raised a brow at him.

"You're not one to hold back your opinion," I said.

He stopped folding a napkin and leveled me with a flinty stare. "You robbed your mother of a big wedding."

Purposefully. When I was married for real, my mother could go wild with planning. I wanted that for her because it would make her happy. There was no way I would have been able to stomach her going all in on something that was a lie from the beginning.

"She had Clara's," I argued.

"She wanted one for you too. If she asks, you'll allow her to throw you a party."

I couldn't fight her on that. What would I even say to get out of it?

"She and Saorise can talk about that."

He folded his arms over his chest. "I'm disappointed you chose to go about getting married this way."

"I know you are." Disappointment was something I was used to from him. He attempted to hide it, but he wasn't the most stellar actor. I may have looked like him, but I was not made in his image, and we were both all too aware of that.

He held his stare for another long beat before sighing and picking up the napkin to fold. "It shouldn't surprise me. You were never a kid who liked to be placed in a box. And now look at you, doing a job you hate, living a life you never wanted. If this is your last act of rebellion—"

"Marrying Saoirse privately wasn't an act of rebellion. It was what we both wanted."

He folded the other three napkins silently then raised his head. "You didn't deny anything else I said."

I tugged the tie around my neck loose. "There's nothing to say. I had thirty-one years to live how I wanted. It's hard to adjust to my new reality, but that doesn't mean I hate it. It will take me time to find my way, but I *will* find it."

He gestured toward the kitchen. "From what I've seen, you picked a good woman to have by your side. Your mom is already in love."

Another sock to the gut. "Saoirse has that way about her."

And I would have to deal with my mother's heartbreak when this marriage dissolved.

———◇———

Dinner with my parents was a lot lighter than I'd expected it to be. My father grumbled over his breading-free chicken breast, and the lack of wine with our meal was obvious, but it wasn't mentioned.

My father was going through his own adjustments. In that way, I understood him all too well.

"How do you like working at Rossi?" Dad asked Saoirse.

She wiped her mouth with her napkin. "I've worked a lot of places, and Rossi is one of my favorites."

"She likes it because of the snacks," I interjected.

Dad cocked his head. "Snacks?"

"The manager of her department brings in bakery treats." I glanced at Saoirse, who nodded along with me in agreement. "She's only staying on for the fresh biscotti."

"It's true. I'd sell my shoe collection for that biscotti."

My brow winged. "You don't have many shoes, so that isn't saying much."

She tapped my chin with her fingertip. "But the shoes I have, I treasure. So, it really is saying a lot."

"We'll have to go shopping, Saoirse. A woman can never have too many shoes," my mother offered.

"I'd love that." Her hand slid down to my shoulder. "Your son has told me about all your beautiful clothing and jewels. He was aghast that I'm not a big jewelry person."

"If I raised him right, he'll remedy that." My mother winked at her then smiled at my father.

The conversation flowed to other topics, including travel. My parents were planning a trip to California in a few months once my dad was given medical clearance to travel.

"You grew up in California, didn't you?" Dad asked.

"I did. And I spent a lot of time at my family ranch in Wyoming too. That's where my dad, brother, his wife, and their kids live."

"A ranch?" He stroked his chin. "Do you ride horses?"

Not knowing the answer to his question, I listened with interest.

"Oh yeah, of course. I was on a pony as soon as I could sit up on my own, and I have my own horse that lives on the ranch. Her name is Athena." She bumped my shoulder with hers. "We'll go riding when we visit. I have a horse in mind for you to ride."

Dad laughed. "Luca's more of a bike rider than a cowboy."

She didn't let his doubt deter her. "He'll learn. And after we go riding, he can book a massage at the resort part of our ranch."

My mother's eyes lit up. "Resort? Now you're speaking my language."

This wasn't real. It wouldn't last. But I decided to put those facts aside and enjoy seeing my parents smiling, happy, and excited for what was to come. I let myself enjoy it too.

It was late by the time we had a chance to talk on our own. My parents had hung out for a while, and neither Saoirse nor I had been in a rush for them to leave. She seemed to genuinely like them, and I was certain I'd be getting a gushing call from my mother about how wonderful my wife was.

I walked into the den after seeing them out. Saoirse was waiting for me on the sectional, a blanket thrown across her lap.

"I haven't seen them this happy in a while," I stated.

"They're lovely. I thought your mother was going to attack me, but she gave me the biggest hug I've had in ages."

"She does that."

"Well, I liked it." She gestured to herself. "I wish I'd known they were coming. I would have tried to be presentable. Jeez."

This was the first time what she was wearing registered. She'd changed out of her work clothes into leggings and a vintage Hard Rock Cafe shirt. Her long hair was pulled back into a loose ponytail, and her face was free of makeup.

Beautiful, as always. She had nothing to worry about.

"I'm sure they understand." I sat down, stretching my arms over the back of the couch, and tugged on the end of her ponytail. "You hadn't been expecting them, and you're relaxing in your own home. If anything, how you looked sold the legitimacy of our relationship."

Her nose crinkled. "The lies just keep stacking up."

My exhale was heavy, and suddenly, so was my head, lolling back on the cushions. "Let's talk about real things. You have a horse named Athena in Wyoming."

"I do."

"Your parents are divorced."

"Yes. It's been fifteen years now."

"Amicable?"

"No. They broke each other."

I closed my eyes. "They're the reason you don't believe in marriage?"

"The dissolution of their marriage was the first seed in my disbelief, yeah. The following fifteen years of bitter heartbreak planted it firmly in my heart."

"What happened?"

"Do you really want to know?"

"I wouldn't have asked if I didn't." Opening my eyes again, I gave her my attention.

"My parents were college sweethearts. Their plan was to live in California after they got married and eventually move to Wyoming to take over the family ranch. My mom kept postponing the move, and as the years went by, I think it became obvious to my dad she wasn't going to keep up her end of the bargain. So, he lived with us part time and part time in Wyoming until he finally left her for good."

Saoirse smoothed her blanket with her palms. "When I was young, my parents were crazy about each other. They were so different, but they worked in a huge way. And then, one day, it just...fell apart. Our family crashed and burned."

"That was it? It was all over?"

She blew out a heavy breath. "I wish. My mother has been hating on my dad ever since, while my dad never moved on from loving her."

"He still loves her fifteen years later?"

"Mmm...yeah. They aren't in the same place often, but when they are, he can't take his eyes off her."

"Then why are they divorced?"

"Do you want to hear the nail in my cynical coffin?"

I grabbed the end of her ponytail, toying with her silky hair. "Give it to me."

"I only found this out as an adult. After years of blaming my mother for splitting up our family, it came to light that my father had cheated on her."

"I thought he was madly in love with her."

"That's the kicker. He is and always has been. But love and marriage are just words. They can be broken on a sad, lonely night in Wyoming."

Her hair slipped between my fingers. I kept mindlessly playing with it until her head fell back and lolled to the side like mine.

"You ever think he knew his marriage was over, but he couldn't be the one to end it, so he chose the nuclear option?" I asked.

"I think a lot of things, Luca. I don't think my dad even knows why he did what he did."

Since we met, Saoirse had been a firecracker. Even when she was mellow, she popped and fizzed. Seeing her go dark, the inherent light inside her dim, sparked a low, simmering panic in me. This wasn't her natural state. It didn't feel right.

"I'm sorry shit went south in your life, pretty girl." I slipped my hand from her hair to cup the side of her neck. "I don't think I like this cynical side of you."

She tipped sideways, pressing against my hand. "I'm multifaceted. I can't be sunshine and rainbows all the time. That would be boring."

"There's certainly nothing boring about you."

The corner of her mouth hitched. "Now that I've spilled my emotional trauma—"

"I think we've barely scratched the surface."

"And that was deep enough for this evening, thank you." She reached for my hand, peeling it off her neck to hold on her knee. The pad of her thumb slid back and forth over my fingertips as she yawned.

"Tired?"

She nodded. "I really love sleep."

That made me laugh. "I've noticed that about you."

"Shut up, Luca." She tossed me a lazy grin. "As I was saying, I may be cynical, but you're a territorial prat."

My brows rose. "Prat? Are you British now?"

"It fits the situation."

"So you say." I tried to yank my hand from her, but she clapped her other hand over it, keeping it on her knee. "Maybe I am territorial. Temporary or not, you are my wife, and I don't appreciate seeing you out alone with another man, especially after you turned down my offer to have lunch together. Now that our relationship is public, I trust it won't happen again."

With a groan, she tossed my hand back at me. "I was alone with him for maybe five minutes while Niddhi and Amelia—who are women, by the way—were in the restroom. If you would have spoken to me or thought before acting, you would have known this."

Her explanation made sense, but I still didn't like the way that guy had been looking at her, getting close to her. I'd set that right. He'd know better in the future.

Now wasn't the time to tell Saoirse any of this though.

"I hear you, and I understand my knee-jerk reaction was misinformed. I don't regret it now that it's over and done with."

"You can't make decisions that involve me without a discussion, Luca. That isn't fair."

"I get that. Believe me, Clara came back to my office after you left and tore me a new asshole. I had to take a call with our legal department while she stood over me. I've been properly chastised."

"Not by me." She folded her arms over her chest. "We'll have to go to Wyoming this weekend, you know. There's no way we can delay that now."

"I told you I'd go. I meant it."

"Okay. Then I should probably give you a crash course on the Kelly family so it seems like we actually know each other." Her jaw cracked when she yawned again.

"I know a lot about you."

"Oh yeah? What do you know about me that you didn't learn from my background check?"

"What you taste like."

Her mouth fell open with a huff and she kicked her foot out from under her blanket, connecting with the side of my leg.

"I know a lot about you too, Luca."

She tried to draw her foot back, but I caught her by the ankle, giving her a sharp tug, which landed her flat on her back. I tugged her again, bringing her legs over my lap, her ass bumping against my thigh.

Leaning over her, I braced a hand beside her head. "What do you think you know?"

"I know you're a brute." She shoved at my chest without any real force.

"First a prat, now a brute. Those words sting, Saorise." I lowered my face close to hers. "What else?"

Her eyes danced with mischief. The little firecracker was all lit up again. "You're a mama's boy."

My mouth hitched. "Guilty as charged. What good Italian boy isn't?"

"It's cute. I like it." Then she lifted her chin. "I know you talk a big game, but there's nothing to back it up."

Rearing back, I stared down at her. "What's that mean?"

"It means you told me we were going to end up fucking, but this is the closest you've been to me unless we're playing a part."

My head tilted. This woman remained a mystery to me. I had no idea where she was going with this except for the obvious. "Are you feeling needy?"

"Not right now. As you know, I can take care of myself. I'm simply making an observation. You're all talk."

Goddamn mystery.

"I don't think you can make a definitive opinion on that subject. Just because it hasn't happened doesn't mean it won't." I trailed my finger along her cheekbone. "I know you're a naughty little fucking tease."

Her mouth spread into a slow grin. "You make it so fun."

Pushing upright, I grabbed her hands and tugged her up with me so she was half sprawled across my lap. "Why are you bringing this up right now?"

"I'm trying to figure you out, Luca. You've made no effort to spend any time with me since we got married, but the second you see me with another man, you go all caveman. You switch between hot and cold in a blink. I'm trying to find a pattern, but I don't think there is one. Who are you, Luca Rossi? I have no earthly idea."

My gut clenched as she laid out the bare facts as she knew them. The things I'd let her see. She wasn't wrong. I was so fucking off-kilter I barely recognized myself.

I took her chin in my hand, tipping her head back. "Luckily, we have two years for you to figure that out. When you do, let me know."

"Cold," she whispered, taking my hand in hers. "So cold."

Before I knew what she had planned, she bit down hard on my fingertip, never breaking eye contact. I didn't pull back, letting her grind her almost-too-big front teeth into my ring finger.

"If you're going to bite it off, do it already," I gritted out.

Something behind her chocolaty eyes lit up, and her teeth were replaced with warm lips and her tongue stroking away the sting she'd caused.

Then it was all gone. Saoirse hopped up from the couch, stretching her arms over her head.

"Glad we had that talk," she chirped. "Good night, husband."

She sauntered out of the den, and my head fell back with a groan.

My finger pulsed to the same rhythm as my rock-hard dick. I'd married a madwoman. Either that or an evil genius.

Most nights, I left the condo to do my own thing without giving her a second thought. Thinking about Saoirse was not what any of this was about. But that little brat had locked herself into the forefront of my mind.

Something told me that was exactly what she'd intended.

Well, she had my fucking attention now. And I looked forward to seeing what she did with it.

CHAPTER SEVENTEEN

Saoirse

"LET ME SEE THE rock. I demand it." I held out my left hand to Rebecca, Elise's extremely extroverted work bestie. She turned my hand back and forth so the lights from the bar glinted off the aquamarine. "Well, that's just gorgeous. I can see why you chose this over a diamond, even though I still love the ring Sam gave me."

Sam was her high school sweetheart, who she never failed to drop a mention of in every conversation.

"Sersh has never been a diamond girl." Elise took my hand, studying my rings. "He did good."

I laughed. "That's because he let me pick it out." I picked up my vodka cran with my free hand while my other hand was passed on to Simon, Elise's other work bestie. They had a habit of going out for drinks after work, and I had a habit of joining them. Since Luca and I were off to Wyoming tomorrow morning, I needed this to relax my jitters.

"The rock is stunning, but I'm disappointed in the sheer lack of romance." Simon was born in the UK and still had a slight British accent that got thicker when he drank or wanted to sound like a royal, looking down his nose at the commoners.

"I don't know." Miles rested his ankle on his knee. "There's something to be said for grabbing your girl, telling her she belongs to you, and marrying her the first chance you get."

If only that was how it had happened. Not that I would have agreed to marry Luca for anything other than a favor, but when Miles put it that way, it made the whole thing sound sexy instead of sordid.

Elise raised a brow at Miles. "Is that your plan?"

He lifted his drink. "You know me and plans, Lisie. We don't mesh. But I'm into Luca's whole vibe. I respect it."

I held back the eye roll since I was supposed to be crazy in love. "Let's see what my father and brother think tomorrow about Luca's vibe."

Deciding that surprising them in person was a recipe for disaster, Luca and I had video called my Wyoming family last night. My brother Lock had done a lot of grunting. My dad had gotten eerily quiet. And my sister-in-law Elena had become teary-eyed, which was *so* not her...which had only made Lock gruntier.

"Luca's known for his charm," Elise said. "I'm sure once the shock is gone, they'll be happy for you."

"These are ranchers, Lise. They don't get charmed." I slugged back my drink and set the empty glass on the table in front of me, signaling our waitress for another. "Anyway, let's talk about something other than me. I'm tired of being the center of attention."

Thankfully, Miles steered the conversation to his house, which he declared was a money pit but refused to throw in the towel and sell it.

"Every weekend, I'm scraping shit, pulling up nails. I've probably inhaled enough asbestos for ten sets of lungs." He casually drank his beer as though that wasn't alarming.

"Asbestos? You're not serious," Elise pressed.

He shrugged. "It's hard to say. I'm definitely inhaling particles of ancient building material."

"There are masks for that, mate," Simon quipped.

"That's it." Rebecca clapped her hands. "Let's have a building party. I'll bring Sam and snacks. Someone else can bring the beer. We'll knock this thing out in a weekend."

Miles winced. "It'll be more like a thousand weekends."

I waved my hand. "My next few weekends are filled anyway."

Elise gave me a pointed stare. "What friend are you helping now?"

"How do you know it's that?"

Her chin lowered. "I know you too well. Out with it."

I took a long swallow of my fresh drink. "Kenji, my friend from when I lived in Japan—"

"Of course you have a friend in Japan." Simon twirled his straw in his drink. "Is there a corner of the world you haven't conquered?"

"Sure there is." I fluttered my lashes at him. "But it's only a matter of time."

Elise rolled her hand. "Get to the point. What are you helping Kenji out with for free when you should be charging him?"

"He's got this pop-up—" The entire table groaned before I even explained what the pop-up business was. And I got their frustration with me. I was feeling it with myself too.

"You have to charge for your time," Elise admonished. "How many hours did you spend helping Maritza plan for her gardening shop?"

A lot. If I counted the time I'd given away for free...well, I didn't mind it. I liked being useful and getting my hands on a new project. But at some point, it turned from offering advice to formulating entire business plans—and that was when it went from helping to being taken advantage of. I was a nice girl, but my niceness only went so far.

"I know, I know. And once I'm done with this pop-up, I'm going to take a step back from free labor. You know, I've been thinking about starting a consulting business for years. The prospect is just so daunting to do on my own—"

Miles set his beer down on the table. "I'm in."

My mouth popped open. "What? You're in on what?"

"Your business idea. Working at my brother's company has been a learning experience, but I can't grow there." He flicked his hand next to his head before I could formulate a response. "I know, I know. You don't take me seriously. But the minute you started talking, it clicked. I want in on this."

Elise looked from Miles to me. "He's an incredibly talented visual marketer. He won't let me call him an artist, but he is. Miles is the lead designer of the Andes stores."

Rebecca and Simon nodded. Since all four of them worked at Andes, Weston's outdoor apparel company, they would have inside knowledge of Miles's skill set. If they agreed with Elise's assessment, I had to believe them.

Elise's brow pulled into a frown. "Are you serious about leaving Andes?"

"You don't know what it's like to live in my brother's shadow," Miles said. "I'm ready to have my own thing."

"Pfft. *I* don't know what it's like? My brother is Elliot Levy, billionaire property genius. Actually, I'm not even certain I know what he does." Elise tapped her chin like she was thinking.

"But you've always done things your way, Lisie. Plus, you don't work for him." Miles turned his attention squarely on me. "I do have skills I can bring to the table. If that's not enough, I have a shitload of money I'll never be able to spend in this lifetime I also bring with me. What do you say?"

I wasn't sure how seriously to take him. "Are you pulling my leg?"

"Not at all." He smoothed his hand down his thigh. "Let's set a time to sit down and talk at a place that doesn't involve alcohol. But I'm letting you know now if you're serious, so am I. This feels right."

As I sat with the idea and drank yet another vodka cran, running it over in my mind again and again, it strangely felt right to me too.

Holy shit.

<hr>

Back at home, I lay in bed, still buzzed from my drinks. I was restless. My things were packed for tomorrow. I'd showered and put on pajamas. The condo was still and quiet. This was the perfect spell for my passing out the moment my head hit the pillow, but my thoughts wouldn't stop racing.

Worries about how my family would take the news weighed on me like bricks.

A fluttering of excitement about possibly starting something with Miles yanked me back up.

The constant gnawing of wondering when Luca would come home ate at me.

We were headed on a four-hour motorcycle ride tomorrow and since I'd rather not end up as roadkill, I needed to be rested.

But I kept circling back to Miles's offer to be my partner. I was trying really hard to temper my excitement—who knew if it would really happen? But I couldn't get over the feeling of being in the right place at the right time. So, of course, my mind blasted off with ideas and lists of all the things that would have to get done for us to truly launch a business together.

It was all I could do not to vault out of bed, crack open my laptop, and start typing up a plan.

Fuck. I really needed to get some sleep.

There was one thing that never failed to quiet my mind. Rolling to my side, I opened the drawer of my bedside table and pulled out my favorite vibrator.

An orgasm or two was exactly what I needed.

Chapter Eighteen

Luca

Luca

I arrived home earlier than usual, hoping for a conversation with Saoirse before our trip tomorrow. But the lights downstairs were off, and the den was dark. She must've gone to bed early.

As I climbed the stairs to the second level, I heard noises coming from her bedroom.

Distinct noises I recognized from the one time she'd made them for me.

Registering her moans of pleasure, my brain dropped out and instinct took the wheel. Charging up the rest of the stairs, I pushed open my wife's cracked door, violence thrumming through my veins.

The scene in front of me was not what I'd expected to see.

Saoirse was alone, her honey hair spread over her crisp, white pillowcase, legs splayed wide. Her hands were frozen, one on her breast, the other holding something pink inside her slick, swollen pussy.

Oh shit.

She lifted her head, her eyes latched on to mine. "I'm busy, Luca. If you're not going to help out, close the door when you leave."

Her head fell back, and her eyes closed. Those frozen hands of hers thawed, slowly working over her flesh.

I should have gone. Left her bedroom, the condo, the fucking city.

Instead, the same instincts from before pushed me forward to the armchair in the corner of her bedroom. I straightened my tie and took a seat.

My view was exquisite. Saoirse's long legs stretched across the mattress, revealing the vibrator sliding in and out of her sleek little pussy. Her hips rose and fell with each thrust, soft yet urgent cries spilling from her parted lips.

It came to an abrupt stop all too soon. Saoirse groaned, yanking the vibrator from her pussy, and jackknifed upright.

"You're distracting me, Luca. I was so close when you wandered in."

"Don't let me stop you."

Her glare was filled with a thousand sharp knives. And trouble. Fucking trouble.

"Fine. I won't let you stop me." She stood from the bed and pulled her tank over her head then shimmied out of her panties. Completely naked, she stalked over to me and leaned down, her tits in my face, her hands braced beside my head. "You want to watch, you can have an up close and personal show."

She spun around and parked her bare ass on my suited lap. Then she fell against me, her back aligning with my chest.

"What are you doing, pretty girl?" My fingers curled over the ends of the arms of the chair. "Asking for trouble?"

One leg draped over my knee, then the other, her feet sliding down my calves. "No, I'm only finishing what you interrupted, and you looked like a nice place to sit."

Ah, Jesus. This girl might have the bubbly girl-next-door act down, but she was a little vixen through and through. She knew exactly what she was doing.

"Far be it from me to deny you anything." I dipped my head, bringing my mouth to the crook of her neck. "Are you going to get started, or are you all talk?"

My lips brushed her skin, sending shivers through her body and a rush of blood to my cock.

Head turned, her nose and mouth whispered across my jaw. "Only one of us is all talk—and it's not me."

She dragged her palm down her center, stopping at her core.

"Touch yourself. Show me you don't need me," I ordered.

Her fingers slowly circled her clit. "Mmm...I don't need you for more than being my chair."

Reaching up, she cupped the back of my neck. "You're a very comfortable chair, except for the thick, hard cock poking my ass."

Releasing my hold on the armrest, I lightly slapped her inner thigh. She jumped then ground her ass hard against me. I sucked in a breath. "Less talking and more riding your hand."

"You're not in charge here." Her nails scraped my nape. "You're my chair."

I nipped at her jaw. "Talk, talk, talk. Fuck yourself, *bella*."

"Like this?" Her knees rose and she tilted her hips, giving me a better view of exactly what she was doing. And what she was doing was plunging two fingers inside herself and slowly sliding them back out.

"Are you going to tell me that satisfies you? Two little fingers?"

She shook her head. "No. I need something thicker." She shoved three fingers inside herself. "Yes, that's better. That's all I need."

I slapped her thigh again. "You're in denial."

She pressed her ass against my cock, grinding down hard enough to make me see stars. "I'm going to come. It doesn't matter how it happens or who does it. The end result is the same."

Slap.

"I think you're having memory problems. I melted you with my tongue."

"Coming is coming," she panted.

Her hips were rocking with the slide of her fingers. It was like getting a private lap dance from the hottest fucking stripper on earth. My dick pulsed behind the zipper of my trousers, which were undoubtedly stretched out beyond repair. Then again, she was soaking them with her pussy juices. They'd have to go in the evidence bag along with the sheets.

I didn't give a single damn.

It took all my self-restraint not to toss her hands aside and take over. To show her how it was really done. But she was baiting me, and there was no way I'd rise to it. If she wanted to give herself a subpar orgasm, she could do that.

We both knew what I could give her would've been so much more satisfying, even if she pretended otherwise.

Her huffs of breath against my neck became shorter, more rapid. The flat plane of her stomach clenched and rippled as she got closer. Her long legs rose and fell with her pleasure.

As maddening as it was not to touch her, there was something to be said for this view. Saoirse's long, lean body all stretched out along mine, her feet digging into the backs of my calves, nipples turned up, begging for a mouth to cover them. I'd done a lot, experienced almost too much, but never anything that could touch how viscerally hot this was. Fully dressed in one of my finest suits, a naked, writhing woman in my lap who wanted nothing from me.

Before I could stop myself, I covered her hand with mine. Her movements stuttered, her mouth falling open against my neck.

"Keep going, pretty girl," I growled low. "I'm riding this out with you."

The heel of her hand hit her clit each time she fucked her fingers. I trailed my fingertips along her outer lips and down to the valley of her ass, which made her jerk and moan into my neck.

"Softest skin, most stubborn girl," I murmured to her. "Let me see you come. Show me how good you can get yourself off."

Like she was following my command, her spine arched, and her cries grew high and frantic. I pressed on her fingers, pushing her deeper into her pussy, which earned me her ass slamming down my throbbing cock.

"Luca," she rasped. "Oh fuck."

Nails dug into my nape as she rode the wave, cresting over and over. Her eyes were slammed shut, her expression rapturous. It was gorgeous and infuriating.

I couldn't even pinpoint exactly why I was angry. I'd had blue balls before, and I'd dealt. I'd never felt like punching a hole in the wall from unmet need. That wasn't what this was.

There was a word on the tip of my tongue for where the anger was coming from, but if I acknowledged I was jealous I didn't own Saoirse's orgasms, I'd be entering dangerous territory.

After a minute or two, her limp body relaxed in my lap. She withdrew her fingers, but we both cupped her between her thighs until she yawned.

"Mmm...I think I can go to sleep now. Everything's quiet."

"Good idea. We have an early start."

Her eyes fluttered open. "You are going to tease me."

Lowering my chin, I stared down at her flushed face and swollen, pink lips. It wouldn't take much to drop a kiss on them. They were practically begging for it.

I scooped her into my arms and walked her to her bed instead. "I think we've done enough teasing tonight."

I laid her down, pulling the sheets up to her chin. The sleepy girl she was snuggled into her pillow without any resistance, her eyelids lowering to half-mast.

I turned away, but she caught the back of my trousers, pulling me back around.

"I'm really looking forward to riding your motorcycle tomorrow," she mumbled.

"Yeah." I grazed her temple with my knuckles. "I am too."

"Good night, Luca." Eyes closing, her lips tipped into a contented little grin.

"Night, wife."

Even after I fucked my fist to thoughts of my wife, I lay awake and alone in bed, nowhere near settled. Any other night, I would have gotten up, gone for a ride on my bike or indulged in other passions, but we had a long ride tomorrow. I'd take chances with my own life but not with Saoirse's. So, I forced myself still, closed my eyes, and waited for sleep to come.

⸺◆⸺

If I'd expected anything to change between us overnight, I would have been wrong. Saoirse's chocolate eyes lit on my bike, and she was all coos and excitement, running her fingers over the seat and bending to check out the chrome.

"Oh, it's pretty." She pressed her hands together beneath her chin. "I didn't know you had this one."

Wearing the leather jacket I'd given her this morning, her long legs encased in black jeans, Saoirse looked like she belonged on a poster hanging in the back of a mechanic's shop.

I patted the seat. "I'm borrowing it for the weekend. It's a better ride for two people. If you end up liking it, I'll buy one for us."

Rossi bikes were works of art, so I appreciated the way Saoirse stroked the leather stitching and admired the shape of the handle-bars.

"It's gorgeous." The light in her eyes brightened. "But what if I want one of my own?"

"Then we'll get you one. Clara rides when she isn't pregnant. You'll have to talk to her about what bike to choose." Folding her hand in mine, I yanked her close. "First step is taking a ride with me. You might hate every second of it."

"I've been on a motorcycle before, Luca."

My mouth flattened, displeased, though I had no idea why I'd assumed she hadn't ridden a motorcycle before. She'd lived ten lives before we'd met. Of course she'd ridden.

And it fucked me to hell thinking of her on the back of someone else's bike. No way they'd been as careful as they should've been. She was lucky she'd come out of it unscathed.

"Never with me. I'm assuming not on this route?"

She shook her head. "Not in this country."

"Good. Then I get your first."

"That you do. First husband, first motorcycle ride in the US." She shoved her helmet on and perched on the seat. The visor was down, so I couldn't see her, but I imagined she was fluttering her lashes at me.

"You really are a little brat, aren't you?"

She nodded her helmeted head. "Lucky you."

Despite the warring pit in my stomach, I found myself laughing. "Get on the bike, *bella*. Time to get on the road."

The ride to Sugar Brush, Wyoming, was exactly the kind I liked, outside the city where I could really open up and let loose. Of course, with Saoirse behind me, I didn't let loose as much as I normally would have, but from the laughter ringing in my ear, she enjoyed every bit of it.

I'd thought we'd have to stop a time or two to give her a break, but she never signaled for it, so we stayed on the road straight through.

As we drew closer to her family's ranch, the terrain became rolling hills and wide-open spaces. Soon, I spotted cattle roaming every-fucking-where, behind low wire fences. Every once in a while, I saw someone riding through the fields on a horse, moving the cattle where he wanted them to be.

Slowing to a crawl, I passed through the entry of Sugar Brush River Ranch and veered off in the direction Saoirse pointed down the road to her family's home.

Since we'd left early, it was just past noon when I rolled the bike to a stop in front of a two-story, sprawling log home. There were rocking chairs and toys on the porch stretching the entire span of the house. Flowers in the beds and a miniature ATV parked on the lawn.

I climbed off first, helping Saoirse off next, holding her hips while she regained her balance. She let herself lean against me, her hands on my chest. I tugged off my helmet, then hers, revealing her grinning face.

"I'm learning to ride," she announced.

"You didn't like riding with me?"

She bounced on her toes. "I loved it. But I want to be able to go whenever I want. Can I? *Please.*"

Pushing her hair back from her face, I shook my head. Not in denial, but because she had her bottom lip pushed out in a pout and it was fucking adorable.

"I told you I'd buy you one, Saoirse. No need to bring out the big guns." I curled my arm around her waist. "Now, are you done delaying? Or are you ready to face the firing squad?"

Before she could answer, the front door swung open, and a massive man filled the doorway.

Looked like it was now or never.

Firing squad it is.

CHAPTER
NINETEEN

Luca

AT FIRST GLANCE, ANYONE would assume Saoirse and her brother's wife, Elena, were the ones who were related. Both were on the tall side, though Saoirse beat Elena by several inches, blonde and beautiful.

But where Saoirse was honey, Elena was ice.

Saoirse wore leather and denim. Elena's clothing looked designer.

Saoirse was down to earth, but Elena was...not.

Saoirse's brother Lachlan "Lock" Kelly, on the other hand, bore no obvious resemblance to his sister. Until we were shaking hands and he looked me square in the eye. The same chocolate brown stared back at me. The three-year-old girl he held in his tree-trunk arm had them too.

"Good drive?" Lock asked.

"Great drive. We came on the bike. Saoirse was a fan."

He grunted. "She's always been an adrenaline junkie. There was a time she would have run away with a circus if she could have found one."

"Still would." Saoirse plucked the little girl from her brother's arms, poking her belly. "Hannah Kelly, have you grown all the way up since the last time I saw you?"

"Yeah. I'm bigger than you." Hannah threw her arms in the air to demonstrate this fact.

"Wow." Saoirse's eyes rounded. "Soon, you're going to be bigger than Daddy."

"*I'm* gonna be bigger than Daddy."

A miniature Lock sidled over, wearing Wranglers and a flannel. I knew from Saoirse this kid was five years old, but he had a valid point. He wasn't as big as Lock, but he was well on his way to being massive. He probably dwarfed the average ten-year-old.

Elena ruffled her son's dirty-blond hair. "Oh, joy. You already eat me out of house and home. How will I manage if you get as big as Daddy?"

The kid shrugged then eyed me up and down. "Are you big?"

I chuckled. "Uh, not as big as your dad."

He crossed his arms and jutted out his chin. "I know."

Elena sighed. "Caleb is somewhat distraught that his favorite aunt got married without running it by him first."

Lock grunted again. "Runs in the family."

Never taking his eyes off me, Caleb walked right over to Saoirse and threw his arms around her middle. "My Aunt Sershie."

Saoirse hugged him back, laughing. "Don't worry, Cay. No one's taking me away from you."

"He can't. He's not big," Caleb declared.

I held up my hands. "I know when I'm defeated."

Elena pointed to the back of the house. "Since you're giving up your wife, come help me with lunch. We'll chat."

It was then I understood that although Lock was the one who could pummel me into tomorrow, Elena was who I needed to impress. I got the sense she didn't stand for bullshit.

I was put to work taking down plates and getting out silverware while Elena made sandwiches and talked.

"Let me give you the down-low on the Kelly fam. Connell is the salt of the earth. If you treat Saoirse right, he's your guy. The day I met him back in college, he basically tucked me in his pocket and told Lachlan he'd be stupid if he lost me." She waved a peanut butter-covered knife in my direction. "Lachlan isn't as easy to please. Saoirse went through some heavy shit when her parents divorced. She got stuck in the middle of their bomb throwing, so naturally, my husband is more protective of her than he might have otherwise been."

"I'm not going to hurt her." That was a promise I felt comfortable making. I'd be good to Saoirse while we were in this arrangement, and when it was over, I'd ensure she was well taken care of.

"Good." Elena turned her back on the sandwiches to face me, crossing her arms over her chest. "Lily's a tough nut. She has certain ideas of what her children's lives should look like. Lachlan was always going to work the ranch, so she goes easy on him—on us. But Saoirse's lifestyle is a sticking point for her. Lily will either view your marriage as another impetuous, poorly thought-out decision, *or* she'll see it as a sign of stability. That's down to you."

I chuckled. I was bewildered by this blunt woman. "Down to me?"

"Yes. Are you going to be a lighthouse for my sister-in-law or an anchor?"

"Explain my choices, and I'll answer."

"A lighthouse is a beacon to follow home, to keep ships safe from crashing, a focal point. On the other hand, an anchor locks a ship in one place and weighs it down."

"Interesting. I always considered anchors a good thing."

She tapped her chin, a brow raised. "Not to someone like Saoirse. Lily was her anchor until Saoirse cut herself free. She doesn't need another one. A lighthouse, on the other hand..."

"I have no intention of changing her. I wouldn't have married her if I didn't appreciate exactly who she is."

That was as true as my promise. I couldn't think of a single other woman I would have entered into this marriage with besides Saoirse. We didn't know each other as well as we should have, but I knew in my bones Saoirse was exactly as honest and forthcoming as she presented herself to be. She didn't abide by artifice. There weren't many people like her. The idea of squashing parts of her to fit her into a box made me uncomfortable, to say the least. It wasn't something I would ever be interested in doing.

"Good. Keep being the lighthouse, Luca." Unfolding her arms, she braced them behind her on the counter. "I told you about everyone else. Now I need to tell you about me. In my past life, I was an angry, mean girl who would cut a bitch for looking at me wrong...and I mean that literally. On occasion, that side of me slips out. I'm telling you right now, if you aren't who you need to be to give Saoirse the kind of life she deserves, you don't have to worry about my father-in-law or husband coming for you. It'll be me on your doorstep with my pink bat—which I am not afraid to use."

I blinked. *What the fuck? Who was this woman?*

"Pink bat?"

She tossed her silvery blonde braid behind her shoulder. "Oh yeah. She's cute, but she packs a powerful swing." She shrugged, her mouth curving into a pleased little grin. "I'm glad we had this talk. Now, for the important question: grape or strawberry jelly?"

I was seated between Hannah and Lock. Saoirse was across from me, between Elena and Caleb, who was alternating between staring daggers at me and resting his head on Saoirse's arm.

"I've been brushin' Athena for you every day," he told her.

"Thank you, honey." She smoothed a hand over the top of his head. "I know she loves all the extra attention from you."

"I brush her too," Hannah announced.

Caleb gave his sister a soft smile. "Yeah, Hannie helps me too. Only sometimes, though. And she puts bows in her hair."

Hannah patted my arm until I looked down at her. She had grape jelly smeared all over her round face. "Thena likes bows."

"I bet she does. Do you wear bows too?" Hannah's hair was long and almost the same shade as her eyes, but it was unadorned, tangled around her shoulders.

Elena clucked her tongue. "The answer is no. She's never kept a bow in her hair. Not even once. It's a travesty. My daughter prefers mud in her hair."

"Next time your parents come to visit, I need pictures of you when you were little." Lock eyed his wife with a warmth that telegraphed his love and devotion for her without saying a word. "Can't wrap my mind around you wearing bows, Ellie."

She held the same warmth for him. "Well, I did, and I was incredibly adorable."

"I have no doubt," he rumbled.

Hannah patted my arm again. "I really like mud."

Lock leaned around me to catch his daughter's eye. "Mud is for the ground. And sometimes your hands."

Hannah shook her head. "Not for my head."

"That's right, baby girl." His tone was a mix of patience and pride. "We get messy enough out in the fields. Let's try not to drive Mama too crazy. Deal?"

Hannah nodded sharply. "Deal." She grinned up at me. "I'm not gonna put mud in my hair."

"I think that's a good idea, Hannah." I pointed to her full plate of food. "Do you like PB&Js? I used to eat them all the time when I was a kid as small as you."

Caleb snorted. "You're still as small as Hannah."

"Cay," Lock admonished. "You gotta take it easy, bud. Maybe try to get to know Luca before you insult him."

Caleb narrowed his eyes on me. "Do you even have a house?"

I nodded. "I do. It's on the top of a really tall building. I can see miles away through my windows."

"Do you have any toys in your house?"

"I don't," I answered. "But if you guys come visit your Aunt Sersh and me, I'll make sure to have some."

Saoirse shot me an amused look. "Luca has motorcycles. Those are his toys."

Caleb's face brightened, then he looked at me and reined in his excitement. The kid was not my fan. "I have my own ATV. Only I can drive it."

"I think I saw it parked out front."

He patted his chest. "That's mine. You're not big enough for it."

"Really? Because I was thinking I'm *too* big to fit." Sure, I shouldn't have been arguing with a five-year-old, but he wanted to tussle, so we'd tussle.

He shook his head hard. "Nope. Your legs can't even reach the pedals."

Elena pushed his plate toward him. "All right, Caleb. Enough grandstanding. Time to eat your lunch."

He picked up his sandwich, staring right at me. "You gotta eat too if you want to be big."

I picked up my own sandwich and took the biggest bite I could, never breaking eye contact. Beside him, Saoirse snickered, clearly taking great joy in our interaction.

Elena moved the conversation away from the kids, telling us about upgrades going on in the resort. From the crash course Saoirse had given me, I knew Elena was the head of marketing while Lock strictly worked on the ranch side of things. My world had always been motorcycles. Learning about other businesses was always interesting to me, especially ones that had been handed down through several generations like ours.

In the middle of grown-up talk, Hannah tugged on my sleeve. "What's up, Hannah?"

She blinked her big brown eyes at me. It did my head in, seeing Saoirse's eyes on this adorable little girl. Made me think this was what *her* daughter might look like. I didn't know what to do with the feelings that came with that though, so I shut that path down and gave my attention to Hannah, who had a bombshell to drop.

"My mama has a baby in her tummy." She did the little kid whisper that wasn't really a whisper at all.

Everyone went still.

Except for Caleb of course. He shook his head at me like *I* was the one who'd spilled the family secret.

Jesus. There was no winning with this kid.

I dipped down closer to Hannah. "Oh yeah? My sister, Clara, has a baby in her tummy too. She's having a little girl like you. It's pretty cool. Don't you think so?"

She nodded. "I'm gonna be a big sister. I'll put bows on the baby."

"What if it's a boy?"

Her mouth twisted as she thought about it. "I'm gonna put *blue* bows on that boy."

"Makes sense. I see you've got all your bases covered."

"Yep. Bases covered."

Lock cleared his throat and addressed his sister, whose cheeks had turned pink, eyes glassy. "We're having another one in about six months."

Saoirse swiped her eyes. "This is the best news." She leaned over and kissed Caleb's head. "More sweethearts for me to love on. I can't wait."

Elena reached behind her son to rub Saoirse's back. "I had planned to tell you, but I'm not surprised my chatty little miss let it fly. So far, she's told two grocery store clerks, her preschool teacher, several of her friends' parents, and everyone she encounters on the ranch. She's only known for three days, but she's managed to tell half the state."

Saoirse laughed. "To be fair, it's not a very populated state." Then she wagged her fingers at Elena. "Now your tears yesterday make sense. You're hormonal."

Elena rolled her eyes. "Oh god, don't call me that. Gross. I'm slightly more prone to eye leakage, and that's all I'll admit to. Besides, I always pictured you getting married on the ranch like we did. You robbed me of my chance to throw you a big wedding."

I had to laugh too. "My father claims I robbed my mother of throwing us a wedding. There's a reason we eloped." I winked at Saoirse, who was recovering from her tears. "Congratulations on the new one that's coming. I look forward to seeing him or her adorned in bows."

Elena's eyes twinkled at her daughter. "I don't think we could stop her from doing it if we tried."

"So we won't," Lock added.

"Hannie puts bows on Daddy," Caleb announced.

Saoirse covered his mouth with her hand. "All right, bud. That's enough secret spilling for one day."

After lunch, which ended with Caleb essentially challenging me to a duel, Saoirse took me on a tour of the grounds in a covered ATV.

"Your nephew has it out for me," I told her.

"Well, he's been my number one man since birth, so it makes sense he wants you dead. He views you as the usurper of his position." She patted my knee. "Just let him tell you he's bigger than you and he'll let his grudge go."

"As it is, I'm halfway to being gaslit into believing he *is* bigger than me. The kid is masterful."

She smiled as she drove us over rolling terrain, her shoulders relaxing as the breeze caught her hair, blowing it away from her face. Wyoming suited her. Or maybe it was being around her family.

I fucking liked how much she unabashedly adored them all. Hated to say it, but with the way she'd described her parents' breakup, I'd assumed the entire family was dysfunctional, but that wasn't the case at all. Lock and Elena were devoted to each other and their kids. Sure, Caleb was one hell of a gaslighter, but he was cool, and Hannah was an adorable, mellow little thing.

"Are you ready to meet my dad?" she asked.

"I'm ready. I'd be surprised if he's any scarier than Elena."

That made her giggle. It was light and airy. I'd never once heard her laugh that way. It must've been the Wyoming effect.

"I guess you'll have to stick around and find out."

I was all in on this lie. Might as well dig myself deeper and meet one more person I was going to walk away from in the end.

CHAPTER TWENTY

Saoirse

CONNELL KELLY DIDN'T BELIEVE in days off.

He hadn't always been that way. When I was younger, we'd spend weekends as a family. Oftentimes, my mother would end up locking herself away in her office and it'd just be me, Lock, and my dad, who'd been a steady, unbendable presence in my life...until he wasn't.

I loved him. I'd never understand him betraying his marriage vows. It had taken me a long, long time to forgive him for it, but I had.

But where he'd once been my hero, now, he was just a man. Fallible like the rest of us.

Now, he worked too hard to avoid making a new life from the dust of his old one.

We found him in the horse barn, talking to a couple hands who worked on the ranch. As soon as Luca and I entered, he finished up and strode straight to me, his arms open, his smile wide, wrapping me up in a hug that could never be duplicated.

"Dad," I sighed into his embrace, all my troubles falling away for the fleeting moments he held me. There was nothing better than a hug from my father.

"Sersh, baby." He pulled back, his hands cupping my shoulders. "You don't look any different." He reached for my left hand, examining it closely. "Ah, there's the difference. You've got a big rock around your finger, my girl. What do you know, what do you know."

I wiggled my hand in his. "I'm still getting used to wearing it." I kissed his cheek then turned, grabbing Luca's hand with my free one. "This is Luca. He's been through the Caleb treatment, so maybe take it easy on him."

He let out a laugh that was only an echo of the huge, boisterous ones from years ago.

"Luca, welcome to Sugar Brush. Have you been on a ranch before?"

They shook hands as Luca answered. "Thank you for having me. And no, I haven't, but I've heard I'm missing out."

"I don't know about that." Dad chuckled. "From the way I hear it, you've been living the high life in Denver. At least until you met my daughter."

Ah, so he'd done a little research into his new son-in-law. Probably not finding the most flattering pieces of info either.

Luca hooked his arm around my waist. "I lived a very different life before Saoirse, one I'm not ashamed of—though I wish like hell it hadn't been documented for anyone to read the bits and pieces the press chose to publish." His fingers curled around my hip, lightly tapping a pattern there. Was he actually nervous? Luca wasn't one to fidget.

I covered my hand with his. "Thank god no one followed me around in my early twenties. I would hate for all my adventures to be on the internet for anyone to Google."

Dad raised his hands. "Point taken. No father wants to see his new son-in-law pictured with all kinds of women, but not many fathers have the opportunity to easily take a microscope to their new son-in-law's past. I'll take what I learned at face value—it's in the past, and Saoirse is your present and future."

"I don't get a clean slate with many people because of who I am, but I appreciate you giving me one, Connell." Luca leaned forward. "And don't worry, Elena has already told me what will happen if I misstep with Saoirse."

That earned a genuine, belly-deep laugh from my dad and a worried look from me. "What did she say?"

Luca grinned at me. "There was something about pink bats."

Dad laughed again. "That girl is a gift to the world. Don't think she's bluffing, though. She isn't."

"I absolutely believed her. It's fortunate I'll never hurt Saoirse."

Dad gave him a long, considering look. "I'll be honest and tell you I was prepared to be pissed off you married my daughter without getting to know her family first. But there's something about the two of you together that eases my worries." He crossed his arms over his chest. "I'm willing to reserve judgment and see how this thing goes."

Luca gave my side a little shake. "That's all I ask."

Dad raised a brow at me. "You still haven't told your mother?"

"No. I'm hoping I can get away with a FaceTime call." I held up my crossed fingers. "Think that'll be enough?"

"Not even close, kid," he rumbled at me. "Good luck with that."

I blew out a heavy breath. That was a chat I couldn't put off much longer but didn't want to think about, so I changed the subject entirely. "Luca's never been on a horse."

Dad's head swiveled from me to Luca. "Is that true?"

Luca nodded. "It is. Not on purpose. I just haven't had the opportunity."

He patted Luca's shoulder. "We'll have to rectify that. You can't be married to a Kelly girl and not be able to chase her down on a horse. Let's get you saddled up."

My father and Luca talked while he gave Luca a lesson on the basics of riding. I spent time with Athena, noting with pleasure how well taken care of she was. I'd have to tell Hannie and Cay they'd been doing an excellent job with my girl.

Even though we asked my dad to join us on a ride around the ranch, he begged off, saying he had too much work to do. We all knew he was trying to give us alone time, which I appreciated. Luca had to be overwhelmed. He was basically a fish out of water here.

This was a lot for a temporary husband to take part in.

We meandered over the acres. Athena was such a sweet girl. She would patiently walk with me all day, never straining to run. That was a good thing, so Dad and I chose our old boy Barney for Luca. Barney didn't do anything in a hurry anymore, but he liked getting out and going for rides, poking his muzzle at everything he saw along the way.

And goddammit if Luca didn't look sexy on old Barney. Though it was his first time, there was nothing clumsy about his ride. In his jeans and fitted T-shirt, the low wind ruffling his hair, he looked like a movie cowboy.

I blamed it on spending my formative years on a ranch, but a cowboy would always, *always* do it for me—even more than a man in a suit. Knowing Luca could pull both off to a T made him doubly dangerous.

We stopped beside the stream that ran through our property and hopped off the horses. Luca rubbed his backside, giving me a frown.

"I don't know if I should be insulted you gave me a senior citizen horse to ride."

"Don't be insulted." I glanced back at Luca as I started for the stream. "He's perfect for beginners and gets along well with Athena."

Luca followed me, standing next to me at the bank of the stream. "It's gorgeous here."

I sucked in a lungful of the freshest air in the world. "Yeah. I'm glad you got to see it."

"Me too." He knocked his arm into mine. "Do you think you'll ever live here?"

"Absolutely not. I love it here, but I could never live so far outside a city. Plus, my family—"

"They're great."

"Yes, they are. I'm lucky. But they'd also suffocate me with their greatness. I'm better at being me when I have space."

"I can't imagine you ever having trouble being yourself."

"You know what it's like to be part of a family that's also a business. Individualism is valued, but it's hard to grasp when your name means a *lot* of people's livelihoods."

"True. I hadn't considered you feeling that same pressure.

"We're no Rossi Motors, but this ranch is a pretty big deal around here."

"I get that now that I'm here."

We were quiet a minute, the sounds of the ranch our only sound-track. But I'd been wondering something since this morning and hadn't had a chance to ask between the motorcycle ride and hanging with my family. This was the first opportunity, so I seized it.

I rounded to face him. "Can I ask you something?"

"Of course. Anything."

"Where did the condoms in my drawer go?"

I'd thought about packing some for this trip...just in case. But when I'd checked my toy drawer, the box I'd *definitely* stashed there was gone, the spot where they'd been empty.

Luca shrugged, shoving his fingers through the side of his hair. "Why would I know anything about that?"

"Because you're the only one who has access to my bedroom." I poked his arm. "Did you take them, Luca? Did you find yourself needing one and decide to steal them from my drawer? I just can't imagine why else you'd—"

He caught my hand, using it to tug me against his chest. "Why would I need a condom, Saoirse? I'm not fucking you, which you're well aware of."

I let out a huff of breath. "I know you're not, so I can't think of any other reason you'd take my condoms other than to use with your hookups."

"Hookups? What exactly are you accusing me of?"

"I'm not accusing you of anything. I'm asking you why you took my condoms."

"To use with the purported hookups I'm having." He wrenched his eyes away from me, focusing somewhere far off in the distance. "I told you I wouldn't do that. I don't go back on my promises."

"Okay." I swallowed hard, taken aback at his adamance. "Then tell me what you did with them."

His jaw rippled as he clenched and unclenched, but he refused to look at me. "Tossed them."

My brow dropped. "But...why?"

"Doesn't matter. You want more, I'll buy them for you."

"They'd be for you too, so, sure, I'm up for that. But in the fu—"

His head whipped around, and his hand flew up to cup my throat. "You still want that?"

"Didn't I make myself clear last night?"

His face closed in on mine, our noses almost brushing. "When you told me you didn't need me?"

"When I sat in your lap naked and *teased* you."

His hand dropped, and he stomped a pace or two away. "*Fuck.*" His hands came up, clasping behind his head.

While he dealt with his existential crisis, I plopped on the ground, took my shoes and socks off, and waded into the stream. At this section, it only came up to my lower calves, but the cool, gently bubbling water was the refreshment I needed. Bending at the waist, I trailed my fingers over the surface, watching small fish wiggle along with the current.

The next thing I knew, my arms were in Luca's grip, and my body was being tugged into his. He stared at me for a moment, suspended in time, then his mouth covered mine.

I whimpered in surprise, and that was all the opening he needed to sweep his tongue deep into my mouth, curling around, injecting his taste into me. And he tasted good. Fresh, clean, wanting. I licked at him, remembering all the details of our first night together.

That turned into my laughing against his lips.

He pulled back. "What's so funny?"

"Nothing. I'm just thinking what it would be like to tell the girl I was when we first met that within two months, she'd be married to you."

"Would that girl have run if she knew?"

I nipped at his bottom lip. "I don't think so. You're not so bad to be married to."

He palmed my ass, jerking me against him. "I wish I'd had a warning. You're an absolute nightmare."

"Hey, asshole, that's not nice."

He took my chin in his other hand, staring at me with dark, hard eyes. "My condo smells like you now, so half the time when I'm home, I'm hard. The other half, I'm finding relief by fucking my hand to my memories of you. Do you think I enjoy being a slave to my body's infatuation with you? It's infuriating."

"I have no idea, Luca. I barely ever see you, so I don't know what you enjoy or how you feel. If this is the reason you're rarely home, then why don't you do something about it?"

He slipped his fingers into the back of my hair, fisting thick strands hard enough to tip my head back, then his mouth covered mine again. His tongue was a whip, lashing between my lips with anger and frustration, making me moan and my knees weak. He kneaded my ass with bruising strength, keeping my belly flush with the thick bulge pressing behind his zipper.

Rocking into me, licking me, squeezing my flesh, we made out with our feet in the stream, our horses grazing nearby, ranch life going on around us. If I thought about it too much, it would have been surreal, but Luca had stolen my ability to latch on to anything cognizant.

God, this man could kiss.

I slipped my hands up the back of his shirt, spreading wide over his warm, smooth skin, and felt my bones melting. I let it happen too, knowing he had me. My knees could have given out, and Luca would have held me upright.

His lips trailed down my throat, sucking and licking. There was nothing gentle about the way he tasted me. This man was taking out the frustration he'd been living with in silence, and every inch of my skin he could reach was his target.

His mouth latched on to the crook of my neck, all teeth and tongue and lips. My toes curled into the bed of the stream, eyes rolling back. Oh god, this was definitely going to leave a mark.

"Luca," I panted, raking my nails into the muscles along his spine. "I can't go back to my dad's house with a hickey."

It took him a few seconds to ease up, his lips ghosting over my throat. "Pretty sure it's too late for that. I would imagine it's not the first time."

"What are you talking about? I was always a good girl."

He slowly raised his head, and I got a good look at his blown-out pupils. "Nothing bad about a husband and wife making out in a stream."

I shoved him gently, but he kept his hold on me. "Says the man who doesn't have to face down his father with a hickey."

Releasing my hair, he carefully pulled it forward so it draped over my shoulders. "There. Now the evidence is hidden. Only you and I know it's there."

"Thank you." I trailed my fingers down his back and brought them to his sides, hooking into his belt loops. "I think we should head back."

His gaze dropped to the sliver of space between us. "I'm going to need a few minutes before I can get back on that horse. Can you get out of my eyesight?"

A laugh burst out of me. "Oh shit. I guess riding Barney won't be too comfortable with an erection."

He shuddered, slamming his eyes shut. "Jesus, Saoirse. Don't say erection. Don't even acknowledge my cock's existence. I'm already burning up here. I don't need you to fan the flames."

"All right." I removed my hands from his waist and tried to take a step back, but he was still very much holding my ass. "You might need to let go of me too, Luca."

He gave my butt another hard squeeze, followed by a quick, sharp slap. "Get out of here."

CHAPTER TWENTY-ONE

Luca

WE TOOK CARE OF the horses. Saoirse made me shovel shit. At first, I thought I was being hazed, but then she did the same thing without a word of complaint, so I sucked it up and took care of old Barney's stall.

As my reward, Saoirse let me hand-feed him some snow peas. I was dubious when I was told they were his favorite treat, but that big, old motherfucker gobbled them right out of my hand and smiled at me, happy as a clam.

I guessed he was cool. I'd sure as hell enjoyed taking a ride on him, even if he was slow as molasses. My pride didn't keep me from admitting—but only to myself—I would have been ass over heels on anything faster.

By the end of our two years together, I was determined to master horseback riding so I didn't get stuck with the horse they gave to small children. And when Saoirse pointed out Ramses, Lock's stallion, who was twice the size of Barney and looked like he could chomp my head off in a single bite, I became even more determined.

No offense to Barney, but I wanted a badass horse like Lock's.

"Oh no."

I whipped around to find Saoirse staring down at her phone in horror.

"What?" Knuckles under her chin, I drew her face up. "What happened?"

"My mother."

My stomach dropped. "Is she okay?"

"She's here."

"Here? Where?"

"In town. She's in Sugar Brush, demanding we have dinner with her, or she'll come to the ranch." Her hand shot out, clutching my arm. "I can't let her come to the ranch. My dad... can't be around her. He—"

"It's fine, pretty girl." I took her hand in mine, angry to find it trembling. This woman had screwed Saoirse up so bad her very presence made her shake. "I'm here with you. We'll have dinner with her. I won't let you do this alone. I promised you that, remember?"

She nodded, her eyes clouded with unshed tears. "I just really don't want her to come here."

"She won't. Let's go get cleaned up. Tell Lock what's going on. Warn your dad if you feel like you have to. Keep it quiet if you don't. I'm with you every step of the way. That's our deal, right?"

It took her a second to respond. Her chin quivered even as she raised it. "Right. That's our deal."

<hr/>

Main Street of Sugar Brush, Wyoming, looked like it had stepped out of a greeting card. Glass-front mom-and-pop shops lined the street, with a few restaurants scattered in between. I rolled down the road on my bike, Saoirse wrapped tightly around my back. She pointed out the pub where we were meeting her mom.

Joy's Elbow Room.

Cute. The whole town was.

I'd never be able to live in a place this small, but in another life, I could see myself spending long weekends here with Saoirse. That would never be us. This was what we had, so I'd take it and enjoy the hell out of the entire Saoirse experience.

I parked the bike, helping Saoirse off, as Lock pulled in beside us. The second his sister had told him their mother was in town, he'd told her he was coming with her. Elena and the kids stayed back, having dinner with Connell.

In the end, Saoirse had decided to tell her dad Lily was in town. The way he went from open and amiable to shuttered and silent told me everything Saoirse had said about her parents was true. They were broken, and she had to witness the continued crumbling of her father.

It struck me deeply. I wondered if her parents even understood what they had done to her. I didn't think I knew a tenth of how far her pain reached, but with her shaking hand in mine, I suspected it was all the way to her core.

Lock patted his sister's back. "It'll be okay. We'll deal with whatever she has to say then go have some ice cream back home."

She listed toward him, her head hitting his shoulder. "Can we skip this and go home now?"

"Nope. Gotta face the music, kid."

I would have recognized Lily as Saoirse's mother without anyone telling me. Willowy and blonde, she'd passed her looks down to her daughter. She was already seated at a round, wooden table that looked like it belonged on a pirate ship, and she wasn't alone. A slim, balding man in a navy suit rose to his feet beside her as we approached.

Saoirse turned her head, speaking lowly to me. "That's Peter, her chief of staff."

"He looks like a jackhole," I muttered.

"He is."

I squeezed her nape, then slid my hand to the small of her back, reminding her I was with her all the way.

Lily pulled Saoirse and Lock into stiff hugs—stiff on her children's part, her embrace was firm and fierce, which took me by surprise. She offered me a warm handshake and an introduction to Peter that thankfully didn't involve touching. I got the vibe this guy had perpetually sweaty hands.

We all sat and got ordering out of the way. Saoirse stared at her menu blindly, so I helped her pick out a burger I thought she'd like. I ordered her a beer too. She needed something to take the edge off, or she'd burst.

"So..." Lily folded her hands on the table, her gaze trailing from me to Saoirse, "I'd like to know why I had to read about your marriage in the Denver Times. Cora sent me the clipping, and I thought it was some sort of practical joke."

I found Saoirse's hand under the table and brought it to my thigh. She wove her fingers between mine and squeezed.

"Obviously, I'd planned to tell you, but the news got out before we expected it to. I'm sorry for that. It wasn't intentional."

"Your mother was very hurt," Peter chimed in.

Lock glared at him. "Why is he here?"

Lily straightened her shoulders. "I don't like traveling alone. Peter volunteered to come with me."

"That doesn't answer why he's sitting here at this table. This doesn't involve him. Saoirse shouldn't have to reveal personal information in front of your employee," Lock stated, his thick arms folded over his chest.

"Peter knows everything. In his position, he has to," Lily answered.

"Bullshit," Lock uttered.

"Peter isn't family, Mother. He's nothing more than a clinger," Saoirse said.

Peter went crimson from his collar to his receding hairline. "Show some respect, young lady. I know that's a foreign concept to you. All that matters is 'living free' or whatever you call your irresponsible life—"

I slammed my hand down on the table, possibly drawing more attention than any of us wanted, but I was past caring. This piece of shit thought he could sit here, disparaging Saoirse, and get away with it? He had a lot to learn about me if he really believed that.

"That's enough. I will not sit here and allow you to speak to my wife that way." I flicked my gaze to her mother. "This ends now, or I am taking my wife out of here, and in the future, you'll have to go through me to speak to her. No one will *ever* disrespect her that way. Not if I have anything to say about it."

Saoirse slipped her hand from mine to press on my chest, the other curling around the back of my shoulders. "It's okay," she whispered next to my ear. "I'm okay."

I turned to her, our noses grazing. "It's not okay. You don't have to accept that."

She nodded. "I know, I know, it's just easier—"

"No."

Lily murmured something to Peter, who then shoved back from the table with a deep scowl on his face. He marched over to the bar on the other side of the room, planting himself where he could watch our table.

Asshole. I knew it at first sight.

"You have to fire that guy," Lock gritted out. "He's a piece of shit."

"He's good at his job," Lily said softly. "But you're right, I shouldn't have brought him to dinner. I'm sorry, Saoirse. What he said was rooted in truth, but the cruel way he said it was unacceptable."

"Rooted in truth?" It took a lot for my anger to rise, but these people had pressed all the right buttons. I was riled. "Excuse me for being blunt, but are you fucking kidding me, Lily? You're telling me you think your daughter is irresponsible...why? Does she live off your dime? Beg for help from anyone? Get herself in trouble? Or does she simply make choices you wouldn't?"

Lock grunted, which I took as agreement. Saoirse remained stiff and silent beside me.

Lily sighed. "I'm sorry this is the first time we're meeting each other, Luca. Neither of us is being cast in the best light—"

"Neither of you?" Lock interjected. "Sorry, Mom, but that's on you. As far as I've seen, all Luca has done is stand up for his wife, as he should. If you want this to continue, you'll have to start over. Otherwise, we're leaving."

"You can't leave. I flew out here for this." She rubbed her lips together. "I'd like to see my grandchildren while I'm here."

Lock chuffed. "We'll see. As of right now, that's not going to happen."

"Oh. Well..." Lily patted her cheek, her gaze flitting over the three of us. "I think Lachlan is right. Let's start fresh. I admit to being upset I'm the last to know about your marriage and started this meeting off on the wrong foot. I'm sorry for the way Peter spoke to you, Saoirse, and even more so, that I implied anything he said was correct."

"It isn't a surprise," Saoirse said.

Her mother's lashes lowered. "That's incredibly unfortunate, but I know it's my fault." She gave us both a tentative smile. "Would you be willing to tell me about your engagement and wedding?"

Saoirse was still leaning against me, so I touched my lips to her temple and murmured next to her ear, "Anything you want, pretty girl."

She exhaled and slipped her hand back into mine before facing her mother. "Luca has pictures. The wedding was just us, but it was beautiful."

Saoirse went on to describe the ceremony, and I found myself listening, hanging on her every word. She wasn't embellishing anything. She took her time explaining the little details, like the color of my suit, how she'd picked her dress, the flowers she'd carried. The setting was the highlight of her story. I passed my phone to Lily for her to scroll through the pictures the judge had taken.

She smiled as she looked. "This is very you, Sersh. You were never a poofy dress kind of girl—and never one for tradition."

"The idea of a poofy dress makes me itchy," Saoirse said. "We just wanted to be married. The ceremony wasn't the important part."

Lily passed the phone back to me and turned to her daughter. "A lot of people lose sight of that. They place too much emphasis on one day and not enough on the lifetime they'll be spending with the other person. I'm hoping the two of you spent enough time together to really agree on what you want your life to look like."

"We did," I assured her. "Saoirse and I are still discovering each other. I hope that never ends. But as far as what our marriage will be, we're in complete agreement."

Lily squared her shoulders, looking back and forth between us. "You seem to have a good head on your shoulders, Luca. And while I'm certain you didn't come here needing my approval, I have to say I like the way you are with my daughter." She gave Lock a soft smile. "And having my son sit beside you tells me he likes the way you are too. He wouldn't be here if he didn't."

Lock made a low sound, which I took as agreement.

"You're right. I didn't come here seeking your approval." I leaned forward, ensuring I had Lily's full attention. "It would be nice for my wife to have an easier relationship with you without the constant pressure of having her choices questioned. I hope your worries ease, knowing she has my unwavering support. If they don't, I hope you find a way to keep them to yourself."

"Well..." Lily straightened her silverware before flicking her eyes back up to mine, "I think I've been properly put in my place. I would love to have an easier relationship with my daughter. With both my kids."

Things calmed between the four of us after that. Lily asked about Caleb and Hannah, and Lock told her about Elena's pregnancy. She seemed genuinely thrilled.

I couldn't get a read on this woman. On the one hand, she made Saoirse stressed and worried. But on the other, there was obvious and genuine love coming from her toward her children.

The one thing I did know was the next time I saw my own mother, she was getting a big hug and "thank you." I'd never appreciated her more than I did now.

When dinner was over, the check paid, all of us made our way toward the exit. Peter was waiting outside, keeping a safe distance.

He wasn't a complete idiot. Only three-quarters of one.

Lily took Lock's hand. "Can I come out to see the kids in the morning before my flight?"

He pushed his shaggy hair off his face. "I don't think you being at the ranch is a good idea."

"Why not? Did Connell tell you not to let me? Because if he did—"

"No, Mom." Saoirse's hands were balled into tight fists. "Dad would never do that, and you know it. Stop trying to draw us into whatever drama is still happening between the two of you in your mind."

Lock clamped down on his mother's shoulder before she could respond. "We'll meet you at the park in the morning. I'll text you a time," he said calmly.

"Fine." Lily smoothed her palm over her already tidy hair. "Will I see you too, Saoirse? Luca?"

"No," I answered. There was no chance I'd let Saoirse put herself through more stress tomorrow. Tonight had been enough. "We have to get back home. We'll say goodbye now."

Everyone said their goodbyes. I shook Lily's hand, uninterested in a hug. Lock patted me on the shoulder, giving me a look that told me he appreciated me taking care of his sister. In turn, I appreciated the hell out of him putting their mother in her place when she'd stepped out of line. It pleased me to know Saoirse had people who were wholeheartedly on her side. As of this weekend, I'd put myself in that corner too.

When I finally got Saoirse alone by my bike, I took her face in my hands. "Tell me what you need."

Her lashes fluttered, falling to her cheeks. "Take me for a long, long ride."

"You got it, pretty girl." I planted a firm kiss on her forehead, then handed her her helmet. I needed this ride too. Maybe as badly as she did. My bike was where I straightened my thoughts. Worked out problems. Chose my next step.

With Saoirse at my back, her arms tight around me, long legs pressed against mine, it was the ride that mattered, and all of the rest fell away.

We drove for at least an hour before turning around and heading back to the ranch. It was past Saoirse's bedtime when we arrived. Climbing off the bike, she stumbled slightly, but I caught her by the elbow, keeping her steady.

"Tired?" I murmured.

"Exhausted."

We were staying in her dad's house, which had been built in a similar log cabin style to Lock and Elena's. The lights were off, so he must've been asleep already.

He was a good guy, but I was relieved not to have to deal with another parent tonight.

Our room was on the same floor as Connell's, so we were careful to be quiet. Saoirse disappeared into the bathroom to get ready for bed while I stayed in the bedroom, shucking off my shirt and changing into pajama bottoms. I settled on the bed we'd be sharing, staring up at the ceiling.

This was supposed to be convenient. A solution to the newfound complexities in my life. But there was nothing convenient about navigating family. Even mine, which was pretty damn functional.

We shouldn't have gotten married. That much was clear—and had been since day one. But I was in this now, and I didn't take my commitments lightly.

I'd stick by my vows and promises.

And I'd hope now that everything was out in the open, things would smooth out, and I wouldn't have to put so much thought into this marriage. We could go about our lives as we'd agreed to in the beginning. Helping each other when needed, lightening the load.

But even with all my regrets, I couldn't say I regretted being here with Saoirse or standing between her and her mother. It'd needed to happen.

The bathroom door opened, and I sat up, ready to take my turn, when I got a look at the woman who walked out.

She'd changed out of her jeans into a short, flowy nightgown with straps so thin, they were barely more than floss.

"What are you wearing?" I barked lowly.

She stopped in her tracks, pressing her folded clothes to her middle. "My pajamas. Why?"

"Is that what you always wear to bed?"

"Yes, Luca. Either this or shorts and a tank. Why are you looking at me like I have three heads?"

"Jesus, Saoirse." I strode up to her, took her nape in my hand. "I have patience for days, but there is going to come a time when it snaps. You are stretching it paper thin by standing in front of me in lingerie, your nipples trying to poke a hole in the thin material barely long enough to cover your pussy and ass, looking like you have no idea what effect you have on me."

Her lips parted, a breathy little pant gusting out. I had to let go of her and walk away before I did something stupid.

Like fuck the hell out of my wife in her father's house.

CHAPTER TWENTY-TWO

Saoirse

LUCA THREW BACK THE sheets to climb into bed with me and came to a dead stop.

"What is this?"

I patted the pillows I'd piled next to me. "A pillow wall for your comfort."

His brow crinkled as he raked his eyes over me. "You changed."

"I had some clothes in the dresser. I don't want you to feel uncomfortable."

I didn't know what I'd been thinking wearing that nightgown. A long time ago, Elena had gotten me in the habit of wearing pretty pajamas, but I should have thought before packing one for this trip. Of course Luca wouldn't want to share a bed with me when I was wearing a silk slip. To me, it was comfortable. To him, it probably looked like I was trying to seduce him.

The sweatpants and T-shirt I had put on felt like they were strangling my legs and drowning my torso, but I could suck it up for one night. Especially after Luca had stood by my side while my mother chose to put her worst foot forward.

Luca picked up the pillows one by one and tossed them aside, then climbed into bed, rolling onto his side to face me.

"You didn't make me uncomfortable, Saoirse. You made my dick hard." He plucked the hem of my loose T-shirt. "This doesn't help."

I shifted to my side too. There was still a good amount of mattress between us. "I can take care of it for you." Reaching out, I laid my hand on his side, just above the waistband of his sleep pants. "Do you want me to touch you? Suck you?"

He caught my hand, pulling it up to his chest. "You're killing me."

"I'm trying to make it better."

"I know you are, pretty girl. And I want all those things. I want to fuck the hell out of you until we're both sore. But there is no way I am going to do that with your father sleeping right down the hall. I need to be able to make you scream, and that is not going to happen here."

His words made me dizzy, sending blood straight to my core. Scissoring my legs back and forth, I was all too aware of the slickness between my folds.

"Are you trying to kill me too?" I choked out.

He huffed, his head falling forward to our clasped hands. "If I have to die, I'm not going alone." His free hand shot out, giving my butt a smack. "Go to sleep so I'm not tempted to defile you in your father's house."

"You can't say filthy things to me, spank my ass, and expect me to fall asleep."

"That is exactly what I expect, sleepy girl. You've had a long, tough day. I saw your tired eyes before I commented on your pajamas. You're wrecked. It's time for you to shut it all off and rest."

"You've had a long, tough day too. Are you going to shut it all off?"

"Eventually." He swatted my butt again. "Go to sleep."

I grinned in the dark. "Fine. You have to let go of my hand first."

He shoved it back at me. "Get out of here."

Laughing softly, I flipped to my other side, giving him my back. A moment later, the blankets were pulled up to my shoulders and tucked around me. I settled down in the warm bed, smiling to myself at the sweetness of the act, the day, which had been mostly good, the house I loved, the ranch that refueled me when I visited. Soon, I was so heavy I had no choice but to fall.

Sometime in the night, I woke warmer than usual. Awareness crept over me little by little. The sound of breathing behind me. A big, hard body against my back. The arm banded firmly around my middle. Luca's legs tangled with mine.

I knew Luca's secret. He was a cuddler.

Closing my eyes again, I snuggled even closer and fell back into a dreamless, peaceful sleep.

When I woke again, it was morning, and I was alone in bed. Light drifted from beneath the bathroom door. That and the sound of the shower running told me where Luca was.

He emerged minutes later, only wearing a pair of jeans, the top button unsnapped. My mouth went dry as I watched him stride across the room to his bag.

He stopped suddenly, turning toward the bed, and found me watching. The corners of his mouth curved.

"I woke up to my cock trying to dig a hole through my pants and yours."

I laughed and sat up, swinging my feet to the floor. "That's because you spent half the night cuddling me."

His hands went to his hips, providing an erotic frame of his low-slung jeans and the V of muscle that disappeared beneath them. A few more inches and things would have gotten even more interesting.

"You don't know that."

Standing up to stretch, I shrugged. "I do. *I* woke up to you holding me in your sleep."

"That doesn't sound like me." He dragged his hand over his mouth. "You didn't push my ass off the bed?"

"Why would I? I liked it." Passing by him, I gave his shoulder a bump. "You should have woken me up with the cock problem. I wouldn't have been offended."

His jaw went tight. "Go take a shower. We need to get on the road."

———— ◆ ————

Luca zipped the leather jacket he'd given me up to my chin and smoothed his hands down my front before handing me my helmet. He'd been broody all morning, rushing me while keeping his distance. We said quick goodbyes to my family, and now we were about to spend four hours with our bodies pressed together.

It was going to be a rough ride.

As soon as he slung his leg over the bike, he grabbed my hands and yanked me against his back without saying a word. That one move hopelessly soaked my panties, and I groaned into his ear.

He revved the engine once, then reached behind me and slapped my ass.

Oh, yeah, he'd definitely heard that.

At least I wasn't going to be the only one uncomfortable.

Luca started on the road, but when he reached the fork that would take us to the highway, he turned toward downtown instead. Within minutes, he was taking a sharp turn into the little travel lodge beside Joy's Elbow Room.

Tearing off his helmet, he jabbed a finger at me. "Stay right there."

Then he marched into the front office.

Unsure of what was happening, I took off my helmet and climbed off the motorcycle, standing beside it. Through the window of the office, I watched Luca push cash across the counter, sign a paper, then the clerk handed him a key.

The first flutters of anticipation crowded my belly.

There was only one reason he'd rent a motel room.

And I was all in.

Luca strode out of the office, his hand reaching out to me. Leaving the bike behind, I went to him, letting him guide me to room 108.

As soon as the door was unlocked, he shoved me inside, kicked it closed, and shrugged out of his jacket.

"Clothes off," he barked.

Even with his harsh order, he carefully unzipped my jacket and slipped it off my shoulders, throwing it on top of his.

Neither of us was careful after that. Something snapped. We were a flurry of movement, tossing clothes aside, kicking off shoes, ripping away everything until we were all skin.

Luca was on me, gripping my nape to spin me away from him and latching on to my throat. He pushed me into the dresser, which was waist height, and bent me so my chest lay across the top.

The next moment, his mouth was on my pussy, eating me so hungrily I couldn't have stopped the bone-deep cry that escaped if I'd tried.

His fingers dug into my thighs, keeping them apart as he fucked me with his tongue. He ate my pussy and ass, his lips and teeth leaving no part of me untouched. Then his fingers joined, thrusting into me deep and hard.

All I could do was grip the sides of the dresser and let him have control over me, what we did, everything. His hold was so firm and unyielding I couldn't even grind against him. I had to take what he gave me.

Thank everything holy Luca was a giver.

He had me boneless and coming in minutes. The sounds he coaxed out of me were animalistic and completely foreign. I had never growled and whined once in my life, but it slipped from me naturally with this man plowing his tongue between my thighs.

"Please, Luca."

His lips were on the juncture between my ass and thigh, sucking hard and nibbling softly. When he finished, he licked a line following the curve of my ass, then he rose behind me, bending over my sprawled torso to bring his mouth beside my ear.

"Please, what, pretty girl?"

I wiggled my hips against him, finally able to move, if only a little. "I need you."

His chuckle was gritty and taunting. "You admit to needing me?"

"Yes. I do. And I want you even more."

His forehead fell to my shoulder blade. "*Fuck.* You can't say that to me if you want me to last."

"I don't care how long you last as long as I get to feel you inside me."

"That's it." His weight lifted off me, fingers curling around my hips, yanking me into his pelvis. I spread my legs without being told, giving him all the space he needed.

One warning was all I got. The head of his cock aligned with my entrance for a fleeting beat before he slammed all the way in, knocking my hip bones into the edge of the dresser and robbing me of breath.

My head reared back, eyes flying wide, and that was when I spotted the mirrored closet facing us, giving me a perfect view of Luca's tightly muscled body dominating mine.

And that was what he was doing. My will was his. My pleasure at his command. He held me how he wanted, thrusting into me with a force that would have been blinding if I hadn't been so fucking enchanted by our reflection.

His teeth captured his bottom lip. His eyes were on me, on the space where we were joined. It was heady knowing that, without a doubt, the focus of his concentration was solely on me. He watched himself pump his thick cock into me over and over while I watched the effect it had on him.

"I've been walking around hard for you since you ruined my sheets." He slid his palm along my spine and trailed back down to my ass, spreading me with his fingers.

"There's only so much I can take, Saoirse. My home smells like you. Now I'm gonna ride my bike with memories of your body wrapped around mine. You're *everywhere*."

"You're everywhere for me too," I panted. "I think about you when I make myself come."

"Good. If you think about anyone else, I'll kill them."

I grinned in delirium. This man was out of his mind. "What if they're famous?"

He smacked my ass. "Don't play with me. Not when I'm inside you."

I arched my ass and moaned as he smacked me again. "But what if I really, *really* like sparkly vampires?"

The growl he let out was feral. "I look good in fangs."

"You're crazy."

Smack. "You made me this way. Little silky nightgown. I'm never sleeping again, knowing you're next door to me wearing that. Christ, Saoirse. You're invading me."

My skin was coated in perspiration, slipping and sliding over the shiny wooden top of the dresser. I scrabbled to keep hold, to find purchase, finally slamming my palms down and pushing back, meeting his thrusts.

"I feel you squeezing me, trying to get me to lose it. You're going to get your wish if you're not careful."

With that, I circled my hips as well as I could in this position, tearing a groan from deep within his chest. If I thought he'd been fucking me hard before, I'd been delusional.

I'd set him off. Unleashed him. He drilled into me, slamming me into the dresser over and over. In the back of my mind, I was aware I'd be bruised and sore later, but dear god, it would be worth it.

My inner walls clamped around him, so close to the edge, I couldn't stop my eyes from closing, losing the intoxicating reflection. Moments later, I lost Luca too.

He pulled out of me, then his fingers tangled in my hair, yanking me upright. His cock was wedged tightly between my cheeks as he rutted and grunted into my ear, louder and louder, until warmth spilled on my skin in spurts. Luca's mouth clamped onto my shoulder, biting down on the muscle while he came and came on me.

Jerking his hips back, he slid his fingers down my crack, over my slick folds, to my throbbing clit. His fingertips circled and his tongue lapped at the sore spot he'd left on my shoulder.

That was all it took for me to find the orgasm I thought I'd lost. My head fell forward, crying his name on a long, breathy moan.

Slowly, Luca's arms shifted to wrap around me, holding me flush with his chest. I covered one hand with mine, the other braced on the dresser, not trusting my knees to hold me up on their own.

Luca's lips touched my temple, and he tucked his face beside mine. "I have to ask you something."

That sounded somewhat ominous. I tipped my head back to see him. "What is it?"

"Did I say shit about being a vampire?"

"You did. Next time, I expect you to wear fangs."

He exhaled, his head falling against mine. "Can't do it. Next time is going to happen in about five minutes, and I'm not willing to leave this room naked in order to hunt down a pair of fangs."

My pussy clenched. "Five minutes?"

"Mmhmm."

Luca lifted me off my feet, carrying me to the shower.

He didn't make good on his promise.

It was more like six minutes.

Chapter Twenty-three

Luca

Saoirse hissed when I helped her off the motorcycle, cupping herself between her thighs. The ride back to Denver hadn't been as smooth as the one out of town. We'd stopped twice to give her a break, but she was still aching.

I didn't like seeing her hurting. Not when it was my fault for being a fucking animal with her. I couldn't feel guilty for that. It was my timing that needed a lot of work. "I'm sorry, pretty girl. I was way too hard on you before going on a long ride."

She shook her head. "I liked it though."

"I was right there. I know you did. I have the claw marks on my back to prove it."

"Shut up, Luca." She bunched the front of my jacket in her fist. "It's okay. I'll live. I might need a break from the motorcycle for a little while, but other than that—"

She squealed when I swooped her up in my arms and headed toward the elevator.

"You're carrying me. Why are you carrying me?"

"Shhh." Stepping into the elevator, I punched the button to our floor. "Let me do it. I need to do something."

"Okay. I'm guessing this is you being sweet." She patted my cheek. "Thank you for carrying me."

"You like this?" I moved my hand to palm her ass, giving it a squeeze.

Her eyes flared. "I liked it when I thought you were being sweet. Now it's clear you were just looking for an excuse to feel me up."

"I don't need an excuse."

An hour later, we'd unpacked, I'd gone through some of the emails I'd neglected while we were away, and Saoirse had showered. She padded into the den, where I was sitting with my laptop on the sectional, plopping down a cushion away.

"I haven't thanked you for the way you stood up for me yesterday."

I clicked the laptop closed, setting it aside. "It was part of our agreement."

"I'm not sure you knew what you were getting into when you agreed, though. My mother is intense and hard to handle. So, thank you, Luca. It meant a lot to me."

"I don't want you thanking me for doing the right thing."

She folded her arms over her chest. "Well, I am. What are you going to do about it?"

I ran my gaze over her long legs and exposed midriff. Her damp hair woven into a braid. The new freckles on her cheeks from all the time we spent outside on the ranch.

She made my place look good.

"Are you spoiling for a fight?"

"Maybe. I'm feeling a little vulnerable from that trip. Lashing out at you seems like a good idea right now."

Leaning over, I slid my hand under her knees, twisting her body sideways so her feet were on my lap. They were soft, her toes painted pale pink, pretty like every other part of her. I took them in my hands, rubbing the tops and soles.

"No lashing when I'm giving you a foot massage," I said. "Tell me why she's like that."

She blew out a long breath and wiggled her toes. "She's always been that way. Exacting. But when she and my dad were together, she was softer. When I wanted to take belly dancing lessons instead of ballet, she started to get pissed, but my dad wrapped his arms around her, kissed her cheek, and said, 'Come on, Lil. Everyone does ballet. Our girl has to dance her own rhythm.' That was all it took. A snuggle, a kiss, and some soft words, and she was giving in."

I shook my head. "They really loved each other."

"Yeah. But it wasn't enough to surmount their fundamental differences. My dad bent for her until he couldn't anymore. Then he did the unforgivable thing, and my mother has never been the same. Neither of them has been."

I pushed the pad of my thumb down the center of her arch, and her eyelids fluttered closed on a sigh.

"How'd belly dancing go?" I asked.

Her eyes stayed closed, but her mouth lifted into a grin. "Awful. I was terrible and dropped out after three classes."

"Damn. I was looking forward to a demonstration."

Her feet vibrated in my hands as she giggled. "If you want to witness the least sexy thing you've ever seen, I can make that happen. I still remember a couple moves."

"I find it hard to believe anything you do isn't sexy."

Her eyes opened and landed on me. "That is quite the compliment, Luca. I'm not going to list all the unsexy things I do to convince you otherwise."

I dug my thumb deep into her foot. "Thank you for that."

With a yelp, she stole her feet from my lap, tucking them beneath her. "That was way too hard, but this is nice. We never do this."

I kicked my legs out, resting my feet on the ottoman. "What?"

"You know, hang out. You're either at work or disappearing to your mystery locations."

"You're right. My schedule is hectic. We're in the initial phase of an internal audit. I've been vetting a new company since my father has used the same one for his entire tenure, and Clara and I felt we should bring in someone new. Then there are the countless meetings, video conferences, emails to return. It leaches most of my time and energy."

"That's understandable. I don't fault you for that. I don't really know what life was like before you took over as CEO, but I get the sense it was nothing like this."

"You have no idea."

"You're right. I don't. This is the most you've told me about *anything*, including what's going on with you currently."

I met her curious gaze. "I don't keep secrets, Saoirse. You've never asked me where I go at night."

Nodding, she swallowed hard. "The night after our wedding, I fell asleep in here. You came in and picked me up."

"I remember."

"You came home freshly showered."

"Did I?" The things I remembered had to do with her. The flower in her hair. Her dress. The ring she gave me. What I did and where I went were only vague memories I'd stored away in the back of my mind.

"You know you did. And since you go to the gym in the morning, I made assumptions I didn't want to have confirmed. I don't ask because I don't want you to say it."

I reared back, really taking her in. I didn't like what she was accusing me of when I'd explicitly told her more than once I wasn't fucking around. More than that, it gnawed at me that she thought that was exactly what I was doing but hadn't called me out on it.

"You truly believe I'm out all night fucking, yet you let me inside you without a condom? Make that make sense, Saoirse."

The back of her hand hit her forehead. "I don't think either of us were thinking clearly when that happened. Obviously, we shouldn't do that again—"

"Oh, we're doing it again." I shot to my feet, holding my hand out to her. She didn't take it. "Come here."

"I'd rather not."

"If you don't, I'll pick your stubborn little ass up." I shook my hand. "Come here."

With a sigh, she slipped her hand into mine, and I yanked her upright. Taking her by the hips, I brought her closer to me.

"You need to understand me. I don't keep secrets, and I don't lie. If you ask me anything, I will tell you the truth. So ask me."

Her lashes were dark, except for the tips, which were so blonde, they were almost clear. She usually wore makeup, so I hadn't noticed until now, looking at her up close.

"Do you take a shower so you don't come home smelling like sex?"

"No."

Her exhale was light, drifting between us. "Where do you go, Luca?"

"Do you want me to show you?"

Her mouth pressed into a hard line, and for a second, I thought she'd deny me, but finally, she nodded once.

So, I took her hand and walked to the entry. I grabbed her flip-flops and my unlaced boots, then we left the apartment, riding the elevator one floor down.

I unlocked the door to my other apartment and pushed it open. Saoirse hesitated beside me.

"Come on. Nothing's going to hurt you." I gave her hand a tug, and after another beat of hesitation, she let me pull her in, and I flicked on the lights.

"This is where I spend my time. My studio."

With her mouth shaped like a pretty little *o*, Saoirse did a slow spin, taking it all in.

When I bought the penthouse a couple years ago, I also bought the one-bedroom below it and gutted it to the studs. Now, it was completely soundproof, with a small, utilitarian kitchen used for cleaning my supplies more than making meals. The bedroom had been made smaller and lined with shelving, where I stored tools, materials, and canvases.

"The sculptures in your living room," she whispered.

I nodded. "They're mine. I made them."

I let her weave around my studio, bending to check everything out, stopping to study completed pieces. She took her time, and I watched.

None of this was a secret from the people who were part of my inner circle. My friends had my pieces in their homes. My parents and sister too. I'd been creating art since I could stand and had been selling a piece here and there under a pseudonym since adulthood.

But no one else had ever entered this space. Saoirse was the first. She was seeing a part of me no one else had. The uncomfortable squirming in my chest took me by surprise. I'd thought I'd show her, lay her curiosity to rest, and that would be that. But as I waited for her to react, I understood why she'd wanted to lash out when I'd asked about her mother.

Without thinking, I'd made her one of my inner circle. She now held a part of me only a few did.

That made me vulnerable to her.

A fact I found I did not like.

Saoirse spun on her toes, facing me. "I can't believe this."

"What can't you believe?"

She strode across the room, and as soon as she could reach me, she shoved my chest. "I can't believe you, Luca. Why wouldn't you just tell me you were going to work in your studio instead of disappearing without a word, *knowing* what I believed you were doing?" She shoved me again. Not hard. Just enough to keep my attention. "I can't believe I've been looking at your sculptures in your living room, trying to figure them out, while I'm living with the freaking artist. I could have just asked you."

"You could have." I caught her hands before she could shove me again. "You can ask me anything."

"I just have to know the right questions to ask." Her eyes narrowed. "You aren't wide open, no matter how many times you say you have no secrets."

"I don't have secrets, but you might be right. I could afford to be a little more open with you." It seemed like I was safe from being shoved again, so I wrapped my hand around her nape. "For the final time, I am not having sex with any other women, and I won't for the duration of this arrangement. My word might not mean anything to you yet, but it will. You will understand, sooner rather than later, if I have anything to say about it. When I tell you I'll do something, you can count on it."

"Okay," she whispered.

I sank my fingers into her hair. "Do you get me, pretty girl? Are you hearing me?"

She nodded. "I do hear you."

"*Finally.*"

She brought back the shoves. "Don't be smug. You may not have been keeping this side of you a secret, but you definitely weren't forthcoming, and you know it."

"Maybe. I've never had someone to answer to. You're the first person I've lived with since college."

"You don't answer to me, but a 'hey, I'm headed down to the studio, see you later' would be nice."

My mouth hitched. "I can handle that."

"We'll see." She pushed off me, forcing me to let her go. "Now, tell me about this place. Do you only sculpt?"

"That's my main medium. I also paint and draw."

Her gaze swept over me. "Do you love it?" She asked this with such complete earnestness I felt compelled to give her the full, raw truth.

"In another life, I'd make a go of this as a career. But I was born a Rossi, and with my last name comes responsibilities. What I do in this studio can't be more than a hobby. That's the way it is."

"I'm not sure that answered my question, Luca."

"That's all I have to give you."

I showed her around, answering her endless stream of questions along the way. She wanted to see every corner, to know what each tool did. I wasn't at all surprised she was so interested. Saoirse lived for experiences, and that was what this was for her: an experience to stack up with the others.

When she was finished with her tour, she started for the door, but I didn't follow. "Aren't you coming?"

I glanced around the space, then at her. "Hey, I'm gonna stay in the studio. See you later."

That made her smile. "See? That wasn't so hard."

"You're right. I'll try to make it a habit."

"Well"—she shifted from one foot to the other—"don't stay up too late. You have work tomorrow."

"Got it. Good night, pretty girl."

"Good night, Luca. Thank you for showing me this."

With that, she left me alone, quietly closing the door behind her, and I blew out a long, heavy breath, shoving my hair off my face.

I should have followed her upstairs. Eaten dinner with her. Made sure she was comfortable after the way I'd taken her this morning. Put her to bed.

But after the weekend of playing the good husband and bringing her into my studio, I needed to be on my own. To re-create the safe space between us we'd pretty much decimated the last few days.

I was only human. Continuing to grow closer to Saoirse would only lead to disaster. I could fuck without feeling. I'd proven that over the course of my life, time and time again. It was everything else I wasn't able to compartmentalize.

But we'd done the hard part. Our family and friends knew. An article or two had been published. It was time to get on with it.

Tomorrow, we'd return to the office and slot back into our roles. All would be right.

CHAPTER TWENTY-FOUR

Saoirse

THE TWO WEEKS AFTER we returned from Wyoming went by fast. My weekdays were filled with working, hanging with Elise in my downtime, and waving at Luca in passing.

Sure, he'd gotten better about telling me where he was going, but he hadn't made any effort to spend time with me. Not that I expected him to. It was just...after our trip, I thought we'd gotten closer. Maybe even heading toward friends...with benefits.

But Luca's walls had gone right back up.

It was for the best. I didn't have the time to miss him when he was gone. I'd spent the past two weekends working at my friend Kenji's pop-up business and several evenings during the week meeting with Miles about our potential partnership, which was beginning to seem more and more real.

That was why I was surprised to receive an email from Luca Monday morning since I had barely said more than a "hello" and "goodbye" to him for days.

To: saoirserossi@rossimotors.com

From: lucarossi@rossimotors.com

Saoirse,

If you are available at lunchtime, please meet me at the Davenport at noon. Room 1019. If you won't be able to make it, let me know and we'll find another time.

Yours,

Luca

I stared at his email, both incensed and turned on. He was so fucking arrogant, assuming I'd jump at the chance to meet him at a hotel. But dear god, did his arrogance do something to me.

I knew he could back up his words with action. Having that taste of Luca left me wanting. And damn him for being right. My toys were fun, but they didn't satisfy me anymore. Not when I knew the heights my body was capable of attaining with his help.

To: lucarossi@rossimotors.com

From: saoirserossi@rossimotors.com

Luca,

I do happen to be free for lunch today. I'm in the mood for a big, thick sandwich. Is that what you were planning to feed me in room 1019? Are you going to cram it down my throat? Will you give me so much it drips down my chin? I really don't want you to stain my top. It's silk. So I might have to take it off first.

I hope that was what you had in mind.

Sincerely,

Your Inconvenient Wife

My busy husband managed to reply within minutes.

To: saoirserossi@rossimotors.com

From: lucarossi@rossimotors.com

Saoirse,

I'll feed you. It won't be a sandwich, but you'll be satisfied when you walk away, you filthy girl.

The only thing inconvenient about you is you're not under my desk with your mouth around me, taking care of the situation you created.

Yours,

Luca

Wetness flooded my panties. How did he do this to me?

To: lucarossi@rossimotors.com

From: saoirserossi@rossimotors.com

Luca,

Hmmm...is that an invitation?

If not, I'll see you at noon.

Sincerely,

Your Inconvenient and Wet Wife

To: saoirserossi@rossimotors.com

From: lucarossi@rossimotors.com

Saoirse,

I wish it was an invitation. Unfortunately, Miller is sitting across from me, and I think he would notice you crawling under my desk.

I'll see you at noon. Make sure you're not wearing panties.

Yours,

Luca

At 12:05, I knocked on the door of room 1019. It was torn open seconds later, and I was yanked inside. It slammed shut as Luca backed me into the wall beside it, huffing at me like an angry bull.

His hips rocked against my belly, and my pulse thrummed.

"Hi," I said softly. "You're a sight for sore eyes."

His hand came up to my jaw, more gentle than I'd expected given the intensity radiating from his pores.

"I want you on your knees."

Dear. Fucking. God.

After our email exchange, I wanted that too, but oh, to hear him say it.

Before I could drop, Luca hitched my skirt up to my hips and ran his fingertips over my lace panties.

Without warning, he hooked his fingers over the flimsy material and ripped them off. I whimpered at the brief sting but didn't protest.

He dangled the red lace beside my face. "I told you not to wear them."

"I wanted to see what you would do if I did."

His fingers wrapped around my neck, the lace of my panties pressing against my throat.

"Always teasing. Get on your knees, pretty girl. Put that teasing mouth to good use."

He dipped down and licked me from collarbone to earlobe, groaning along the way. My knees went weak, which was useful when dropping to them.

Once I was there, I became desperate. Saliva pooled on my tongue. My fingers worked his belt, fumbling around. Luca took mercy on me, unbuckling it himself. I managed to undo his pants, yanking them and his briefs down his hips.

His dick was thick and so hard it was pulsing. I wasted no time curling my fingers around the base and wrapping my lips around the wide head.

Luca and I groaned in tandem. He was so hot and silky on my tongue. The taste of his flesh mixed with precum curled my toes. Giving head wasn't really my thing, but I wanted to give it to him more than I wanted to find my own release.

His fingers delved into my hair, holding the sides of my head in his palms. He didn't shove me down his length or try to take over. He let me do my thing, grunting with satisfaction when I took him all the way down my throat.

Something knocked against the wall. When I looked up, I saw it was his head. He'd let it fall back, and his face was slack with pleasure.

"That feels so good, pretty girl. You don't know how badly I needed this with you." His hips rocked, sliding his cock along my tongue. "I've been thinking about this. About you. Couldn't go another day without having you."

I hummed in agreement. I'd been thinking about this too. At night, when he returned from his studio, I pictured him walking into my room and spreading my legs to bury his face there. I rode my vibrator, imagining it was him. It was never enough though.

His fingers slipped from my hair to press on my chin. My mouth opened, and he slipped out, slick with my saliva.

"Get on the bed, Saoirse. Clothes off, hands and knees."

He helped me up and pressed a hard kiss to my lips, then pushed me toward the bed with a smack on my ass. I shed my shirt, top, and bra and positioned myself how he wanted me.

Luca followed, spreading me with his fingers first, then his tongue. God, he was so good at this. I'd never felt anything like it. His passion and hunger flew me straight to the moon. My nails raked at the sheets. I was helpless to his mouth. He could have told me to jump off a bridge right now and I would have.

He had me trembling in minutes, core throbbing, panting his name. I rutted into his mouth, wordlessly begging for more, to never, ever stop.

Pleasure slammed into me, and my arms collapsed beneath me.

"Luca, Luca, *please*."

"I know," he murmured against me. "I have you. I feel it too."

There was pressure at my entrance, followed by the slide of his fingers into me. Then his tongue went back to work, lapping at my quivering flesh while he pumped and curled his fingers. And when he hit that spot inside me that made my belly ache and spine arch like an alley cat, he grunted with satisfaction and stayed there. Pressure built and built, making me feel so full I thought I might burst. I told him that. Told him I was close and had lost my sense of control.

He promised he had me. Vowed not to stop. And he kept pressing, stroking, massaging that one magic spot until I snapped.

My entire body quaked when the release came, and moisture flooded my thighs.

"That's it, pretty girl. That's fucking gorgeous."

Luca moved over me, his fingers slipping out even as I continued coming. But I wasn't empty for long. He took hold of my hips and slid into me in one long, smooth stroke. I was so wet my body gave no resistance to his filling me to the hilt.

"Yes. This is what I've been needing." He started to thrust, deep and slow, opening me up to him even more. Still helpless, barely supporting myself on my boneless arms, I let it happen, knowing he would take care of me and make it good.

"So wet," he murmured. "These sheets are going in the evidence bag too."

"Shut up and fuck me, Luca."

He slammed into me with enough force to knock the wind out of me. "I'm doing all the work here. Never knew you were such a lazy lay."

I grinned into the sheets. He had me there, but it was his own fault. "That's because you killed me."

"You're hot for a dead woman." His thumb slid down the valley of my ass, spreading me wide. "Even your tight little hole is pretty. Did you know that?"

"I don't spend much time looking there."

He pressed his thumb into me, making me moan. "I plan to spend a lot of time looking at it. Licking it. Fucking it." I moaned again. This man had the filthiest mouth. "Do you like that idea?"

All I could do was nod.

"I'd fuck your pretty little ass right now if I had lube. Don't want to tear you apart. I want you to like it as much as I know I will."

I reached back, clutching his wrist, needing more of a connection to him. "You talk a lot when you should be fucking me harder."

He slowed then pulled out all the way. My protest died on my tongue as Luca flipped me onto my back, giving me a good look at how much he disliked my last tease. The scowl on his gorgeous face sent goose bumps racing down my arms.

"You want it hard, pretty girl?" All his teasing had fallen away. This was dark Luca. Sexual demon Luca.

I reached for him. "Yes, please."

He lifted my legs, folding me in half, my thighs pressed against my chest, my ankles draped over his shoulders, and filled me up with his thick cock.

He wrapped a hand around my throat as he drove into me. He had me at his mercy, and I had never been more turned on in my life.

He fucked me like that until I was panting. Sweaty. Tears leaking from my eyes.

I grasped his shoulders, clawing him, begging him to keep going, to give me a break, to stop, to never let it end. Thankfully, he didn't listen to anything I said because I had lost all sense.

Even in my delirium, I watched him. So powerful above me. Intense and determined. He watched me back, pupils blown so wide, his eyes were like black tunnels. It only made him more demon-like.

Through it all, there was no question he was here with me. This was about us. Working out our attraction, the tension thick in our home, even when we weren't near each other. This was two weeks of absence coming to a head, exploding in this wild, grappling *need*.

Before I was ready, my walls were clamping around him, and my spine bowed. Luca's hand slipped from my throat to cup my crown as I fell apart around him.

"That's it. So pretty when you come." He shuddered, his hips snapping against mine. "I can't resist you. Can't fight it."

He slammed into me as deep as he could and held himself there, his head thrown back, mouth open. My inner muscles fluttered and pulsed, pulling his hot release from him and into my body.

He fell to the side, bringing me with him. Legs tangled, his cock planted inside me, we lay there panting, working to catch our breaths. My skin was slick with perspiration and our combined releases. My heart hammered in my chest. I was a complete mess, but I couldn't remember a time I'd felt this satisfied.

Luca started to chuckle, and I dragged an eyelid open to see what was so funny.

"You better not be laughing at me," I warned.

"I'm not." He shoved my sweaty hair off my face and leaned in to give me a soft kiss. "I'm thinking I have a meeting in probably less than thirty minutes with our European division and I'm lying here reeking of sex and sweat."

"I have to go sit in a cubicle reeking of sex and sweat. I don't know who has it worse."

His laughter died. "No, you're not going back there like this. No one else gets to know where you spent your lunch hour."

Luca and I showered together. He scrubbed my body, taking extra care between my thighs. He told me it was so I didn't get my hair wet, but I thought he just liked doing it, especially since he dried me off afterward. And when we were all dressed, he straightened my clothes and smoothed my skirt down my hips.

I raised a brow at him. "When you ripped my panties off, I bet you weren't thinking about sending me back to the office for the rest of the day."

"Shit." He palmed my ass, giving it a rough squeeze. "Keep your legs crossed."

"I wasn't planning on flashing my coworkers."

"You should have stopped me."

I laughed. "And somehow it's my fault? I don't think there was any stopping you."

He scowled at me, tugging me out of the room. "Yes. All of this is your fault."

"I'm sorry." I wasn't. I kept giggling as he dragged me to the elevator, and he kept glaring at me. Once we were inside, he started to crowd me against the wall, but a cute old couple got on one floor down, so Luca was forced to act civilized.

Conveniently, the Davenport was only two blocks from our office. Luca took my hand and tucked it in the crook of his arm as we walked together. It felt old-fashioned but sweet, so I let it go without making light of the gesture.

At the Rossi building, Luca ushered me into the executive elevator, sighing once we were alone again.

"Thank you for meeting me." He scanned me from under heavy lids. "The last two weeks have been demanding. I really needed that."

"I needed it too." I touched the tip of my toe to his. "You know, you can just knock on my door…"

"No." He slipped his hands in his pockets. "This has to be separate from everything else. Doing it at home—"

"Blurs the lines," I filled in. "That would be a marriage thing. Meeting in hotels is—"

This time, he filled in for me. "Something else." He glanced up at the rising numbers then back to me. "I need you Friday evening. Frank Goldman—he sits on Rossi's board—"

"I know who he is." I'd researched my husband's business like any proper, inconvenient wife would.

"Good, good." Luca nodded. "He's throwing a birthday cocktail party for his wife. Knowing Frank, it won't be formal."

"Well, I happen to be free, and I'm sure I can scrounge up something to wear."

"You don't need to scrounge. Anything you want, you can have. Go shopping if you want something new."

I skimmed my hand down his front. "I'm only kidding about scrounging. I promise not to look like I walked out of a thrift store."

With a huff, he caught me by the waist, reeled me in, and kissed the side of my head. "Get out of this elevator before I think too hard about the fact that you're not wearing panties and give in to the urge to spank your bare, sassy ass."

I almost asked him to give in to the urge, but the elevator doors slid open before I could, which was for the best. I had work to do, and there were most certainly security cameras recording everything.

"See you at home, husband."

He mumbled something under his breath that sounded an awful lot like, "You're asking for it," but I couldn't be sure.

I must have been smiling as I strolled past Niddhi's desk. She cocked her head at me and smiled back. "Good lunch?"

I paused, pressing a hand to my stomach. My inner muscles clenched, still feeling the ghost of Luca inside me.

"It was a great lunch."

CHAPTER TWENTY-FIVE

Luca

Running late for Frank's party, I asked Saoirse to meet me outside our building, where I was waiting by the car. She appeared a minute later, pausing to have a chat with our doorman on her way out, giving me the opportunity to take in what exactly she'd *scrounged up* to wear.

Her dress fit as if it had been sculpted to the shape of her body. Black, with long sleeves, it hit her midthigh. Modest on some women. On Saoirse, miles of legs were on display, her spiked heels only making them longer.

All that made my throat go dry, but when she turned to finally face me, tossing her blonde waves over her shoulder, smiling like seeing me was the high point of her day, my heart rate became erratic.

Straightening, I reached out my hand. She slipped her palm against mine and tipped her face to the side, offering me her cheek. Cupping her nape, I brought her the rest of the way in and touched my lips to her jaw, then the corner of her mouth. I would have tasted her lips, but they were painted cherry red. Off-limits to me for now.

"Gorgeous."

Her smile widened. "I wanted to look good on your arm." She slid her fingers along my lapel. "No one wears all black the way you do."

Pleasure shot through me. I'd taken the time to change my shirt, ridding myself of the starched white button-down in favor of black on black. I'd done it knowing Saoirse would appreciate it, remembering the way she had the night we met.

"I wanted to look like I deserved you on my arm."

Her lashes fluttered. "Smooth, Luca. No wonder you had to marry me. Women must have dropped like flies around you when you turned on that kind of charm."

All that pleasure plummeted like lead. I jerked my chin. "Get in the car, Saoirse."

She slid in the back of the limo, and I climbed in beside her, placing the small bag I'd brought with me on her lap.

"I wasn't sure what you were wearing tonight, so I brought choices. You can decide which goes best."

She peered in the bag. "What did you do?" Reaching in, she plucked up the two black velvet boxes and carefully opened each one. Inside the first was a necklace with multicolored gems. The second held platinum and ruby chandelier earrings.

"The earrings, I think."

She turned to me with wide eyes. "Luca...you've already bought me so much jewelry."

"And yet, you're not wearing it." Scooting closer to her, I traced a finger over the necklace. "What do you think? Earrings or necklace?"

She rubbed her lips together, a small puff of air releasing. "They're really beautiful. I don't know what to say. No one's ever—Luca, this is..."

Taking her chin between my fingers, I raked my gaze over her. She'd taken her time getting ready for me. Her hair had been straight this morning, but now it was in soft, perfect waves. Her makeup was flawless. Thick lashes, highlighted cheeks, smoky eyes, those cherry lips. It pleased me to no end that she'd put in this much effort for me. Giving her jewelry was the least I could do. A drop in the bucket compared to the sudden urge I had to give her everything.

"It's not too much, and I'm really fucking glad no one has ever," I told her. "Choose which you'd like to wear tonight. You'll keep them both and wear the other piece another night."

Her exhale grazed my hand. "I think...you're right. The earrings will look best with my dress." She slipped them in her ears and pushed her hair away from her face. "What do you think?"

"Perfect." Unable to resist putting my mouth on her, I dipped my head to the crook of her neck and trailed my lips up the graceful column of her neck. The earrings were extravagant. On another woman, they might have been too much. But with Saoirse's height and timeless beauty, they were made for her.

She sighed as I sucked the hollow beneath her jaw. "If you give me a hickey, I'm not going in there."

Darting my tongue out, I gave her smooth skin a lick, and fuck if she didn't taste sweet. I hadn't been able to find time for a repeat of our lunchtime hotel meeting this week, and it had been too long. I was craving her. "It's a husband's right to suck his wife's neck."

Laughing, she shoved me away, and I went because she was right. A hickey wasn't the right accessory for tonight.

"You can suck my neck later," she promised. "Time to act respectable. I think we're here."

Frank was one of the few board members I actually liked. Part businessman, part biker, he had more of a live-and-let-live attitude than the rest of the board. He was keen to see what I could do with Rossi rather than pushing me to follow in my father's exact footsteps.

He welcomed Saoirse and me into his townhome with genuine warmth. His wife Shira, who was probably thirty years younger than him, stood stiffly at his side. How he had ended up with an ice queen, I couldn't say, but the two of them couldn't have been more opposite.

Frank took Saoirse from me, giving her a bear hug. "I've heard all about you, Saoirse Rossi." He held her by the shoulders at arm's length, giving her a grin. "I can see why Luca fell so fast and locked you down."

She didn't miss a beat. "It was entirely mutual. Have you *seen* my husband?"

Frank burst out laughing. "Can't say Luca's my type, but I get the appeal. Women are into that whole suave, Italian thing. Lucky for me, my Shira liked my personality enough to marry me. Let me introduce you." Frank waved me off. "Go, mingle. Saoirse, Shira, and I are going to have a chat."

Just like that, Frank stole my wife.

Maybe I didn't like this motherfucker.

If he hadn't been pushing sixty, we would have had a problem. Then again, Saoirse seemed happy to go off with them. This was exactly why I'd married her. She was doing her job, and from the emerging smile on Shira's face, doing it well.

———◦———

A while later, Clara and Miller arrived, and my sister found me at the bar.

Clara raised a brow. "Did you come alone? Saoirse said she'd be here with you."

"Saoirse said?" I muttered. "When did you speak to my wife?"

She flicked her fingers. "She mentioned it when the three of us went shopping during lunch on Wednesday."

"Three of you?"

Her eyes rolled like I was stupid. "Yes. Your wife, our mother, and me. That makes three."

"Ah." I tugged on my collar. "Right. I wasn't counting you."

She gave my shoulder a slug, and I was relieved I'd played it off. Wednesday, I'd had a working lunch with the auditing company going over some of our accounts. Saoirse had never mentioned what she'd been doing. Of course, I'd never asked.

What kind of husband was I, fake or not, when I put no effort into this marriage? My wife was mingling, getting to know my family, dressing up for me, and all I could do was change my shirt in the back of the limo? If we shared a bed, I wouldn't have been surprised to be kicked out of it.

Clara took a sip of her sparkling water and sighed. Something in the sound put me on alert.

"Are you feeling okay?"

Nodding, she smoothed her hand over her stomach. "Tired. Miller and I are somewhat at odds, so—"

Taking her by the shoulder, I drew her away from the few people nearby so we could have privacy. "Why are you at odds?"

She sucked in a deep breath, her gaze traveling across the room where Miller was speaking to Frank and a few other men.

"He's so distracted lately. I've been trying to get his opinion on things for the baby. Cribs, nursery decor, that sort of thing. Bigger things too, like childcare and his paternity leave, but he's been blanking on me. I'm at my wits' end, and he won't give me any feedback. At this point, I'll be making every decision on my own."

I frowned. Miller was a dipshit, but as far as I'd known, he'd always been decent to Clara. "Would you like me to speak to him? If he's too busy to concentrate on his family, we need to reprioritize his responsibilities at work."

"Oh god, no." She grabbed my arm. "Please, please don't say anything. If he thought I came to you as his boss and not my brother, he would be humiliated."

"Well, I'm both. I can't really unravel the two roles."

"Just be my brother tonight, Luca. Give me a pat on the head and remind me I still have months to prepare." As my hand traveled toward her head, she swatted it away. "I meant metaphorically. Do *not* actually pat me on the head."

Chuckling, I squeezed her shoulder. "All right. Then I'll remind you you're the most competent human being I know. You could have a baby in a cave and pull it off without missing a beat."

"And I'm dewy and glowing, right?"

"Yes, Clara. You're very dewy and extremely glowing."

She rolled her eyes. "Good talk, Luca. Crisis averted." Exhaling, she steeled her spine. "All right. I'm going to do my duty and mingle."

"Damn. We can't stay back here and make fun of people like we used to at Mom and Dad's parties?"

That made her laugh, giving me a small dose of relief. If Clara could laugh at my stupid jokes, it couldn't be all that bad. Still, I'd be keeping an eye on Miller. If he didn't step up, we *would* be having that chat.

Saoirse found me while I was in a group of Frank's friends who were CEOs and business owners. They were discussing the volatility of a New York bank when she slipped her arm around mine and leaned into my side.

I turned to her, pleased for the hundredth time to have this woman on the same level as me. Her face and eyes were breathtaking to look at, and drinking her in straight on was a heady, addictive experience.

"Did you find a drink?" I murmured in her ear.

"I did." She gave my arm a shake. "Are you having a good time?"

"Mmhmm. You?"

"Great."

Attention fell on Saoirse as conversation died off, and I introduced her around. Her easy, affable confidence made me proud to call her mine. Her goal was to make me look good, and the truth was, she elevated me. I looked *better* with her beside me.

She chatted away with the other men, telling them about her family's ranch, which kept them following her every word. I was enchanted and already knew everything she was saying from firsthand experience.

Clara and Miller joined us after a while, and Saoirse and my sister fell into another conversation. Someone who'd worked at Rossi years ago was waving to me from the other side of the room. Saoirse told me to go, and Clara promised to guard her with her life. Miller just stood there like a useless bookend. But that was Miller. No surprise.

———◦———

Saoirse, Clara, and Shira were having a grand time, so I ventured to the bar after my former coworker was pulled away. While I waited for my drink, someone snuck up behind me and laid a hand on my shoulder. Seconds before she spoke, I breathed in a whiff of jasmine, and my stomach clenched with dread.

"Luca, funny seeing you here."

I turned, putting on a polite smile for Frank's daughter. "Francesca. I thought you were living in Paris."

That was the only reason I'd felt comfortable bringing Saoirse tonight. I'd made the mistake of taking Francesca to bed a few years ago. Now, every time our paths crossed, her attempts to lure me in for a repeat were unsubtle and off-putting. There was no way I would willingly expose Saoirse to it.

Francesca hadn't dropped her hand, merely sliding it down my arm. "Keeping up with me, are you?" A practiced, throaty giggle fell then disappeared like it had never been there. "Yes, I'm still living in Paris, but Dad asked me to be here for my step-monster's big three-oh. How could I refuse?"

"Probably best if he doesn't hear you call her that."

"Oh, please. He married a woman three years older than me who barely speaks. What did he expect?" She gave my arm a squeeze. "It's been too long since we've run into each other. Tell me what you've been up to, handsome."

I took her hand in mine and lowered it to her side. "I'm married."

She burst out laughing, this one real and boisterous. I cringed at the heads no doubt turning our way and took a subtle step away from her. The last thing I needed was for anyone to get the idea I was flirting with Francesca.

Especially Saoirse, who I'd lost sight of.

When I didn't join Francesca's laughter, it slowly waned. "Oh my god. You're not serious, are you?"

I nodded once, folding my arms over my chest so my ring was visible. She homed in on it, her eyes flaring.

"I'm very serious. My wife is here somewhere. Actually, I should be looking for her."

Francesca patted her rosy cheek, and her mouth pulled tight. "You'll have to introduce us. I would *love* to see the woman who tamed you."

My nostrils flared, and another hit of heavy jasmine assaulted me. "We'll see. Have a good evening."

With that, I brushed by her and went in search of my wife.

CHAPTER
TWENTY-SIX
Saoirse

Some people didn't enjoy themselves at parties where they didn't know anyone, but that wasn't me. My mother said I could make friends with a brick wall, and although I always thought she meant it in a negative light, it was true, and I liked that aspect of myself.

I was having a great time. With Clara here, the company was wonderful, and every time my earrings swayed, I was reminded of how sweet Luca had been in the limo.

I'd just broken away from Clara and Shira to find him when I stopped dead in my tracks. A gorgeous brunette had her hands all over my husband. I watched him stand there, not removing her hands, and bile rose in my throat.

I couldn't watch them together for another second.

Swiveling in the opposite direction, I made my way into the kitchen and poured myself a glass of water to cool off. Too bad I couldn't pour it over my brain, which was sizzling.

Whatever our relationship might've been in private, in public, Luca was supposed to be mine, which meant no sexy brunettes pawing all over him. I hated that I had to witness that, and even worse, I hated that I wasn't able to see how much worse it got. Who knew? They could've been making out right now. Licking whiskey off each other's hot bodies. Fucking on the—

"Oh. Hello."

My downward spiral was interrupted by Miller stutter-stepping into the kitchen.

"Hey, Miller."

He gestured to the empty kitchen. "Is this a party for one, or may I join you?"

"Of course you can join me." I held up my glass, pleased at the interruption, even if it meant having to spend time with Miller. "I was having a glass of water. Wild times."

He filled up his own glass and leaned his hip against the counter across from me. His smile was stiff and didn't reach his eyes. "Sometimes these things get overwhelming and I need to find a quiet spot to take a break."

"You and Clara really balance each other since she seems to enjoy socializing."

"She does." He lifted his glass to his lips. "It's always been a bone of contention between us."

"That's too bad." Although Clara and I had become friendly over the past couple weeks, we weren't so close I should have been hearing about marital problems, especially not from her husband, who I barely knew. I tried to steer us to safer waters. "Do you enjoy working at Rossi?"

His brow dropped, and I immediately knew I shouldn't have gone in this direction. "In normal circumstances, I would answer wholeheartedly yes. But with the upheaval lately—"

"You mean Luca taking over?"

His jaw jutted out. "Not simply that. It's all the changes. I don't do well with change, especially when they're unneeded. And Luca doesn't take my advice—"

"I'm sure that isn't true. He's just incredibly busy."

Miller set his glass on the counter and took two steps closer to me. "By any chance, has he mentioned my concerns over the Grave Business Report? They are persistent in running articles about Rossi. More importantly, our financial situation—and not in a flattering light. It's aggravating. I've told Luca we have to do something about them. We can't let this go on."

I knew right away Luca had never mentioned this publication, but I pretended to rack my brain to appease Miller, who was beginning to get twitchy.

"I'm sorry, Miller. I can't say I've heard of them. But Luca and I don't talk a lot about business."

He scratched the back of his head and looked away. "No, I don't suppose you do." Then he squared his shoulders. "I should go find Clara. Good evening."

He walked out, leaving me alone once again, confused how Clara could be married to a man like that. I'd yet to find a redeeming quality about him.

Taking a deep breath, I gathered my calm and decided to head out to the party. But the doorway was blocked by a frowning Luca.

"I've been looking for you," he claimed.

"I've been here."

"I see that. What's so exciting about the kitchen?" He came toward me, the corners of his mouth curved like he was amused. Well, he was the only one.

I spread my arms out, showcasing the counters. "Look at this place. It's pristine and polished. No husbands being mauled by hot women in short dresses anywhere in sight."

I expected him to stop, to ask me what I was talking about, but I was wrong. He ate the small distance still between us and hooked me around the waist, dragging me flush against his chest.

"Are you being a brat?" He used his smooth, charming voice that made my thighs quake. Luckily, my brain wasn't such a floozy.

"Nope. I didn't like you allowing that woman to touch you."

He jerked me even tighter to his front. "That was Frank's daughter, Francesca. If you would have stayed a second longer, you would have seen me removing her hand and telling her I'm married."

"Well—" I was too worked up to back down now, even though I thoroughly believed him. "Why did she seem to think she had the right to touch you like that?"

"She doesn't."

My brows drew together. He hadn't answered the question. "Have you fucked that girl?"

"Yes. One time, years ago."

I raised my chin. "Would you fuck her tonight if I weren't here?"

"No. I'm not interested in her."

"Who are you interested in?"

Slowly, he trailed his hold on me lower and lower until he was palming my ass. "I can't seem to think about anyone else but my wife."

"As it should be." I gripped the lapels of his jacket. "Don't let women touch you, Luca. You wouldn't like it if the roles were reversed, would you?"

He squeezed my cheek just shy of too hard. "Do you really have to ask that? The answer is no. No one touches you but me."

"That's fine with me. When you touch me, I come."

His mouth hitched. "And you like coming."

"You make it so good for me." I tilted my hips into his, and his thick erection prodded my stomach. "I'm ready to go."

He gave my butt a light swat. "Me too. Come on, pretty girl."

Luca walked me through the party, quickly saying our goodbyes. He made a point to parade me by Francesca, but he didn't look at her. He couldn't since he was busy running his nose through my hair and murmuring how lucky he was to have me beside him. *I* looked at her, though. And maybe it was petty, but I didn't even try to stop the smirk that curved my lips.

Try touching my husband again and see what happens, Frannie.

In minutes, we were shut inside the limo, the divider firmly up. As soon as the limo was moving, so was I.

On my knees, I climbed astride Luca. "Please tell me this car is outside the confines of our agreement."

"Does this look like home to you? Sit on my cock and let me feel how wet you are."

He gripped my thighs, his palms sliding to the insides to spread them wider, bringing me down to the bulge in his pants. We both moaned when we connected.

"God, I can feel your heat." He hooked his finger into the crotch of my panties and gathered them to the side so he could trail another finger along my wet slit. "Soaked. My girl gets wet when she's jealous."

I shook my head, throwing his words back at him. "Not jealous. Territorial."

Two fingers plunged into me as he gripped my nape, holding me there. "Then claim your territory, pretty girl. Take what you need."

"I need to come." I rocked my hips to the rhythm he fucked me with his fingers, confident he'd get me there.

"I've got you. I'll take you there."

He sucked my neck, thrust and stroked my pussy, and held me close. That must have been the magic formula since I was flying out of my skin in no time. And Luca kept going, lapping at my throat, circling my clit until I was whimpering and writhing, begging for his cock.

My dress was dragged down, off my arms and chest. Lips surrounding my nipples, my head thrown back. Luca's pants were unzipped, his cock wedged between my folds. Each time he sucked, I rocked over his thick length, hitting my clit, covering him with my arousal.

We taunted each other, coming close, but never all the way, until it was too much. I needed him, and from the rumbling groans vibrating Luca's chest, he needed me just as badly.

He took me by the hips, lifting me like a feather, and placed me on his cock. I sank all the way down with his help, and when our pelvises connected, we ignited. Clashing mouths, grappling hands, slapping skin. We fucked each other like our lives depended on it.

I still had the memory of that woman with her hands on Luca's arm, so I might have dug my nails into his neck harder than I would have otherwise. He didn't complain. If anything, he sucked on my lips with extra force and shoved me down on his cock like he intended to meld me with it.

My head fell back as I came around him. He slapped me on the ass and covered my mouth to muffle my cries. In the moment, I didn't care who heard me, but in the back of my mind, I was thankful Luca had.

"Yes, *yes*," he gritted out. "Do you have any idea how fucking beautiful you are when you let go?"

He wasn't waiting for an answer from me, but I gave him one anyway. "Not as half as beautiful as you when you pump your cum inside me."

He groaned, his head thumping against the headrest. "You're killing me. I'm going to fill this pussy up until it's overflowing. Then I'm going to stuff all my cum back up there, so you take every drop. Don't waste any of it."

"Give it to me, Luca. Stop talking and paint my pussy. I need it."

He slammed me down on his cock like I was his personal toy, and I loved it. Loved how he owned my body and made me feel like I was fully his and he was promising to take care of me.

My thighs quivered as another wave of pleasure swept through me until I was sinking beneath it, lost. Luca's groans were like thunder, cracking the electric air around us.

He buried his face in my throat as he fucked me in earnest. I held him there, my arms around his head and shoulders, melting under the heat of his breath on my skin.

Luca drove into me from beneath like we were all alone in a big bed—not the back of a limo, crawling through city traffic. My body was under his control. His grip on my hips was ironclad, lifting and dropping me down to meet his upward thrusts. He was giving me a fantasy in real life. Better than I could have dreamed up. Being taken by Luca in the back of a limo made saying "yes" to him worth it, though I was thoroughly ruined for anyone else. No one would ever measure up to Luca Rossi.

For a brief moment, regret tried to sneak through the cracks of my psyche when I thought about a future that wouldn't include Luca. But this wasn't a time for sadness and thoughts. Luca fucked my thoughts away, leaving only euphoria as my body reached yet another peak.

When we fell, we went together. Moans mingling, panting breaths exchanged, pleasure binding our fiery bodies, if only for this one wild, fleeting moment.

I fell against him, giving him all my weight. Still deep inside me, Luca idly stroked my hair as we both caught our breath.

"There's no way the driver didn't hear that," I murmured.

"Mmm. I pay him enough money not to listen." He curled a lock of my hair around his finger. "I like that you didn't even try to be quiet."

"I did try." I lifted my head from his shoulder with great effort. He'd liquefied my bones. "It's just that I failed."

He laughed softly. "I doubt you fail at much, so I'll take it."

"You're right. I don't give up, so I can't fail."

"Pretty, persistent girl. You even managed to melt Shira's icy facade."

"She isn't icy. She's very, very shy. You'd know that if you weren't so quick to judge."

"Hmmm. Something to think about. Now...let's get you off my dick so I can thank you for coming with me tonight."

I snorted a laugh and patted his cheek. "I like you, Luca Rossi."

He unwound my hair so he could drag his finger along my jaw. "I like you too, Saoirse Rossi."

The funny thing was, it didn't even sound strange to hear his name attached to mine anymore.

CHAPTER TWENTY-SEVEN

Luca

I CRACKED ONE EYE open. Seven thirty a.m. An ungodly hour for a Saturday. But the persistent tapping on my door had dragged me out of my much-needed sleep.

"The condo better be burning down," I called in the direction of the closed door.

Saoirse's muffled laugh came from the other side, then she pushed it open, peeking her head into my dark room.

"Hi."

I cracked the other eye, taking her in. She was fully dressed and far too bright-eyed.

"You don't look like you crawled through smoke to get to my bedroom, so I'm assuming there's no fire."

With a soft laugh, she strode across the room and plopped down beside me on the bed, pushing my hair off my forehead. That small gesture was all it took for most of my grouchiness to fade.

"This is the last farmers' market of the season. I wanted to see if you'd like to come with me."

I would have liked her to climb into my bed and wrap her lips around my cock. Or put her head on my chest while I slept. None of my preferred activities involved me getting out of this bed before ten.

"As much fun as that sounds, I'm going to have to pass." I closed my eyes, hoping she'd leave me in peace.

"Mmm...too bad. I noticed you really like the cheese I bought you, even though you never mentioned it. I was going to buy you more, but now..."

The genuine disappointment in her voice woke me up a little more. My eyes opened so I could look at her in the dim light. She stroked my hair off my forehead again and sighed.

"Okay, I'll let you sleep. You need it. And I'll even bring you some cheese." She leaned down and pressed a kiss to my cheek. "See you later, Luca."

She was on her feet when I remembered the fucking honey guy. The man she'd been reeling in for months. He'd see her in her pretty little dress, probably spend time with her, make her laugh, all while I lay in bed.

"Hold on."

She swiveled around. "Are you coming?"

"Yeah. I'm coming."

⸺⸺◦⸺⸺

Spending time with Saoirse was easy. We strolled through the market, no direction in mind. She pointed out her favorite booths, introducing me to people she'd come to know. Each time she told another person we were married, they gifted us something—from apples to jam to a small, carved-wood ring holder.

She wandered ahead of me while I got stuck talking to the cheese guy about motorcycles. I kept one eye on her, so I didn't miss when she stopped at a booth and the man running it walked around to her side to give her a hug. The massive fucker even lifted her off her feet.

Honey guy. Spinning my wife around. Making her smile. She'd been reeling him in, and it appeared he'd been caught.

Barely saying goodbye to the person I was speaking to, I charged in their direction. He'd set her on her feet but was still far too close when I reached them.

I slipped my arm around her waist, pulling her back against my chest. She yelped, turning her head to look at me.

"Oh god, Luca, you surprised me."

I squeezed her hip. "Introduce me to your friend, Saoirse."

"Oh, of course. Luca, this is Mick. Mick, this is Luca."

Mick had torn his eyes off Saoirse to study me, and I studied his overgrown Viking man bun, wannabe hipster ass right back. His jaw rippled when he landed on my fingers curled around Saoirse's waist.

"Mick, of course." I rocked back on my heels. "My wife has told me all about you and your honey."

His gaze lifted to Saoirse's. "You're married?"

"I am." She held up her left hand, wiggling her fingers. "We got married a little over a month ago. It was a whirlwind."

He folded his arms over his big chest. "I wondered where you'd been."

I chuckled. "I've been keeping my wife busy." He could let his little imagination run wild by guessing exactly what I'd been keeping her busy doing.

He grunted, not bothering to acknowledge me in any other way. "Congratulations. I wish I'd known."

"Now you do," I said flatly.

Saoirse laid her hand over mine and drove her elbow into my side. "Thank you, Mick. As I said, it's been a whirlwind. Sorry I haven't been by in a few weeks. I made sure I had time to stop by today since it'll be a while before I see everyone again."

"Thanks for coming." He averted his gaze, eyeing the slowly streaming crowd. "It's a busy day. Gotta get back to it. Pick something out if you want. My wedding gift to you."

He turned his back on her and returned to his place behind his table. Saoirse stared after him for a moment before removing my hand from her hip. Instead of dropping it, she wove her fingers between mine and tipped her head to the side.

"Come on. There's more to see," she said as she pulled me along.

"You okay?"

She lifted a shoulder. "I feel bad for stringing him along. I could tell he was disappointed."

When we were far enough away from Mick and his honey, I tugged Saoirse to the side between two booths and wrapped my arms around her waist. She slid her hands up my chest to curl them around my neck.

"Here's the thing, pretty girl: Mick had his chance and didn't take it. He saw you, gorgeous fucking you, and didn't do everything he could to have you for himself. That alone tells me he's not good enough for you. The douchey man bun and his sad little pout sealed the deal. Don't feel bad for moving on. If he's disappointed, that's on him."

She scooted closer and pressed a hard kiss to my lips. "That was exactly what I needed to hear." She kissed me again. "Thank you for coming with me, Luca. I would have had a guilt spiral if you hadn't set me straight."

She went in for another kiss, but this time, I caught the back of her head, keeping her mouth sealed to mine. What started as a hard, closed-mouth kiss melted, her lips parting for my tongue to sweep inside. Always mindful we were outside, in view of anyone who cared to look, I kissed her with slow, gentle caresses, licking away any residual sadness. Saoirse didn't get to be sad over other men in front of me. I'd cure her of that quickly and with precision.

She pulled away first. "I bought you something."

I huffed a laugh. "When did you do that? I always had my eye on you."

"I'm sneaky like that." She reached into her canvas bag, pulled out a small package wrapped in white tissue paper, and handed it to me. "I saw it and decided you needed it."

I flipped the package over, frowning. Saoirse trailed her fingertip over my knuckles.

"Why do you seem confused?"

My frown deepened. "I'm..."

"Just open it. It's not jewels like you keep giving me. It's only a little something."

Tearing the tape carefully, I unfolded the paper, revealing a small pewter motorcycle attached to a key chain. Though it fit in the center of my palm, I immediately recognized it was a model of a Rossi bike from my grandfather's day.

"It's an M50 Road Knight."

She leaned in, peering at my hand. "Is it? I saw it had a Rossi symbol."

I closed the paper, replacing the tape, and tucked the package in my pocket. "Thank you."

Her head canted. "Is it me you're not good at accepting gifts from, or is it a general thing?"

"What do you mean?"

"Well, it began with the cheese board. You've never said a single word about that. Then your wedding ring. You barely looked at it. And now this. I know the key chain is small, but you gave it a glance, then put it away. It's a pattern, but I wonder if it's specific to me or not."

"I didn't realize I was doing that."

"You are."

I took the key chain out and unwrapped it, wadding the paper up, and attached it to the house key in my pocket.

"My grandfather rode this bike. He took me for a ride on it when I was a kid. My first ride. You didn't know that, but it took me aback. I needed a minute to recover my equilibrium." I clutched the key chain in my fist. "Thank you for giving me this. I'll think about him when I unlock my door."

"That's a good thing, I assume?"

"Great thing," I answered. "As for the cheese board, I ate the hell out of the cheese. The board is on my counter. You noticed I'm sure."

"I did."

"When you gave it to me, I wasn't sure about you. No one gives me gifts out of the blue, and you handed me something you had put a lot of thought into at what was supposed to be our first meeting. You threw me off balance, as you have a tendency to do."

She crinkled her nose. "I don't. Do I?"

I smoothed my fingertip down her nose. "You do, pretty girl." I glanced at my ring. That wasn't something I wanted to talk about. "I'll try to do better next time."

She arched a brow. "Assuming there'll be a next time."

Taking her chin between my fingers, I tipped her head slightly. "Knowing you, there will be."

A slow smile spread across her face. "Fine. Gift giving is my love language. I can't help it, so prepare, Luca. I *will* give you thoughtful presents."

A lightness I hadn't had for months bloomed in my chest. All because of Saoirse. Even though I continued to mess up. Even though I was absent more often than not and incredibly deficient at accepting gifts. She continued being this...fucking brilliant surprise.

"I'll be ready. Promise, pretty girl."

———— ◦◦ ————

Saoirse had me drive her to a café where I learned she'd been working for the past two weekends, helping out a friend.

I'd pictured the friend as someone like Elise, but I was far off the mark. When I pulled up to the curb, Kenji—a tattooed, rock star–looking Japanese guy—was leaning against the brick wall beside the café, one booted foot kicked up.

"There are lots of other people working with you, right?" I eyed the handsome motherfucker, wondering if he was Saoirse's type.

"Yes. Well, it's Kenji, me, and his brother, Riku. He hired some other people to work with him next weekend, but—" She squeaked when I pulled away from the curb. "What are you doing?"

"Finding a parking spot. I'm coming in with you. I'd like to meet the man you've been spending so much time with."

I felt her boring holes in the side of my head.

"Did you even notice I wasn't home?"

My fingers tightened on the steering wheel. "Of course I knew you were out. I didn't know what you were doing. Now I do. I'm going to meet Kenji. You don't mind, do you?"

"I don't mind as long as you're nice."

I pulled into a parking lot two blocks from the café. "Oh, I'll be nice."

And I would, as long as Kenji didn't look at my wife like the honey guy did. I found it hard to believe he was happy in the friendzone with Saoirse, but we'd see.

Besides, I was curious about what she'd been up to over the past couple weeks. Now seemed like a great time to find out.

CHAPTER
TWENTY-EIGHT

Saoirse

I TAPPED LUCA ON the shoulder. He pulled his attention from his computer to snake his arm around my back, his hand dangerously close to my ass.

"This is your thirty-minute check-in," I chirped. "Are you making progress?"

"Strangely, yes." He shoved his fingers through his hair. "I got through five employee surveys."

"Good job." I patted his shoulder. "I'll be back in thirty minutes to check in with you again."

Kenji had brought his pop-up business from Japan, testing it out in a temporary space to see if it worked with Americans. Customers used a workspace in the café and requested to be checked on by the staff at predetermined intervals to ensure they were staying on task.

The past three weekends had been packed, convincing Kenji this business model might really work here. Ping-ponging between customers, serving coffee and check-ins, I agreed with him.

Luca had spent all of Saturday, and now Sunday, working in the café. These two days were the most time we'd spent together since Wyoming. At first, I'd been a little annoyed he stuck around. To me, it'd felt like he didn't trust me. But I was beginning to believe he was using his territorialism as an excuse to spend time with me—which I didn't mind at all.

I liked my husband.

A half hour later, I circled back to Luca with a coffee, sliding it in front of him.

"How's my good boy doing?" I whispered to him.

He growled at me. "I'm thinking of all the bad, bad things I'll be doing with you as soon as I have the chance."

"Which won't be tonight if you don't get through more employee surveys."

He winced. "You're a taskmaster."

"I am." I shoved his shoulder. "Now, get back to work or I'll be forced to crack the whip."

"Yes, mistress."

"Oh god. Yes, yes, *yes.*"

Luca's hand gripped my shoulder, the other held my ass cheek. "Don't move, pretty girl. Don't fucking move."

My back opening burned and stretched from Luca's thick cock breaching it and sliding into me. I clawed at the couch cushions, keeping still for him everywhere else, tamping down every instinct telling me to rock into him.

"You're so tight," he gritted out. "So hot and tight."

I shook my head, tears welling in my eyes. Not because it hurt but from the intensity.

"You won't fit."

As soon as we left Kenji's, Luca drove us to the Davenport, herded me to *our* room, and ordered me to strip. By the time he bent me over the arm of the couch, I was shaking and soaked. Dropping to his knees behind me, he buried his face between my thighs, taking me over the edge again and again until I was delirious. Then he announced it was time for him to take my ass, and I'd had no objections.

His hand rained a smack on my ass. "Don't doubt me, Saoirse."

My doubts lay in my ability to handle him, not in Luca. He could work me into a frenzy in three licks. Even a filthy look would do.

"Just fuck me already," I squeezed out. "Prove it to me."

He slapped me again. "Don't rush me. I plan to enjoy this." To illustrate how unrushed he was, he retreated, then slid in at a snail's pace, going a little farther this time. "You have the prettiest little hole and fuck if it's not clamping around me like a fist."

"Stop talking about my asshole and fuck it."

He leaned over my back, gripping my hair at the crown. His lips were near my ear, whispering taunts. "You're not in charge here, pretty girl. Right now, I own you, and I'll talk about all the parts of you I'm obsessed with whenever I want. Here's a hint: it's all of you, so we're gonna be here for a while."

I had no sassy comeback. Not when he chose that moment to push the rest of the way inside me, his hips flush with my backside. A wobbly moan was the best I could do, but that really said it all.

Luca slid one hand around my front to play with my nipple, rolling the hardened bud between his fingers. The other held on to my hip as he started to build up a steady rhythm. Still slow and gentle, but dear god, was it good.

"Keep going," I panted.

"Don't need to worry about that. I couldn't stop if I tried."

Flesh met flesh. Pleasure thrummed in my veins. Luca's hands owned my body, trailing over my curves, stroking my live-wire flesh. In his hold, I was unbound, crying out with a voice I'd never used. Grasping, clawing, helpless. He drove into me, harder now but precise. Never taking it too far.

My toes curled into the carpet.

My mouth went slack.

I pushed back, meeting his purposeful thrusts.

Our skin slapped, and Luca murmured all the words I needed to hear. Even in my helplessness, he told me I had the power. He couldn't contain his attraction to me. Inside me, he was found. He thought about this, us together, when we were apart.

"My fuckable little wife," he grunted. "Pretty ass, perfect tits. Could fuck you for days and still want more."

"Try it," I begged.

"You'd have me lose my company, would you?"

That earned me another spanking. I threw my head back and moaned so loud it rattled the walls. He spanked me some more and powered into me, taking my breath away.

"It would be worth it," Luca answered himself.

"Screw capitalism. It's not even that good." I had no idea what I was saying, but it earned me a deep thrust and Luca's fingers on my clit, so it must have been right.

His thumb rolled my clit, the other fingers sliding into my slick pussy, filling me up beyond anything I'd ever known. To the brim and then some. My breath came in short pants. There was no room for my lungs to expand.

"What are you doing to me?" I cried, my head floaty.

"Exactly what you need."

He was right. So, so right. After two days of jealousy and flirtation, I did need this. Luca took me out of my head, out of my goddamn skin, and conquered me the way only he could.

It wasn't forever, but for now, I was so very his.

I'd never wanted to be anyone's, but I loved belonging to Luca Rossi.

With that thought, my inner walls clamped down around him, and I soared into another climax. Panting, yelling, writhing, my body seized, my heart trying to beat right out of my chest.

Luca grunted, low and feral, his grip digging into my hips as he rode the wild wave with me until he finally allowed himself to fall. Hot spurts filled my back channel, and my own arousal flooded past his fingers, rolling down my thighs.

As soon as he finished, he slid out of me and carried me to the bathroom, somehow steady on his feet when I wasn't certain I even had feet any longer. He even took the time to tell me it was too bad he couldn't add the carpet to the evidence bag since I'd surely dripped all over it.

Funny man.

We showered together, and Luca washed me like he always did. Careful, gentle, thorough, especially between my legs. Then he dried me just as carefully and bundled me under the covers in bed, crawling in beside me.

I blinked at him. "What are you doing?" We didn't get in bed after. We got dressed and left.

Luca was on his back, as relaxed as could be, his hands behind his head. "I was thinking I might lie here for a while then order room service."

"Why?"

His brow crinkled. "Why not? I paid for the whole night. They're not going to kick us out when the hour's up. It's not that kind of place."

"You're so rude." I kicked him, but he captured my foot beneath his calf.

"And you're usually nicer after I make you come." He reached down to cup my pussy, sliding one finger along my slit. Despite being a little sore and a lot sated, goose bumps sprouted along my limbs, and heat pulsed in my core. "Hmm...is my pretty girl not satisfied?"

"I won't be able to walk if you satisfy me more than you already have." I wrapped my fingers around his wrist. "You've trained me to respond to you. I can't help it."

His mouth hitched. "I like that. Because I have to tell you, one whiff of your scent and I'm hard. It pisses me off sometimes, but knowing you're just as needy for me makes it an easier pill to swallow."

"And willing, Luca. I'm needy and willing." I pressed his hand against my heated core. "You're the one who put boundaries up. Things would be a lot easier without them."

His dark gaze swept my face, and he shook his head. "No. As tempting as it would be to bend you over the kitchen table whenever the mood strikes, those boundaries are necessary for me."

"Okay."

Rolling away from him so he couldn't read the disappointment etched on my face, I grabbed the room service menu from the nightstand. I couldn't even say why I was so disappointed. Sex with Luca was great, and I wanted more of it, but that shouldn't have caused this pang in my belly.

He followed me, his chest flush with my back, chin on my shoulder. "Hungry?" Knuckles dragged from my navel to my core and back up.

"Mmm. Starved, actually."

He kissed me below the ear. "Are we good, pretty girl?"

Twisting my neck to see him, I smiled. "We're perfect."

But now that the pang was there, I was all too aware of it.

I poked the menu. "I'm going to get a milkshake."

"Perfect," he whispered.

Just freaking perfect.

CHAPTER
TWENTY-NINE

Luca

ELLIOT'S ASSISTANT OFFERED ME a small, tight smile as I approached from the elevator.

"Hello, Catherine."

She tucked a lock of her neat auburn hair behind her ear. "Good afternoon, Mr. Rossi."

Catherine had been working for Elliot for a few months. Her smiles were always small and tight, but her posture was perfect—a contrast to the typical beaten-down spines of his previous assistants.

I nodded toward Elliot's closed office door. "How's he doing today?"

She stacked one hand on top of the other on her desk. "I haven't noticed anything out of the ordinary. Mr. Levy is always busy."

Tapping the edge of her desk, I grinned. "I get it. I've known him since college. The guy never changes."

I was lucky to pin him down for lunch today. He didn't normally stop for longer than it took him to consume enough sustenance to power him for the rest of the day, so going out anywhere was a stretch. But things had been off between us since I'd gotten married.

Our gym meetups had been quieter—which was saying something since Elliot wasn't exactly a fount of conversation.

Being at odds with Elliot didn't work for me. It was time to end it and move on.

Catherine stood from her desk and turned to the side, giving me a view of her small bump.

"Hey, congratulations."

She swiveled back to me, her brows popping. "Oh." Her hand flew to her belly. "Thanks. I'm not used to people noticing yet. It only started happening this week."

"I have a pregnant sister, so maybe I'm more attuned to it these days."

Her smile was a little looser this time. "Well, congratulations on becoming an uncle. I'll let Mr. Levy know you're here."

<hr />

Lunch with Elliot meant takeout in his conference room. Weston joined us too. He was just as difficult to pin down as Elliot, though he actually had some flexibility.

I couldn't say much about their schedules, though. My lunches the past few weeks had been spent at the Davenport if I found room in the day. Not meeting Saoirse today hadn't been easy, especially knowing it would be another twenty-four hours until I let myself have her again.

But now wasn't the time to think about that. I'd drive myself crazy with it later.

"How's Elise?" I asked Weston.

"Excellent. I'll be asking her to move in with me as soon as I'm certain she'll say yes."

I dipped my salmon roll in soy sauce. "Why wouldn't she say yes?"

"It's too soon." He cocked his head, addressing Elliot. "Don't you think?"

Elliot drummed his fingers on the table. "If you think you're worthy of living with my sister, then ask her. She'll tell you if it's too soon."

I laughed. "You didn't think through what it would be like to have Elliot Levy as a brother-in-law, did you?"

Weston's mouth twitched. "To be honest, I wasn't thinking about Elliot at all when I went for Elise."

"Maybe you should have," Elliot gruffed.

"Then he would have missed out on living under the constant threat of you murdering him if he messes up. What fun would that be?" I popped an eel roll into my mouth. "By the way, Elliot, what are you going to do when Catherine goes on maternity leave? Is she already training her replacement?"

Judging by the size of her bump, she had months to go, but I wouldn't have been surprised if Elliot already had her prepping someone else to work under his exacting demands.

Surprisingly, a deep crevice was carved between his brows. "What are you talking about? Catherine isn't pregnant."

"Uh..." Weston and I exchanged a look. Elliot wasn't the most personable man, and I had a distinct feeling he didn't get to know his employees, but I found it hard to believe he'd missed that detail about his own assistant. "She is. We had a conversation about it when I arrived."

The crevice deepened. "She hasn't discussed this with me."

Weston chuffed. "I don't think she's required to discuss her pregnancy with you."

I nodded. "Actually, I think there are laws that specifically say she's not required to discuss it with you."

"Wasn't there a reason for this lunch besides mocking me?" Elliot tapped his chopsticks against the table, clearly done talking about his assistant. That was fine with me, though I looked forward to how thrown off balance he would be during her maternity leave.

"Yeah, that was." I wiped my mouth with my napkin. "I need a PI referral."

Neither Weston nor Elliot spoke. They were waiting for me to expand on my request, but I was still deciding how much I wanted to say.

To be honest, I was still sorting through the conversation Clara and I had this morning.

Clara walked in and flung herself into one of the chairs in front of my desk.

"Good morning to you," I said, barely looking up from my computer.

"I think Miller's cheating on me."

That got me to look up. "What makes you think that?"

"A feeling. He's more distracted than ever. Secretive with his phone. He's coming home late when I know he's not at the office." Her chin wobbled as she broke off and looked away. "I might be crazy, Luc. I asked him, and he swore he's not being unfaithful and never would be, but something's going on with him—"

"I'll talk to him."

"No." She cradled her belly. "No, I'm probably wrong. I don't want to blow everything up on a feeling."

I decided to expand. "Clara's dumb fuck of a husband might be cheating. *Or* he might be innocent and Clara's hormones are running wild."

Elliot shifted, resting his elbow on the table. "I have contacts. I'll send you names."

"What are you going to do if you find something?" Weston asked.

My fingers curled tight into my palm. "I'll cross that bridge when I come to it. I've always known Miller was an idiot—"

Weston frowned. "He's your CFO."

"He's good with numbers. That, I trust him with." I dragged my hand down my face, frustrated to be in this position. "I used to think I trusted him with my sister too. Even if he isn't betraying her, he's stressing her out, which makes him an idiot."

"You're not letting this stand, are you?" Elliot intoned. He didn't play around when it came to his sister. Elise's ex-boyfriend had mistreated her, and he'd basically extracted her from her old life without a trace. I was certain he expected my response to be no less mercenary for my sister.

"I won't. First, I need to gather facts. Once I know for sure, I'll do what needs to be done."

Elliot dipped his chin. "I have contacts for that too, if you need them."

Weston slowly shook his head. "I've known you since we were little kids, but in times like these, I question if I even know you at all."

I chuckled. "Does it really surprise you that Elliot has a contact for every situation that might arise?"

Elliot lifted a shoulder. "It's simply good planning."

"For every contingency," I added.

"Exactly," he agreed.

Weston let out a sigh. "Is everything else going well? Happy wife, happy life?"

"Yeah, all is well on the marriage front." I smoothed my tie, only half-guilty at the lie I kept telling these two men. "Being married to Saoirse is easier than I ever expected."

That part wasn't a lie.

"I'm glad. There aren't many women like Saoirse out there." Weston pointed his chopsticks at me. "But if you could tell your wife to stop poaching my employees, that would be great. I'm already losing Miles to her. She can't take any others."

I shot him a bemused grin. "What do you mean?"

He waved me off, picking up a piece of sushi. "I'm only kidding. To be honest, I haven't seen Miles as enthusiastic and committed to anything since they started planning their business. I don't want to do anything to dampen that. If they want to take Simon and Rebecca, they can have them. Although, I draw the line at Elise. She's staying at Andes."

In the back of my mind, I remembered Saoirse vaguely mentioning working on something with Miles, but that was all it was. Vague.

I worked hard at schooling my expression. If Elliot or Weston had any idea how out of touch I was with my own wife, they would know none of this was real.

But it wasn't confusion I had to work to fight off. It was disappointment.

Not in Saoirse but in myself.

I shouldn't have been sitting across from my best friends, learning important information about my wife from them. I obviously hadn't made it clear to Saoirse that I was interested in more than fucking her.

We were in this thing together.

And what kind of teammate was I to not know what was going on with my other half?

A shit one.

We'd be talking tonight.

CHAPTER THIRTY

Saoirse

I WAS IN THE den reading a book when Luca arrived home. Instead of going directly upstairs like he normally did, he startled me by popping his head in.

"Hey."

I lowered my Kindle. "Hello, you."

Luca was yanking his tie loose from his throat. With his hair slightly disheveled and the thick stubble lining his jaw, he was a sight for sore eyes. I'd gotten used to our too-brief meetings during the day. He hadn't been free today, and I'd been surprised at how fiercely disappointed I'd been when he'd told me.

I'd missed him.

"Did you eat dinner?" he asked.

"I did. You?"

"I ate at my desk." He drummed his fingers on the doorway's molding. "I'm going to get changed then head down to the studio."

His usual routine, though stopping to tell me his plans was new. "Okay. Have fun."

He paused, sweeping his gaze over me. "Join me?"

"In your studio?"

"Yeah. You can bring your Kindle. Hang out with me for a while."

I hopped up from the couch before he finished asking. "Yes. Yes, I want to."

He did another sweep of me, and from the way his eyes went heavy-lidded, I remembered I was wearing my pajamas—a tiny pair of shorts and a cami.

I grinned. This man had seen me naked and bent in half, so it both amused and pleased me he was affected by what I wore. "I'll change too."

He grunted. "Good idea."

Luca put me on the love seat in his studio, and he sat on a stool with a big drawing pad in his lap, facing me.

"What are you drawing?" I asked.

"You, so don't move."

I burst out laughing. "No, really."

"Really. I've been trying to draw you using a picture, but I haven't gotten it right. You're going to be my live model."

I tilted my head, trying to read how serious he was. "Are you joking?"

"Not joking." He flipped the page of his drawing pad, holding it up for me to see the sketch. I recognized myself immediately, and my heart stuttered. He really had been drawing me. "It's not my best work."

My eyes rounded. "You drew me. No one's ever drawn me."

"Shame," he muttered. "You're art in motion. You deserve to be committed to canvas for eternity."

"Luca..." My heart had traveled up to my throat. How did this man manage to keep surprising me?

"Tell me about the business you're starting with Miles."

My mouth fell open at the abrupt change of subject. "What?"

He tapped the eraser of his pencil on his pad. "Weston mentioned you poaching his employees. Imagine being me, having no earthly idea what he was talking about. I sit in this studio at night, trying to capture your image. I spend an hour a day inside you. But I don't know you."

"You want to?"

"Of course I do. I'm sorry if I never made that clear."

I rubbed my lips together, vulnerable under his close scrutiny. "It's not like I've been exactly open with you about what Miles and I are planning. Part of me still can't believe we're really doing this. If he weren't involved in it with me, I'm sure I would have given up on it already."

"Weston said he's enthusiastic."

"He is." I put my Kindle down and leaned my elbows on my knees. "We're going to start a business consulting company. New businesses will come to us, and we'll build plans for their launch. We'll also rework current businesses that need help."

I told him everything Miles and I had discussed. The spaces we'd looked at for our offices. The budget we'd worked out. Miles's monetary contribution. Our roles in the company. Luca listened to me intently, nodding along as I spoke.

He asked me questions, not as a challenge, but as if he truly wanted to know more. And as I explained in deeper detail, I gained confidence in the direction Miles and I were going.

"It's a big risk," I said.

"And commitment." He set his drawing pad aside and crossed the room to sit beside me.

"Yes. A bigger commitment than I've ever made." I almost said *except for marrying you*, but that wasn't true. We had an expiration date. Running a business wouldn't.

"It means you'll be staying in Denver."

I nodded. "Well, we could really work with businesses anywhere, but...yeah. Our home base will definitely be here, and at least in the beginning, our focus will be here too."

He reached over and picked up a lock of my hair, absently running it between his fingers. "No more bouncing around jobs."

"I don't think I'll be bored. We'll constantly be doing something new."

"Do you know when you'll be launching?"

"We haven't decided yet. We want to make sure we're truly ready before we begin. Although Kenji told me he'd be our first client, so..."

He huffed, "*Kenji*," then muttered something about his stupid tattoos. I had to stifle my grin at his *territorialism*—not *jealousy*.

"Tell me you'll be charging Kenji."

My mouth fell open. "Of course I will. Why would you think I wouldn't?"

"Have you ever charged any of the friends you've helped in the past?"

"Well, no, but—"

"Did Kenji pay you to work at his pop-up?"

"I kept my tips."

He gave my hair a gentle tug. "I won't allow you to sacrifice yourself any longer, Saoirse. I know that's your whole vibe, but—"

"What are you talking about? That's not my vibe."

The look he leveled me with said *get real*. "The first time I met you, you'd purposely spilled your drink on yourself to allow a woman who wasn't even your friend to be the center of attention. Don't tell me it's not your vibe."

"I wouldn't call it a vibe..." But he wasn't wrong. "Anyway, you're lucky I'm the way I am since you're benefiting from it."

His chest made a rumbling sound. "I hope you've found it's worth it."

"The orgasms more than make up for having you as a ball and chain."

This time, the tug was less than gentle. "I'm serious, Saoirse. Recognize your worth. You have valuable knowledge Kenji and the rest of the people have taken advantage of when they should be paying for it."

"And they will. That's why Miles is my partner. He'll be the one to discuss money since I'm apparently incapable of it."

"You're capable of anything."

I sucked in a sharp gasp. The confidence in his low tone settled in my chest.

Luca believed in me.

He really, truly believed in me.

"I'm terrified, Luca."

"You have no reason to be."

"I don't?" I sputtered a laugh. "I have been thinking about doing something like this for years. And now that I am, I wonder who the hell I think I am to have the audacity to believe I can. I can't even imagine telling my mother about any of this. I can almost hear her reaction now."

"Her reaction doesn't matter. You're Saoirse Rossi."

My nose scrunched while my stomach whooshed. "I like when you call me that."

"Mmm." He wrapped my hair around his finger. "Listen to me, pretty girl. You grew up with the Kelly name and all the expectations that came with it. But the thing is, you'll never be your mother's image. She's got Peter to take up that mantle. You won't be your father's image either. Lock has that taken care of."

"Yeah," I whispered.

"You're Saoirse Rossi now. You get to start anew and be the woman *you* want to be. There are no expectations, no pressure. It's up to you to shape your path. I want you to know I'm fucking proud of you. I admire the strength it takes to strike out on your own. You might be scared, but I've got your back, so there's no need for you to fear."

I had to bite the inside of my cheek to stop myself from crying. Luca was being sweet and freaking wonderful. I didn't want to make him regret it by bursting into tears.

"I think that was exactly what I needed to hear." I shifted to sit sideways so I could brush his hair from his forehead and drop my hand to cup his jaw. "I have your back too, you know. You can lay your shitty days on me, or rant, or whatever you need. I want to be that for you too."

He leaned his face into my palm and slowly exhaled. "I could get used to you way too easily."

"I'm not going away, even when this is over." My stomach twisted at the thought. "So get used to me."

"Don't think I have a choice." His intense gaze locked on mine. "I'm going to draw you now. Are you up for sitting still for me?"

"I'm not one to be still." I stroked my fingers along the rough stubble on his cheek. "But for you, I'll try."

"That's all I ask."

⸻ ◆ ⸻

The next night, Luca came home and invited me down to his studio with him. Even though we had been able to spend our lunch at the Davenport, he still wanted to hang out.

The night after that, he went upstairs first to change, and disappointment flooded my veins. But then he stopped in the den and asked me if I wanted to go for a ride.

Of course I did.

We rode through the dark, my arms tight around him, and when he was able, he patted my thigh or squeezed my hands. Being on the back of Luca's motorcycle was one of the sexiest experiences I'd ever had. There was something about the powerful machine, combined with his utter confidence in handling it and being wrapped around him, that majorly did it for me.

He took me to his studio when we got back. I lounged on the love seat with my feet hanging over the arm, watching him as he sketched, a lock of hair hanging over his forehead, his teeth clamped down on his full bottom lip.

I pressed my thighs together, but it was no use. I was much too turned on from that ride. There would be no relief until I slid between my sheets and took care of myself.

For now, I'd look at this gorgeous man and edge myself into oblivion.

"How can you work in an office? You're meant for the wild."

With a sigh, he lowered his pad. "That's what I thought. When my dad got sick and I was thrust into this role, I thought I was losing myself."

"You don't think so now?"

He shook his head. "I was free before, but I was stagnant, living a life I'd outgrown just to show how much control I had over my choices. The truth is, everything I did was because I *didn't* have control. I didn't want my father's role, and I still don't. I'm not him, and I won't ever be. Now that I have real control, I'm finally getting to decide how I want to fit this job into my life. I can still be me. Paint, draw, fuck, ride, and take on the title I was born to have."

"It's too bad you figured that out after you took on an inconvenient wife."

His nostrils flared. "You piss me off when you call yourself that."

"I'm only repeating your words, Luca."

"And I was an idiot to say it. I'm steady right now *because* of you. This marriage has given me the breathing room to concentrate on running Rossi and not losing myself. There is nothing inconvenient about being married to you. Even if you didn't let me have your sweet pussy every day, I'd say the same."

My face flooded with heat that trickled down to my chest. This man managed to make me blush with his filthiness while also feeling valued as a person. It was a first for me. I'd already known Luca had set the standard for sex, but he was now raising the bar for how I was treated so high I wasn't sure another man would ever reach it.

I was standing in the kitchen, eating a bowl of ice cream, when Luca prowled in.

"Come on."

I waved my spoon. "I'm busy."

"Bring it with you."

I twisted my lips. "Go without me. I—"

Before I could finish teasing him, he scooped me in his arms. I squealed, reaching out blindly for my bowl. With a laugh, he dipped me toward the counter so I could grab it then swooped me down to the studio.

"I can walk, you know."

"I'm well aware of your legs, Saoirse. But this is easier. Far less sass."

"You like my sass."

His hand shifted to grope my butt. "I think you're mistaken. I said I like your *ass*."

"Oh, I definitely know you like my ass. You stare at it like a perv and fuck it like a fiend."

He set me down in front of the door to the studio, pressing me against it. "And how is your ass feeling, pretty girl?"

I let my head fall back against the door and rocked my hips against his. "Utterly ravaged. You're a monster."

It had been awkward to go back to the office after he'd worked me over at the Davenport, but so very worth it. No one handled my body as well as Luca did. He'd gotten me hooked. The one frustrating part was we only had an hour a day we were allowed to indulge.

He trailed his knuckles along my jaw. "Don't you forget it."

We took our spots, me on the couch with my ice cream, Luca sketching. He'd shifted to his easel this time, working with charcoal.

"Can I see?" I asked.

"Nope."

My spoon paused midair. "You won't let me see?"

He looked at me over the easel, his mouth twitching. "Nope."

"Are you being mean on purpose?"

"I'm not being mean. I'm at the point where I don't want you to see until it's finished. Can't you be patient? You'll be rewarded for it."

"Fine, if you insist. I'll just sit here eating my ice cream while you keep secrets."

He snorted. "Don't be a brat. You'll be in for it tomorrow if you choose to continue."

I kicked my leg out, swinging it over the arm of the love seat. "I'll take my chances. By the time you let yourself put your hands on me tomorrow, your annoyance will have waned."

"Don't bet on it, pretty girl. When it comes to my hand and your ass, my desire for them to connect never lessens."

"Hmm." I twirled a finger in my hair. "It's just really unfortunate you have to wait until tomorrow. But you're the boss…"

He shot me a narrow-eyed glare over the easel. "I'm actually not that easily manipulated."

"Then I suppose I'll just continue driving you crazy since I already know what's in store for me."

He tore his eyes from me to concentrate on his drawing. I could see his free hand twitching on his knee, and it made me giddy. It wasn't that I wanted Luca to cross the lines he'd drawn. They were important to him, and in the end, I had to respect that. However, I was perfectly willing to frustrate him as much as I could.

Luca interrupted the quiet a little while later. "I've been wondering."

"What's that?" I swung my legs around to sit up, crossing them beneath me.

"Why haven't you gotten your cat?"

"Simple." I tapped my fingertips on my chin. "I want you to go with me to choose it."

"You do?"

"Of course. I can't choose a cat who hates you since it will be living in your house."

"Your house," Luca murmured.

"Our shared house. Right. We've been busy, and I'm not in a rush. So, when we both have time to spare, we'll go to a shelter."

"What if I hate all the cats?" Luca flicked his eyes to me, a smile playing on his lips.

"I'd be more worried about all the cats hating you."

"What?" He rose from his stool, his hands on his hips. "I'm insulted."

"You are not."

He flung himself onto the couch beside me. "I could make a joke about pussy loving me."

I scrunched my nose. "But you wouldn't because that would be gross."

He kicked his legs out straight, his hands joined behind his head. "It would be beneath me. I'd never do such a thing." Then he turned his head toward me. "I'd be glad to go with you, pretty girl. Name the time, and I'll make room in my schedule for you."

"Okay."

A sudden wave of emotion clogged my throat, preventing me from saying anything more. I couldn't really pinpoint if it was due to the prospect of finally having a cat of my own or that Luca wanted to come with me.

What I did know was there was something big blooming inside me. Something new and unexpected I never would have had without Luca Rossi.

CHAPTER
THIRTY-ONE

Saoirse

"Hey, Niddhi."

Niddhi looked up from her computer and smiled. "Hey, Sersh."

I swirled the iced latte I'd picked up on the way back from the Davenport. "I feel like we haven't caught up in forever. Are you doing anything fun this weekend?"

She lifted a shoulder, her eyes darting to the side. "I have a date with a guy I met on Hinge. It's a second date, actually."

Despite the piles of work waiting for me, I sat down in the chair beside Niddhi's desk to get the scoop on this guy. Ever since Luca and I had started our lunch dates, I hadn't been as in touch with my coworkers as I had in the beginning.

It didn't help that there hadn't been a happy hour for a few weeks. Every time I asked about them, Niddhi explained too many people hadn't been able to make it, so they hadn't been happening.

Disappointing but understandable.

I'd been asked to temp for another month, so hopefully, happy hours would start up again because I missed the combination of camaraderie mixed with alcohol.

After work, I settled in the den at home. With my laptop on my legs, I absently scrolled through Insta, and that was when I figured out what happened to happy hour.

I'd clicked from Niddhi's account to Charlie's, then Amelia's.

My heart sputtered when I viewed Amelia's story.

Happy hour hadn't stopped.

I hadn't been invited.

The proof was on my screen. Amelia, surrounded by most of my coworkers, all holding their glasses up and smiling. I could picture their waitress telling them to say "TGIF." before snapping the picture.

I'd been stupid to think happy hours had simply stopped. Of course they were having them. They just didn't want me there.

Tears welled in my eyes, which was ridiculous. They weren't my friends. Only my temporary coworkers. But I couldn't help my feelings being hurt. I couldn't remember a time I'd felt so excluded.

"Good evening, pretty girl. I was able to break away early, and I thought we could grab dinn—" Luca broke off when I looked up at him, his brow immediately dropping. "Why are you crying?"

I swiped my eyes with the backs of my hands. "I'm not. It's nothing."

He sat down next to me, glaring at my computer as if he could find the source of my sadness and destroy it.

"It can't be nothing if you're crying. Tell me what it is, Saoirse."

"Please, Luca. I'm overreacting over something silly."

He took my hand in his. "Tell me anyway. I won't think it's silly."

I sniffled and clicked on Amelia's story again, turning the screen so Luca could see. "They had happy hour without me."

His eyes darted over the picture, taking it in. "These are the people who work in your department?"

"Yeah. Niddhi said there hadn't been a happy hour in a while, but she was sparing my feelings." I sucked in a shuddering breath, hating myself for being so sad about this. "They don't want me there."

"What the fuck?" Luca seethed. "Who wouldn't want you with them? Are they all idiots? I have idiots working for me?"

"No, I'm sure it's because they want to unwind and talk about work, but they probably don't feel comfortable doing that with me there since we're married." I swiped my eye again. "It's fine. I'm fine. Everything's fine."

"It isn't fine." His jaw worked as he gritted his molars. Then, without another word, he strode from the room.

When he didn't come back, I closed my laptop and went into the bathroom to wash my face and attempt to get ahold of my emotions. This really was silly. Not worth wasting tears over.

My phone buzzed in my pocket. I took it out, reading a message from Clara.

Clara: *Please tell your husband he CANNOT ban all after-work fraternization.*

Clara: *Seriously, Saoirse. Stop him before he sends out this email. He's begging for a lawsuit.*

Me: *What email?*

Clara: *Oh, thank god you're by your phone. Luca just sent me a draft of an email he wants to send to the entire company, banning all fraternization outside work hours. He's clearly lost the plot.*

Me: *He's home. I'll go talk to him. Don't worry, I'll take care of it.*

Clara: *Why do I have a feeling this has something to do with you?*
Me: *I think it might. But I've got it handled.*
Clara: *Tell him if he sends out that email, I'm firing him as uncle.*
Me: *I'll let him know!! xx*

———◆———

I found Luca in his home office, boring holes into his computer monitor. Crossing the room, he watched me approach. When I rounded the desk, he pushed back, giving me room to slide onto his lap.

I hadn't spent any time in this room, nor had I ever been in this position with him, but it was as natural as breathing, especially when his arms closed around me.

"What are you doing, Luca Rossi?"

His eyes searched mine. "Your feelings are hurt."

"They are. But you can't burn down your entire company to make up for it."

His brows drew together in a hard line. "That's where you're wrong. I can and I will."

I shook my head and stroked his tight jaw. "You can, but you won't. Clara texted in a panic."

He grunted, holding me tighter. "I did what she asked and sent her the draft of my email before sending it to the rest of the company. She repays me by going to my wife?"

"She thinks you've lost your mind."

His huff of breath brushed my neck. "When I walked in and saw you crying, your little chin wobbling, I did feel like I was losing my mind. I need to fix it, Saoirse. I won't let you be hurt."

"You know you can't send that email." My fingers moved to his hair, carving lines through the side. "You've already made me feel better by giving a shit. Your irrationality soothes me."

He made a grunting sound. "You like seeing me go crazy over your tears?"

"I like knowing you care."

With a sigh, he tucked his head beneath my jaw, pressing a kiss on my throat. "I knew she wouldn't let me send it."

I snorted, already lighter in his arms. "Did it feel good to write it?"

"Nothing feels good when you're sad. I fucking hate it."

We held each other, and I slid my fingers through his hair. His breath was warm and slow on my skin, his fingers soft and rhythmic, trailing along my spine.

"I can't work at Rossi anymore," I whispered.

His hands stilled. "You can."

"I think it's obvious I can't."

"I want you in the same building as me."

"We do live together. It isn't as if I won't see you."

He raised his head, glaring at me the same way he'd glared at his monitor. I'd replaced it as his enemy, which made me want to laugh, but I held it in since I didn't think he'd take kindly to it.

"I don't want you working for someone else," he stated.

I shook my head. "I don't want to work for anyone else. I'm hoping my rich husband will keep me afloat so I can throw myself into starting my business. I've been delaying jumping in with both feet, but I think this is the push I needed. It's time."

"You don't have to hope, Saoirse. Anything you need, I'll give it to you. What about office space? I'll clear out the office beside mine. You can have it."

"In the Rossi building?" He nodded in all seriousness, which made me sputter a laugh. "Isn't that Miller's office?"

"Say the word, and he's out."

Laughing again, I patted his chest. "Poor Miller. I think Clara might object to you kicking her husband out of his office."

"She'd get over it."

"Luca,"—I dropped my forehead to his—"you're being sweet. Crazy, yes, but very, very sweet."

He squeezed my butt in response.

"I'm not going to work in the Rossi building."

He sighed. "I know, and it pisses me off."

"Maybe I'll take over this office."

He leaned back in his chair, eyeing me. "You can have it. I barely use it anyway. I like the idea of you working here."

"With Miles."

That made his lip curl. "I have to accept that?"

"You do. He's my partner."

"*I'm* your partner. Miles is your coworker."

"Sure." I brushed his hair from his forehead. "You're really good at cheering me up, you know."

"I'm not done. Go get changed. I'm taking you to dinner."

I perked up. "Can we go on the bike?"

His lips curved as he looked at me with his bedroom eyes. "Anything you want, pretty girl."

Why did I actually believe he meant that wholeheartedly?

CHAPTER THIRTY-TWO

Luca

THE NEXT MORNING, I woke up still as pissed off as I'd been the night before.

The email I'd pounded out hadn't helped.

Saoirse soothing me—soothing *me*—hadn't touched it.

Going for a ride hadn't been the release it normally was.

Spending a quiet night with my wife in a cozy restaurant had been nice as hell, but I'd still been left with a roiling anger beneath my skin.

I couldn't massacre all the people who'd put tears in her eyes. Neither Clara nor Saoirse would allow me to destroy my company as vengeance, which was extremely irritating.

So, I found myself sitting on the side of Saoirse's bed while she slept, only making minor attempts to wake her up.

Stroking her cheek.

Sliding my fingers through her hair.

Trailing my knuckle along her arm.

Pulling the sheets back to look at her in her silky nightgown.

I thought I was getting away with it until her lips curled into a smile. "What are you doing, crazy man?" she croaked out, her eyes still firmly closed.

"How do you know it's me?"

She rolled to her side, nuzzling her face on my thigh. "Only you would sneak into my room to poke and prod me."

"I also spent some time looking at your tits."

Her laugh was muffled by my leg. "You might be pervy, but at least you're honest." She rolled to her back, her eyes fluttering open. "Good morning, you."

"Morning, pretty girl."

"Why are you in my bedroom, sir?"

"I'm waking you up, wife. We have places to be."

She glanced at the time and turned back to me with a furrow between her light brows. "The places better have coffee and donuts, or I'm not getting out of bed."

"I can make that happen." I peeled her sheet the rest of the way off her, which was a mistake. Her nightgown had ridden up to the tops of her thighs, revealing her bare little pussy. "*Fuck*. No underwear? Really?"

She tugged the scrap of material down and sat up, draping her legs over mine. "You sneak into my bedroom, you're bound to see more than you expected." Then she made sure to rub her calf against my dick, which was now standing at full attention. "Now you have to deal with the consequences of your actions."

"I came in here with the intent to cheer you up," I gruffed.

"You have. Look at me smiling." She pressed her calf against me again. "I'm just returning the favor by cheering your dick up."

I caught her leg and tossed it off me. It was a necessity. Otherwise, I'd have her flat on the mattress, spreading her legs instead. For a moment, I couldn't remember why that was a bad idea.

But then I remembered.

Boundaries.

Temporary.

Convenience.

If I crossed the line now, when my emotions were already heightened, who knew how many others I'd cross?

I stood from Saoirse's bed, adjusting the bulge behind my zipper.

"I'll be waiting downstairs."

———◦———

Saoirse was miffed we took my car instead of the motorcycle, but when I pulled up in front of the animal shelter after taking her out for breakfast, she squealed with delight.

Her fingers dug into my bicep. "Are we getting a cat?"

I pried her hand off me and nipped at her fingertips. "If you find one you like, then yes, we're getting a cat."

We had the place to ourselves, thanks to a generous donation from Rossi Motors. Saoirse was soon buried in cats, and I questioned my choice of bringing her here.

Did I want to live with five cats if she couldn't part from any of them?

Hell no.

Would I be able to say no?

Absolutely not.

Luckily, Saoirse had more sense than me. She homed in on the one cat who decided I made for a good climbing post and clawed its way up my leg until I had no choice but to hold it in my arms.

Orange. Scruffy. Missing half an ear. The thing was a mess.

Saoirse gasped. "Oh my god. He's so cute." She scratched beneath its chin, and the thing's tail swished, hitting me in the face. "You're a beautiful boy, aren't you? You are. And you like Luca, don't you? I do too. You have good taste, buddy."

I had to clear the thickness from my throat. How did hearing her tell a fucking cat that she liked me make me feel like my collar was three sizes too small?

"How do you know it's a boy?" I asked.

"Orange cats are almost always male," she said.

"You know a lot about cats?"

She stroked the orange fur, a smile curling her lips. "I've wanted one forever. I used to check out books from the library about taking care of them when I was little. Back then, I still thought my mother's mind could be changed. My dad tried to convince me the barn cats on the ranch were my pets, but they barely wanted anything to do with humans. They definitely wouldn't have let me put them in a dress."

I turned to the side, taking the cat out of her reach. "He's not wearing a dress."

The woman who ran the shelter came toward us. "I see you've met Clementine. Isn't she sweet?"

"*She*? I thought orange cats were always boys," Saoirse said.

"Eighty percent of the time, they are," the woman replied. "Clem is an exception to the rule. She really does have a lovely temperament, but no one's taken her home yet due to her slightly rough appearance."

I cleared my throat again, this time in indignation. Whoever hadn't chosen this cat was clearly an idiot. "There isn't anything wrong with her."

Saoirse cuddled in next to us, kissing the top of Clem's head. "She's a princess and obviously has great taste."

The women agreed, shooting me a wink, and said she'd give us time to play with Clementine. The three of us ended up sitting on the floor of a private room, getting to know each other.

Clem was just as affectionate with Saoirse, which was important. This was her cat, after all.

In the back of my mind, I knew I was digging myself into a hole it would fucking suck to climb out of. There wasn't a single doubt in my mind I was going to fall in love with this creature and break my own heart when I had to say goodbye to her at the end of my and Saoirse's arrangement. At the same time, I couldn't say no to this.

Not when I pictured Saoirse as a little girl with stacks of cat books, promising to take care of the cat all by herself and being shot down time and time again.

She was getting her damn cat.

Fuck my heart. It would recover.

The smile on Saoirse's face made whatever I had in store worth it.

I knew that because when I looked at her and our previously unwanted cat, I was calm. My urge to destroy and maim had quieted. The future might be painful. I might regret these decisions down the line. But for now, everything was right.

———◦———

My parents came for lunch on Sunday. Saoirse and my mother cooked together. Clementine sat in my father's lap while we watched the game in the den.

He looked good. Miles better than he had a few months ago. But I'd never forget he wasn't invincible. My big, strong, capable father had nearly been brought down by his own body.

The four of us sat down to eat together while Clem checked out her new climbing tower.

My mother shook her head. "A cat. I never pictured you having a cat, Luc."

Dad wiped his pants off. "You'll have to invest in lint rollers by the case."

Saoirse lit up as she told them how Clementine had chosen me. "She climbed him like a tree. And when the woman in charge of the shelter implied there was something wrong with Clem, you should have seen Luca. It was like she was talking about his child."

My dad grunted. "I'd hardly call a missing ear something wrong. Who are these people who said that?"

My mother laughed. "Do you see where he gets it from?"

Saoirse's cheeks were rosy when she grinned at me. "I do. Who knew Luca had such a mushy heart?"

"I did," Mom declared. "You can't be a beautiful artist without feeling things deeply. When he was a little boy, he once came to me with tears in his eyes. When I asked him why he was upset, he said he wasn't sad. He told me he'd been thinking about me, Clara, and Dad, and his heart got so big it felt like his chest was going to burst. As he got older, he disguised that side of him behind his cool-guy front, but I know what lies beneath."

"I do too. Aren't we lucky?"

Saoirse squeezed my leg under the table, keeping her focus on my mom. Thank Christ, because I remembered the incident she was talking about. My mother undersold the dramatics of eight-year-old Luca. I'd been sobbing, almost hysterical, over how much I loved my family.

Weird kid.

At least I hid it better now.

Dad wiped his mouth. "Are you finding time for that these days?"

"That?" I leaned back in my chair. "You mean my art?"

"Mmm. From what Clara says, you're at Rossi later than her most days."

"You're checking up on me?" It came out harsher than intended, but this was a sore line of questioning. While my mother had cultivated my little artist heart, my father had never quite understood me. He was all facts and numbers. It made him a great CEO, but I didn't work the same way and never would.

His brow winged. "I had a conversation with my daughter, Luca. You came up in conversation. I'm not spying on you. I'm interested in both you and my company."

"*My* company," I corrected.

"Not because you want it."

My arms folded over my chest. "Does it matter why it's mine? The fact is it is. And since you're checking up on me, I presume you're watching our stock prices."

"Of course I am. I have a vested interest in Rossi. That's my retirement. My legacy."

"Mine too," I replied.

"There's no need for you to get your back up, Luca. I'm not telling you how to run things. I'm not going to wedge my way back in. Rossi is yours. I should be able to ask questions without it being viewed as an attack on you." Dad folded his arms too, mirroring my pose.

"Then ask me."

He cocked his head. "I would. If our conversations didn't devolve into you feeling like I don't trust your decision-making abilities."

I huffed. "Do you?"

"I do, or I wouldn't have put my full support behind you." He gestured to Saoirse. "I trusted you implicitly, even when you were in the throes of rebelling. I always knew you would rise to the role when it was time. And look at you, taking the reins of Rossi without faltering even though it came a lot sooner than either of us expected. You married a beautiful woman, and you're making a home with her. I knew you had this in you, Luca."

"I'll never be you."

Mom spoke up. "No one wants you to be your father. *He* certainly doesn't."

Dad nodded sharply. "I have Clara as my clone. I don't need two."

My mother reached across the table, palm up. Slowly, Dad unfolded his arms to meet her in the middle, enfolding her hand in his.

"Rossi needed a breath of fresh air," Mom said. "And your father needed a reason to step down. He won't admit either, but he knows I'm right."

Dad grunted again, his mouth pulling into a frown, but the way he looked at her was soft as always, and he held her hand tight, not denying her opinion.

Bless that fucking cat. Clementine chose that moment to walk right up to a small succulent in a clay pot sitting on the edge of a shelf and bat it with her paw. It plummeted to the floor while she watched, shattering into a million pieces. Then she sat on her princess ass and started grooming herself as if she hadn't just committed mayhem for no good reason.

———◆———

After my parents left, Saoirse and I ended up in the den, with Clem passed out on the couch between us.

"I think you needed to have that conversation with your dad," she said.

I grunted, which made her laugh. My eyes narrowed. "What?"

"You sounded exactly like him."

"I'm nothing like him."

"Okay." She absently stroked Clementine's back. "Your parents are really in love. It's nice to see. I think my parents were like that when I was young, but life..."

"I once heard my mother tell Clara the key to her long and happy marriage is choosing each other. The choice didn't happen only once at the altar. They have continued to choose each other throughout their lives together."

Saoirse nodded slowly. "My parents chose each other once, then let the chips fall where they may after." She slung her foot over mine, where it rested on the ottoman. "When you get married for real, you'll have to remember that. Choose her and keep choosing her."

My mother had been right. I'd gotten a lot better at dealing with my emotions over the years. They didn't burst out of me anymore. They were there, contained but just as powerful.

And what my wife just said to me? I felt that *deep*.

CHAPTER THIRTY-THREE

Luca

"BEND OVER. HANDS AROUND your ankles."

Saoirse arched a brow at me. "No hello? How are you?"

Her ass was asking for my hand, so I gave her what she wanted, smacking her bare flesh. "I'm not really in the mood for jokes."

Not with her standing in front of me naked, her clothes puddled on the carpet. Not when it had been over a week since I'd been inside her.

Saoirse finished her tenure at Rossi three weeks ago. Miles had timed his departure from Andes to coincide with hers. Since then, they'd thrown themselves into their business, which they'd dubbed Peak Strategies.

I respected that they didn't want to cash in on their family names, but a feral part of me wished Saoirse had used Rossi. Not for me to claim her business, but so anyone who met with her would know *she* was claimed. The big rock she wore on her finger wasn't enough for me.

Neither was the time we were able to spend together.

Not working in the same building meant our lunch meetings were more difficult to arrange. Saoirse and Miles used the condo as their office, and I was strapped to my desk at Rossi, in the midst of an internal audit on top of my regular duties.

Breaking away during the day had become mostly impossible.

Our evenings had been spent either working, spending time with my family, or at client dinners.

Which was why it had been a week since we'd done this. Six days too long. Especially when I lived day in, day out with this woman. Her scent. Her long legs. Tiny pajamas. Sensual presence. I spent more time hard than not.

My boundaries were so fucking blurred I barely saw them. This one was the last one standing. We slept apart. We didn't fuck at home.

But I was playing a losing game.

A battle I could already see the outcome of, and I wouldn't be the winner.

I was sure of that as I slid into my wife and my eyes rolled back from the sheer euphoria of being enveloped in her perfect, slick heat.

She was bent in half for me. Crying my name as my pelvis met her ass. Clenching around me and drawing me in for more.

But it wasn't enough.

I pulled out and spun her around, standing her up straight. "Come here."

We moved to the bed, my back against the headboard, Saoirse in my lap, my cock deep inside her. She rocked her hips, taking me deep, then retreating, the velvet glide of her inner walls eliciting vibrating groans from me.

"There's my girl." I cupped the back of her head and dipped my lips to hers. She opened for me, touching her tongue to mine. She was as sweet as ever, delicious, exciting, yet familiar.

Her forehead rolled against mine. "I missed you."

"Good god, did I miss you."

"Maybe you weren't so off base trying to give me Miller's office."

I groaned again, but it wasn't from pleasure. "Never say his name again while I'm inside you."

She laughed, which made her clench around me. "Sorry, babe. I just meant I hate not seeing you during the day. You got me used to having you."

My mouth covered hers again. It was impossible to stay away. Cupping her breasts, I twisted her nipples between my fingers. She whimpered, and I swallowed it down.

"Luca," she panted. "You feel so good."

"You feel like the best dream, pretty girl." I slid my hands to her hips and pressed her down on me. "You have to go harder. Ride me like you missed me."

"I told you I did." She reached over me, gripping the top of the headboard for leverage. "You can have me any time you want, you know. I'm yours."

But we both knew that wasn't true. Everything I had with her was borrowed. What she gave me of herself would be taken back in the end.

The thought sent a wave of anger over me. I slammed her down on my cock and raised my hips. One hand slapped down on my shoulder, nails digging into me as she gasped and moaned.

"Yes, Luca, yes. I need it like that."

My hand came down on her ass. "You'll get it how I give it to you."

Her nails raked up the side of my neck. "Don't be mean. I want my sweet Luca as you pound my pussy."

"Filthy little mouth." I nipped at her bottom lip. "Driving me crazy."

She moaned and ground down on me, taking me deep and keeping me there. "I played with myself last night. I leaned against the wall between our rooms so I could be close to you when I came."

It took all my willpower not to squeeze my eyes shut. This woman was going to be the end of me. "I thought I heard you moaning."

"I bet you did. I didn't hide it. I wanted you to burst in and watch me like you did before."

"Fuck, Saoirse." I thrust into her from below, spearing my cock into her wet heat over and over.

Her little ass slapped against me, her wild eyes locked with mine. We worked each other, taking out the weeklong frustration with nails and teeth and tongues. But it was more than just fucking, and it had been for a long time. This was a release of the feelings we didn't say. A chance to be close that wasn't allowed in any other way.

It would be over in no time.

And I'd want it all over again.

I wanted more than this.

Everything might have been enough.

But I'd have to settle for this. Her body being mine. Her eyes on me. My name on her lips. My seed coating her. My claim on Saoirse might have been temporary, but it was powerful. She was mine, and I was so fucking hers, I couldn't see straight.

"I'm going to come." As if I couldn't already feel her swelling and pulsing.

"I know your body, pretty girl. I'm ready for you."

She took me as far as she could and rocked against me, her clit hitting my pelvis. Her head lolled back, giving me the opening I needed to suck her throat and bite down on the crook of her neck.

I waited for her to begin the fall before I allowed myself to let go and join her. Arms wrapped around slick bodies, we embraced, holding on as powerful shudders traveled from her body to mine. Air was in short supply, so we shared it, heaving lungfuls at each other. Hot and thready, passing back and forth.

Minutes passed, breathing became somewhat normal, and I found myself flat on my back with Saoirse sprawled on top of me.

"Clem sat in her window sling this morning," Saoirse said.

I raised my head. "She did? Did you take a picture?"

"Of course I did." She rolled to the side to grab her phone from the nightstand and turned it on to show me the screen.

Our cat. I couldn't deny Clementine was as much mine as Saoirse's. She was Velcro, either attached to me or her. She wasn't a cat who needed space.

I'd bought her a sling that attached to the windows in the living room, thinking she'd like to look out at the city. So far, she'd only sat in it for a second or two before frantically meowing like we were lighting her tail on fire.

But there she was on Saoirse's phone, relaxed and regal, like the princess she was, curled up in the sling, her tail lazily hanging off the side.

"How long did she stay there?" I asked.

"An hour. She fell asleep there. I think she would have stayed longer, but Miles started singing 'Mo Money Mo Problems,' and she woke up."

Turning the screen off, I tossed the phone aside. "Miles saw her in the sling?"

"Yeah." She trailed her fingers along my chest. "Are you jealous?"

"Territorial. He shouldn't get to see my cat in the sling *I* bought her before I do."

"I told him to close his eyes."

"Good."

She snorted. "I was kidding about that. At least you'll be happy to know Clem still doesn't like him."

"Did she scratch him?"

"No. How could you think she'd ever do something that violent? She just gives him the cold shoulder and swishes her tail at him."

"As she should."

Saoirse patted my chest then dropped a kiss over my heart. "She knows who her Daddy is."

I grunted. "Don't patronize me."

"I would never." She kissed me again. "Now, tell me about the dinner you're taking me to tonight. Who am I impressing?"

I rolled so I was on top of her, spreading her legs to fit myself between them. Our noses were tip to tip, and I dragged mine along hers.

"The only one you have to impress is me, and that's a given."

Her smile was white lightning up close. "I like you so much, Luca."

"Then put your lips on me and show me."

CHAPTER THIRTY-FOUR

Saoirse

CLEM WOVE BETWEEN MY feet as I walked. When we got her two months ago, this maneuver of hers nearly sent me sprawling. But we'd worked out a system—she did what she wanted, and I learned to adapt.

Luca walked through the front door just as I passed the entry. Clem immediately detached from me to attach to him.

"Hello, you."

"Hey, pretty girl."

He picked Clem up and crossed to me, dropping a quick kiss to my cheek, even though I was aching for so much more. Luca was steadfast in his determination to keep our physical interactions outside of our home, and I hated it with the passion of a thousand burning suns.

I constantly missed him, even when he was right in front of me.

It was like having half of him.

Not that I was a sex fiend. It was more that I was a Luca fiend. I would have settled for a cuddle, but he wouldn't even give me that.

I played off my disappointment, arching a brow. "Are you talking to me or the cat?"

He kissed the top of Clem's head. "You're my pretty girl. Clementine is my princess."

I leaned into the two of them, stealing a little bit of contact. "As it should be. By the way, Clara's spending the night."

Luca's head jerked up. "What? Why?"

My shoulder lifted. "She said she can't get comfortable in her own bed and has been dreaming about your guest bed. I told her of course she can spend the night at our place. As many nights as she needs."

Clara was a month away from her due date. She hadn't really slowed down, despite the beach ball she was carrying in front, and she *never* complained. So, when she called me this afternoon and her voice cracked when she told me how tired she was, I immediately invited her. How could I not?

Luca put Clem down so he could shove his hands into his hair. "It's going to look awfully strange when you and I don't share a bedroom."

I curled my fingers around his wrists, pulling his hands down to his side. "I sent Miles home early so I could clean out every trace of myself from my bedroom and move my things to your room. I'm sorry to tell you, you'll have to share your bed with me for a night or two, but I've heard I sleep like a corpse, so it shouldn't be too much of a burden."

Luca didn't look any less relieved. If anything, he seemed to be horrified, which was a dagger to my chest. I was starved for him, and he was reacting like sharing a bed with me was his worst nightmare.

"Fucking Clara," he muttered. "How long is she staying?"

"She didn't say." I chewed on the inside of my cheek while he bored holes into the floor. "I'm not picky about where I sleep. I'll just sleep on the flo—"

"You're not sleeping on the floor, Saoirse." He glared at me like I was enemy number one. "We managed just fine in Wyoming, we'll be fine here too. It just took me a minute to come to terms with it."

Dear god. He had to come to terms with sleeping with me. I didn't think he realized how awful that sounded. Luca wasn't a cruel person, and he made his affection for me obvious. We had become good friends over the past few months, but that was where it ended for him.

Besides the hotel sex, of course.

I'd fallen for him.

I hadn't meant to. It hadn't been part of the plan. But it had been impossible not to.

⸺◆⸺

I walked out of the bathroom in sweatpants and Luca's T-shirt. My skin already itched from all the extra fabric, but it was for the best. Wearing my normal skimpy pajamas didn't really seem fair to either of us.

Luca was in bed, his back against the headboard, laptop on his legs. He glanced at me over the screen.

"What are you wearing?" he groused.

"My pajamas." I climbed into bed, situating myself on the edge, and grabbed my Kindle.

He'd been grumpy with me all night, though he was sweet to Clara, making sure she had everything she needed in the guest room down the hall. She hadn't even peeked into my bedroom, so moving all my things probably hadn't been necessary, but it was better safe than sorry.

Luca was still looking at me. "Those aren't your pajamas."

I plucked at my T-shirt. "I borrowed this. I promise to wash it before I return it."

"I don't mind my clothes smelling like you, Saoirse. I'm wondering why you're wearing them."

"It's better this way."

I turned on my Kindle, blindly flipping the pages while he stared. Eventually, he looked away from me, returning his attention to his computer.

In my head, I rolled to Luca's side of the bed and snuggled into his side while I read and he worked. In my fantasy, every once in a while, he'd reach over, stroke my hair, or drop a kiss on the top of my head.

Instead, we spent the next hour in silence, a cold stretch of mattress between us. Eventually, I gave in and said good night. I couldn't stand one more minute of this strained atmosphere.

Besides, I *was* tired. Starting a new company was no joke. Peak Strategies officially had two clients. Kenji and a tech startup. Actual strangers had hired us. Miles and I had been throwing our whole selves into this venture.

The problem was I couldn't get comfortable. My legs felt like they were tangled in fabric, and my shirt kept twisting around my torso every time I moved. But I couldn't stop moving because I was being suffocated by my own pajamas.

So, I turned.

Rolled.

Flopped.

Sighed out my frustrations.

"Is this you sleeping like a corpse?" Luca had closed his laptop and turned off the lights a while ago. I'd assumed he was asleep. Obviously, I'd been wrong.

"Sorry. I'm trying to get comfortable. I'll be still."

I tried. I really did. I lay there until Luca's breathing evened out and tried to convince myself it was soothing. And it was. It was just that I felt like I had ropes around my legs.

I decided to kick off my sweatpants. I was under the covers, so he wouldn't see if he happened to wake up before me.

Raising my hips, I wiggled the loose pants down. They were around my knees when Luca cleared his throat.

"What's happening now?"

I shoved them the rest of the way off. "I took off my pants."

"Is this a seduction technique I'm unaware of?"

"It's not. I thought you were asleep."

"I was, but then the bed started rocking and rolling."

I snorted, rubbing my bare legs on the smooth sheets. Much better. "You're being dramatic."

"Says the woman flailing about. Just put on your regular pajamas. I can control myself."

"I was being thoughtful, Luca. There's no need to be rude about it. Anyway, I'm fine now that I took my pants off. I'll survive the night."

He made a grumbling sound. "Go to sleep."

"I plan to when you stop talking to me."

He went quiet then, and I stared up at the ceiling, trying to force myself not to wish for his arms around me.

Eventually, I fell asleep.

I woke to a hand on my bare breast and my back cradled against a hard chest. Luca's hot breath was on my neck, and in his sleep, his thumb rubbed my beaded nipple.

"You took your shirt off," he murmured.

Okay, not sleeping.

I opened my eyes, peering down at myself. I was naked except for my underwear.

"Shit. I don't remember doing that."

His laugh was gritty and low. "You really hate wearing clothes to bed."

"Despise it." I wiggled back to steal some of his heat. "How did we end up in this position?"

"I woke up here."

"And you didn't immediately vault out of the bed?"

His teeth nipped my shoulder. "Are you complaining?"

"Just asking. I have no complaints at all."

We stayed like that, Luca holding me and stroking my breast, me pretty much basking in the contact. He was aroused, and my panties were soaked, but neither of us made a move to take it further.

In a lot of ways, this was as far as we'd ever gone. The intimacy of these quiet moments soaked beneath my skin and embedded in my heart. I wanted this, but I was so afraid to voice it. Luca had been explicit in what this was and wasn't, and he hadn't wavered from that.

Was this wavering?

I shut my eyes, closed off my thoughts, and enjoyed the unparalleled bliss of waking in this man's arms.

———— ◆◇◆ ————

Clara showed no signs of going home. This was her third night here, and judging by how clear her eyes had been the last two mornings, she really was resting better in our guest room.

Neither Luca nor I could possibly begrudge her presence. Clementine had taken to her also, curling around her belly when Clara sat down, purring to her little heart's content.

I slipped between the sheets wearing a black satin nightgown. It was my longest, least embellished gown. But Luca looked at me like I was armed to the teeth.

He was on his back, reading a novel. I'd learned Luca preferred science fiction. But he rested it on his chest to look at me.

"Hey, you," I said softly.

With a sigh, he knocked his book to the floor and opened his arms. "Come here."

Without a single beat of hesitation, I threw myself onto him. My leg draped over his, arm curled around his bare middle, my head snuggled on his shoulder. Locking his hand on my hip, he dragged me a little closer.

Neither of us said a word about what we were doing. It was like we both knew if we did, it would break the spell. We would have remembered why this was off-limits.

I wasn't going to be the one to replace the space between us. Luca would have to kick me across the mattress to be rid of me.

"I'm worried about Clara."

His sudden speech startled me. "About her pregnancy?"

"Not so much that. She's handling the physical stuff pretty well. A while ago, she came to me and told me something was off with Miller. She'd asked him if he was cheating, which he denied."

I shuddered. "I can't picture Clara sleeping with Miller, let alone anyone else."

His grip tightened. "Please don't try. I'm already horrified when I think about how she got knocked up."

That made me laugh a little. "Has she said anything else lately?"

"No, and that's why I'm worried. Every time I've tried to broach the subject, she shuts me down. I was hoping things were better. Hell, I even hired a PI who'd found nothing on him. But she's here."

"And he's not," I filled in.

"Yeah." His chest rose when he sucked in a deep breath. "I'm at a fucking loss. If she doesn't open up to me, how do I help her?"

I raised my head, looking at his worried face. "Give her space and support. Let her stay here without questioning why. It's not so bad having her here, is it?"

The anger in his gaze ebbed as his eyes flowed over me. He reached up and tucked a lock of my hair behind my ear, then dragged his knuckles along my jaw.

I didn't breathe as he touched me with a gentleness that was foreign and reverent.

"It's not so bad, right?" I whispered.

"No," he agreed. "It isn't bad at all."

He cupped my crown, drawing me down to him. Our lips met in a tentative caress. Testing the waters. Taking a sip, then another.

But I was so thirsty for Luca that one sip or a hundred would never be enough.

At first, all we did was kiss and kiss and kiss. Slow and soft. Deep and searching. Fingers in hair. My hand over his heart. His holding me tight against him.

We were careful with one another in a way we had never been. I was achy, like I had the flu. My need for Luca's touch had seeped into my bones. Each slide of his hand over my silky nightgown soothed.

But it was when he shifted us so his chest was on top of mine that I melted and tension flowed out of me in ragged rivers.

Words weren't spoken. There was no discussion when he slipped my nightgown off and lowered his sleep pants. Our heated skin melded like it was always meant to be touching.

Luca didn't command me. I didn't sass him. This was different than all the other times, yet exactly the same. His body knew mine. We were drawn to each other in a way I'd never been drawn to anyone else. Even as we broke the rules in Luca's quiet, dimly lit bedroom, that hadn't changed. He held my strings, and I danced for him, though it was a languid, sultry *pas de deux* instead of the usual fiery tango.

Luca pressed my thighs apart as he buried his face between them. I covered my mouth with the back of my hand, muffling the moans he elicited from me with the flat of his tongue on my slick, swollen flesh. In the back of my mind, I still feared if I was too loud, the spell would break.

And I would die if the spell broke.

When I reached my peak, Luca's palm traveled up my torso and rested over my thrashing heart. The heart he'd unknowingly unlocked and set free.

I crumbled then. Crumbled and fell even harder for this man.

When he climbed over me and stared down at my face, I thought there was no way he couldn't read the magnitude of my feelings for him. But if he did, he showed no signs. He remained intense and focused on me, fitting himself inside me in one smooth stroke.

He moved above me, into me, advancing and retreating, but never for long. As soon as he slid out, he pushed back in, somehow deeper every time. When we weren't kissing, we were caressing, stroking, touching. Eyes locked, panting breaths exchanging air that wasn't mine or his but ours.

Luca wasn't in love with me. He cared for me, though. Deeply, tenderly. And he was showing me without any restraint.

I wasn't certain the unbound emotions running rampant within me could be called love either. But I suspected that was what this was, and I couldn't keep them neatly tucked away.

I didn't want to terrify him either.

So, I closed my eyes and kissed him hard, looping my arms around his neck, locking my legs around his middle.

I told him with my body that I wanted him, wanted him, wanted him.

He answered by giving me more and more and more.

We came together with a kiss that was more exaltation than a meeting of lips. I said Luca's name with my tongue on his. He uttered mine in the fluttering pecks he placed on my lips. My neck arched, lifting my chin, my cries of pleasure ringing from me like bells in a tower. Luca's head bowed next to mine, so we were cheek to cheek, and his groans became a chorus with my cries until there was nothing left but the echoes of us.

We stayed connected even as Luca rolled us to our sides. I scuttled closer, my leg over his hip, keeping him there.

"Don't move," I murmured, hiding my face in his chest.

"I don't think I could if I wanted to." His lips touched the top of my head, exactly as they did in my fantasies.

"Just a little while longer. Stay."

"I'm not going anywhere, pretty girl."

I fell asleep with Luca inside me, around me, over me.

I had never slept better in my life.

CHAPTER THIRTY-FIVE

Saoirse

ON THE FOURTH MORNING of Clara's stay, I found her in the kitchen making breakfast. Luca had already left for work, so I was surprised to see her there. She was normally at the office before him.

"Going in late?" I asked.

She groaned, her hand resting on her belly. "I was moving slowly this morning."

"I think you have a perfectly reasonable excuse for slowing down in general."

She waved me off. "Nonsense. I'll have three months of maternity leave, and no doubt I'll be climbing the walls by the end of it. I don't want to begin that earlier than I have to. Besides, my job isn't very physically taxing. It's the whole heaving myself from bed and making myself presentable that takes twice as much energy as it used to."

I slid in next to her, wrapping my arm around her shoulders and squeezing. "Well, you look absolutely gorgeous, if that makes you feel any better."

She knocked her head against my shoulder and grinned. "Coming from my gorgeous sister-in-law, it does indeed. Although, I rue the day I have to see you walking around glowing and pregnant. You're so tall, I bet your bump will be tiny, and I'll seethe with jealousy. I just know it."

When I didn't laugh, Clara turned her sharp eyes on me. I gave her the warmest smile I could muster.

I hated lying any more than I had to, so I answered carefully. "I'm not sure when that will happen."

Her hand flew to her mouth. "Oh, look at me, speaking out of turn. It's this baby in me, sucking my brains out. Before this, I never would have presumed a woman had plans to become a mother. Forgive me?"

"Of course I forgive you. You didn't do anything wrong."

Flustered, I made myself busy pouring a cup of coffee. Miles would be here soon to start our workday. We had a meeting with Kenji, so I needed to grab breakfast before everything started rolling.

Then I remembered how worried Luca was about his sister. She hadn't been receptive to him prying into her marriage, but maybe she'd talk to me.

"Will you be here again tonight?" I was going for casual, peering at her over my steaming coffee.

Clara leaned her hip on the counter. "If it's okay, I'd like to stay another night."

"You don't have to ask, Clara. We talked about it last night and agreed how much we like having you here."

Her brow winged. "My brother doesn't mind me intruding on his newly wedded bliss?"

I laughed. "He really doesn't." I set my mug on the counter and opened a box of granola. "Do you think Miller would like to stay over too? We'd love to have him."

"Oh, no, that's okay, I—" she cut herself off, turning toward the sink. Suddenly, she was interested in washing her plate and glass. I'd struck a nerve.

"I'm sorry. If you want to talk, I'm here, but I won't press." I made a show of pouring my granola into a bowl so she would relax. I wasn't going to badger her.

Then she turned around with tears in her eyes. "I don't know what's going on." She swiped at her face with the backs of her hands. "I was convinced he was cheating because something's been so off with him. But once I confronted him about it, he promised me he wasn't, and since then, he's made a concerted effort to be a good husband. He's been so attentive...I gaslit myself into believing I was the crazy one."

I went to her, took her hands in mine, and pulled her into the living room. We sat together on the sofa no one ever sat on. Clementine showed up to take her spot wrapped around Clara's belly.

Clara cooed at Clem for a moment, stroking her soft fur, then she took a deep breath and spilled everything.

"Miller's assistant came to me on Monday. She was buying a car, so they ran her credit report and there was a credit card listed on it that didn't belong to her. Naturally, she panicked and looked into it. The card is in her name, but the address is ours. Mine and Miller's."

My heart lodged in my throat. I had no earthly idea where this was going, but it couldn't be anywhere good.

"Did you confront him?" I asked.

"No. I haven't yet. But I did some digging and found the credit card's statement. He paid for flowers delivered to a woman named Theresa Graves in Tennessee. He sent a book to her address too. I don't get it. I just don't. Miller doesn't know anyone in Tennessee.

He hasn't been on any trips. I don't know what to think. And I'm afraid, Saoirse. I have to know, but I don't want to ask."

I wanted to help. The urge was so strong I could barely sit still. "Luca can talk to him."

"No," she snapped. "Absolutely not. Luca will kill him with his bare hands if he finds out—" She gasped, her chest rising sharply. Clementine mewed and butted her head against Clara. After a moment, Clara dug her fingers into Clem's fur, soothing them both. "I looked at Miller's phone a few days ago. I only had a few minutes, but I clicked on his email app, and it was logged in to an account I didn't know he had."

She cut herself off, her lips pressing together in a straight line.

"You can't go on like this. I hate seeing you so upset."

Her shining, tear-filled eyes met mine. "What if you talk to him? You could meet him for coffee, maybe tell him you want to talk to him about baby stuff and try to get the truth out of him."

The idea was crazy. Miller and I had next to no relationship. Why would he confide in me? But Clara was so distraught. If there was even the smallest chance I could help her, I had to do it.

"Okay. I'll try."

She exhaled, her shoulders curving forward. "Thank you so much."

Her relief was palpable. I wrapped my arms around her because she really looked like she could have used a hug.

"Of course, Clara. You shouldn't be under this kind of stress."

"I appreciate that you care." She pulled back and took a deep breath. "Please don't tell Luca until we have all the facts. My brother will get himself arrested if he finds out."

"I don't want to keep secrets from him."

She shook her head. "No, I understand. But can you wait until afterward? And let me tell him once we know for sure."

My stomach squirmed with discomfort, but I agreed. I'd let Clara be the one to tell Luca what was going on since this was her marriage and life. It was only fair for her to get to choose the timing.

I'd just sat down at my desk Monday morning when Luca sent me an email.

To: saoirserossi@peakstrategies.com

From: lucarossi@rossimotors.com

Saoirse,

I had a cancellation today and I want to take you to lunch. This isn't a euphemism. I want to sit across from you and eat food together. I have enough time. I can meet you close to home if that's easier.

Tell me you're free.

Yours,

Luca

I smiled as I read the email, even as my heart sank. I'd have to decline since I'd already made plans to meet Miller—which I was dreading like getting a filling without Novocaine. I'd already been pissed at Miller for being such a shithole husband his wife had asked me to intervene, but now I was doubly mad because I was going to miss out on spending time with Luca.

I couldn't knock the grin off my face, though. It had become something of a constant since the week before when Luca had thrown out the rules. Clara had gone to stay with her parents on Saturday, which I thought would mean I'd be returning to my bedroom. But when I tried, Luca scooped me up and threw me on his bed.

We didn't talk about the change. It just...was.

"Tell me the joke."

I jerked back, surprised by Miles's voice. I shouldn't have been. We shared an office, and I'd let him into the condo only a half hour ago. I'd known he was in the room with me, but I'd been so busy daydreaming about Luca I'd forgotten I wasn't alone.

"There's no joke," I said.

He parked his butt on the edge of my desk, a habit he'd carried over from his days working with Elise at Andes. Miles and I were both talkers. We quickly realized in order to get anything done, we had to learn to ignore each other or else we'd spend hours chattering instead of working.

"It might be me being paranoid, but I see you smiling at your computer like a little loon, and I think you're talking trash about me."

Laughing, I leaned back in my chair, folding my arms over my chest. "That is *definitely* you being paranoid. There's no question."

His eyes narrowed. "You're not going to tell me?"

I would have, but he was amusing me, so I drew out the torture. "I don't want to hurt your feelings."

"That's it. This partnership is dissolved." He picked up a blank piece of printer paper and ripped it down the middle.

"That wasn't our contract."

He crumpled the piece while staring me dead in the eye. "That was symbolic. It's dissolved in my heart."

I fell sideways in a fit of giggles. Working with Miles Aldrich was one of the best decisions I'd ever made.

He scowled at me through my laughter. "I'm not amused, Sershie."

Sobering somewhat, I waved my hands between us. "I'm sorry, I'm sorry. I would never talk trash about you other than your abysmal taste in food trucks."

His chin jutted. "I stand by Ludwig's taco stand."

"That's because you're a maniac. No one else wants sauerkraut tacos."

"More for me." His hand came down on my desk. "Now, tell me what had you grinning before I order sauerkraut tacos every day for the next month and eat them in front of you."

I almost dry-heaved at the memory of the smell. One time was enough. They were banned from the condo.

"Just a sweet email from my husband, that's all."

He threw his hands up. "You couldn't have said that?"

"I could have, but we were having fun."

"*You* were having fun. You know, I see why you and Elise are friends. Both of you have demon hearts. It's a good thing I get along well with evil women."

"Go back to your desk and rest easy with the knowledge that I would never trash-talk you."

He hopped up and shot me a dimple-popping grin. "I never doubted you, Sershie."

When I was alone again, I replied to Luca's email, stretching the truth as far as I could. I wouldn't lie to him if I didn't have to.

To: lucarossi@rossimotors.com

From: saoirserossi@peakstrategies.com

Luca,

I would love to sit across from you and eat food together. Sadly, and I really am sad about it, I won't be able to make it today.

Miles and I are going to view that shared office space I told you about. I'll pop in on you when we're done. Are office kisses allowed? Because I plan to give you several.

Sincerely,

Your Inconvenient Wife

Biting my lip, I hit send. His hand would be twitchy when he read how I'd signed it. He hated me calling myself that. But he'd married a woman who liked provoking her husband's twitchy hand.

I looked forward to seeing what he'd do about it.

My lightness vanished as soon as I remembered my impending meeting with Miller.

Freaking Miller. Ruining everything.

I walked out of lunch with Miller none the wiser.

He was squirrelly, evasive, and oddly sweaty. He asked me a lot about Clara's state of being. She hadn't come into the office today, so he was worried. From the dark circles around his eyes, it looked like he'd been worried for a while.

But when I outright asked him if he was cheating, he flatly denied it...and I believed him.

Something was off. Very, very off. He wouldn't tell me what it was, and I couldn't even begin to guess. But I truly didn't think there was another woman. He loved his wife, even if he was screwing up big time.

I texted Clara on my walk from the café to the Rossi building.

Me: *I just left lunch with Miller. He says he isn't cheating, and maybe I'm stupid, but I believe him.*

Clara: *Did you ask him about Theresa Graves? The flowers? The book?*

Me: *I did. He acted like he had no idea what I was talking about. And when I showed him the credit card statement you gave me, he said there must be some mistake.*

Clara: *Oh, no. Why can't he just be honest?*

Me: *I don't think he's going to be honest with you. You're going to have to decide what you want to do without having all the answers. I'm sorry.*

Clara: *No, don't be sorry. You went above and beyond your sisterly duty for me. I will never be able to repay you. Thank you for everything.*

Me: *You don't have to thank me. When will you tell Luca?*

Clara: *I'll tell him soon. I need to get my thoughts straight first.*

Me: *Please do it as soon as possible. I'm no good at secrets.*

Clara: *I will. I promise. I'll talk to him this week.*

I slid my phone back into my purse and looked up at the Rossi building in front of me. My stomach somersaulted, knowing Luca was in there, waiting for me.

I hated not being able to talk to him about this, but I trusted Clara would tell him soon. As long as Luca didn't ask me a direct question about what was going on, I wouldn't have to lie. Since I was terrible at lying and hated doing it, I kept my fingers crossed as I walked inside to find my husband.

CHAPTER
THIRTY-SIX

Luca

MY HAND CAME DOWN on Saoirse's sassy ass. "You're not inconvenient. Say it."

She squirmed in my lap, her face buried in my throat. "I'm not inconvenient."

"You *are* a fucking menace, though." I smacked her again, making her yelp.

"I'm a fucking menace."

I smacked her again. "I'm not having sex with you in my office. There are far too many people nearby for me to do what I want to do with you. Now, I'll have to work the rest of the day with half my blood supply in my dick because of you."

I felt her grin against my throat. "You didn't have to spank me."

"You had it coming, and you know it."

I'd been disappointed Saoirse hadn't been able to join me for lunch, but when she appeared at my doorway a few minutes ago, that fell away. Holding her in my lap more than made up for not having her company earlier.

I pressed a knuckle beneath her chin, drawing her out of my throat so I could look at her. I'd woken up to this face for a week now, and not a single part of me wanted to go back to waking up alone.

"How was the office space?" I asked.

"We liked it. I don't know if we're ready to sign on yet, though. We were more just getting a feel for what was out there."

"Did you and Miles grab lunch, or are you hungry?"

Her nose scrunched. "I'm not hungry."

There was a strained quality to her answer that brought me to attention. "Did you eat?"

"Mmhmm." Her eyes darted to the side, and her hands clenched on her thighs.

"Was that a yes?"

"Yes, Luca. I ate."

"With Miles...?"

She huffed, turning away from me. "Yes. Miles and I both ate. He's actually probably wondering why I'm not back at work. I should go."

I caught her before she could slip off my lap, holding her flush to my chest. "Is everything okay?"

"Of course it is. I only meant to stop in for a minute, though. I need to head back to work." Her lips pressed against the side of my throat, and she nuzzled me with her nose. "I'll see you tonight."

She wanted to go, so I let her. But she'd raised my alarm bells. I knew my wife. She was an awful liar, and just now, I was almost certain she'd lied about something.

Approaching Saoirse from behind, I swallowed her in an embrace. Her head fell back against my shoulder with a sigh.

"What are you making, pretty girl?"

I'd arrived home, welcomed by Clementine and the scent of garlic and spices. After giving my cat a good pat, I followed my nose to the kitchen, where Saoirse was standing at the stove. She wasn't exactly a domestic goddess, but she cooked well, and my mother had taught her a few of my favorite dishes from childhood.

I had no complaints and considered myself lucky.

"Salmon and asparagus." She tilted her head to the side to meet my eyes. "I wasn't sure if you'd be home in time to eat with me."

"Are you glad I am?"

"Always."

Leaning down, I dropped a kiss on her lips. "I'm starving. Are you hungry?"

"Mmhmm. Give me a few minutes and I'll feed you."

I slid my hand down to her lower stomach, splaying my fingers wide. "What did you have for lunch?"

Her breath stuttered. It was quick, and if I hadn't been holding her, I wouldn't have noticed. But I had noticed, and once again, I went alert.

"A terrible curry chicken sandwich at this café near Rossi. I'll have to check what the name was so you can make sure you never eat there."

Reaching around her, I turned off the stove. Saoirse yelped when I spun her to face me.

"Yeah, that's bullshit."

Her mouth fell open. "What? I don't—"

I tapped her lips. "You don't lie. You're really bad at it. You're lying to me now, and I want to know why." She tried to turn her head, but I caught her chin, keeping her in place, so she clamped her mouth shut. "Are you really going to do this? I'm standing in front of you, telling you I *know* you're keeping something from me, and you're—"

"I promised Clara," she snapped. "Okay? I promised her I wouldn't say anything."

Taking her hand in mine, I dragged her out of the kitchen and pulled her with me to the den. This was where she was comfortable. Where she relaxed.

If she was going to go back on her promise—and she was—it would happen here, where everything was soft and away from the hot stove and sharp knives in the kitchen.

"Luca, I can't do this. Talk to Clara. I'm going to finish dinner."

She started to rise, but I tugged her right back down, holding both her hands in mine.

"No. I could give a fuck about dinner. Clara shouldn't have put you in this position and she knows it. You know it too. I don't know why you would agree to lie for her—"

"She's your sister." Saoirse yanked her hands out of mine and folded her arms over her chest. My pretty girl was pissed, but she had to have known it would come down to this.

Still, I softened at her reasoning. Saoirse understood the importance of family in the same way I did. Her willingness to go above and beyond to help Clara simply because she was my sister affected me on a visceral level. It made me want to take this woman in my arms and hold her and tell her not to worry about anything.

That she could keep her secrets and continue with her lies without explanation.

But that would never happen.

I could let a lot of things slide, but lying wasn't one of them.

"I appreciate you're trying to protect and help Clara, but she was out of line to ask you to keep something from me. You don't come between a husband and wife. Clara was wrong to do that. I need you to talk to me, Saoirse. No more lies."

For a second, I thought she wasn't going to tell me. Her teeth clamped down hard on her bottom lip, and her gaze shifted to the side, to the ceiling, to my balled hands, until finally, it landed on me.

"Clara asked me to talk to Miller. I had lunch with him today. I really did eat a terrible curry chicken sandwich."

Closing my eyes, I released a slow exhale so I didn't allow my anger to get the better of me before deciding just how pissed to be and where to aim it.

"Why did you have lunch with Miller?"

Her fingers flexed on her arms. "She is afraid he's cheating on her, but of course you know that. But something else happened. Miller opened a secret credit card in his assistant's name and used it to send flowers and a book to this woman in Tennessee. Clara didn't want you to know. She was afraid you would kill him."

"He's fucking someone in Tennessee?"

I would kill him. I absolutely would. If not with my bare hands, then I would make use of one of Elliot's shadowy contacts. I didn't know for a fact that he knew hit men, but I would be surprised if he didn't know how to hire one.

And Miller would fucking die if he hurt Clara. If he stepped out on her, he would wake up with his shriveled dick in his mouth. He should have known better than to fuck with a Rossi. Clara might have wanted peace and a nonviolent resolution, but we weren't the same in that regard.

Saoirse quickly shook her head. "No. I don't believe he is. I think—" She sucked in a deep breath. "Obviously, I'm not a mental health professional, but I left our lunch with the impression Miller is stressed to the point that he's unwell. And I don't really know how to pinpoint why I think this, except something was off. More than his worries over Clara leaving him."

I gnashed my molars down, clenching my jaw. This wasn't the time for me to say all the filth running through my mind. Saoirse had a tender heart. She was worried about his mental health. All I cared about was my family—and as far as I was concerned, from here on out, that did not include Miller.

"Do you have the name of the woman in Tennessee?"

She nodded. "I'm scared to give it to you. I know you want to burn it all down, but you can't."

I knew she was right. All the fantasies of hiring a hit man and drawing Miller's blood were just that: fantasies. There was too much at stake. My hands were tied by my responsibilities.

Just because I couldn't kill him didn't mean I couldn't ruin him in all other ways.

"Give me the name and I'll send it to my PI." Uncrossing her arms, I tugged her toward me. She came the rest of the way on her own, curling up in my lap.

"Don't touch him," she whispered.

"The only promise I can make is not to touch him until I have all the facts." I dusted my knuckle along her cheek and stroked a lock of her hair away from her face. "I'm going to take care of this. It isn't your problem anymore."

Her palm was warm and soft on my jaw. "I wanted to be the one to take care of it. I thought I could."

"You did good, pretty girl." I dropped a peck on her forehead. "You helped my sister and did what you were able to. I'm thankful for that. But you have to understand you can't do this again. We don't lie to each other. It fucks me up knowing you're capable of it."

"I'm obviously not capable of it." Her nose crinkled the way it always did when she was uncomfortable...or lied. "You found me out right away."

I tapped her lips with my fingertip. "It was your intention, though. I have to admit, that hurts."

She flew into motion, banding her arms around me and burying her face in my throat. Her lips moved against my skin.

"I feel like shit, Luca. I'm sick over this." Her fingers gripped my shirt as she dug in closer. "I'm sorry I hurt you. It doesn't matter if I meant to or not. I did, and I'm so sorry."

Her fierce reaction to my pain took me aback. She'd taken my anger in stride, but the second I'd said I was hurt, she was holding me, apologizing to me, trembling in my arms.

"Saoirse. Look at me."

Her head came up, revealing a flushed face and watery eyes. "I'm sorry, Luca."

I took her quivering chin in my hand. "Promise never to hide anything from me again and I'll forgive you."

Her lashes lowered, and one lone tear tracked down her cheek. "I promise. I hate this so much. There is absolutely no way I want to repeat this. We don't keep things from each other."

I wiped her tear on my thumb and sucked it off. "No, we don't. And we don't cry over each other unless they're tears of happiness. Got it?"

"I got it."

"No spilling wine on yourself. You can't say yes at your own expense."

"No spilling wine," she echoed.

"You better mean that."

She sucked in a shaky breath, and it rattled my heart. "I mean it, Luca."

She leaned in and pressed her lips to mine. Cupping the back of her head, I held her there while I *really* kissed my wife, letting her taste the salt on my tongue from her tears and replacing it with all her sweet.

Miller would be dealt with. And soon. But right now, I needed to concentrate on what was most important in this moment, and that was making things right with my wife.

CHAPTER THIRTY-SEVEN

Saoirse

LUCA LED ME DOWN to his studio.

We hadn't been hanging out there as much. Instead, we had dinner together, took rides on his bike, played with Clem.

That didn't mean Luca didn't go there on his own. He did. Only now, he spent an hour or two in his studio instead of the whole evening.

My hand was still shaky in his when he pulled me inside. The only reason I hadn't burst into tears in the den was because this wasn't about me. Luca had been hurt. I was the wielder of the weapon that had injured him. It wasn't his job to comfort me when I was in the wrong.

Suck it up, buttercup.

Luca was being sweeter than I deserved, but who was I to tell him he couldn't be?

"I made you something," he said.

"What? You did?"

"Yes. It started with the sketch I couldn't get right."

"The sketch of me," I murmured.

"Mmhmm. Then capturing you became something of an obsession."

It was on the tip of my tongue to tell him he'd captured me months ago. That I was his and had no intention of escaping my binds anytime soon.

But of course, that wasn't what he'd meant.

His hand was warm around mine as he pulled me deeper into the studio. "Then I realized my pretty girl can't be captured. When I stopped trying to confine you to one thing, I was unblocked. And...well, you'll see."

The walls had been covered in paint splatters and dents but otherwise bare. Now, they were home to drawings, paintings, and chrome-dipped sculptures.

First, I went to my shining silver profile. It was hollow and one-sided, allowing it to be hung from the wall. There was a flower tucked over my ear, and my hair was whirling swirls of metal cascading behind me. My chin was tipped up, and my mouth was stretched into a wide smile.

Luca stood behind me, clutching my hips. His fingers latched around my bones, attaching himself to me like a snapped button.

"You have questions?" he asked softly.

I nodded, but nothing came out, which made him chuckle and hold me a little tighter. But dear god, his gravity was the only thing keeping my feet on the ground. I needed his tether, or the lightness in my bones would betray me.

We moved together to the next piece, which was a pencil sketch of the same pose. Profile, hair blowing, smile. I reached out to touch it but stopped myself. When I dropped my hand, Luca picked it up and placed my fingertips on the paper.

"It's from a picture the judge took," he murmured beside my ear.

"The pictures you've kept from me since that day."

"I didn't know you wanted them."

I turned my head, glimpsing at him over my shoulder. "I do."

He hummed. "Now I don't know if I want to share them."

I leaned my back against his chest and tipped my face to the side to kiss his jaw. "Send them to me when you want me to have them."

We slid over to the watercolor painting. I was reading in this one. My legs hung over the side of the couch, one finger twirling the end of a lock of hair. This must have been based on one of the many evenings I'd spent with him in the studio.

My heart stretched my chest, making it feel tight and overstuffed. My tongue was too big for my mouth, and my brain had shrunk to the size of a pea. I couldn't form words, much less get them out.

Luca shifted me to the next sketch, then the next. There were at least ten pencil or charcoal sketches of me reading in various poses. Always relaxed and serene. Was that really what my face looked like or how Luca saw me?

I thought back to the nights we'd spent here when he'd finally let me into his private world. Something had settled in me. An anxiousness I'd been battling. Luca had noticed it and immortalized that feeling on paper.

The last thing hanging on the wall was a chrome-dipped sculpture of two hands. I recognized our rings. These were our hands.

"I took that from one of the pictures too. I liked the dichotomy of your fine bones and my—"

I spun around and crashed my mouth against his. His response was immediate, taking me in his arms and kissing me back with soul-melting fervor.

I had done nothing in this life to deserve any of this. Not the art. The thoughtfulness. This man. Especially not today, when I'd screwed up in such a big way.

He had to know this was too much. I wasn't meant to have something like this. I couldn't begin to fathom how to accept it.

"Luca," I cried against his demanding lips. I had to tell him since he clearly didn't know. "I don't deserve this."

His fingers wound in the back of my hair, roughly fisting it. A rumble vibrated his chest. "You don't get to decide that, do you? It's me who decides. For months, you've been the only thing that's inspired me. My pretty fucking girl. You're all I want to paint and sculpt, and I'll do that until I'm satisfied."

He tapped my lips when I opened them to deny him. "No more arguing. It's time for you to tell me how much you like all this."

I clutched at his shirt, reeling myself into his warmth. "I fucking love it, Luca. I've never seen myself the way you do."

"You will, one day. I'm not anywhere done with you." His hand skimmed down my side to cup my breast. "Next, I'm going to sculpt these, which means I need you modeling for me naked. It could take hours, probably days. You'll have to lie there and let me look at you."

I pressed my lips together to hold back my grin. Leave it to Luca to lighten my mood. He had that way about him, and I loved him for it.

I loved him for it.

I really did love this man. And looking around this studio made me think he might have loved me too.

We weren't supposed to fall in love. I couldn't even begin to consider what this would mean for our agreement. But Luca's mouth slammed into mine, bringing me back to the present and away from the what-ifs.

This man saw me. He understood me like no one ever had. When things died down and Clara was taken care of, we would talk.

If Luca loved me too, then we could figure out what that meant together.

But right now, I needed to show him how vital he was to me and how special he'd made me feel in the best way I knew how.

With my body. My whispered sighs. My arms around him. My mouth on his lips. This was a language in which both of us could say all we wanted without fear and listen without argument.

We spoke that way for hours. Until everything had been said.

Then Luca curled around me in his bed, between cool sheets, and kissed me good night.

CHAPTER THIRTY-EIGHT

Luca

ONCE MY PRIVATE INVESTIGATOR pulled the first thread, Miller's secret life began to unravel.

It was worse than I could have imagined.

He wasn't cheating, but I almost wished he was.

Miller Fairfield was a fucked-up man.

I couldn't even wrap my head around this stranger who'd been my brother-in-law for years. Had I ever known him?

Within three days, it was all laid out in front of me, and I was staggered by the extent of his depravity. This went beyond what the detective in Tennessee had suspected, and as of today, everything had been turned over to the FBI.

All I wanted to do was go home, sink inside my wife, and forget everything I'd learned. But I was no good. Too angry. Too bitter and confused to go home to Saoirse. She knew what was going on, though, and had promised to be waiting for me whenever I came home.

My fucking wife.

Elliot and Weston dropped everything to meet me for a drink. They both had companies to run, but I didn't hesitate to ask them to leave early. Neither asked why. They showed up at the bar I'd named at four thirty sharp. Weston was doing better about a work-life balance, but Elliot rarely left work before eight p.m.

Yet he showed like he always did when push came to shove.

I was already one drink in. It had been necessary to settle my blood before I spilled all the ugliness everywhere.

I let them down half their drinks before I started talking.

"Miller has been cyberstalking and harassing a couple who run a business blog in Tennessee for the last six months."

Elliot put his glass down on the table. "Fuck."

Weston rubbed the deep line between his brows. "Why the hell has he been doing that?"

I shrugged, but my shoulders were too heavy to lift far. "This is all information I'm getting from the investigator, who's been in contact with the detective working on the case. Theresa and Albert Graves run the Grave Business Report."

Elliot frowned. "I've never heard of it."

"Neither have I," Weston agreed.

"That's because only a few thousand people read it. I have no fucking clue how Miller found it, but the Graves' published a few scathing articles about Rossi's quarterly earnings report and the fluctuation of our stock prices. They had some things to say when I took over as CEO, but, hell, so did a lot of other journalists. I don't know why Miller picked this blog to become obsessed with, but he did."

Weston shoved his fingers through his hair. "What did he do exactly?"

"The harassment started with their email address being sub-scribed to things like the Satanic Temple, Nashville Kink Night, the Green Party...stupid, annoying shit. But annoying in the sense that they were bombarded day after day. And it didn't stop there. The anonymous social media threats were next. *Shut down or go down,* basically. Then he doxxed their address online. He listed it for free puppies, on hookup sites, as the host of a swingers' party...and people were showing up at their door."

"Jesus," Elliot uttered. "Is he really that stupid?"

I shook my head. "I don't know what was going through his mind. Maybe he snapped, had a mental break. I don't give a damn. He terrorized these people. When Clara finds out—"

Weston clamped a hand on my shoulder. "When she finds out, you'll be there for her."

"She's having his baby in less than a month." My head fell, even heavier than my shoulders. "He sent them a pig fetus. Dead rats. Insects. But the worst part...the very worst part—he had a funeral arrangement delivered to the husband. And the following day, he sent him a book called *Life After the Death of a Spouse.* This couple is in their sixties. The detective said the husband had to be hospitalized with an irregular heartbeat due to the stress of all this. Miller could have really killed this man."

Weston blew out a heavy breath. "Holy hell. I know he's never been your favorite person, but this is next level."

"He wasn't my favorite person because I thought he was bland, not psychopathic." I raised my head even though there was a knife lodged in my skull. "I don't have any idea what the next step is. What am I supposed to do? There's no manual on this."

Elliot swirled his drink, the ice clinking. Of the three of us, he was the least ruffled, but that was Elliot. His way of showing he cared was coming in, taking care of what needed to be taken care of in the smoothest way possible, and always being there like an unmovable mountain.

"I'll put you in touch with a crisis team. Rossi will need a plan on the corporate level. Trust them to implement one for the company. On a personal level, I don't doubt you'll handle it. Be there for Clara. Take care of anything she needs without question."

Weston nodded along with what Elliot was saying. "And in the dustup, don't neglect Saoirse and your relationship. No matter how big the crisis, you can't put that on hold. Let her be there to lean on."

Weston spoke from experience. When Andes had gone through a crisis, he'd put his complete focus into fixing it, leaving Elise alone in the dark. I wouldn't repeat his mistakes.

I had a rough road ahead of me. When this went public, all hell was going to break loose. My only hope was to keep it quiet for as long as we could.

"Us too," Elliot said. "Anything you need, contacts you require, we're here. You're not handling this alone, even if it feels like it."

"I know I'm not." I swallowed the thick lump in my throat. "Never once have I not felt you at my back."

Elliot lifted his chin. "Good. Don't doubt it."

Saoirse was waiting for me with her arms open when I arrived. I fell into them, into her, clutching her like the only buoy in the center of a maelstrom at sea. Neither of us could control how badly we would be battered, but if I held on to her, I'd see the other side of this.

I was sure of that to my bones.

"I'm sorry," she whispered.

"I know, pretty girl."

Her fingers curled into the back of my shirt. "Tell me how to make it better for you."

Heaving an exhale, I rolled my forehead on hers. "You're doing it. All the ugly is waiting for me, but it doesn't weigh as much right now. That's all you. Stay with me."

"You don't have to ask."

My mouth twitched. First almost-smile of the day, and of course, she was the one to draw it out of me.

"I didn't."

She let out a breathy laugh. "Come snuggle with me in the den."

"Lead the way."

Before I'd walked in this door, I'd had fucking on my mind. Hard and rough. Making her scream. Taking my frustrations out on her body. Satisfying the empty place in me by making her come over and over until we were both so exhausted that sleep took us over.

But then she climbed into my lap and covered us both with one of the throws I'd bought with her in mind. My head fell back on the cushions. Saoirse tucked her face in my throat and stroked my jaw with her fingertips.

This was peace.

The flip side of the coin.

Beyond these walls was chaos I would have to face, but that didn't touch us. Not when we were together like this. She took my frustrations by being here. The empty place in me was filled with her presence.

Damn this woman.

She'd made it so that living without her would be a painful, ugly reality. I wasn't interested in experiencing that. Not now, not two years from now. Whether Saoirse liked it or not, she was mine. She could fight me on it, but that wouldn't change the fact that I was keeping her. That was what she got for blunting all the sharp and smoothing out the rough. She'd gotten me hooked on her. Going back to life before her didn't hold even an ounce of attraction.

"I can't do this without you," I told her.

"You could, Luca. I know you could. But I'm here. It's my job to make your life easier, so that's what I'm going to do."

A barb pierced my gut. Her job?

Tucking my knuckle beneath her chin, I drew her face up so I could look at her. Her full lips curved into a slow, easy smile.

"I'm not a job."

"Luca." Her palm flattened on my cheek. "Of course you're not a job. I meant my job as your wife. The way I care for you goes way beyond the agreement we made. I hope that's obvious."

That should have made me feel better, but I wasn't thinking about agreements when I had her in my arms. I was thinking about keeping her forever.

When all I did was frown, Saoirse shifted so she was straddling my legs and took my face in both hands.

"I'm here for you, Luca. If you want quiet, I'll be quiet. If you want to yell and fight, we can do that. I know this shit with Miller and Clara is killing you. You don't have to say it. I can see it in your face. But I want to be your soft place to land because you're mine. That's not a job or an agreement. It's because we care for each other. Don't turn away from me because I said the wrong thing. Please let me be here for you. Let me make it easier."

Reaching up, I took her chin between two fingers. "You're not working a job when we're together."

She shook her head. "No. This is real."

"Don't say that again."

"I won't." Her fingers traced the downturned edges of my mouth. "You're my favorite yes."

Releasing a shuddering breath, I slammed my eyes shut. I was maddeningly in love with this woman. More vulnerable than I was comfortable being. But there was no helping it.

Saoirse Rossi was my wife.

Two years wasn't going to be close to enough time with her.

I was beginning to believe two lifetimes wouldn't cut it either.

CHAPTER THIRTY-NINE

Luca

THE SHOULDER OF MY shirt was stiff and damp from hours of my sister's tears. My guts had been raked and twisted from her sobs and the pain she hadn't even begun to hold back.

I'd been the one to tell her what Miller had done.

Clara chose to kill the messenger by throwing herself into my arms and letting me feel every ounce of her turmoil. She keened her husband's name. Begged for me to make it untrue. Bargained for me to cover for him. Then screamed he should never see the light of day again.

Our parents couldn't comfort her. My mother tried to tell her to be calm for the sake of the baby, but Clara was inconsolable. She cradled her belly and rasped her apologies to the baby kicking inside her.

My father dealt with his own rage. Like me, he wanted blood. He'd taken Miller in as his son-in-law, had treated him like family, given him an executive position at Rossi, all for Miller to spit in his face.

I'd spent the day with them. Holding Clara. Telling my father he had to calm down, or he'd end up having a second heart attack. Forcing my mother to sit down before she ran herself into the ground.

Saoirse had asked me if I'd wanted her to come, but I'd declined. Instinct told me Clara needed privacy to express her grief without restraint. Saoirse could come tomorrow, or the next day, when Clara was ready for her brand of comfort. And she would be. Even though she'd barely been coherent, Clara had asked about Saoirse.

"You should be with her," she said, shoving at me with weak arms.

"She's fine, Clara. Saoirse's working today, but she's been texting, checking in on you."

Her head fell on my chest. "You're such a good husband. Promise me you won't hide anything from her. Promise me you won't hurt her like this."

"I promise I won't hurt her."

A great rolling sob racked her body. "Miller wasn't supposed to hurt me. I know you never liked him, but I loved him so much. He was sweet to me and—"

If I had the chance, I didn't know how I'd be able to stop myself from killing him. Lucky for Miller, he turned himself in to the FBI last night. Based on my private investigator's contacts within the bureau, Miller confessed to everything. Even more than what had been uncovered.

In the part of me that hadn't been charred by cynicism, I wondered if he'd turned himself in for Clara's sake. If he felt guilty for putting her through this.

But that was probably giving him too much credit. Most likely, he'd sensed the blade dropping. Turning himself in was the only way he could save his own neck. No doubt his attorney would be angling for a plea deal.

When I entered my condo after my never-ending day with my family, all I wanted was a replay of last night, My wife in my arms. Her hands on my face. Sweet words in my ear.

But I was greeted with laughter. Saoirse's and Miles's.

That wasn't uncommon since they began working together. To be honest, it had always put a smile on my face because it meant Saoirse was happy.

Tonight, it was nails on a chalkboard. All the hairs on my arms stood on end. My immediate, gut-churning reaction was betrayal. How could she be laughing when I'd spent the day holding together my crumbling family?

My logical side knew these feelings were irrational. But that side of me had been worked to fucking death today. All that was working now was my hindbrain, which took major offense to another man making my wife happy on today of all days.

It only got worse when Miles came strolling out of their shared office with Clementine in his arms.

My fucking cat.

"Hey, I thought I heard the front door." Miles grinned and stroked Clem's back. The little traitor barely glanced at me.

"I'm surprised you heard me." I tossed my keys and phone down in the ceramic bowl Saoirse had added to the small table in the entryway. "Is your workday over?"

"Yeah. We've been done for a while. We were just hanging out. I'm gonna head home, though." He gave Clementine a kiss, then set her on the ground. "By the way, remind your wife to move her stuff out of the apartment. If there's anything left when I move in, it's mine."

My hand froze midway to my face. What the hell was he going on about?

Luckily for me, Miles was a talker, so he filled me in without asking.

"Have you been to Elise and Saoirse's place? It's sweet. The views are killer, and my big ass fits in the bathtub, no problem. I'm only living there temporarily while the lead paint gets removed from my house's walls. Apparently, that's dangerous or something. Don't tell Saoirse, but I used one of her candles last night. And her bubble bath." He laughed at himself and clapped me on the shoulder. "All right. Good to see you. Have a nice weekend."

Miles exited without waiting for me to say goodbye. Which was good because I was still trying to wrap my head around what he'd just said.

Clem meowed at my feet, so I bent down and picked her up. As I straightened, Saoirse emerged from her office, striding toward me with a worried pinch in her brow.

"Hey. You look like you need to sit down." Cupping the back of my neck, she placed a soft, lingering kiss on my lips. "Come sit down with me."

"You never moved all your things here."

Her head canted, the pinch in her brow deepening. "What do you mean?"

"Miles wants me to remind you to move your things out of your apartment. You never really moved in here."

"Well, yes. I left some of my belongings there since we still had the place for a while—"

"And you had one foot out the door this entire time."

"No. That isn't true. I uprooted myself to move into *your* place. We barely knew each other then. I left a few things there, but my foot isn't out the door." She put her hand on top of mine, which was on Clem's back. I looked down at our woven fingers, feeling no comfort. "Can we go sit down? I know you have to be exhausted from today, and I want to—"

"Where are your rings?"

"What?" Her wide eyes flicked from mine to her hand. "Oh, I don't know. I guess I forgot to put them on this morning."

I had to put Clem down on the floor before I lost it. I'd been on the edge when I walked in. Pressure coming at me from all sides. Expectations I had no choice but to meet. Saoirse told me just last night she'd be my soft place to land, but there was nothing comforting about knowing the woman I loved could easily walk out the door whenever she wanted. Hell, she was only halfway here, even now.

"I haven't taken my ring off since we got married."

She touched her forehead. "I'm sorry. It was an accident. You know I normally wear them, but things have been out of the ordinary lately and it slipped my mind."

"All day."

Her lips pursed like she'd sucked on something sour. "Yes, apparently so. I spent my day fretting for you, and when I wasn't doing that, I was texting you, or Miles was talking me out of getting in my car to go to you."

"Miles? Did you tell him what's going on?"

Suddenly, I couldn't stand that he'd been here with her. He got parts of her I didn't. While I'd been watching my sister's world fall apart, he'd been making her laugh.

I had no say in it. She could do what she wanted, and I'd be expected to carry on. Hold it all together.

"No, of course not." She stepped into me and clutched my folded arms. "Luca, please. Come sit down. Let me get you a drink and we can talk about this. Or whatever you want, I just—"

"When the two years are over, do you still plan to walk away from me?"

The plea in her eyes and the thin line her lips pressed into gave me my answer.

"I don't—why are we talking about this now?" She cupped the side of my neck and pressed her chest to my arms. "Neither of us knows what will happen, but I don't want to be anywhere else but here. I want to be with you, Luca. Isn't that enough?"

"Do you love me?"

She nodded sharply, immediately. "I do. I love you very much. Do you love me?"

"Madly." My jaw rippled with everything I was holding back. "Which is why I'm ending our agreement."

She sucked in a harsh breath. "Why does loving me mean the end of our agreement?"

Unfolding my arms, I took her face in my hands. "Because you're my wife. That's real to me, and fuck, maybe it always has been, but I can't go on loving you like this if I don't have any guarantees. I have to know I'm your husband in every sense of the word. Tell me our marriage is real to you."

"Luca," she breathed. "This isn't the time."

"No." I dropped her face, taking a step back. "You said it's your job to make my life easier. Well...this is it. I'm asking for your promise that this is real to you. No more agreement. It's me and you, husband and wife."

She turned her head, but not before her eyes filled with tears. I knew what the answer would be before I asked, but knowing and seeing it live and in color were two different things.

"I can't do that right now." She touched her delicate fingertips to her lips. "When this is all over, we can—"

"Say yes." I shoved my fingers into my hair, a throb like nothing I'd ever felt surging through my skull. "I'm asking you to say yes."

She shook her head, still facing away. "I'm not doing this right now. Not like this."

She didn't get it. It had to be now. Everything else was unsettled. The foundation of my world was crumbling, and all I could do was apply duct tape and throw a wish up to the stars it would hold. Things I knew to be true were lies. Up was down and down was up.

I needed her to be the one unchanging thing I could count on. If I was worried I was going to lose her when some arbitrary date came along, how did I deal with the thousand other things I had to?

"Say yes, Saoirse." I yanked at the collar of my shirt. It was too fucking tight for the knot in my throat. Somewhere in the condo, my phone rang, but there was no one else I wanted to talk to, so it barely registered. "Look at me and say yes."

She wouldn't give me her face, so I walked around her until she had no choice but to see me. Her eyes flared, but she wouldn't say the word. Her teeth dug into her bottom lip, trapping her answers inside.

"I am asking you to say yes." I slapped my chest in frustration. "I'm telling you I need it."

"I love you," she whispered.

There was a hurricane inside me. Wild and uncontrollable, shaking my knees and balling my fists. A deluge of exhaustion and anger warred in my brain. My sister's cries echoed like rolling thunder in my ears. I had to yell to make myself heard over it all.

"Then say yes."

Saoirse flinched, taking a step away from me. "Stop it, Luca."

My phone began ringing again, driving a spike into my aching head.

"You say yes to everyone else. You dropped everything to work for another man for *free*. But you won't say yes to me? You love me and you won't say yes?"

Her shoulders jumped and bunched around her ears, which told me I was louder than I'd meant to be, but everything was swirling out of control. She was supposed to be my fucking buoy. My soft place. And I couldn't get a grasp on her. On anything.

Tears were rolling down her cheeks when her eyes locked on mine. "You're asking me to spill wine on myself."

That brought me to a dead stop.

"What?" But I'd heard her—and everything behind those words.

"If I said yes to you, it would be to make you happy. And god, Luca, I want to make you happy. I would do anything for you to feel that way."

I finished her thought since I knew exactly where she was going with it. "But not at your own expense, right? Being married to me for real would mean spilling wine on yourself. That's how you see it."

My phone rang again. This was the third or fourth time. Saoirse and I both turned in the direction of the grating sound.

"You should get that," she whispered.

"We're not finished talking." But the phone wouldn't stop ringing. In a moment of clarity, I remembered the crisis currently happening outside these walls.

I walked back to the entry. Seeing my dad's name on the screen drew me up tight. Something was wrong.

"Hello?"

"Thank Christ," he uttered. "You need to get down to Davis Memorial as soon as you can. Clara's been in a car accident and they're taking her into surgery to deliver the baby."

Blood drained from my face. "No. Accident?"

"I'll explain it when you get here. She's going to need all of us around her."

My heartbeat whooshed in my ears. "I'll be there. Davis Memorial."

Saoirse was beside me when I hung up, concern etched on the face I loved more than anything but could barely look at.

"Clara's in the hospital. I need to go."

She nodded. "Okay. Let me get my shoes."

"I don't have time to wait. My sister needs me."

She murmured a protest, but it was too late. I was already gone.

CHAPTER FORTY

Saoirse

I DROVE MYSELF TO the hospital, only a few minutes behind Luca.

But once I arrived, I didn't know what to do. I wanted to be there for him more than anything, but he was so very mad at me. I wasn't happy with him either, but I could forgive him because I knew he was hurting.

I texted Luca to let him know I had arrived then took a seat in the lobby and waited.

And waited.

At some point, I must have nodded off because something woke me up. A touch, or maybe a presence. It didn't matter. When I opened my eyes, Luca was standing in front of me.

His scruff was thicker. His eyes were hollow and bloodshot. His clothes and hair were disheveled, which was so incredibly unlike him. He looked beautiful, though. Sad, but a sight for sore eyes, as he always was.

"Clara?" I croaked.

He nodded. "She has a concussion and fractured collarbone. She's asleep and hasn't met her daughter yet."

I swallowed back my tears and focused on my relief. "And the baby?"

"In the NICU, but she looks good." He cupped his nape. "You should go."

I climbed to my feet, wishing he'd open his arms so I could walk into them. "I want to be here. If you guys need anything, I—"

"No, Saoirse. I'm not going to allow my family to get used to you being around when we both know it's temporary."

It hurt. The hard look in his eyes. The distance he forced between us. We *weren't* temporary, even if he believed that right now. The way I loved him wasn't going away. We owed each other a conversation, more than one, but it wasn't going to happen now. Not when emotions were high and defenses were even higher.

"But I would like to help if I can. I can stay down here and be on call if a need arises. I won't get in the way."

"You're not getting it." Luca's jaw flexed and rippled before he spat out five words that vaporized every ounce of my hope we could find a way through this, striking me to my core. "I don't want you here."

My heart lodged in my throat, so big, I couldn't breathe more than a wisp of air. My mouth attempted to form a brave smile, but it probably looked insane. Luca wasn't focused on me. His eyes were distant. Like I wasn't there anymore.

He didn't want me. Not here or anywhere.

"Okay," I rasped. "I'll go. Tell Clara congratulations for me when she wakes up."

I hesitated for a beat, giving us both a chance to change our minds. Luca remained impassive and far, far away, and I couldn't stay for another second.

I left without another word, charging through the lobby and out the front doors. I wasn't looking where I was going and ran straight into someone heading inside. They caught me by the biceps, steadying me.

"Saoirse?"

I focused on the man in front of me. "Elliot. I'm—"

"You're crying."

"Am I?" I touched my cheeks, shocked to find them wet. I thought I'd been holding back my tears.

"Is Clara...?"

"Oh." My eyes rounded. "No, Clara is okay. That's not—she's okay, and I'm just leaving. It's good you're here for Luca. He needs a friend."

Elliot hadn't let go of me. "Why the hell are you leaving him? What he needs is his wife."

I shook my head, letting my eyes fall to the floor. "He doesn't want me here."

His fingers tightened around my arms before letting go and giving them a gentle rub. When he spoke, though, he was all business. "Okay. I'll check on Luca. Do you need me to arrange a ride home for you?"

"No. I'm fine. I drove myself."

He peered at me with a pinched expression. "Are you sure that's safe? You're upset."

I drew in a deep breath. I knew Elliot Levy well enough to know he wouldn't let me leave his sight if he believed I was a danger to myself or others. His mother had died in a car accident, so he didn't take driving recklessly lightly.

"I'm good, Elliot. I just need to get home."

It took a few more minutes to convince him, but he finally let me go. I drove carefully, probably more than I would have if I hadn't had Elliot's disapproving glare on my mind. I didn't want to hear his shit if I crashed my car, so I made sure I didn't out of spite.

Even heartbroken, I couldn't let Elliot Levy get the best of me.

Hours later, I still didn't know what to do. Luca hadn't come back, and the walls of our home were closing in. Being squeezed like this, I couldn't sleep or think. I wanted him to come home so we could talk, but I dreaded it at the same time. He'd told me in no uncertain terms he didn't want me around.

It was his way or nothing.

There was no one for me to talk to about this with. Any other situation, I would have been drinking wine with Elise, singing Dolly Parton songs until my voice gave out, and letting her mop my tears. But I couldn't do that. If I did, I'd have to admit to our lie.

I needed space to arrange my thoughts and decide how to go on from here. I couldn't be here when Luca came home.

Not now.

Not when I didn't know what to say to him or what happened next.

So, I packed a bag and wrote him a note. Then I gave Clementine some snuggles and arranged for our doorman to check on her until Luca returned.

As much as I wanted to hop on a plane and move somewhere on the other side of the globe, I couldn't do that. I had responsibilities here now, so I wasn't leaving forever.

Just for now.

CHAPTER FORTY-ONE

Saoirse

By NINE O'CLOCK THAT evening, I was at Joy's Elbow Room, throwing back a beer with my sister-in-law. Country music filtered over the din of conversation around us. Couples danced. Friends played darts. Our small table was an island of misery in the midst of the revelry.

Well, I was miserable. Elena was staring at me with barely restrained impatience. She didn't have a lot of it on a normal basis, but pregnancy sucked the rest right out of her.

Once I'd arrived in Wyoming, I'd spent the afternoon snuggling the kids, riding Athena, and avoiding questions. Elena had put her foot down after dinner.

She wasn't demanding answers, but I knew I wasn't getting out of this town without spilling my guts. Deep down, that was probably why I came here. Elena wasn't exactly a neutral party, but exposing the truth to her wouldn't blow up my and Luca's friend group.

All it took was one beer, and I was ready to talk.

When I started, everything poured out at once.

"My marriage to Luca is an arrangement. He basically needed a wife for his image, and I needed my mother off my back about dating. He asked me to marry him for two years, and I said yes because...well, you know how I am. I always say yes. But he told me from the beginning he wanted to settle down and have a real marriage eventually, and I explained my anti-marriage stance. We're two people with fundamentally different beliefs about that. It should have been simple. I thought it would be."

I waved my empty glass at our passing waitress. One beer wasn't going to cut it. It had only begun to blur the raw edges of my eviscerated heart. I was going for full-on numbness.

Elena folded her arms, raised a brow, and waited for me to continue, so I did.

"We fell in love. It wasn't on purpose, but it happened, and it was beautiful, El. Being with Luca is as easy as breathing. Most of the time, I forgot about our arrangement. He was just mine, and I was his. But then Clara—that's his sister—had a crisis in her marriage. Her husband turned out to be this despicable human, and Luca has had to hold the weight of his family while everything fell apart."

A full beer was placed in front of me. With grateful hands, I picked it up and took a long pull. Elena swung her crossed leg and waited for me to continue.

"He came home last night, and I could tell he wasn't himself. He found out I still had some things at my apartment, plus I wasn't wearing my rings, and he accused me of having one foot out the door. He was so mad he wouldn't listen to anything I said. Then he told me he loved me for the first time. I love him too. How could I not? I've never loved a man the way I do him. But then...he demanded to make our marriage real. He wanted me to say yes right then and there, *knowing* how I feel about marriage. And I couldn't, Elena. Of course I couldn't."

My head fell into my hands, too heavy to hold upright. "Then Clara got into a car accident, so Luca had to rush to the hospital. He wouldn't let me come, but I followed him anyway. And he—"

My throat was too tight to get the words out. Elena laid her hand on mine, giving it a firm squeeze. My sister-in-law wasn't the most demonstrative person. If I was getting a handhold, I must have truly looked miserable.

"He told me he didn't want me. He told me to go."

I ached. Dear god, did I ache. What was I supposed to do? I never should have agreed to any of this. How could I go back to Denver, share Sunday brunch with my friends, and face Luca again and again? I already knew I wouldn't be able to. Time wouldn't be enough.

I would never get over him.

How could I? He'd loved me so well. No other man would ever be able to touch the place inside me he'd carved for himself. It would be empty without his claim on it.

"Is that it?" Elena dug around in her purse and withdrew a plastic tube I recognized all too well.

I held my hand out, and she shook a cannabis gummy into my palm, then tossed the tube back in her bag.

"What do you mean, is that it?" I almost shrieked. Hadn't she been listening? "I just told you I'm heartbroken."

"But why? I don't understand the problem. Your husband wants to be married to you. You're already married. Nothing has to change."

Maybe I'd had too many beers. She was confusing me. "But...it was an arrangement. It wasn't real."

Shaking her head, she chuffed. "Were you committed to each other?"

I nodded.

"And you already said you're in love."

I nodded again, slowly chewing on my gummy.

"You adopted a cat together."

"Clementine." I missed her, and it hadn't even been twenty-four hours. Thankfully, the doorman had texted me pictures of her when he checked on her.

Elena leaned in. "The sex is...good?"

"Good doesn't even come close to describing it."

Her lips curved. "You met each other's families."

"Yes, but it was part of the agreement—"

She flicked her fingers, dismissing me. "I'm assuming this marriage is legal, right?"

"Yes, of course."

"Then what's the problem? You're married to a man who fucks you right, loves you and your cat, is good to you, rich as God, hot as hell...I don't get it."

How had Elena managed to twist my mind around so thoroughly that I was beginning to not understand my own problems? Was she a witch?

Maybe it was the weed...and beer.

"I don't believe in marriage?" Yeah, it had come out as a question. I doubted myself at this point.

Elena laughed. "Do you even know what you believe? You know, your brother tried to use your parents as an excuse to dump me."

I sat back in my chair, heart sinking. "I remember that." That was a decade ago, and I still recall telling Lock he was being an idiot for breaking up with Elena. Thankfully, he pulled his head out of his ass quickly and she forgave him. I might have made my dad adopt her so she could have still been my sister if he hadn't.

"Then you'll also remember it didn't work. He figured out very quickly how stupid it was to use his parents' mistakes as an excuse not to live the life he wanted. I see you doing the same *after* you had front-row seats to Lachlan fumbling the bag, and I can't help wondering why you're being stupid too. Is this fear?"

I flinched from the pummeling she'd given me. "You're being mean."

"No, I'm being blunt."

And this was exactly why I came to Elena. She never pulled punches. She wouldn't coddle me and tell me my decisions were right if they were dead wrong.

"I've never wanted to be married."

She arched a brow. "And yet, you are."

"But it's not real."

"You keep saying that. I don't think that word means what you think it means."

"I only married Luca because there was an end date. He's the one who changed what we agreed on. He didn't even want to have a conversation about it. It was his way or nothing."

"And you honestly chose nothing?"

"I don't believe in marriage," I whispered.

"It's not a fairy tale, babe. It's an agreement between two people, which is what you and Luca have. Was it fair for him to change the details? No, of course not. It sounds like he was a total jackass."

"He yelled at me."

Because he'd been in pain. My Luca had been hurting and angry. If I hadn't been there, he would have yelled at the walls. Taken his fury out on a canvas or mounds of clay. But it had been me. And I wasn't a wall or clay. I was a woman with out-of-control feelings, shaky knees, a rattling heart.

Her eyes narrowed. "Did he hurt you?"

"No. I didn't love being yelled at, but I wasn't afraid of him."

Aching for him. Confused by him. Needy for him. Angry at him. Never afraid of him.

"Good. I would hate for Lachlan to have to murder him."

"He would." My brother didn't play when it came to the women he loved.

She nodded. "Not a question. Your father would probably get in on it as well."

"There is no need for violence." My head was beginning to feel lighter, as were my troubles. The gummy was working its magic. "I don't think you'll see him again anyway."

Elena sighed and picked up her sparkling water, giving it a swirl. Then she reached for my hand. "I want to dance. If I go out there alone, I'll end up having to fend off a lonely rancher or two, so you'll have to dance with me."

The gummy had loosened me up just enough that I let her drag me to my feet and over to the dance floor. Everyone was doing some line dance I didn't know, but I joined in anyway. Soon, I was swept up in it, shuffling and spinning, probably doing it all wrong, but I didn't give a damn. It was something other than being miserable, so I latched on to it with both hands.

One song blended with the next. Elena and I danced together, and any time a guy so much as glanced our way, she bared her teeth. Even pregnant, she attracted attention. That might've been because she had a whole "Evil Elsa" thing going. Scary but hot.

We spun until we were dizzy and had bounced ourselves sweaty. Eventually, we bellied up to the bar for another drink.

A pretty bartender with black hair and bright-blue eyes rested her elbows on the bar and grinned.

"What'll it be?" she asked.

Elena patted my head. "Joy, this is Saoirse. Saoirse, Joy."

I waved at Joy, who I assumed was the owner since her name was all over the place, and she waved back.

"Saoirse doesn't believe in marriage," Elena said.

Joy nodded at my rings. "Pity for your husband."

I hid my hand behind my back. Elena cackled. "Right? I told her you can't *not* believe in marriage when you're literally married. Anyway, Saoirse needs a shot. Something sweet and strong, please. And I'll have another seltzer."

Joy saluted Elena. "I got you."

Elena turned to me while Joy poured our drinks. "You know, I was suspicious when you called to tell us you'd eloped. All the time I've known you, you've been adamantly against getting married. But then you showed up here with Luca, and I saw how he looked at you. Then he was so patient with Caleb, who'd challenged him at every turn, and I thought, 'Saoirse might have landed a good one.'"

"He is good," I agreed.

Joy slid us our drinks and moved along. I swallowed the sweet liquid, exhaling as it fired down my throat and warmed my chest.

"I think he's good for you." Elena took a gulp of her seltzer and wiped her mouth with the back of her hand. "He's your lighthouse."

"My—what?"

"Sometimes I worry about you, babe. You've been directionless for a long time while calling it freedom and adventure. Those are good things, but I see you using your adventurous spirit as a cover for your fear of committing to *anything*. Not a job, a city, a home. But since Luca came into your life, you've committed. You started the business you've been thinking about for years. You have the cat you always wanted. And you fell in love. Head over heels. I think being with Luca has allowed you to feel secure enough to grab on to the things you've always wanted. You can explore uncharted waters because he's your beacon home. Do you even know how rare that is? To have someone who really sees you, values you, and supports you?"

Tears welled in my eyes. I couldn't cry at the bar at Joy's Elbow Room. I absolutely refused. So, I bit down on the inside of my cheek until I got myself under control.

"I love him very much," I rasped. "But I don't know how to navigate this. How do I move past these feelings I've had for so long?"

"You have to talk to each other." She curled her arm around my shoulders. "He was wrong for forcing your hand and then being cruel to you when you couldn't say what he wanted you to say. But there's no way around this. You have to work through it. And that will only happen if you both are willing."

I leaned my head against hers. "I don't know if he's willing."

"You won't know until you face him, babe. Running will only get you so far."

I wasn't ready to give up on Luca.

But I also wasn't ready to face him either. Not when I still didn't know if I was capable of being what he wanted me to be.

If he even wanted me at all.

CHAPTER
FORTY-TWO

Luca

IT SEEMED IMPOSSIBLE FOR there to be anything wrong in the world when I held my niece in my arms.

I was the second one to hold her. Clara hadn't wanted to give her up, which I understood. I tried my best to play the part Miller would have, taking pictures of every moment and making sure Clara was as comfortable as possible.

Time was nothing but an abstract theory in the hospital. I dozed every once in a while and ate the leftovers from Clara's tray. Our parents hovered at first, but our father needed to rest for his own health, so I was the one who stayed overnight with her.

While Clara napped, my niece squirmed in her bassinet, so I took her out and cradled her against my chest. Antonella Rossi—Nellie—made this crooked world straight again. I'd loved her before we'd even met, but I had never experienced anything like looking into her tiny, round face and feeling like I was falling and sinking at the same time.

"I'll make it right for you," I whispered. "When you need me, I'll always be there, Nellie baby. Uncle Luca loves you."

Her lips puckered, and long lashes brushed her cheeks. That was enough of a reaction for me. Anything she did was fucking amazing.

———•◦•———

By day three, my sister and mother kicked me out. According to them, I was a walking zombie. And maybe I was. But the fact was, I preferred camping out in the hospital to facing the unknown outside of it.

Elliot was waiting for me out front. As much as I didn't want to be dependent on anyone, I hadn't slept in days, and I had no business driving.

"How is the baby?" he asked once I was buckled.

"She's healthy. Eating like a champ." I sighed, scrubbing a hand over my face. "I hate that she was born in the midst of a shit show."

"Clara will rally."

I nodded. My sister was more than capable of handling motherhood. This wasn't her plan, and her heart was broken, but she was determined. When Clara was determined, whatever she wanted to make happen, she did. That was who she was.

"She's already rallying."

His thumbs tapped on the wheel as he drove through the quiet streets of Denver. It was early. Not many people were out yet. The more distance we put between us and the hospital, the more my mental fog lifted. It was like emerging from a days'-long fugue state and clarity was returning little by little.

"I saw Saoirse leaving the hospital."

I whipped my head in his direction. "When?"

"The first night. She asked me to be there for you since you didn't want her there."

This sinking sensation was nothing like the one I'd had when holding Nellie. This was being pulled under by quicksand, compressing my chest until I couldn't breathe. I'd pushed everything but Clara and the baby from my mind in the haze of all that had been going on, and it all came slamming back.

"I can't talk about that right now."

Normally, that would be all I needed to say to get Elliot to back off, but not this time. He stayed silent for all of a minute.

"I've known Saoirse for a long time now, and I have never seen her like that. She looked like a kicked dog. And I think you did the kicking."

The edge in his tone had me sitting up straight. Something about it prickled my senses, alerting me.

"We had a disagreement."

He huffed. "Is that what you call telling your wife she can't be at the hospital?" He glanced at me through narrowed eyes. "I've known you a long time too, and I never thought you had it in you to be cruel."

"Cruel? You have no idea what happened between us."

"Did she do something worth treating her like garbage? Is that what you're telling me?"

I opened my mouth to say yes, but nothing came out. The raw truth was Saoirse hadn't done anything wrong. It was all on me. I'd been the one to demand things of her I had no right to. I lost my temper and yelled. I spoke to her like she was nothing when she was exactly the opposite.

"No. She didn't," I admitted, and it was like chewing glass. It wasn't her fault she didn't want the same things I did. She'd been honest from the beginning. I was the one who'd deviated from the arrangement.

"I don't care what you do. Find a way to fix it."

The same awareness prickled. I recognized it now. *Territorialism.* "Why are you so concerned about my wife? Are you lining up to take my place or something?"

Elliot burst into laughter, which was a rare sight. "Oh, you're so far gone. I'll let that slide since you haven't slept in days. Once you're rested, I expect you'll recognize how wrong what you just said was on every level."

"You're right. That was out of line. I'm just surprised at your level of care over Saoirse."

His fingers flexed on the steering wheel, but that was the only sign he was pissed at me. "There are very few people who are important to me. Elise is one of them. You're another. Being *her* best friend and *your* wife, Saoirse falls into that category because of who she is to you both. I don't want to have to explain to my sister why her best friend's husband dicked her over. So fix it before it comes to that."

"I don't know if it can be fixed."

"You're a smooth talker. I don't doubt you have it in you."

Elliot left me with that vote of confidence, and since it was the only confidence I had, I took it.

The doorman smiled and waved at me as I walked in. I would have kept going with a nod if he hadn't called me over.

"You're back, Mr. Rossi?"

I cocked my head, unsure why he was asking. We didn't usually exchange niceties. "I'm back."

"That's great. Don't worry about Clementine. I kept her company the last few days. Easy as pie."

I stared at him, unsure if my exhaustion was confusing me more than I thought. "You took care of my cat?"

He nodded slowly, his brow furrowing. "Sure. Mrs. Rossi asked me to. Did I do something wrong?"

I stepped back, shaking my head. *What the fuck?* Why would Saoirse have asked this guy to take care of Clem?

Needing to go upstairs and get to the bottom of what was going on, I offered a quick thanks and strode to the elevator, punching the button for the penthouse.

The minute I walked in the door, Clementine came striding up to me. I scooped her into my arms and kissed the top of her head.

"Where's your mother?"

She meowed, which wasn't any help. But I didn't need my cat to tell me the condo was empty. Saoirse's presence was unmistakable, and this morning, it was absent. If not for Clem, I would have said my home felt hollowed out.

But maybe that was just me.

I had to get my life together. With Miller gone and Clara out on leave, Rossi needed me to be there more than ever. I should have been taking a power nap, a quick shower, throwing on a suit, and heading into the office. It was the responsible thing to do.

Duty to my family and my company had me swaying on my feet. I needed to make a move, but which way?

I really only had to think for a few seconds before my choice was obvious.

My next move would be in the direction of Saoirse, wherever she had gone.

Carrying Clem through the condo, I searched for clues. My stomach clenched with disappointment at the empty den. I'd been holding out hope I'd find her in there.

Clem jumped out of my arms when I entered our bedroom. Saoirse's scent hung in the air but nowhere near strong enough for my liking. She'd invaded every corner of my home. Of me. And I never wanted to go back to the cobwebs that had been there before. She'd brought so much light and sweetness.

There was a sheet of paper in the center of our bed. Unmissable. I sat down on the edge and picked it up. My hand shook as I read.

Luca,

I'm going to spend some time in Wyoming to give us both the space I think we need. I'll be working from the ranch for the next two weeks. When I come back, I hope we can sit down and have a conversation about where we go from here. If you want to end the arrangement completely, I understand. There won't be any hard feelings on my end.

If you need anything, or if something changes with Clara and the baby, please let me know and I'll be back as soon as I can get there. No matter what happens with us, I'll always be there if you need me.

I want you to know I really do love you. I'm sorry we ended things on bad terms. I'm pretty shattered over this, to be honest.

Be well. I'll talk to you soon.

Sincerely,

Your Inconvenient Wife

⸺◆⸺

Why the hell did this sound like a goodbye?

Because you told her to go, motherfucker.

We weren't finished. Not by a long shot. And there was no way I was waiting two weeks to have a conversation with my wife.

Especially when she'd signed her letter like that. My hand twitched with the need to remind her there was *nothing* inconvenient about her, despite what I had said.

I rubbed my thumb over my wedding band and slipped it off to look at the inscription I'd discovered the day we got married.

The day I knew I had gotten in over my head.

I turned on my phone. There were a thousand calls to return. A million emails to read. I ignored them all to press on Saoirse's contact, opening our text thread. She hadn't texted me since she'd arrived at the hospital and had spent hours waiting in the lobby for an update. Even though I'd told her not to come and then callously dismissed her when she did anyway.

What the hell had I done? Panic to get on the road, to get to my wife, clawed at my chest. But if I got behind the wheel now, I'd be putting others in danger.

I sent her a text to let her know what was happening.

Me: *I'll be in Wyoming tonight, and then I'm coming for you.*

CHAPTER
FORTY-THREE

Luca

I ARRIVED IN SUGAR Brush just before five. There was plenty of daylight left, so if I had to hunt my wife down, I would. But I'd hunt for her in the pitch black with only my other senses to rely on if that was what it came down to. The urge to find her and keep her was stronger than my own self-preservation at this point.

I parked and started for the barn, deciding that was the best place to begin my search. If Saoirse wasn't in there, maybe Lock or Connell could point me to her.

Before I could get there, a mini ATV came out of nowhere, cutting off my path. To avoid getting run over, I had to jump back a few steps.

Caleb and Hannah Kelly blinked up at me from their little vehicle. Hannah was grinning and giggling. "Uncle Luca!" she squealed.

"Hey, Hannie," I greeted while rubbing my chest to get my startled heart under control. "Fancy meeting you here."

"I have a bow." She opened her hand and held it up to show me. "Put it on, please."

Seeing no other choice, I took the bright-pink bow from her. She watched me carefully and with an edge of menace until I slid the clip into my hair.

"Good?" I tipped my head to the side to give her a good look.

She nodded. "I love it, Uncle Luca!"

Caleb had his arms crossed and a deep frown on his chubby little face. "What are *you* doing here?"

"I'm here to talk to your Aunt Saoirse. Have you seen her?"

"Why?"

I narrowed my eyes at him. "She's my wife."

His lip curled into a snarl. "I heard my mommy say you made Aunt Sershie sad."

Hannah nodded. "Aunt Sershie cried."

I'd known I'd made her sad. I wasn't even surprised she'd cried. But there was something about these kids delivering the news that was a dagger to the heart.

"I'm here to tell her I'm very sorry for making her sad. Think you could tell me where she is?" I asked as calmly as I could.

Caleb jutted out his chin. "Are you going to make her cry again?"

"I really hope not."

The kid looked me square in the eye. "Aunt Sershie is on Mars, and she forgot her phone. Sorry."

"Mars, huh? Maybe I'll wait for her to come back."

He chuffed. "You gotta go home now cuz we don't have a bed that'll fit you. They're all way too big for you."

Then he put his mini ATV in gear and stepped on the gas, zipping away while Hannah squealed and waved at me over her shoulder.

Apparently, Caleb was going to be my nemesis. I could live with that until I got Saoirse back. Then, I'd spend some time winning our nephew over. He'd be an Uncle Luca fan before he turned six, and I'd convince him I wasn't fucking small.

I found Lock in the barn. If he was surprised to see me, he didn't show it. We shook hands in silence, and he waited for me to speak.

"I'm told Saoirse has left for Mars."

Lock grunted. "You had a Caleb run-in, I take it."

"I did."

"He's not pleased with the state his aunt arrived in. She put on a brave face for him, but he's not stupid." Lock folded his tree trunk arms, sending the distinct message he wasn't impressed with me either.

"I've come to fix the mess I made. I would have been here sooner, but I've been with my sister in the hospital."

The hardness in his gaze softened a fraction. "How is she?"

"Doing as well as can be expected. She and Nellie will be going home tomorrow."

He lifted his chin. "Glad to hear that."

"Is Saoirse—"

"Look, Luca. My wife and I don't have secrets from each other, which means after Saoirse unloaded on Elena, Elena unloaded on me. The origins of your marriage won't go any further if that's how you want it. To be frank, I don't give a damn how things started between you. What I care about is where you go from here."

I nodded in agreement, unsurprised Saoirse had spilled everything to Elena. I was glad she had someone to confide in.

"That's what I care about too. That's why I'm here."

Eyeing me, Lock wrapped his thick fingers around the end of a shovel. "I'm sure Saoirse has shared some of the ugliness she grew up witnessing. I got out, went away to college, and she was left in the middle of it. If she's gun-shy about marriage, she has every reason to be. If you're not able to understand her reticence, you're not the man for her."

His blunt tone made me grimace. "I do understand it. I'm here to tell her I do."

His fingers flexed around the shovel. "Don't let her get away with making excuses out of fear. If you allow her to convince herself she doesn't deserve what she really wants, she'll live with regret forever. I know because I almost did it to myself, and I would have been *nothing* without Ellie."

"I don't even know if she wants to see me, but I'll try, man. I'll keep trying."

"She'll want to see you," he gruffed. "You're going to need to get on a horse to find her. Remember how to ride?"

"Uh…" I scratched the back of my neck and scanned the horses in the stalls behind him, landing on my old friend, Barney. "It's like riding a bike, right?"

Lock pushed out a rumbling chuckle. "Sure. That's one way to look at it." He started toward Barney, but before I could take a step to follow him, he spun back around and leveled me with a hard stare. "One more thing. If I ever hear about you yelling at my sister the way you did a few days ago, you will deal with me. I'm not a violent man, but when it comes to my family, I don't play games. Got me?"

"I got you, Lock." I didn't look away from him. "Give me time, and I'll show you you don't have to worry about Saoirse with me. That's never going to happen again."

He nodded once. "Good. Now, help me get Barney set up and I'll point you toward Saoirse."

CHAPTER
FORTY-FOUR

Saoirse

I'D SPENT THE DAY out in the fields with my father. He'd given me half his tasks, and we'd still managed to have more than enough work for both of us.

More than ever, I understood his need to be busy. When I was checking fences and moving cattle from one field to another, I didn't have time to think about the life I was missing.

The *man* I was missing.

Dad headed back to the barn, but I wasn't quite ready to be around the rest of my family, so I rode Athena to our favorite spot by the stream and let her graze while I dipped my feet in the water. The cold ripples around my tired legs were heavenly. I stood there, my face tipped to the endless sky, and closed my eyes.

I loved it here, but I could never live here. The peacefulness of wide-open spaces made for a beautiful place to retreat to, but the city was where I belonged.

A few more days, and I'd go back. I'd said in the letter I'd left for Luca I'd be gone for two weeks, but I was hoping he'd be open to speaking before then.

I wondered if he missed me the way I missed him.

Was he thinking about me, or was he relieved I was gone? The possibility of the latter was a punch to the gut.

Either way, I had to face what was to come. Being at the ranch was a much-needed respite, but I needed answers more than anything.

The sound of grunting and cursing brought me out of my reverie. I opened my eyes, surprised to see someone riding in my direction. Well...lumbering was a more apt description. Barney didn't go faster than a turtle these days.

Who the hell was riding Barney?

Another curse, and the rider in all black listed to the side until he tumbled in slow motion all the way off. Barney came to a halt, nudging the man with his nose.

Alarmed, I scampered out of the stream and hurried over to them. "Are you okay?" I called.

The man in black sat up, shoving his hair out of his face, giving me my first clear view of him. My feet stopped moving, and my jaw dropped.

"That wasn't exactly the entrance I'd planned on making." Luca got to his feet and brushed himself off, then he started toward me.

"Are you hurt?"

The corner of his mouth hitched. "Nothing but my pride."

I hadn't moved. My mind was still trying to reconcile that the man I'd just been thinking about was right here in person, with a pink bow in his hair, no less. He must have run into Hannah.

"You're here." I whispered it, not really even meaning to say it aloud, but Luca heard me.

"I'm here. I'm beginning to think Lock was fucking with me with that saddle and that damn horse, but I can't be mad. He got me here." He stopped a foot away from me, scanning me from head to toe. I was dirty and a little sweaty, with a trucker hat on my head and Elena's boots on my feet. "You look like a cowgirl."

"You look like a dream." I squeezed my eyes shut, then cracked them open, finding him right where he was. "But you're really here. What are you doing here?"

His brows drew together in a straight line. "Did you really think I'd wait two weeks to talk to you?" He shook his head, huffing, and spread his arms wide. "You wanted space. You have it. Look at all the space around you. The thing is, I'm going to be joining you in your space."

"That's not how space works."

"That's how it's going to work for us." He reached out, taking my hand in his. "Come sit with me so we can talk."

"I tried doing that with you, but you weren't interested."

His hold on my hand tightened, and his thumb moved to my ring finger like a magnet.

"Where are your rings?" An echo of the last time we did this, but his tone held no accusation now.

I wiggled my fingers in his. "It's not smart to wear rings when I'm working around the ranch. They're in a little pouch beside my bed, safe and sound."

His eyes were soft on mine. "Are you going to put them on later?"

My breath caught at his loaded question. "Do you want me to?"

He exhaled through his nose. "Let's sit down."

Trying not to panic, I let him lead me to the grass by the stream. We sat down side by side. Luca's long legs were stretched out in front of him. Mine were tucked against my chest, my arms around them.

He stroked his fingers along my ponytail, then ghosted his hand down the length of my spine.

"You need to know I'm so fucking sorry for how I treated you."

I turned to him, my chin on my arms. "Okay."

"I could offer excuses like stress, the circumstances, but you already know what was going on because you were standing by my side the whole way. As you have been from the beginning."

"You've been standing with me too," I said.

"I've tried, pretty girl, but I know I let you down this time."

I didn't know what to say to that. He wasn't wrong.

Luca sighed. "I thought I could do this arrangement with you. But I messed up and fell in love with you, despite my efforts to avoid it. We never should have done this."

Oh, that hurt too badly to reply. He watched me with sorrowful eyes, but I couldn't bring myself to argue or tell him he was wrong. He'd driven all the way here, so clearly, his mind was made up.

"When you walked out in your pink dress on our wedding day, I could barely look at you. And then you had this ring for me, a ring I would have chosen for myself if I'd had the opportunity, and acknowledging it had felt too big. That whole day had felt too fucking big. How'd it feel to you?"

I sucked in a shaky breath. "I asked you what you thought of my dress, and you said, 'I suspect you know exactly how you look.' I can still hear you saying that. But then you gave me roses and kissed me like you meant it." I shrugged. "It was confusing."

"Saoirse." He nudged me beneath my chin. "I could barely look at you in that dress because you looked like my wife. I was trying to distance myself from you, the ceremony, the entire event, but it was impossible. All of it felt real to me. The orchid in your hair, our kiss, the fucking pictures I've stared at every single day since. Every time I pushed you away, it was to protect myself because I have been falling in love with you since we met. And I have always believed you when you said marriage wasn't for you. I respect that."

I pulled away from him. "But you didn't. You made demands of me that weren't fair."

"I know." His rejected hand curved around my jaw, refusing to break contact with me. "I'm not ashamed to admit I got scared. I'm only ashamed of how I handled it. You have been my constant, pretty girl. With Clara's world crumbling, I saw how easy it was to lose everything, and I panicked. I made demands I had no right to make. Now that I'm on the other side of it, I know I was wrong, one hundred percent."

"I know something about fear," I told him.

His jaw rippled with tension. "I know you do, and I'm sorry for that. I never want you to be afraid of me."

"I'm not." I held his gaze, ensuring he was listening. No matter how this day ended, I needed him to know he didn't scare me. "Even when you were yelling, I knew you wouldn't hurt me. I understood what was going on. If you'd given me time to think, to talk instead of giving ultimatums, things could have worked out differently."

His nod was beaten down and sorry. "Right. I'd go back and do a lot differently if I could."

"Like never marrying me," I supplied.

He heaved a great breath. "I can't regret getting to be your husband, Saoirse, but yes. If I could change things, we never would have gotten married."

Tears sprung to my eyes before I could blink. "So, what do we do now? How do we move forward?"

"I want you to come back to Denver with me." Luca's words were shaky and low, like he was struggling to get them out. "On Monday, we can start the divorce process."

There was no stopping the choking sob that fell from my lips. "Well, I guess it's a good thing I never gave up that apartment, huh?"

"Saoirse. You mistake me." Luca was on his knees, both hands cupping my face. "You're not going anywhere. I'm keeping you forever."

I clutched his wrists but didn't push him away. The strength to do so had fled long ago. "But you want a divorce."

His brows furrowed. "You don't want to be married. I'm giving you what you want, pretty girl, but that doesn't mean we're through. You're always going to be mine."

"Luca," I whispered. My tears were flowing freely now and gathering my thoughts was difficult when I felt like I was being jerked left and right.

"After our wedding ceremony, I took my ring off and noticed the inscription. 'Partners in crime.'" His thumb swiped one tear after another as he looked at me like I was precious. "That's what we are, Saoirse. We committed a crime and got away with it. I can't have you going off on your own, living your life without me, when you could tell our secret to anyone you please. No, I'm going to need to be by your side, making sure you keep your pretty little mouth shut. You're not leaving me."

I thought I'd been cute getting his ring inscribed that way. But he'd never said a word about it. I'd never known he'd even noticed it. Yet, now he was telling me...

Oh god.

I pushed up to my knees so we were face to face and braced my hands on his chest.

"I don't believe in marriage as an institution. A contract is only as good as the promises behind it." My fingers curled, grasping his shirt in my fists. "The thing is, now, I mean the promises I made to you on your balcony. I want to be your partner in this crime until we see our last sunset."

With a growl, he wrapped my ponytail around his fingers and tipped my face to his. "That sounds like almost long enough."

I shoved at his chest, but he had a tight hold of me and didn't go anywhere. Not that I really wanted him to. "If you ever suggest divorce again, I'm not going to be happy. I'm your *wife*, Luca. I won't be downgraded."

His head cocked. "But you don't want to be married."

"I didn't want to be forced into an answer when everything was up in the air. I've had days to think about everything now and Elena to explain to me how stupid I was being."

"Thank god for Elena," he uttered. I tried to shove him again, but he caught my hand and brought it to his lips. "I love you deeply, Saoirse Rossi. I'll take you any way I can have you, but I'd really fucking prefer to keep you as my wife forevermore. No time limits. No arrangements. Just you and me, making promises and keeping them. Choosing each other again and again."

"I love you too, Luca. And I choose you." I reached up, slid the bow from his hair, and showed it to him.

With a grunt, he snagged it and tossed it behind him, then pulled me flush to his chest. "I can't believe I just declared my undying love to you with a pink bow in my hair."

I grinned even as he lowered his mouth to mine. "That made me forgive you before you even said a word."

"I'll thank Hannah later."

I laughed into his kiss, which curled my toes and dried up the last of my tears. He held me gently, kissing me thoroughly, for all the days we'd missed each other. It went on and on while the stream trickled by and my heart beat more surely than it ever had.

Once he'd kissed me breathless, he drew back, his eyes sliding back and forth between mine.

"You haven't said yes."

I raised a brow. "What was the question again?"

"To staying married without contracts or end dates. Just you and me, partners in crime and our crazy, wonderful life. What do you think, pretty girl—are you in?"

I bit down on my bottom lip and let my gaze drift over him. There were very few yeses I regretted. I always found something of value in my experiences. But the day I said yes to Luca Rossi for the first time stood apart from all the rest. Over the past few months, I'd gotten more from that yes than any other.

Luca had given me passion. Art. Beauty. Family. Oh, had he given me family. I already knew the Rossis would always be my favorite people.

Through Luca, I'd found stability. Freedom to pursue my passions. Understanding and support when I needed them, and a push when I needed that more.

With Luca's arms around me and his body aligned with mine, I'd discovered a level of pleasure I'd never known existed.

At Luca's side, we'd adopted a cat. The cat of my dreams. My Clementine.

In Luca, I'd found a friend unlike any I'd ever had. He made me laugh and think. His adventurous spirit matched my own. His tender heart made him so very easy to love.

The crazy thing was, we were only just beginning. This yes had already given me so much, yet there was *so* much more to come.

I nodded first, then I said the word. "Yes."

His eyes flared. "Yes? You're in?"

I took his face in my hands and rubbed my nose along his. "I'm so very in."

It was the easiest yes I'd ever said.

EPILOGUE

Luca

One Year Later

"YOU'VE MADE GOOD CHOICES."

Saoirse stopped midstride, raising a questioning brow. "I like to think so, but I sense you're commenting on something specific."

I patted the arm of her desk chair. "I will be replacing my chair with this model as soon as possible."

She sauntered over to where I sat behind her new desk, putting an extra swing in her hips. "Oh, you like my chair, do you?"

"Mmhmm." As soon as she was within arm's reach, I grabbed her and pulled her into my lap. She circled her arms around my neck and crossed one leg over the other. "I like your chair even better now."

"You know I have a million things to do before everyone arrives."

I rubbed my palm along her thigh and placed a soft kiss to the curve of her neck. "I'll let you get back to running around checking on things you've already checked a hundred times after you sit with me a minute."

She relaxed against me, letting out a sigh. "You're exaggerating."

"Okay." I touched her throat with my lips again. "You've checked things fifty times."

"Maybe. I just want everything to look perfect."

"It does, pretty girl. You and Miles are going to blow everyone away."

Peak Strategies was a little over a year old. In that time, Miles and Saoirse had steadily grown their business, gaining clients and a reputation in and outside of Denver. Up until this point, they'd been mainly working from our condo and renting conference rooms in shared office space when they needed it.

They'd finally agreed they needed more room and their own official office. I used my connections to secure them a space in the building beside Rossi's. It was for my own selfish purposes—working in close proximity made lunch breaks at the Davenport possible.

My wife and I now fucked whenever and wherever the mood struck, but a part of me missed our secret trysts. Although I'd settled into my CEO role, knowing I got to sink inside my wife in the middle of the day made my job much more enjoyable. I had plans for us to relive our early days as often as possible now that I'd have her nearby.

But I was getting ahead of myself. Tonight wasn't about business or even about me. Saoirse and Miles were throwing a party to celebrate and show off their new digs. Within the hour, clients and friends would be arriving, and my wife was a fluttering bundle of nerves.

"I shouldn't have invited my mother." Saoirse wrung her hands. "That was a mistake."

I took her hands in mine, kissing her fingertips one at a time. "She'll be fine. Lily Smythe-Kelly would never make a scene in public, and I'll ensure she doesn't have the chance to make one in private."

Understanding Lily wasn't something on my agenda. I didn't care why she was the way she was. All that mattered was how she treated my wife. The first time I walked in on Saoirse attempting to defend herself against her mother's criticism, I calmly took the phone from her, told Lily Saoirse wouldn't be speaking to her again until she was ready to apologize and be civil, and hung up. Neither woman had been angry. Saoirse had thanked me for defending her, and Lily had apologized the next day.

Since then, she'd gotten better. Not perfect. Far from it. But better.

"My bodyguard." Saoirse snuggled into me with a sigh. "At least she's leaving Peter at home."

Saoirse had mostly come to terms with the fact that she would never be close to her mother. Luckily, my mom had taken her under her wing, treating her like a second daughter. Which worked well since Clara thought of Saoirse as her sister.

Like I knew she would, Saoirse had supported Clara in all ways over the last year. Times had been rough, and some days still were, but Clara was divorced from Miller, who was serving his time in federal prison. Our auditors had uncovered that Miller had embezzled over a million dollars from Rossi, so his sentence was even steeper with those charges added.

Nellie was thriving without that dick in her life. She looked like a little clone of Clara, so we all pretended Miller had had nothing to do with her origins.

My niece was also obsessed with her aunt. She had managed to babble an adorable form of "Sershie" while she hadn't come close to forming my name. The guy who'd held her when she'd been all gooey and brand new.

Not that I was upset by that or anything.

Most days, I was pretty certain all my family liked my wife more than me, and I didn't blame them for it. After all, I liked her more than anyone else too.

"Tell me what else you're worried about, and I'll reassure you."

She talked, and I listened, which in the end, was what she'd needed.

Miles strolled into Saoirse's office, tugging at his tie with a deep frown on his face. "I look like an idiot."

Saoirse laughed. "You look dapper."

Miles cocked his head, looking at me. I nodded. "I agree. The suit works. Glad you finally hit up my tailor."

His spine straightened, and he twisted side to side to show off his light-gray trousers and jacket, which had been custom made for him. "The suit is the absolute shit. I love it. I may sleep in it. It's the tie I can't get on board with. Sersh made me wear it, but I feel like I'm wearing a noose. Some people aren't meant for such formality." He pointed to himself. "Hi. I'm some people."

"I think you have to listen to Saoirse. She knows what she's talking about."

Miles dropped his hands from his tie and tucked them in his pockets, sighing in defeat. "Fine. I'll do it for the 'gram. But don't expect me to wear a tie to work just because we have a fancy office. It's not happening."

Saoirse laughed. "I'm always relieved when you wear actual pants to work."

Miles rocked back on his heels. "Jesus, will you let that drop? I wore shorts *one time*—"

"To a meeting with a prospective client," she added.

His eyes narrowed. "We don't know that my shorts were the reason they didn't sign with us."

"I'm sure they didn't help. You just *had* to show off your calves."

I nuzzled my nose into her hair. "To be fair, Miles does have exceptionally nice calves."

Saoirse slapped my shoulder. "Don't encourage him."

Miles finger gunned me. "Thanks, man. Always knew you were a real one. Now, I'll leave you two in peace to christen the office or whatever you were doing before I walked in here."

Saoirse groaned at his retreating back. "If I didn't love him, I'd kill him," she muttered.

"If *I* didn't love *you*, I'd kill him for being loved by you," I said.

I stole another kiss, then she was off again, expelling her nervous energy by pacing and speaking with the caterers. It wasn't often that Saoirse got nervous, but this was important to her.

She'd been like this before our vow renewal too. My mother had gotten her wish. Saoirse had let her help plan a celebration for our one-year anniversary. It had been a lot more low-key than she probably would have liked, but we all ended up happy.

Connell got his first dance with his daughter.

Elena helped my mother plan everything with baby Phoebe on her hip.

Hannah sprinkled flowers, and Caleb passed out programs. And while Caleb wasn't fully on board with me, he'd been calling me small less and less these days, so I took that as a sign I was winning him over. He had even lowered himself to having a sleepover at our condo twice in the last year. I figured one or two more times, and he'd be putty in my hands.

I picked up the frame from Saoirse's desk. There were two photos side by side. One from our wedding where we were laughing with each other. The second was at our vow renewal in Wyoming. Saoirse had worn her pink dress with a flower tucked behind her ear. She took my breath away, always, but that dress had done a fucking number on me. I'd already asked her to wear it for me every year. Since she was a good girl, she very easily said "yes." She'd definitely get something out of the experience. Multiple somethings.

I ran my finger over the picture of us in Wyoming. We'd said our vows in a rustic chapel on the ranch in front of fifty friends and family, sun streaming through the stained-glass windows, giddy smiles on our faces.

It hadn't been a do-over. We hadn't needed one of those. The first time had been perfect because it was what had made us *us*.

Standing in front of everyone at the renewal had only reaffirmed what we had already worked out for ourselves: we chose each other, and we would keep choosing each other until our last sunset.

Read Lock and Elena's story in Sweet Like Poison:

https://mybook.to/SweetLikePoison

PLAYLIST

"In Agreement" Lizzy McAlpine

"Lie to Me" 5 Seconds of Summer

"Hard Feelings/Loveless" Lorde

"Too Close" Melanie Martinez

"Teeth" 5 Seconds of Summer

"Bulletproof" Melanie Martinez

"The Show" Melanie Martinez

"Breezeblocks" alt-J

"To Be Alone With You" Sufjan Stevens

"Tribulation" Matt Maeson

"The Night We Met" Lord Huron

"I Come Apart" A$AP Rocky, Florence Welch

"BITE" Troy Sivan

"Would That I" Hozier

"The same" mehro

"From the Dining Table" Harry Styles

"Glue Myself Shut" Noah Kahan

"Video Games" Lana Del Ray

"Fuck It I Love You" Lana Del Ray

"Everybody Wants To Love You" Japanese Breakfast

"Yours To Keep" Jordan Mackampa

https://open.spotify.com/playlist/0Q8Mzjc3Gwrd7JjG1PK9b R?si=f43d043e15b14053

Stay In Touch

Come find me in my reader group!
https://www.facebook.com/groups/JuliaWolfReaders

THANK YOU TO...

THIS BOOK HAS BEEN on my mind since I first wrote Saoirse's character in her big brother's book, Sweet Like Poison. Lock and Elena become beloved characters to both me and my readers, so I knew I couldn't quit them and their family. The Harder They Fall series exists because of Saoirse. I built this series around her so I could tell her story.

I hope I did justice to her and her family. I'm pretty satisfied with all the happily ever afters I created.

I have to thank my husband for helping me come up with Miller's crime. I was going to write something boring like embezzlement, when my husband mentioned a story he'd seen on "60 Minutes". My mind started whirring, I did a little research, and *boom*, Miller's storyline was born.

I have to thank my girl, Kate Farlow, for creating my covers and being patient with me when I'm indecisive and not bursting with enthusiasm. I promise, I LOVE it. I just show it quietly!

Thank you to Alley, Laura, and CoraLee for letting me pop in to our chat with random thoughts and worries and always replying. I love our randomness.

Thank you to the Booktokers/Bookstagrammers who shared the hell out of Dear Grumpy Boss. You guys really made it soar in ways I couldn't have come close to doing on my own.

Thank you to Kristie for your unwavering support and the Tik-Tok you made which pushed DGB into the top 40. I can't tell you how much I love everything about you!

As always, thank you to my readers. You are the best of the best. I never feel pressure or get mean emails or comments from you guys. How did I get so lucky? IDK, but I love you to the moon and back!

ABOUT JULIA

JULIA WOLF IS A bestselling contemporary romance author. She writes bad boys with big hearts and strong, independent heroines. Julia enjoys reading romance just as much as she loves writing it. Whether reading or writing, she likes the emotions to run high and the heat to be scorching.

Julia lives in Maryland with her three crazy, beautiful kids and her patient husband who she's slowly converting to a romance reader, one book at a time.

Visit my website:

http://www.juliawolfwrites.com

Made in the USA
Las Vegas, NV
17 September 2023

77639582R00221